Rhythms of Resilience

BOOK 2
HEALING HEARTS SERIES

ALEXANDRA PALCHAK

Cover design by: A. Palchak

ISBN: 979-8-9924396-6-3 (Paperback)

ISBN: 979-8-9924396-4-9 (Hardcover)

ISBN: 979-8-9924396-5-6 (eBook)

Library of Congress Control Number: 2025923757

Printed in the U.S.A.

Acknowledgements

Writing this second book while managing demanding IT projects, maintaining my training discipline, and nurturing my three children proved harder than the first. I considered postponing the release, but writing, like martial arts, is my therapy—my way of mentally detaching from stress and finding clarity. This book exists because the same people who believed in Book 1 stayed with me through a harder journey.

To Joe, my champion and the man who shows me daily what true fatherhood looks like—thank you for being my safe harbor. Like Chris in this story, you've proven that family is built through choice and devotion, not biology. Thank you for understanding when I inhabited difficult headspaces and for always bringing me back to the light.

To my children, Chantal, Isabella, and Joseph Jr.—watching you grow taught me everything I needed to write about Louise's resilience. You remind me daily that children see through pretense to the love underneath. Your presence kept me grounded when this story took me to dark places.

To my Taekwondo family—thank you for proving that physical training and creative expression are both essential therapies. The discipline you've instilled helped me push through the hardest scenes and find this story's heart.

To every reader who returned for this second chapter—thank you for your courage. This book asks harder questions than the first, exploring betrayal, manipulation, and the painful reality that sometimes those who should protect us are the ones we need protection from.

Like Chris and Leah, I learned that surviving the storm means discovering what you're truly made of. Real families are forged in fire, not just formed by blood.

This story is dedicated to everyone who has defended their chosen family, set boundaries with toxic relatives, and discovered that loyalty without love is just another kind of prison. Most of all, it's dedicated to my family—my fortress and my home.

With fierce love and deeper gratitude,
Alexandra Arias-Palchak

Contents

CHAPTER 1

Shadows in the Light

The late summer morning seeped through half-drawn blinds, painting stripes of golden light across cardboard boxes still labeled in Leah's precise handwriting. Their new kitchen smelled of coffee and remnants of last night's take-out - neither of them having summoned the energy to properly cook after returning from their honeymoon. The granite countertops had disappeared beneath a landscape of partially unpacked wedding gifts and displaced everyday items searching for their new homes.

Leah's fingers trailed along the box edges, seeking the familiar dents and scratches of Kate's recipe tin. The blue container had moved with her through so many transitions - from her first cramped dorm room where she'd hidden morning sickness from disapproving professors, through the tiny rental where she and Louise first became a family after she'd withdrawn from pre-med, into Kate's house during those raw months after the funeral. Each relocation was marked by her best friend's handwritten recipes, the cards growing soft at the edges from years of handling, margins filled with Kate's distinctive scrawl: "Add more vanilla!" and "Don't tell your mom I changed her pie crust recipe!"

"It has to be here somewhere," Leah muttered, pushing aside a crystal bowl still wrapped in newspaper. The movement dislodged a heavy white album perched precariously near the counter's edge. It fell with a dull thud,

1

spilling their wedding photos across the hardwood floor like scattered memories.

She knelt to gather them, her hands hovering over moments caught in glossy paper: Chris teaching Louise to slow dance, Mary dabbing tears during the ceremony, Terry's tight smile as she hugged the new bride. The images blurred slightly as Leah blinked back unexpected tears. Not sad ones, exactly, but heavy with the weight of change, of families merging and shifting, of the empty space where Kate should have stood as her maid of honor, should have been there to whisper irreverent commentary during the ceremony, should have danced with Louise at the reception.

Then her fingers brushed against a photo that sent ice through her veins. The man in the tailored suit stood at the reception's periphery, his presence so carefully calculated it nearly blended into the background. In the joy of their wedding day, she'd dismissed him as another member of Chris's expansive family circle, or perhaps one of her father's business associates paying respects. But now, with Wallace & Associates' letter lying heavy in her desk drawer upstairs, his watchful stance took on a more sinister cast.

She studied his face, noting how his eyes scanned the room even as he appeared absorbed in his champagne glass. The familiar predatory assessment in his gaze reminded her of the times she'd accompanied her father to Miller Financial as a child, before she understood what it meant when small family businesses disappeared overnight, before her own dreams of medical school dissolved in the face of unexpected motherhood and hard choices.

"Hey, beautiful." Chris's voice, still rough with sleep, startled her from her reverie. He leaned against the doorframe in worn pajama pants and yesterday's t-shirt, hair charmingly disheveled. "You're up early for someone who was complaining about jet lag last night."

Leah slid the suspicious photo into her pocket before rising, pasting on a smile that didn't quite reach her eyes. "Couldn't sleep. Thought I'd try to find Kate's recipe tin - Louise has been begging for those chocolate chip cookies."

Chris crossed the kitchen, his bare feet silent on the cool hardwood. He wrapped his arms around her from behind, chin resting on her shoulder as they both surveyed the chaos of unpacking. "The blue one? Pretty sure I saw it in one of the boxes marked 'Personal' in the study."

"Of course," Leah said, letting out a breath that was half laugh, half sigh. "Kate never did stay where she was supposed to." The words caught in her throat, heavy with the finality of that truth.

Chris tightened his embrace slightly, reading the tension in her shoulders. "Like someone else I know," he murmured, pressing a kiss to her temple. "You okay? Really okay?"

The concern in his voice made her chest ache. She turned in his arms, studying his face - so open, so genuine, so different from the calculated masks she'd grown up navigating. The photo burned in her pocket like a secret, but she forced herself to smile. "Just tired. And maybe a little overwhelmed by all this unpacking." The words carried an echo of other overwhelming moments - textbooks abandoned mid-semester, hospital volunteers' scrubs carefully folded away, dreams deferred but not forgotten.

"We'll tackle it together," he promised, gesturing at the boxes. "After we get Louise to preschool and I handle my morning lessons. Speaking of which..." He glanced at the kitchen clock.

"Go shower," Leah said, pushing him gently toward the stairs. "I'll wake Louise."

Once his footsteps faded upstairs, she pulled out the photo again. The mysterious man seemed to stare back at her through the glossy paper, his presence a warning she'd failed to read in the bright chaos of her wedding day. Something about him - the careful positioning, the watchful eyes behind the sociable smile - stirred memories of her father's business world, of the predators who wore perfect suits and carried briefcases instead of teeth. She carefully tucked it into her planner between parent-teacher conference reminders and choir practice schedules - danger hidden among the mundane, just like at her wedding.

The morning sun caught her wedding ring as she headed upstairs, sending prisms dancing across family photos lining the wall. The rainbow lights skipped across Louise's baby pictures, Chris's graduation portrait, a candid

3

of Kate mid-laugh at Christmas years ago. Family. Home. Love. Everything she'd fought to build, everything she'd protect.

Kate's voice seemed to whisper from memory: "Sometimes the best defense is seeing the fight coming." Leah squared her shoulders, touch lingering on Kate's photograph. She couldn't save her best friend from the cancer that ultimately took her, but she'd be damned if she let hidden threats destroy the family she was building now.

Louise's sleepy voice drifted down the hallway: "Mama? Is it school day?"

"Coming, sweet girl," Leah called back, her tone carefully light. The recipe tin could wait. Right now, her daughter needed breakfast, Chris needed his missing guitar picks, and their new home needed to become the sanctuary they'd planned - no matter what shadows might be gathering at the edges of their happiness.

She climbed the stairs, leaving the scattered wedding photos behind, each step a quiet promise: They would not break what she had built. They would not take what she had earned. They would not destroy what she protected. The morning sun streamed through windows they hadn't had time to wash, casting imperfect light on their imperfect beginning. Beautiful despite its shadows, precious because of its costs, and worth protecting at any price. Leah touched her wedding ring, feeling its weight like a talisman against all the things she'd lost - and all the things she refused to lose again.

Late afternoon sun filtered through the venetian blinds in Atty. Williams' office, casting striped shadows that reminded Leah of prison bars. The leather chair beneath her felt too large, too formal, its cool surface offering no comfort against the knot of anxiety tightening in her chest. Family photos lined Williams' walls – children's graduations, little league games, moments of genuine joy that made the manila envelope on the desk seem even more obscene in its sterility.

RHYTHMS OF RESILIENCE

Her fingers trembled as she smoothed her skirt, a gesture Kate would have recognized as her tell for mounting panic. The Wallace & Associates letter sat between them, the same heavy cream paper that had arrived the day before her wedding. Its timing hadn't been accidental, she realized now. Nothing in this carefully orchestrated dance ever was.

"Tell me about the surveillance first," Williams said, her voice carrying a quiet authority that somehow made the room feel safer. "You mentioned noticing someone at the wedding?"

Leah's hand shook slightly as she withdrew the image, hating how easily fear could still make her fingers unreliable. "I almost missed him entirely." The photograph felt like evidence of her failure to protect their happiness. "He was so careful to blend in."

Williams studied the image while Leah twisted her wedding ring, a habit she'd developed whenever she felt lost. The attorney's expression remained carefully neutral, but something in her eyes made Leah's throat tighten.

"Professional work," Williams noted. "High-end equipment." She tapped the man's carefully positioned stance. "This isn't amateur hour. Someone invested significant resources."

Metal touched Leah's tongue – the familiar taste of fear she'd known too often since becoming a mother. "Ryan's watching us." Her voice sounded smaller than she intended. "Gathering evidence while pretending to respect his choice to walk away."

"Family court cases often involve surveillance," Williams said gently, reaching for the Wallace & Associates letter. "Let's look at what we're actually dealing with."

The words hadn't changed since Leah first read them, yet they seemed to pulse with new menace in the afternoon light:

"Dear Ms. Miller, This correspondence serves as formal notice that our client, Mr. Ryan Matthews, despite his prior voluntary relinquishment of parental rights, intends to petition the court regarding minor child Louise Danielle Miller..."

5

Williams read silently while Leah tried to remember how to breathe normally. Kate's voice whispered from memory: "Fear only wins if you let it choose your path."

"The timing isn't coincidental," Williams said finally. "Serving this the day before your wedding – they wanted to destabilize you at a vulnerable moment."

"It almost worked." Leah's admission came out barely above a whisper. "I almost postponed everything."

"But you didn't." Williams' tone carried no judgment, only observation.

"Louise deserved to see joy win." The words surprised Leah with their quiet certainty. "Just once, I wanted fear to lose."

Williams set the letter down with deliberate care. "'Be advised that any attempts to relocate with the minor child...' They're trying to trap you in place while they build their case."

"He signed away his rights." Leah's voice caught between plea and protest. "He walked away when things got hard. How can they possibly—"

"Money," Williams interrupted gently. "Notice the emphasis on 'financial stability' and 'enhanced opportunities.' They're building a narrative about resources."

"While he gathers evidence." Leah's hands curled into fists in her lap, an unfamiliar anger warming her fear-chilled fingers. "All those times I felt watched at church, at Louise's school..."

"They expect you to panic." Williams' steady gaze anchored her. "To make emotional decisions they can use against you."

"Like I did before?" The question carried years of weight. "Running from medical school, letting Ryan sign away his rights without a fight?"

"Those were survival choices, Leah." Something maternal touched Williams' expression. "What matters is what you choose now."

The antique clock's steady heartbeat filled the silence. Leah watched Williams study her face, the attorney's eyes carrying the weight of similar stories witnessed across decades of family law. Shadows from the venetian blinds striped the desk between them like prison bars, a fitting metaphor for how trapped Leah felt in this moment.

Williams's chair creaked - a small sound that somehow carried the gravity of decision. Her hand moved to the desk drawer with deliberate care, the kind of measured movement Leah recognized from her own moments of steeling herself for difficult conversations with Louise. The drawer's hinges whispered protest, and Williams withdrew a legal pad.

The yellow paper caught afternoon light, its blank surface both promise and threat. Williams uncapped her pen, the small click echoing like a starting gun. Her hand hovered over the pristine page, waiting.

"Start at the beginning," Williams said, her voice carrying the same steady authority that had first drawn Leah to her practice. "Every interaction. Every whispered comment. Every moment you felt watched but couldn't prove it." She paused, letting the weight of what she was asking settle between them. "Even the things that seem small. Sometimes the most subtle threats leave the deepest wounds."

Leah's fingers found her wedding ring, twisting it like a worry stone. The metal had warmed to her skin, carrying the memory of Chris's trembling hands as he'd slipped it on her finger. Before the Wallace & Associates letter. Before the man in the tailored suit. Before their joy had acquired shadows.

"We'll build this carefully," Williams continued, her pen now touching paper. "Like assembling evidence for a jury. Each piece matters. Each detail counts." She looked up, her gaze anchoring Leah against the tide of memory and fear. "Together, we'll create something they can't dismiss."

The clock marked another moment. Another breath. Another chance to choose between silence and fight.

Leah straightened in her chair, shoulders squaring against the weight of what came next. Her voice, when it came, carried the strength of steel wrapped in silk. "It started at the wedding reception..."

Sunlight caught the edge of a family photo on Williams' desk – her children's graduation pictures lined up like silent witnesses. Leah felt Kate's presence in that moment, her best friend's fierce protective instinct echoing through memory: "Some battles choose you. The trick is letting them teach you your own strength."

The metal of her wedding ring had warmed against her skin, a small comfort in this sterile space. She had survived by running once, choices made in desperate moments that still echoed through her dreams. But now, watching the afternoon light paint Williams' legal pad in shades of possibility, Leah felt something shifting beneath her fear – not the bright flame of defiance, but the quiet, steady warmth of resolve. This time, she would find her voice. One careful truth at a time.

Sunday morning light filtered through gauzy curtains, casting a honeyed glow across the breakfast nook where Chris, Leah, and Louise had established their weekend ritual. The air held traces of cinnamon and coffee, mingling with the lingering sweetness of the french toast Louise had helped prepare – her small hands carefully dipping bread into egg mixture under Chris's patient guidance. Their laughter still echoed in the kitchen, a counterpoint to the gentle classical music drifting from Chris's beloved vintage record player.

Leah watched from her perch at the counter, coffee mug warming her hands, as Chris helped Louise practice her piece for next week's student recital. Their heads bent together over the child-sized guitar, created a tableau that still caught in her throat sometimes. The simple intimacy of these moments felt like a gift she hadn't dared hope for during those early days of single motherhood.

"Remember what we talked about with the finger placement?" Chris demonstrated on his own guitar, his movements slow and deliberate. "Like this – see how my hand forms an arch?"

Louise's face scrunched in concentration as she adjusted her grip. "Like a rainbow bridge for the music to travel on?"

"Exactly like that." Chris's smile carried the warmth of genuine pride. "That's a beautiful way to think about it. Where did you learn to describe things so poetically?"

"Mommy said autie Kate used to make up stories about everything." Louise's fingers found the right position, muscle memory beginning to take hold. "She said it made the world more magical."

A familiar ache bloomed in Leah's chest at the mention of Kate, but it was softer now, wrapped in the comfort of sharing these memories with her daughter. Chris glanced up, reading the emotion in her expression with the intuition that still amazed her. His eyes held understanding, acceptance of the ghost that would always dance at the edges of their happiness.

"Your Aunt Kate was right," he said, reaching over to tuck a stray curl behind Louise's ear. "And you know what? I think she'd love how you're making your own magic with music."

The morning light caught Louise's smile, transforming it into something luminous. "Can we play the special song? The one you wrote for Mommy?"

"After you show me that finger exercise one more time," Chris bargained, his teaching instincts seamlessly woven into their family dynamic. "Good habits first, then the fun stuff."

Leah set her coffee down, moving to join them at the table. The wooden surface bore the comfortable marks of their daily life – water rings from countless cups of tea, tiny scratches from Louise's art projects, circular indentations from Chris's coffee mug during late-night composition sessions. Each imperfection told a story of their growing connection, of separate lives weaving into something stronger.

As Louise worked through her exercises, Leah's fingers absently traced the edge of the Wallace & Associates letter hidden beneath yesterday's mail. The heavy cream paper carried an institutional weight that threatened to crack their Sunday morning peace. But here, in this sunlit corner of their world, the threat felt distant. Chris's hand found hers under the table, a gesture so natural she sometimes wondered if he could read the tension in her shoulders before she recognized it herself.

"Mommy, look!" Louise's excited voice pulled Leah back to the present. "I did it without any mistakes!"

"Beautiful," Leah murmured, forcing her thoughts away from legal letterhead and surveillance photos. "You're becoming quite the musician."

"Like Daddy?" Louise's hopeful question carried echoes of acceptance of belonging she'd discovered in Chris's patient guidance.

"Exactly like Daddy," Leah assured her, catching the flash of emotion across Chris's face – pride and protectiveness intertwined.

Chris reached for his guitar, the opening notes of their song rising like a shield against unseen storms. Louise abandoned her practice to crawl into Leah's lap, small body radiating warmth as they listened to the melody Chris had written for their first dance as husband and wife. The music wrapped around them like a blanket, creating a bubble of safety that almost – almost – let Leah forget about the gathering clouds on their horizon.

"Why don't we have a private concert?" Leah suggested, her voice deliberately light. "Just us, up in the music room?"

Louise's eager nod spoke volumes about her desire to preserve their intimate family moments. Chris packed away both guitars, his movements carrying the weight of choices not yet confronted. They climbed the stairs together, each step a quiet affirmation of their bond.

The music room – once a spare bedroom – had become their sanctuary. Afternoon light played across the wall of instruments, each one representing a piece of Chris's journey from uncertain student to confident teacher. Louise's smaller instruments had their own corner, arranged with the same respect given to Chris's professional gear. Family photos lined the walls, capturing moments of genuine joy: Louise's first attempt at the piano, Chris teaching her to read music, their impromptu living room concerts.

As Chris began to play again, Leah studied her daughter's face in profile. Louise's expression held the same transported peace she wore during their bedtime reading, the same complete trust she showed when falling asleep in Chris's arms. This was their reality – not the carefully staged family moments others might orchestrate, not the traditional roles some insisted were the only path to stability.

The music swelled, Chris's original composition speaking of love that chose its own shape, of family bonds forged through understanding rather than obligation. Louise hummed along, her clear voice rising with innocent confidence. Leah held them both in her heart, memorizing the moment like a photograph: the quality of light, the texture of Louise's hair against her cheek, the way Chris's hands moved across the strings with both strength and tenderness.

The song ended on a gentle note of hope, leaving them wrapped in a silence that felt like a promise – whatever storms gathered, they would weather them together.

Louise clapped with genuine delight, her joy unmarred by adult complexities. "Again, Daddy? Please?"

Chris's smile held no trace of tension. "Always, sweet girl. As many times as you want."

Leah leaned back, letting the next song wash over her like a blessing. They had built this – this imperfect, beautiful life that refused to fit neatly into anyone else's template. And she would fight with everything she had to protect it, starting with the letter burning a hole in her desk drawer downstairs. But that was for tomorrow. Today, they had music and sunlight, love and laughter, a family of their own making.

The phone rang downstairs, its shrill tone cutting through their musical sanctuary. All three of them stilled, the outside world intruding on their carefully constructed peace.

"Let it go to voicemail," Chris said quietly, his fingers never stopping their gentle movement across the guitar strings.

But the damage was done. The reminder that their bubble of safety was temporary, that forces beyond their control were already in motion. Leah pulled Louise closer, breathing in the scent of her daughter's hair, holding fast to this moment before whatever message waited downstairs could shatter their Sunday morning tranquility.

The music continued, a defiant act of joy in the face of gathering uncertainty.

CHAPTER 2

Awakenings

*THREE MONTHS EARLIER, BEFORE THE
WEDDING, BEFORE THE LETTER...*

R yan Matthews stood in the doorway of his father's home office, the termination agreement clutched in his hand like a condemned man's final appeal. Judge Matthews's study held the gravitas of a courtroom in its wood-paneled walls and leather-bound legal volumes, a fitting sanctuary for the confession burning in Ryan's throat.

Late afternoon light filtered through half-drawn blinds, casting amber stripes across the judge's silver hair as he looked up from his desk. The moment of recognition, of seeing his son framed in doorway shadows, softened the judicial severity around his eyes, but only briefly.

"Ryan." His father's voice carried the measured neutrality he'd perfected through decades on the bench. "This is unexpected."

Ryan's fingers tightened around the document, its edges soft from handling that had begun as occasional, guilty curiosity and evolved into obsessive examination. Each crease marked a moment of awakening regret, each wrinkle a reminder of choices made in haste and repented at leisure.

"I need your help." The words emerged thicker than intended, weighted with implications Ryan hadn't fully confronted until this moment. "Professionally. Legally. Financially."

Judge Matthews removed his reading glasses with deliberate care, placing them on the open brief before him. The gesture bought time, a tactic Ryan recognized from childhood interrogations about broken windows and missed curfews. "I've been retired for three years."

"But your connections remain intact." Ryan stepped into the room, the familiar scent of leather and old books wrapping around him like remembered security. On the walls, framed photographs tracked his achievements—engineering school honors, the prestigious Tesla internship, professional headshots—each one a testament to expectations he'd once fulfilled before disappointing them all.

His father gestured toward the leather chair opposite his desk. Ryan sat, placing the document between them like evidence in a trial neither had anticipated. Judge Matthews touched it with a single finger, his expression shifting as he read the title: "Voluntary Termination of Parental Rights."

"What is this?" The question came slowly, each word measured with judicial precision.

Ryan swallowed hard, his throat suddenly dry. "I have a daughter."

The silence that followed seemed to swallow all sound in the room, even the antique clock's ticking momentarily suspended in the gravity of the revelation.

"A daughter." His father repeated the words as if testing their veracity. "You have a child I've never heard about."

Ryan nodded, his eyes fixed on the document. "Her name is Louise. She's almost four."

Judge Matthews's hand flattened against the desk, steadying himself. "Four years. You've kept this from us for four years?"

"I never told you about Leah's pregnancy." The confession began to spill out, years of secrecy crumbling under the weight of his father's stunned expression. "I was in my junior year of engineering school. I'd just secured that Tesla internship. My grad school applications were perfect. Everything was finally falling into place..."

"And a child didn't fit into that picture." His father's voice held no question, only a dawning understanding that cut deeper than any accusation.

Ryan's shoulders slumped, the careful posture he'd maintained throughout his career momentarily abandoned. "I made a terrible mistake in college. Cheated on Leah at that party before finals. She found out, broke things off immediately."

"The Miller girl? John Miller's daughter?"

Ryan nodded. "Four months after our breakup, she told me she was pregnant. She'd already dropped out of pre-med by then—she was brilliant, you know, top of her class before—" He stopped, realizing how hollow his praise sounded against the backdrop of his abandonment. "She decided to keep the baby, even though it meant giving up medical school."

Judge Matthews's expression darkened. "And you?"

"I told her I didn't want any part of it." The words hung in the air, their ugliness impossible to soften. "Two days later, her lawyer sent over this agreement. I signed it without even reading the fine print."

His father's hand moved to the document, turning it to examine the signatures at the bottom. "Voluntary termination. Before the child was even born."

Ryan nodded, unable to meet his father's eyes. "I was scared. Ambitious. Selfish."

The weight of that admission settled between them like a physical presence. Judge Matthews leaned back in his chair, the leather creaking with familiar protest. His fingers drummed once against the desk, a tell Ryan remembered from childhood—the unconscious gesture that preceded his father's most difficult verdicts.

"Why keep this from us?" The question carried layers Judge Matthews hadn't yet fully excavated. "Why hide her existence from your own family?"

Ryan's laugh held no humor. "Isn't it what you always wanted? 'Focus on your career, son. Everything else is just noise.' I took that literally, I guess."

The words landed like a physical blow. Judge Matthews's face flushed with sudden anger, his palm striking the desk with unexpected force. "Don't you dare put this on me!" His voice rose, judicial control fracturing for a rare moment. "I never—NEVER—would have encouraged you to abandon your child. To deny us our grandchild. To hide her existence like some shameful secret!"

The outburst echoed through the study, bouncing off leather spines and mahogany surfaces. Ryan flinched, recognizing the profound hurt beneath his father's fury. This wasn't merely disappointment in Ryan's choices—this was the raw wound of discovering that precious years with a grandchild had been stolen through deception.

Judge Matthews rose abruptly, moving to the window where late sunlight caught the silver in his hair. His shoulders carried a new weight, the burden of reconciling the son he thought he knew with this stranger who had hidden such fundamental truths. The silence stretched between them, filled with the ticking of the antique clock and the distant sound of traffic beyond the window.

A grandchild, Judge Matthews thought, the words cycling through his consciousness like a mantra both wonderful and terrible. *Margaret and I have a grandchild we've never met.* But alongside the longing came something more troubling—the recognition that this child had built a life, formed attachments, created her own understanding of family. The magnitude of what had been stolen from them pressed against his chest, yet so did the weight of what disruption might steal from her.

He thought of Margaret, how they'd tried for years to give Ryan a sibling after his birth. Three miscarriages in five years had finally convinced them that Ryan would be their only child—their miracle, as Margaret often called him. She'd poured all her maternal energy into their son, but he'd seen her wistful glances at families with multiple children, the way she'd quietly put away the baby clothes she'd optimistically saved. After

Ryan's evasion about serious relationships became a pattern, Margaret had stopped asking about marriage and grandchildren altogether, though he'd caught her sometimes watching children at the park with a longing she thought no one noticed. The realization that Louise had existed all this time, that Margaret's dream of a grandchild to spoil and nurture had been real but hidden, created a hollow ache in his chest.

"She's four years old," he said quietly, still facing the window. The words emerged as much for his own processing as for Ryan's understanding. Four years of Christmas mornings without small hands tearing paper. Four years of missed bedtime stories, scraped knees that needed grandfather kisses, the thousand tiny moments that built the architecture of love between generations. But also four years of another man's lullabies, another family's traditions, bonds that had grown deep and strong in their absence.

Judge Matthews turned back to face his son, studying Ryan's face with the analytical precision that had served him throughout his judicial career. What he saw there wasn't the callous young man who had signed away his rights, but someone genuinely tortured by the magnitude of his mistakes. The slump of Ryan's shoulders, the way his fingers worried at the document's edges, the carefully contained anguish in his expression—these spoke to genuine regret rather than opportunistic manipulation. Yet regret alone couldn't justify the destruction such a case might bring.

"And now?" The question emerged softer than before, judicial assessment tempering paternal disappointment.

"Now I regret it every day." Ryan's voice cracked, emotion finally breaking through the carefully constructed facade he'd maintained for four years. "I see her sometimes, from a distance. She looks like mom around the eyes. She's beautiful and bright and creative, and I've missed everything. Her first words. Her first steps. Everything."

Judge Matthews returned to his chair. His legal mind began working despite his emotional turmoil, decades of family court experience automatically cataloguing the complexities ahead. Voluntary termination agreements were notoriously difficult to overturn. Courts viewed them as sacred, the final word in cases where biological parents chose to step

17

aside. But precedent existed for exceptional circumstances, for cases where fundamental fairness demanded reconsideration. Yet each legal pathway led through terrain that could devastate an innocent child.

"You mentioned seeing her," Judge Matthews said carefully, his voice carrying the weight of judicial caution. "Where? How?"

Ryan reached for his phone with trembling fingers. "Wallace had someone take photographs. For the case." He scrolled to images he'd studied until they were burned into his memory: Louise on a playground swing, her smile carefree; Louise painting at an easel, her expression intent with creative focus.

Judge Matthews accepted the phone with reluctant hands, as if the device might somehow make this impossible situation more real. The judicial mask that had served him for three decades began to crack as he studied the first image. The child's dark hair caught sunlight like Margaret's always had, and those eyes—dear God, those were unmistakably Margaret's eyes, the same shape and depth and startling intelligence.

Judge Matthews swiped through the photographs with growing wonder and pain. Each image revealed new details—the delicate arch of eyebrows that echoed Margaret's face, the way the child held her head with unconscious dignity that spoke to good breeding, the bright curiosity in her expression that reminded him powerfully of Ryan at that age, before disappointment and ambition had hardened his features. But in each photograph, he also saw something else—a child who appeared loved, secure, untroubled by the legal storm gathering around her young life.

"My God," he whispered, his voice catching on the words. "She does have Margaret's eyes."

The admission seemed to crack something fundamental within his carefully constructed composure. This wasn't merely Ryan's abandoned responsibility—this was family blood, Matthews lineage, the continuation of something precious that had been severed without their knowledge or consent. Yet she was also a little girl who had never known their names, who had built her understanding of family around other faces, other voices, other love.

RHYTHMS OF RESILIENCE

Judge Matthews set the phone down carefully. "Professional surveillance. High-end equipment." His gaze sharpened on his son. "Do you have any idea what Wallace & Associates charges for this level of investigation?"

"Fifty thousand for the retainer," Ryan admitted, the number still staggering even after he'd written the check. "Another fifteen for the surveillance and initial case preparation. They estimate the full custody challenge could run to six figures if it goes to appeal."

Judge Matthews's face paled slightly. "You've already spent sixty-five thousand dollars?"

"I had to know if I had a case before coming to you," Ryan said quietly. "They've been working on this for three weeks. The surveillance, the legal research, analyzing the termination agreement for vulnerabilities. They're confident, Dad. Wallace himself said this is winnable."

"What does Wallace say about your chances?" His question emerged laden with judicial caution rather than paternal enthusiasm.

"That it's an uphill battle. These agreements are designed to be permanent. But there might be procedural issues we could leverage. Questions about duress or full disclosure." Ryan hesitated.

Judge Matthews's expression shifted. "Wallace & Associates? Ryan, their retainer alone—"

"I know what they cost." Ryan's voice carried a calculated edge rather than defensive pride. "I've been saving. My consulting work has been good, and I've already liquidated most of my investments." He paused, meeting his father's eyes directly. "But I'll run out of funds within two months if this goes to court. That's why I'm here. Wallace says we have a real shot at this, but only if we can sustain the fight through appeals if necessary. I need your resources, Dad. Your connections. Your expertise."

The admission hung between them—not heroic sacrifice but pragmatic calculation. Ryan had started this battle, but he needed his father's war chest to finish it.

Judge Matthews studied his son with new understanding. This wasn't impulsive desperation but strategic planning. Ryan had done his research, hired the best firm, gathered evidence—and now recognized the limits of his own resources.

"How much are we talking about?" Judge Matthews asked, his tone shifting to something more businesslike.

"Wallace estimates two hundred thousand if it goes to full custody hearing and appeals," Ryan said, the astronomical figure delivered with the flatness of someone who had already absorbed its impact. "Maybe more if they mount a strong defense. I can cover another twenty, maybe thirty thousand. But after that..." He gestured helplessly.

Judge Matthews nodded slowly, his mind moving through the financial and legal labyrinth ahead with careful consideration of every potential cost. Wallace & Associates had an excellent reputation, particularly in family law. More importantly, James Wallace owed him several substantial favors from their shared work on judicial reform committees. Those connections might prove invaluable in ways that extended beyond mere funding.

"Ryan," he said carefully, leaning forward with the gravity of judicial pronouncement, "I need you to understand what you're asking. Not just of me, but of that little girl."

Ryan's hopeful expression flickered with uncertainty.

"Leah will fight you on this," Judge Matthews continued, his voice carrying both warning and deep concern. "She'll fight with everything she has to protect what she's built. The man who's been raising Louise—he'll see you as a threat to his family. This won't be a gentle legal proceeding."

"I know," Ryan said, though his father suspected he couldn't yet fully comprehend the emotional battlefield they would be entering.

"Do you?" Judge Matthews pressed, his judicial experience informing every word. "Because this isn't just about adults making difficult choices. This is about a four-year-old child who will be subjected to psychological evaluations, court interviews, the scrutiny of strangers determining her fate. She'll be asked questions about loyalty and love that no child should have to answer."

Ryan's face paled as the reality began to penetrate his strategic certainty.

"That little girl has lived her entire conscious life believing she knows who her family is," Judge Matthews continued relentlessly. "Your legal challenge will shake the foundation of her world. Are you prepared to take responsibility for that damage?"

The weight of that reality settled over Ryan like a physical presence. For the first time, genuine doubt flickered across his features—uncertainty about whether his desire for fatherhood was worth the disruption it would cause to Louise's established life.

Judge Matthews recognized that hesitation and found it encouraging rather than discouraging. The Ryan who had signed away his rights five years ago wouldn't have paused to consider the child's perspective. This man, struggling with the ethical implications of his choices, seemed capable of genuine growth. But capability and reality were different territories entirely.

"I've spent four years thinking about what I lost," Ryan said finally, his voice smaller than before. "But I believe Louise deserves to know me. To know our family. To understand where she comes from."

Our family. The phrase resonated in Judge Matthews' chest, carrying all the weight of missed Christmases and unspoken lullabies. He thought of Margaret again, imagining her face when she would learn about Louise. The initial shock would give way to fierce protectiveness, maternal instincts extending instantly to encompass this unknown grandchild. Margaret would want to fight for Louise's place in their family with every fiber of her being. But she would also, he knew, be devastated by the thought of causing Louise pain through their legal battle.

Judge Matthews removed his glasses, pinching the bridge of his nose. "I'll help with the expenses," he said finally, each word extracted with visible effort. "I have connections at Wallace's firm. Professional relationships built over decades of judicial work. And savings that can cover what you can't."

The relief that flooded Ryan's expression was immediately tempered by the gravity in his father's continued voice.

"But understand this, Ryan." Judge Matthews leaned forward, his tone carrying the absolute authority of three decades on the bench. "My help comes with conditions that are non-negotiable."

Ryan straightened, recognizing the shift to judicial pronouncement.

"First, this case will be conducted with absolute integrity. No dirty tactics. No character assassination. No using that child as a weapon against the people who've loved her." His voice hardened with each condition. "If I discover you've authorized anything that deliberately harms Louise's emotional wellbeing, I withdraw my support immediately."

"I would never—"

"Second," Judge Matthews continued without pause, "at the first sign that this legal process is damaging Louise—and I mean the first sign—we reassess. Her wellbeing takes precedence over our desires. Always."

Ryan nodded, though uncertainty flickered in his expression.

"And third," Judge Matthews concluded, his voice softening with paternal concern, "you need to prepare yourself for the possibility that what's best for Louise might not be what you want. If the court determines she should remain where she is, you accept that decision with grace."

The conditions hung between them like a legal contract written in familial bonds rather than courtroom language. Judge Matthews studied his son's face, searching for signs of the selfishness that had characterized Ryan's earlier choices.

"I understand," Ryan said finally, and something in his tone suggested he genuinely grasped the weight of what his father was offering—not just financial support, but conditional alliance in a battle that could destroy as much as it might restore.

Judge Matthews nodded slowly, the movement carrying the weight of judicial decision rendered. "I'll call Wallace tomorrow morning. Let him know I'm coming on board financially. We'll schedule a meeting for next week to review their strategy." His expression hardened slightly. "And I'll make it clear that my support comes with conditions."

As Ryan prepared to leave, Judge Matthews watched his son with careful assessment. The young man who had walked into this office carrying shame and regret was departing with something resembling hope, but it was hope tempered by newfound understanding of the complexities ahead—and the recognition that his father's resources, not his own sacrifice, would determine the outcome.

"We'll tell your mother together," Judge Matthews decided. "Tonight. But we'll also tell her about the conditions I've set. She needs to understand that our help isn't unconditional."

Ryan paused at the doorway, turning back with gratitude and trepidation evident in his features. "Dad? Thank you. For giving me this chance. For giving Louise this chance to know her family."

"Don't thank me yet," Judge Matthews replied quietly. "Thank me when we've navigated this without destroying anyone. Especially her."

After Ryan left, Judge Matthews remained in his study, surrounded by legal volumes and family photographs. The termination agreement lay before him like a challenge, its clinical language unable to diminish either his longing to know his granddaughter or his fear of what that knowledge might cost her.

Judge Matthews made the call to Wallace & Associates the next morning. The senior partner's tone shifted noticeably when he learned that Judge Matthews—former family court judge with three decades of experience—would be funding and advising on Ryan's case. What had been a standard custody challenge suddenly carried the weight of judicial expertise and unlimited resources. Over the following two months, Wallace's team worked with methodical precision: more surveillance photographs documenting Louise's daily routines, deeper background investigations into Leah's history, exhaustive analysis of every clause in the termination agreement. They built their case like architects constructing a cathedral—each piece carefully placed, each argument meticulously researched. "We get one shot at this," Wallace reminded Ryan at their fifth meeting. "When we file, it needs to be ironclad." That ironclad filing came in the form of a cream-colored envelope delivered to Leah Miller's doorstep the day before she would marry Chris Johnson, the day before she believed her new life would truly begin. The letter's arrival, timed for maximum disruption, would shatter that belief like glass against stone.

Morrison's office smelled of stale coffee and old paper. Tyler sat across from the private investigator, who slid a folder across the scarred desk without preamble.

"Found what you asked for," Morrison said. "About John Miller's timing."

Tyler opened the folder. A newspaper clipping showed his father standing before Johnson & Sons' storefront. The headline read "Local Business Legacy." The date made his stomach turn.

"Six months before the collapse," he said.

Morrison nodded. "Miller Financial's team started targeting your father's suppliers that same week. Bank records confirm it." He pointed to another document. "These timestamps show a coordinated effort."

Tyler's hands tightened on the papers. "They planned it. Systematically."

"The evidence shows deliberate timing," Morrison said, his tone neutral. "Whether it was personal or just business strategy, I can't say."

"It was personal." Tyler's voice hardened. "And now his daughter is in our family."

Morrison pulled out more documents. Surveillance photos of Leah with Louise. Church records. Chris's music program schedules.

"About your brother's wife," Morrison said. "Here's what I found."

Tyler leaned forward.

"Leah Miller joined St. Michael's parish three months before she met Chris. Started attending the music program where he taught. They met at a Sunday social when her daughter was six months old."

"In the same town where her father destroyed our business." Tyler's jaw tightened. "That's not coincidence."

"Could be." Morrison's expression remained professionally blank. "Small town. Single mother looking for community support. Your brother teaches music. Her daughter needed childcare during services."

"Or it was calculated." Tyler stood, pacing. "Miller tactics are patient. Systematic."

Morrison closed his folder. "I'm giving you facts. The interpretation is yours." He paused, met Tyler's eyes directly. "For what it's worth? The evidence suggests coincidence. I don't see signs of coordination between Leah and her father. No unusual communication patterns. No financial connections. She withdrew from pre-med when she got pregnant—gave up everything, actually. Doesn't fit the profile of someone executing a long-term plan."

"You don't know Miller tactics like I do," Tyler said.

"Maybe not." Morrison stood. "But I've been doing this twenty years. When people are coordinating something, there are always traces. I'm not finding them here."

Tyler grabbed the folder. "Keep digging. There's something we're missing."

"I'll document what I find," Morrison said. "But Tyler—be careful you're not seeing patterns that aren't there."

"Just do your job." Tyler headed for the door. "Watch her. Every interaction. Every phone call. Every church meeting."

Morrison nodded. "You'll get your reports."

After Tyler left, Morrison returned to his desk. He looked at the folder's contents once more—a young woman who'd sacrificed medical school for motherhood, who worked part-time to support her daughter, who'd found community in a church where a kind music teacher had welcomed them both.

Sometimes, Morrison thought, the simplest explanation was the right one.

But Tyler Johnson wasn't interested in simple explanations. Not when it came to the Miller family.

2002

Sunset bled through Johnson & Sons' storefront windows as seventeen-year-old Tyler stood beside the service counter. Miller Financial's associates moved through the shop with clinical efficiency, their clipboards transforming his inheritance into mere assets to be liquidated.

Tyler's fingers found the worn depression in the counter where his grandfather had stood for forty years. The shallow groove held the weight of countless transactions, each one a promise kept between neighbors. Now strangers assigned dollar values to everything his family had built.

"Daddy? Can I play with the train set while we wait?"

Chris's voice cut through the inventory recitation. At six years old, his brother didn't understand what was happening. His Batman shirt bore chocolate smudges from Aunt Terry's stress-baking.

Their father's pen hesitated above the documents, his Adam's apple working against his starched collar. Tom Johnson had never been a man for suits—today's felt like a uniform for defeat.

"No, buddy," their father managed. "The train set's packed away."

Tyler watched Chris's face crumple. The Christmas train display had been a Johnson & Sons tradition, transforming their shop into something magical each December.

"But you said I could help set it up for Christmas," Chris persisted, his lower lip trembling. "You promised."

The word 'promised' broke something behind their father's eyes. Tyler moved with protective instincts that would define him forever, kneeling beside Chris.

"How about you help me count inventory instead?" Tyler forced enthusiasm into his voice. "We could make it a game."

Chris's dark eyes searched Tyler's face. "Is this for the new store?"

There would be no new store. Tyler swallowed against the truth. "It's for the records."

In the stockroom, Chris handled each Christmas ornament with reverent care, unaware this might be their final Christmas here. Tyler watched his brother's small hands, so trusting, so innocent.

"Tyler?" Chris whispered. "Are we in trouble? Did we do something bad?"

The angel ornament—purchased by their mother when the shop opened—felt fragile in Tyler's hands. "No, buddy. You didn't do anything wrong."

Through the walls, fragments of conversation drifted: "Asset liquidation." "Inventory valuation." "Transition team." Each phrase hammered another nail into their family legacy's coffin.

When the final walkthrough began, the lead associate's heels clicked against worn floorboards. "The transition team takes possession tomorrow morning," she announced.

Chris tugged at Tyler's sleeve. "Is Santa still coming to the store this year?"

Every December, Johnson & Sons became a community center where Santa arrived through their modified skylight, delighting children whose parents couldn't afford mall photography.

Tyler knelt to meet his brother's gaze. "Santa will find us wherever we are. Different doesn't mean worse."

He knew it was a lie. Different would mean worse—smaller, diminished. But Chris needed to believe.

Their father's signature completed the final document. The key turned with terrible finality.

On the sidewalk outside, Tyler paused to look back through darkened windows at empty shelves that had once held the promise of his future. The Miller Financial car purred away, its expensive engine mocking the practical reliability his father had always valued.

Tyler stood with Chris and their father beneath flickering streetlights, three generations united by loss.

"Let's go home," their father said, the words carrying no warmth.

Tyler lingered for one final moment, his reflection staring back from the cold glass—a young man aged by circumstances beyond his choosing, already hardening into someone his grandfather might not recognize.

In his pocket, Chris's forgotten toy train pressed against his hip. At seventeen, Tyler made two promises that would define his life: never again would he watch his family break while others profited, and never again would he trust that good intentions were armor against the world's cruelty.

Some lessons could only be learned once. The trick was ensuring you never needed to learn them again.

CHAPTER 3

Blood and Loyalty

E vening light filtered through Terry's lace curtains, casting a honeycomb pattern across her immaculate living room. Tyler stood with his back to the window, his shadow stretching between them like a dark bridge. Morrison's folder lay unopened on the polished coffee table, its crisp manila edges a stark intrusion against the mahogany surface that Terry insisted on polishing each Tuesday after Bible study.

"You're saying John Miller did this on purpose?" Terry's voice carried a note of theatrical shock as her fingers clutched her cross pendant. "Executed your family's business?"

Tyler shifted his weight, uncertainty creeping along his spine. The evidence seemed clear in Morrison's office, surrounded by professional assessments and cold documentation. Here, in the warm glow of his aunt's living room, the theory felt both essential and somehow fragile—a glass figure he feared might shatter under scrutiny.

"Morrison found records. Meetings. Timelines." He tapped the folder with one finger. "It looks deliberate. But I'm still trying to understand if Leah's connection to Chris is just... unfortunate coincidence."

ALEXANDRA PALCHAK

The admission cost him something—an acknowledgment of doubt where certainty would have been more comfortable. The possibility that Leah might be innocent of her father's sins existed alongside his discomfort at her presence in their family. Both truths occupied the same troubled space in his chest.

Terry's eyes widened with the light of revelation, the simple cause-and-effect connections forming in her mind with enviable speed. Where Tyler struggled with nuance, Terry found immediate clarity.

"Well, it certainly explains why she's wormed her way into Chris's life," she pronounced with sudden conviction. "If only Mary had told me that Leah is the daughter of the man who destroyed your family's business! I could have stopped this marriage before it went too far."

"I'm just so mad at Mary," Terry continued, emotional currents shifting with dizzying speed.

The indignation in her voice struck a discordant note. Not because Tyler disagreed with her conclusion—he'd harbored similar suspicions—but because her certainty seemed unearned, built on emotional reaction rather than careful assessment.

Terry moved to the window, adjusting her curtain with practiced precision. "That girl has always seemed wrong for our family. She just doesn't fit in." Her reflection ghosted against the darkening glass, features sharpened by resentment. "I know she's smart and all, according to Chris, but there is something about her that irritates me down to my bones. Now I know why."

Tyler heard the personal edge in Terry's critique—a glimpse of the real source of her dislike beneath her proclaimed concern for Chris. The revelation made him uncomfortable, though he couldn't dismiss her suspicions entirely. His own unease with Leah stemmed from family loyalty and painful history—yet he wondered how much of his judgment might also be colored by pettier emotions.

"Chris doesn't see it," Tyler said, finding safer ground in their shared concern for his brother. "He never looks beneath the surface."

"Never!" Terry seized on this alignment with surprising force. "His heart will be the end of him. Remember Rachael? And Jennifer? Both cheated on him, and he never saw the signs that were clear to everyone else. What makes Leah any different than those women?"

The examples hung between them, Tyler recognizing the partial truth in Terry's assessment. Chris had always been willing to see the best in people, even at his own expense. Yet the comparison between those failed relationships and his marriage to Leah felt imperfect—a forced connection that papered over important distinctions.

Tyler watched his aunt's indignation build, her face flushing with the righteous anger that had fueled countless church committee confrontations. Despite her limited education, Terry wielded social influence with surprising effectiveness—building alliances, spreading concerns, and orchestrating group responses to perceived threats.

"I need to tell Kourtney and Randy right away," she declared, already reaching for her phone. "Randy knows all about business and stuff. He'll understand what this means."

Tyler placed his hand over hers, stopping her. "Not yet. Morrison's still investigating. We need to be careful with the information."

Terry's face fell momentarily before brightening with a new thought. "We need to protect Chris. He's too trusting. Too nice. Just like your father was before the store closed."

The comparison sent a jolt of genuine pain through Tyler's chest. The memory of his father's defeated expression the day they locked Johnson & Sons for the final time remained visceral—a wound that still bled when pressed.

"What about Ryan Matthews?" Terry asked, her question showing unexpected strategic awareness. "Louise's real daddy. You said lawyers are involved?"

"Yes. Wallace & Associates is building a case." Tyler observed the calculation that transformed Terry's expression. "They want to challenge the termination agreement."

"Well!" Terry's eyebrows shot up, a smile spreading across her face. "That's interesting timing, isn't it? Almost like God's provision."

The implication hung unspoken between them—that Louise's removal from Leah's care might be a desired outcome. The casual cruelty of this assessment—the readiness to tear a child from the only home she'd known—sent an uncomfortable chill through Tyler. He shared Terry's suspicion of Leah but balked at the collateral damage Terry seemed willing to accept.

"Louise is innocent in all this," he said quietly.

"Of course she is, bless her heart," Terry agreed without hesitation. "But it's a complicated situation." She closed the folder with delicate precision, her movements carrying the weight of decision. "I'll start a prayer circle for 'family concerns.' Nobody can object to prayer, can they? And during prayer, people share things." Her smile carried a cunning that surprised Tyler. "Important things about parenting choices and stability."

A car passed outside, headlights briefly illuminating Terry's face before returning it to shadow. In that fleeting brightness, Tyler glimpsed something that unsettled him—not the calculated malice he might have expected, but absolute conviction in her own righteousness. Terry truly believed her actions were protective rather than destructive, guided by moral certainty untroubled by complexity.

"If Ryan Matthews is truly worried about his little girl..." Terry let the sentence hang unfinished, its implication clear.

"He should have all the information," Tyler completed, understanding the dangerous alliance taking shape between them.

Terry's smile widened. "For the family's sake," she said softly. "For Chris."

The evening had settled fully outside, darkness embracing the neighborhood in its blanket. Within Terry's living room, the lamps cast pools of golden light that didn't quite reach the corners. Shadows gathered there, witnesses to the unholy communion of purpose forming in their midst.

32

Tyler studied a family photograph on the side table—Chris at his high school graduation, his smile genuine and unguarded. The image made something twist in his chest, a complex emotion that blended love and fear and fierce protection. His certainty wavered again. Was Leah truly part of some calculated revenge, or simply the daughter of a man whose business practices had once destroyed their family? The distinction mattered, yet in this moment, bathed in Terry's righteous certainty, the nuance began to blur.

"I'll tell you what," Terry said, moving to her desk where her leather-bound planner lay open. "I'm going to start writing down every little thing that seems off." Her pen moved across the page with surprising determination. "We need documentation. That's what they call it on those crime shows. Documentation."

Tyler watched his aunt's methodical recording with mixed emotions. Her approach was simplistic yet dangerous in its potential impact. The intellectual limitations that made others dismiss Terry also made her impervious to doubt—a quality that gave her actions a frightening momentum.

"You'll keep me updated on what that detective finds?" Terry asked, looking up from her notes.

"I will," Tyler promised, the weight of that commitment settling on his shoulders.

As he prepared to leave, Terry followed him to the door, her hand catching his arm with surprising strength. "We're doing the right thing," she insisted, needing the reassurance despite her proclaimed certainty. "That girl shouldn't be in our family after what her father did."

The simplicity of her statement captured the essence of her worldview—a place where complex situations were reduced to straightforward moral equations untroubled by nuance. Tyler envied her certainty even as he questioned its foundation.

"Good night, Aunt Terry," he said, stepping into the autumn evening.

"Thursday prayer circle," she reminded him. "Four o'clock. We can talk more then."

As Tyler walked to his car, streetlights cast his shadow long against the sidewalk. The burden of Morrison's folder under his arm felt heavier than its physical weight warranted. The certainty he'd felt in the investigator's office had fractured during his conversation with Terry, doubt seeping through the cracks.

He started the engine, its quiet purr a counterpoint to the discord in his thoughts. In his rearview mirror, Terry still stood in her doorway, a sentinel against perceived threats, guardian of a family legacy she only partially understood. Her simpler view of the situation—Leah as enemy, Chris as victim—lacked the nuance that troubled Tyler's thoughts.

Was Leah connected to her father's sins? Logic suggested no. But the ache in his chest when he remembered his father's defeat demanded someone pay the debt. Even if that someone was just a little girl when Johnson & Sons closed its doors forever.

As he drove away, Terry's curtains closed like an eyelid over a watchful eye. Whether blind or visionary remained to be seen. The alliance with Terry troubled Tyler even as he embraced its purpose. Her methods would be blunt where precision was needed, her understanding limited where complexity demanded care.

Yet her absolute conviction carried its own power. A force that would gather momentum in prayer circles and church committees, in family gatherings and community events. Terry might not understand the battle's nuance, but she would fight it with unwavering certainty.

Tyler turned onto the main road, Morrison's folder a silent passenger beside him. Somewhere between Terry's simplistic vendetta and his own conflicted suspicions lay a dangerous path forward—one that promised protection but might deliver destruction instead.

Whatever grew from this night's work would bear fruit in the coming seasons. Whether that harvest would bring healing or deeper wounds remained to be seen.

Evening light bathed Mary's garden in molten gold, each ray illuminating the roses she had tended through twenty-three seasons of marriage. Her clippers moved with precision, severing spent blooms to encourage new growth—a metaphor she had lived by, though perhaps understood too late. The familiar ritual anchored her thoughts against the growing certainty that this peaceful sanctuary would soon become a battlefield.

The geraniums had spilled beyond their designated borders, nature's gentle rebellion against her careful planning. She smiled at their persistence, thinking of Chris and his music that had never fit Tom's practical expectations, his heart that stretched beyond safe boundaries. In marrying Leah, he had followed that expansive heart again. Mary respected him for it, even as she sensed the storm gathering.

Heels struck the flagstone path with deliberate percussion—sharp, purposeful, carrying judgment in their cadence. Mary's hands stilled, though she didn't turn. Some confrontations announced themselves through posture alone.

"Mary." Terry's voice sliced through the garden's gentle acoustics.

"I wasn't expecting you today." Mary continued her pruning, each cut a small act of defiance against the interruption.

Terry positioned herself, arms crossed, her pressed linen ensemble speaking of deliberate preparation. The cross pendant at her throat caught the fading light like a small accusation.

"I've just had a very interesting conversation with Tyler."

Mary's clippers paused mid-cut, her face remaining turned toward the roses. "Is that so?"

"About John Miller."

The name dropped between them like smoke, heavy with old wounds and unfinished business. Mary resumed her careful work, removing another withered bloom. "What about him?"

"You knew." Terry's voice tightened with accusation barely restrained. "You knew Leah is his daughter."

Mary set down her clippers, brushing soil from her palms while gathering scattered thoughts. The confrontation she had hoped to avoid had arrived with inevitable precision.

"Yes." She rose slowly, joints protesting the movement. "I knew."

"And you didn't tell me."

Mary faced her sister directly, cataloging the high color in Terry's cheeks, the narrowed eyes, the righteous indignation that had fueled her interventions throughout their shared lifetime.

"It wasn't relevant."

"Wasn't relevant?" Terry's voice climbed with incredulous fury. "The daughter of the man who destroyed Johnson & Sons marries into our family, and you don't think that's relevant?"

A robin alighted on the nearby birdbath, dipping its beak with serene indifference to human conflicts. Mary envied its simple focus, its freedom from the complex loyalties that bound families in invisible chains.

"I wanted to know Leah as herself," Mary kept her voice steady. "Not as John Miller's daughter."

"How convenient." Terry stepped closer, invading the careful space between them. "Meanwhile, she wormed her way into Chris's life. Into this family. Using whatever manipulation tactics her father taught her."

Mary's fingers curled against her palms, nails pressing crescents into flesh. "Leah was barely more than a baby when Johnson & Sons closed."

Terry dismissed this with an impatient gesture. "That doesn't change who her father is. What her family did to ours."

"We've made our peace with John." Mary's voice remained quiet but carried steel beneath its surface. "Tom and I both. After Chris and Leah got engaged."

Terry's face registered genuine shock. "You sat down with that man? After what he did?"

Mary turned back to her roses, needing their thorned beauty to steady her trembling hands. "Leah found papers in John's office while helping him move. She and Chris came to us together. We talked. It was... healing."

"Healing?" Terry spat the word like poison. "There's no healing from what that man did. He executed your husband's business. Deliberately."

"We've moved beyond that now." Mary deadheaded another rose with perhaps too much force. "We've all made peace with the past."

"Without telling me. Without telling any of us." The hurt beneath Terry's indignation pierced through, revealing deeper wounds. "I'm family too."

Mary softened despite herself. "It was private. Between the people directly involved."

"I'm Chris's godmother." Terry's voice quavered with genuine pain. "I had a right to know."

The word 'right' hung between them, weighted with decades of assumed authority, of Terry's belief that family membership granted unlimited access to others' decisions.

"The past is settled," Mary said, turning to face her sister. "What matters now is Chris's happiness. He loves Leah. She makes him happy."

"Happiness built on lies isn't real happiness."

"What lies has Leah told?" Mary challenged, rare confrontation entering her tone. "Has she hidden her past from Chris?"

Terry stepped back slightly. "Tyler says Morrison found evidence. Documents. John Miller targeted your husband's business specifically."

"We know." Mary's simple statement deflated Terry momentarily. "John admitted it. Tom has forgiven him. I've forgiven him."

"How can you forgive what he took from your family?" Terry's incomprehension reflected the fundamental chasm between the sisters—Mary's capacity for healing against Terry's determination to nurse grievances.

"Because holding onto anger only hurts us." Mary gestured toward her garden. "Like these plants—sometimes you must prune away dead parts to allow new growth."

Terry's laugh held bitter edges. "Very poetic. Meanwhile, his daughter plays house with Chris and that child that isn't even his."

The casual cruelty burned through Mary's composure. "That 'child' is my granddaughter in every way that matters."

"She's Ryan Matthews' daughter." Terry's eyes gleamed with newfound triumph. "And he wants her back. Wallace & Associates doesn't come cheap."

Mary's chest constricted. "What are you talking about?"

"Ryan Matthews wants his daughter back. He's challenging the termination agreement."

Mary studied her sister's face, searching for signs of speculation rather than fact. Finding none, she asked quietly, "Does Chris know?"

"Of course he knows." Terry's satisfaction radiated like heat. "But he didn't tell you, did he? Our open, honest Chris keeping secrets from his own mother."

The revelation stung, though Mary understood her son's protective instincts. Chris had always processed struggles privately, finding voice through music rather than words.

"Leah cut ties with Ryan before Louise was born," Mary said. "He signed away his rights."

"Well, he's walking back now." Terry smoothed her immaculate blouse. "Poor Chris has no idea what he's gotten into. An ugly custody battle in the first year of marriage? That boy's always been blinded by love."

Mary removed her gardening gloves, the evening suddenly cold against her skin. "Chris is stronger than you give him credit for."

"He's going to need to be. With a wife whose father destroyed his family's legacy and an ex-boyfriend fighting for custody of a child Chris foolishly thinks is his."

"Louise is his in every way that matters." Mary's voice hardened, rare steel emerging. "And Leah is part of our family now. Whether you accept that or not."

"Blood matters, Mary." Terry touched a rose petal with incongruous gentleness. "Family matters. Real family."

"Chris loves that child deeply." Mary's soft voice carried iron beneath silk. "And whatever you're planning, you need to stop before you tear Chris apart in the process."

Terry looked genuinely startled by such directness. "I'm protecting him. Him and Louise both."

"From what? A mother who loves her? A father who chose her? A family that welcomes her?" Mary stepped closer, decades of deference dissolving in the face of this threat. "Your 'protection' will destroy what he loves most."

"You're not seeing clearly." Terry adjusted her cross pendant defensively. "A prayer circle for family concerns. Documentation of troubling patterns. Sharing information with people who need to know. That's all I'm doing."

Each innocent phrase carried ominous undertones. Mary had witnessed Terry's "prayer circles" destroy reputations, seen her "documentation" transform minor incidents into damning patterns.

"You need to be careful," Mary chose her words precisely. "Interfering in a marriage has consequences."

"So does allowing a Miller to destroy another Johnson."

The stark framing chilled Mary despite the warm evening. In Terry's mind, battle lines had crystallized. Leah represented the enemy, regardless of individual character or actions.

"I've started keeping notes," Terry continued, producing a small notebook. "Instances where Louise seems unhappy. Her absences from church functions."

Mary glimpsed pages filled with Terry's rounded handwriting. Date. Time. Observation. The methodical surveillance struck her as more disturbing than emotional outbursts.

"Terry." Mary kept her voice gentle. "This isn't healthy."

"What isn't healthy is letting that girl raise another man's child while hiding who she really is."

"She's not hiding anything." Mary's patience stretched thin. "Chris knew exactly who she was when he married her. He chose her anyway."

"Then he's a fool."

"He's in love." Mary corrected. "Something you might understand if you'd ever allowed yourself to be vulnerable enough to truly know another person."

The unusual barb found its mark. Terry's face flushed with hurt before hardening again.

"Tyler meets with Morrison again tomorrow," Terry said, voice clipped. "The evidence is mounting. John Miller's business practices, Leah's sudden appearance in Chris's life, now Ryan seeking custody... it all connects."

Mary felt an invisible line being crossed. "What exactly are you and Tyler planning?"

"Just gathering information." Terry's smile never reached her eyes. "Someone needs to document what's really happening in that household."

The vague threat chilled Mary more than specific accusations might have. "Document what, exactly?"

"Patterns." Terry's certainty remained unshaken. "Ways that child might be better served elsewhere."

"Chris is her family."

"Chris is being used."

Mary turned away, unable to bear her sister's certainty. The garden she had cultivated for decades suddenly felt exposed, vulnerable to invasion.

"I thought you should know what's coming," Terry continued. "As a courtesy between sisters. I've already spoken with Kourtney and Sarah. The prayer circle meets Thursday."

The casual mention of recruiting family members sent fresh unease through Mary's chest. Terry never acted alone—she built consensus, created impressions of community concern rather than personal vendetta.

"Don't do this." Mary's words emerged softer than intended.

"It's already begun." Terry glanced at her watch. "I should go. Ladies' Auxiliary meeting at seven."

She paused at the garden gate. "You should have told me, Mary. About Leah being John Miller's daughter. I could have stopped this marriage before Chris got attached to another man's child."

Mary watched her sister's retreating figure, heels clicking with triumphant finality. The sun had nearly set, casting long shadows across her carefully tended flowers. Beauty suddenly seemed fragile against gathering darkness.

She sank onto the garden bench, legs unsteady. Terry and Tyler together formed a dangerous alliance—Terry's social influence combined with Tyler's investigation creating a weapon aimed at Chris and Leah's marriage.

Mary touched a rose petal, its velvet softness incongruous against her calloused fingertips. She had always believed in nurturing rather than forcing, in trusting loved ones to make their own choices.

But Terry operated differently—pruning ruthlessly, removing perceived threats, shaping family connections according to her vision rather than natural growth. All under the banner of protection and Christian concern.

Night insects began their evening chorus as darkness claimed the garden. Mary remained seated, mind racing through potential interventions. Warning Chris seemed obvious, but how without overstepping? He was a grown man who had chosen privacy. Respecting that while protecting his happiness required delicate balance.

Her phone chimed with a text notification. The church group chat showed Terry's message: "Emergency prayer circle for family concerns, Thursday at 4. All sisters welcome. Discretion essential."

The machinery of interference had begun turning. Mary looked back at her roses, standing sentinel in gathering darkness. She had always been more gardener than warrior. For Chris's sake, for Leah and Louise, she would need to become both.

Light appeared in the upstairs window—Tom wondering why she remained outside after sunset. Her husband who had found strength to forgive John Miller, who had rebuilt without bitterness, who had welcomed Leah with genuine warmth.

Mary rose slowly, knowledge weighing her shoulders. She would speak with Tom tonight, form their own alliance against the storm gathering around their son's marriage. Find ways to protect not just Louise, but the family Chris had chosen to build.

For years, Mary had maintained peace by stepping aside, allowing Terry's stronger personality to dominate. That quiet acquiescence had preserved surface harmony while strengthening dangerous undercurrents. Now those currents threatened to pull her son under.

Mary gathered her gardening tools with hands that had learned growth required both nurturing and vigilance. Sometimes, to save what you loved, you had to fight those who claimed to protect it.

The house windows glowed with warm light, promising sanctuary from coming conflict. Mary moved toward that light, each step carrying the weight of resolve. Terry had declared war in protection's name. Mary would answer with different strength—born not from judgment but acceptance, not from fear but love.

Battle lines had been drawn across her carefully tended garden, across the family she had nurtured as lovingly as her roses. Mary touched her garden shears one final time before heading inside. Some battles chose you. The trick was finding courage to fight them on your own terms.

CHAPTER 4

Unexpected Allies

The chlorine hit Ashley's lungs with familiar sharpness. She'd coached at this pool for four years, building the life she'd remade from shattered athletic dreams. Her clipboard trembled as she read the name again: Louise Miller. Parent/Guardian: Leah Miller Johnson.

Ashley's gaze snapped to the observation area. There she sat, hair shorter now but with that same straight-backed poise that had haunted Ashley's high school nightmares. Leah Miller - now Johnson - absorbed in her phone, unaware of the past she'd just dropped into Ashley's carefully reconstructed present.

A splash from the shallow end yanked Ashley back to reality. The memory of Coach Stevens' voice echoed across fifteen years: "Peterson, you're three-tenths of a second over qualifying time. I'm sorry, but you didn't make the cut." While perfect Leah Miller had sailed through tryouts, claiming another space Ashley couldn't reach.

"Level One swimmers, please line up at the edge." Ashley forced her voice steady, professional.

Six children scrambled to obey, their feet pattering against wet concrete. Louise emerged from the group, small for her age but moving with unconscious grace. Dark curls, bright eyes, and - Ashley's chest constricted - that same fluid confidence Leah had possessed at sixteen, the day Ashley had watched tryouts from the bleachers, burning with shame.

The memory rose like bile.

"Maybe if you'd trained harder over the summer..." Her father's disappointment had cut deeper than Coach Stevens' rejection. "Miller's girl never misses morning practice. That's why she's varsity material, and you're..." The unfinished sentence had echoed through years of dreams.

"Miss Ashley?" Louise's voice pulled her back. "Can I go first?"

The eagerness in those eyes belonged purely to Louise. Ashley exhaled. "Sure, sweetie. Show me your best streamline position."

Louise stretched her arms overhead, fingers interlocked, chin tucked. Natural instinct for the water. Ashley made notes, her professional mask firmly in place. Out of the corner of her eye, she caught Leah looking up, finally registering who stood at the pool's edge with her daughter.

Recognition flickered across Leah's face. Ashley watched her former classmate's shoulders tense, then deliberately relax - a subtle tell that some memories never fully submerged. How many times had Ashley whispered cutting remarks in locker rooms, spread rumors about performance enhancers, tried to tarnish the golden girl's shine?

"Good job, Louise. Now float on your back for me."

Louise complied, spreading her arms like wings. The late afternoon light filtered through high windows, casting ripple patterns across her peaceful face. No tension, no awareness of the undertow of adult complications swirling beneath the surface.

Ashley recorded her observations in swift, precise strokes. Excellent body position. Natural buoyancy. Strong potential. The clinical language helped maintain distance, but each note felt like marking scores on a competition that had started long before Louise's first splash.

"She's a natural."

Leah's voice, closer now, sent tiny shockwaves across Ashley's practiced calm. She turned to find her former rival standing at a careful distance, close enough for conversation but far enough to acknowledge the years between them.

"She is." Ashley kept her tone professional. "Her instincts in the water are..." She stopped, swallowing the word 'perfect,' remembering how that word had once been a weapon she'd wielded against Leah.

"Like someone else at that age?" The question carried no edge, just a weariness Ashley hadn't expected.

Their eyes met briefly. Ashley saw something new in Leah's face - fine lines of worry, a softness that had replaced the sharp ambition of youth. A mother's face now, where once there had been only a competitor's mask.

"Thank you for evaluating her." Leah's words fell into the space between them. "I know there are other instructors..."

"I'm the best qualified." Ashley's response came too quick, too sharp. Old defenses rising. She drew a breath, tried again. "I mean, I specialize in beginners. Building proper foundation is crucial."

Louise paddled to the edge, beaming. "Mommy, did you see? I floated!"

"I saw, baby." Leah's whole being softened as she knelt by the pool. "You're doing so well."

The pride in Leah's voice sparked something unexpected in Ashley's chest - not the familiar bitter taste of old rivalry, but a strange ache as she watched this intimate moment between mother and daughter. This Leah was someone new, someone Ashley had never competed against: a mother whose greatest victory seemed to be her daughter's simple joy in floating.

"Okay, Louise, let's try a few kicks with the board." Ashley handed over a foam kickboard, their fingers brushing. "Keep your legs straight but relaxed."

Louise pushed off with perfect form.

"She's not afraid of the deep end," Leah noted quietly.

"No." Ashley watched Louise kick steadily toward the center. "She trusts herself in the water. Unlike I did." the unspoken words caught in her throat.

The lesson continued, each exercise revealing more of Louise's potential. Ashley maintained her professional distance, but increasingly found herself seeing mother and daughter as they were now, not as reflections of the past.

Other parents arrived for the next class. Ashley wrapped up her evaluation, writing final notes as Louise changed in the locker room.

"I'll have her in Tuesday's beginner group," Ashley said, handing Leah the registration form. Their fingers almost touched, like tentative olive branches extending across a chlorine-scented divide.

"Thank you." Leah hesitated, then added, "It's good to see you, Ashley."

The words held no artifice, no social nicety. Just simple truth that cracked something open in Ashley's carefully maintained walls.

"You too." She meant it, surprising herself.

Louise bounded back, wet curls dripping. "Can I come back tomorrow?"

"Tuesdays and Thursdays," Ashley found herself smiling. "We'll start with the basics."

"The basics are important," Leah said softly, and Ashley heard the peace offering in her tone.

Ashley hesitated, the fluorescent lights casting her shadow long across the damp concrete. "Actually, before you go... there's something else." The professional veneer slipped slightly, revealing an unexpected protectiveness that surprised even her.

Leah stilled, her hand instinctively finding Louise's shoulder.

"Last week, a woman came by asking specifically about Louise's lessons." Ashley's voice dropped, mindful of the child's attentive ears. "Said her name was Terry. When I told her I couldn't disclose student information, she claimed to be Louise's 'great aunt.'"

Something shifted in Leah's expression – a subtle hardening around the eyes, a tightening of her jaw muscles that transformed her face from open to guarded in the space of a heartbeat.

"What else did she want to know?" Leah's question came measured, carefully controlled, but Ashley recognized the undercurrent of alarm. It resonated with the same frequency as her own father's disapproval – a note she'd learned to identify from across rooms, through closed doors.

"Louise's progress. When she attends. Who brings her." Ashley shrugged, aiming for casualness that didn't quite land. "I didn't tell her anything, of course. It seemed... off."

Leah nodded, her fingers absently stroking Louise's damp curls. "Thank you for letting me know."

The three simple words carried weight that belied their simplicity. In the silence that followed, Ashley recognized something she'd never noticed in their shared past – vulnerability beneath Leah's composed exterior, a protective fierceness that had nothing to do with competition and everything to do with love.

"Mommy, who's Terry?" Louise looked up, curiosity bright in her eyes.

"It's aunt Terry, daddy's aunt, sweetheart." Leah's smile appeared practiced, perfected for her daughter's benefit. "Let's get you dried off before you catch cold."

They walked toward separate exits, the sound of splashing following them out. Ashley paused at her office door, watching Leah guide Louise toward the parking lot with gentle touches and shared laughter, though now she noticed the subtle vigilance in Leah's posture, the way her eyes scanned the parking lot before stepping fully outside.

The late sun caught the water drops falling from Louise's hair, turning them to tiny prisms. A snapshot of connection Ashley had never imagined for herself, too busy chasing trophies and times to consider other measures of success – and now, perhaps, a fragility to that connection she hadn't previously perceived.

Ashley thought of the drawer in her desk, still holding the stopwatch that had measured her failure at tryouts. She'd been polishing that old wound for so long, she'd forgotten what it felt like to simply love the water, the way Louise did now - pure and uncomplicated by competition. And something else stirred beneath the surface of her consciousness – a protective instinct she hadn't anticipated feeling toward the daughter of her former rival.

She opened her laptop to update the class roster. Louise Miller, Tuesdays and Thursdays, 4:00 PM. Level One Beginner. Coach: Ashley Peterson.

The cursor blinked steadily, like a metronome counting the distance between past and present. Ashley began to type her evaluation, each word a small step toward something new, something that felt, unexpectedly, like the beginning of healing. Not just from the old wounds of competition, but from the narrow vision of success that had blinded her to other possibilities, other ways of finding meaning in the water's embrace.

She hesitated, fingers hovering over the keys, then added a private note to Louise's file: *No information to be shared with extended family without direct parent authorization.*

The manila envelope arrived with Tuesday's mail, unremarkable among bills and flyers. Chris set it on the kitchen counter without a second glance, his attention focused on Louise's animated recounting of her art class triumph—a watercolor butterfly that had earned praise from Miss Rodriguez.

Leah stood at the sink, evening light painting copper streaks across her shoulders as she rinsed dinner plates. The familiar rhythm of their domestic choreography continued its steady beat against the soundtrack of late summer crickets beyond their kitchen window. Louise's giggles still echoed from the living room where Chris had left her building an elaborate castle from wooden blocks.

"Anything interesting?" Leah nodded toward the mail while loading the dishwasher, each plate finding its designated slot with the precision born of countless repetitions.

"Nothing much." Chris sorted through envelopes with casual efficiency. "Electric bill. Church newsletter. Something from the dentist." He paused at the unmarked manila envelope, its weight more substantial than typical junk mail. "This doesn't have a return address."

The plate in Leah's hands grew slippery with soap residue. Something in his tone—a subtle shift from casual to curious—made her stomach tighten with the instinctive wariness that had haunted her since the Wallace & Associates letter arrived before their wedding.

"Probably advertising," she offered, though uncertainty threaded through her voice. Since Ryan's legal challenge had materialized, every unmarked envelope carried potential threat.

Chris's fingers hovered over the metal clasp, hesitation written in the careful stillness of his shoulders. The refrigerator hummed. The kitchen clock ticked. Ordinary sounds suddenly rendered strange by mounting tension.

He opened the clasp with deliberate care, as if the envelope might contain something more volatile than paper. The contents spilled across their flour-dusted counter in a cascade of glossy squares, each image catching the light like accusations made manifest.

"What is—" The question died in Leah's throat.

Louise on the playground swing, her smile carefree and unguarded. Chris teaching her guitar on their front porch, both heads bent over the small instrument with identical concentration. Leah helping with finger painting at the kitchen table, her face animated with shared delight in Louise's creativity. Private moments captured through telephoto lenses and transformed into evidence.

The familiar transformed into the sinister through the simple act of documentation. Chris's hand flattened against the counter, tendons standing rigid as he absorbed the violation contained in these seemingly innocent images.

"They've been watching us," Leah whispered, her voice barely audible above the dishwasher's mechanical rhythm.

More photos emerged from the envelope's depths. Louise at preschool, Chris and Leah at Sunday service, their family at the grocery store—mundane moments of their life together now carrying the weight of surveillance. Each image timestamped in clinical white text, transforming their daily existence into a case study.

"For how long?" Chris lifted a photo of Louise feeding ducks at the park, her face luminous with simple joy. The image should have captured a perfect family moment; instead, it felt like evidence of their vulnerability.

Leah sifted through the photographs with trembling fingers, her medical training attempting to impose analytical distance on the violation spreading across their counter. "The oldest timestamp is from three weeks ago," she managed, her voice steadying as she focused on concrete details.

The calculation struck them both simultaneously—their joy as newlyweds had been shadowed from its inception by invisible watchers. The weight of that realization settled between them.

Chris lifted a photo of Louise feeding ducks at the park, her face luminous with simple joy. Another showed her at the grocery store. One captured her fourth birthday celebration at the rec center a few weeks ago, intimate and small, just family, before everything had become complicated.

"The Wallace & Associates letter mentioned 'documentation of current living conditions,'" Chris said, his voice hardening with each word. "This is what they meant."

A folded note had been tucked beneath the photographs, its presence almost an afterthought. Chris extracted it carefully.

"'For your information. Multiple copies exist. More to come.'" He read the words aloud. "No signature."

The language matched the detached professionalism of the surveillance itself—emotional terrorism disguised as legal procedure.

"It's not just Wallace & Associates," Leah said suddenly, her mind racing through recent conversations, connecting dots she'd dismissed as coincidence. "Chris, Ashley told me something today at Louise's swim lesson."

Chris looked up from the photographs, confusion flickering across his features. "Ashley? What does she have to do with this?"

"She said Terry came to the rec center last week." Leah's voice gained strength as she processed the implications. "Introduced herself as Louise's 'great aunt' and asked questions about her schedule, her progress."

The words hung between them, another violation layered atop the evidence spread across their counter. Chris's expression shifted from confusion to something more complex—recognition warring with denial.

"Terry was at Louise's swim lesson?" He set down the photograph he'd been holding, his movements suddenly careful, deliberate. "When?"

"Ashley said it was last Tuesday. She thought it was odd because Terry claimed to be family but had never been there before." Leah watched Chris's face, cataloguing the subtle changes—the way his jaw tightened, the slight furrow that appeared between his brows. "She asked about Louise's attendance patterns, who usually picks her up."

"That doesn't sound like Terry," Chris said, but uncertainty colored his tone. "She's always been interested in Louise's activities."

"Interested enough to show up unannounced and interrogate her swim instructor?" The question emerged sharper than Leah intended. "Without asking us first?"

Chris moved to the window, his reflection ghostlike against the gathering dusk. "Maybe she was just... curious. You know how she is about family events."

"This wasn't a family event, Chris." Leah gathered several photographs, their glossy surfaces reflecting kitchen light like accusations. "This was surveillance. Just like these photos."

The connection hung between them, invisible threads weaving a pattern Leah could see with increasing clarity while Chris seemed determined to dismiss.

"You think Terry is working with Ryan's lawyers?" The question emerged reluctantly, as if voicing it might make it true.

"I think the timing is suspicious." Leah spread the photographs in chronological order, their timestamps creating a narrative of escalating observation. "Ashley said Terry was asking very specific questions. The kind lawyers would want answered."

Thunder rumbled in the distance, the first harbinger of the storm moving toward them. Chris remained at the window, his shoulders carrying new tension.

"Terry would never—" He stopped, the denial incomplete. "She's opinionated, sometimes difficult, but she loves Louise."

"Does she?" Leah's question carried no accusation, only genuine uncertainty. "Or does she love the idea of Louise belonging to your family in a way that excludes me?"

The observation struck something vital in Chris. His reflection in the window seemed to waver, like a photograph underwater. "What are you saying?"

"I'm saying that someone close to us is *possibly* feeding information to Ryan's team." Leah's voice gained certainty as the pieces aligned. "Someone with access to Louise's schedule, her activities, our routines."

Chris turned from the window, his face a careful composition of reason wrestling with uncomfortable possibility. "Even if Terry asked some questions, that doesn't mean she's collaborating with Ryan."

"Then why didn't she tell us?" The question cut through his rationalization with surgical precision. "Why approach Ashley directly instead of asking us about Louise's progress?"

The kitchen fell silent except for the mechanical hum of appliances and the approaching storm. Chris studied the photographs again, as if their glossy surfaces might reveal different truths under renewed scrutiny.

"I'll talk to my mother," he said finally, the offer emerging like a compromise with uncertainty. "See if she knows why Terry might be... asking around."

"You think she'll tell you the truth?" Leah couldn't mask the skepticism that edged her voice. "If Terry is involved in something like this?"

"Mom doesn't lie." Chris's certainty carried the weight of lifetime experience. "She might not volunteer information, but she won't lie directly."

Leah nodded, accepting this small concession while her mind continued cataloguing connections—Terry's questions at the swim center, the professional quality of the surveillance photos, the clinical language of Ryan's legal correspondence. Patterns emerging like constellations, invisible until viewed from the proper angle.

"These photos feel different," she said, touching one image of Louise at the grocery store. "More intimate than what a private investigator would capture."

"What do you mean?"

"The angles. The proximity." Leah lifted several photos, studying their composition. "Some of these were taken from very close range. Almost like..."

"Like someone she knew," Chris completed, understanding dawning in his expression despite his resistance to the implications.

The storm had arrived, rain beginning to fall in gentle percussion against their windows. The sound created white noise around their conversation, a natural shelter for words too dangerous for the surveilled world they now inhabited.

"We need to be more careful," Leah said, gathering the photographs into a neat stack. "About who we trust. About what we share."

"I'll call Mom tonight," Chris promised, his voice carrying new resolve. "Get to the bottom of this."

"And if she confirms that Terry has been asking questions?"

Chris was quiet for a long moment, studying his daughter's laughter captured in glossy surveillance images. When he spoke, his voice held a weight Leah had never heard before.

"Then we'll know where we stand."

Lightning flickered beyond the window, illuminating their yard in stark white flashes. The storm had arrived in earnest now, nature's percussion matching the emotional turbulence that had claimed their evening routine.

"We should document everything ourselves," Leah said, her analytical mind engaging with the tactical challenge ahead. "Every interaction with Louise, every family moment, every sign of her happiness and security with us."

"Turn their own weapon around," Chris agreed, though something in his expression suggested he was still processing the possibility that this weapon might be wielded by his own family.

They gathered the photographs from the counter, each image a violation transformed into evidence of bonds that transcended documentation. The kitchen that had witnessed countless family dinners, homework sessions, and midnight conversations now felt exposed, vulnerable to invisible eyes that might be watching even now.

But beneath the violation lay something stronger—the recognition that what they had built together could withstand scrutiny, that their love for Louise was worth documenting, worth defending, worth whatever battles—legal or familial—might come.

The photographs remained in their neat stack, no longer accusations but affirmations. Evidence not of their vulnerability but of their strength. Proof that some bonds, once formed through daily acts of love and presence, could survive even the most calculated attempts to sever them.

The storm continued outside, but inside their kitchen, something had shifted from defensive fear to purposeful resolve. Whatever forces were gathering against them—whether legal teams or family members or both—they would face them together.

Their family was worth fighting for. The truth would have to be enough.

Darkness gathered in the corners of their bedroom, held at bay only by the soft glow of bedside lamps. In this half-illuminated space, Chris and Leah moved with the practiced choreography of intimacy, even as invisible fault lines spread beneath the surface of their unity.

Chris sat on the edge of the bed, fingers mapping the topography of their quilt. Three days had passed since the surveillance photos arrived. Three days since his hurried conversation with his mother, where he'd laid the unsettling images across her worn tablecloth.

Mary's reaction lingered in his memory like an unresolved chord. Not shock or outrage, but something far more troubling—a momentary flash of recognition quickly masked by maternal concern. When he'd asked directly—"Could anyone in our family be involved in this?"—her denial came too quickly, too emphatically.

"Absolutely not," she'd insisted, gathering the photos with hands that moved too precisely to be casual. "Family protects family, Chris. You know that."

But it was what followed that haunted him now: her sudden pivot to discussing church committee meetings, her offer to make fresh coffee though neither had finished their first cup, the way her eyes never quite met his as she assured him, "Terry would never do something like this."

"I've been thinking," he said, breaking the weighted silence. "Maybe we should call my dad."

Leah stood at the dresser, methodically removing her earrings. The precise movements of her fingers betrayed no tremor, though beneath her skin, a familiar vibration of threat pulsed—the same cold certainty she'd experienced when discovering Ryan's deception.

"Your father would tell Tyler." She placed the earrings in their designated compartment. "And Tyler would tell Terry."

Chris watched her reflection in the mirror. "And that's bad because...?"

"Because someone in your family is possibly feeding information to Ryan." The words emerged more sharply than she'd intended.

"You don't know that." His voice remained soft, which somehow made the disagreement harder to navigate. No anger to push against, just this gentle certainty that felt like a wall between them.

"I know your mother was evasive when you showed her the photos." Leah turned to face him directly. "I know Terry asks Louise about 'her real daddy' when she thinks I can't hear."

"She's just trying to help Louise process—"

"She's mining for information, Chris." Leah leaned against the dresser, arms crossed tight against her chest. "Information that somehow reaches Ryan's legal team."

Three days of simmering suspicion had crystallized into near-certainty for her. Each interaction with the Henderson side of Chris's family now appeared in stark relief, past moments recontextualized as links in a chain leading directly to those surveillance photos.

Chris stood and moved to the window. Streetlights cast rectangular patterns across the floor. "So you think my mother's family is conspiring against us? Against Louise?" The hurt in his voice was genuine, unmasked.

"Not conspiring." She chose her words with care. "But Terry has an agenda. And others follow her lead."

His shoulders stiffened. "Even my mom?"

"Your mother loves you," Leah said finally. "But she's spent a lifetime avoiding conflict with Terry."

Chris turned to look at her, his expression caught between defense and recognition. "When I showed Mom the photos, she practically recited Terry's virtues like a prayer. Said there was 'absolutely no possibility' anyone in our family could be involved."

"And that didn't strike you as strange?" Leah raised an eyebrow. "That emphasis feels like overcompensation."

Chris moved back to the edge of the bed. His weight made the mattress dip, a physical manifestation of the heaviness settling in his chest.

"When I was sixteen," Leah said, her voice softening, "my father took me to a medical research gala where he was being honored for a donation."

Chris looked up, momentarily thrown by the apparent change in subject.

"I had just won the state championship in swimming and received perfect SAT scores." She perched beside him, close but not touching. "I'd worked so hard for those achievements—not only because my father expected it, but because I wanted medicine more than anything."

"During his speech, he spoke about 'the Miller legacy of excellence.'" Her fingers traced invisible lanes on the quilt between them. "He referenced my accomplishments as evidence of strategic parenting, of superior genetic potential."

"Later that night, I overheard him with colleagues." A subtle tightness appeared at the corner of her mouth. "He spoke about me like I was the culmination of a carefully managed investment. The phrase he used was 'calculated developmental optimization.'"

"I achieved exactly what I wanted," she continued, "but in that moment, I understood I had also fulfilled exactly what he required. The line between my ambitions and his expectations had become so blurred I couldn't distinguish where one ended and the other began."

"Why does that matter now?" Chris asked softly.

"Because I wasn't his daughter in that moment. I was his evidence." Leah met his eyes. "Proof of his exceptional guidance. His superior genetics. His success."

Understanding began to form in Chris's expression.

"The way Terry examines Louise's artwork—" Leah's words came faster now. "The questions about her vocabulary, her analytical skills. The constant comparisons to Henderson family traits."

"That's just family stuff," Chris protested, but the conviction in his voice had dimmed. "Everyone does that."

"Not everyone uses a child to fulfill an agenda." Leah's hand found his, a physical connection despite their diverging perspectives. "Not everyone sees a little girl as a possession to be reclaimed."

Chris withdrew his hand, standing abruptly. "So what are you suggesting? That we cut them off? Change churches? Deny Louise the only extended family she's ever known?"

His agitation manifested in restless movement, pacing the limited space between bed and window.

"Not cut them off," she said carefully. "But maybe we limit unsupervised time. Maybe we're selective about which gatherings we attend."

"Maybe we stop trusting the people who have supported us from the beginning." He stopped pacing, facing her with hands spread in frustration. "The people who welcomed you and Louise without question."

"Without question," Leah repeated softly. "Have you ever wondered why, Chris? Why there were no questions?"

The words landed with unexpected force. Chris's expression shifted, defensive certainty giving way to the first hint of doubt before hardening again.

"What are you saying, exactly?" His voice had dropped to barely above a whisper.

"I'm saying that sometimes welcome isn't the same as acceptance." Leah held his gaze steadily. "Sometimes it's reconnaissance."

The analog clock on their nightstand ticked in the silence that followed. Chris stared at his hands, callused fingertips that could coax beauty from guitar strings now lying uselessly in his lap.

"The day I showed my mom the photos," he said slowly, "there was this moment..."

Leah waited, giving him space to unravel the memory.

"She started talking about how Terry had always been the 'protector' of the family. Said she sometimes goes too far, but 'always with the best intentions.'"

"That sounds like preparation for a defense," Leah said quietly.

"Then she just... shut down the conversation." Chris looked up, confusion etched across his features. "Started talking about church committee meetings, upcoming family birthdays—anything but those photos."

"Your mother suspects something," Leah said gently. "But she's choosing not to know for certain. That way, she doesn't have to act."

Chris stood again, moving to his guitar case. His fingers hovered over the latches but didn't open them.

"You're wrong." The words came quietly but with unmistakable finality. He turned to face her, something new hardening in his expression. "My family would never do this."

"Chris—"

"No." He cut her off, the gentleness she'd always known in him temporarily eclipsed by defensive loyalty. "You're seeing patterns that aren't there because you expect betrayal. Your father shaped you to be suspicious, to always look for hidden agendas."

Leah felt the words like a physical blow. "That's not fair."

"Isn't it?" His voice remained quiet, which somehow made the accusation worse. "Ryan abandoned you. Your father manipulated you. Now you're looking for that same pattern in my family."

"I'm looking at evidence," she countered, her own voice rising slightly. "The timing of these photos. Terry's questions. Your mother's strange reaction."

"Coincidences." He shook his head, conviction hardening his features. "My aunt can be overbearing, but she loves Louise. My mother avoids conflict, but she would never betray us."

The distance between them expanded beyond physical measure. Leah stood, moving to her side of the bed with deliberate steps. "You're refusing to see what's right in front of you because it hurts too much."

"And you're inventing conspiracies because trusting people scares you." The words emerged with quiet precision, aimed with unerring accuracy at her most vulnerable places.

Silence fell between them, heavy with accusation and hurt. Leah slipped beneath the covers, turning away from his side of the bed. After a moment, she heard him sigh, then the soft click of his lamp switching off. The mattress dipped as he got in beside her, maintaining a careful distance that felt like miles.

No goodnight. No touch. No reconciliation.

In the darkness, Leah stared at the wall, listening to Chris's breathing—not yet the deep rhythm of sleep, but the controlled pattern of someone deliberately holding their emotions in check. Her mind raced through every interaction with Terry, every seemingly innocent question about Louise's activities.

Behind her, Chris lay equally awake, his thoughts circling around his mother's strange behavior, Terry's lifelong pattern of control, the undeniable timing of the surveillance photos. But allowing himself to believe what Leah suggested meant accepting that his entire understanding of family was built on unstable ground.

The night stretched between them like a widening sea, each adrift on separate islands of certainty and doubt. For the first time since they'd begun sharing this bed, they fell asleep without resolving their disagreement, without reaching for each other across the divide.

Outside their window, a car drove past, its headlights briefly illuminating the ceiling before sliding away, leaving deeper darkness in its wake.

CHAPTER 5

Fault Lines

M orning light spilled across the bedroom floor, painting stripes of gold against the wall where their wedding photo hung slightly askew. Leah watched the dust motes dance in the sunbeams, each particle following invisible currents before settling on surfaces she'd need to clean later. The empty space beside her had grown cold, the sheets bearing the ghostly impression of Chris's body, a reminder of how they'd fallen asleep last night – back to back, the inches between them stretching like miles.

Their first real argument hung in the air, invisible but palpable as morning humidity. She could almost see the words suspended above the bed, unresolved and raw. Chris's voice echoed in her memory: *"You're inventing conspiracies because trusting people scares you."* The accusation had struck with unerring precision, finding the tender place where her father's legacy of suspicion met her own history of abandonment.

Leah's gaze traced the crown molding to avoid looking at their wedding photo. The joy captured there felt distant this morning, a happiness that belonged to different people – ones who hadn't yet faced betrayal from within the family they were building.

Downstairs, cabinet doors opened and closed. Coffee mugs clinked against countertops. Chris moving through his morning routine with the precise timing of a man avoiding confrontation. Usually, he'd wake her with a kiss, Louise sandwiched between them in a morning cuddle that had become their ritual. Today, he'd slipped from bed before dawn, leaving silence where there should have been laughter.

She pushed herself upright, feet finding the cool hardwood. Her reflection in the vanity mirror looked tired, shadows beneath her eyes testament to restless sleep. In the hallway, she paused outside Louise's room. Their daughter slept soundly, small fists curled against her pillow, oblivious to the fault lines spreading beneath their family's foundation.

By the time Leah reached the kitchen, Chris had already poured his coffee into a travel mug. His laptop bag rested by the door, guitar case leaning against it – everything arranged for a swift exit to his music classes at the elementary school.

"Morning." His voice carried the hollow politeness of strangers in an elevator. He glanced up briefly, then returned to buttering toast with studied concentration.

"Morning." She moved to the coffee maker, the familiar routine suddenly awkward, each gesture self-conscious under the weight of unresolved tension. "You're leaving early."

"Early faculty meeting." The lie settled between them, fragile as blown glass. There was no meeting; she knew his schedule as intimately as her own.

Leah poured coffee with steady hands that belied her inner trembling. "Louise has swimming lessons after school. I can pick her up."

"I'll do it." His response came too quickly, the eagerness to escape their shared space barely concealed. "Ashley said she's making good progress."

The mention of Ashley – once Leah's high school nemesis, now Louise's surprising ally – hung between them. Even this innocuous subject carried landmines of hidden meaning: Ashley had noticed Terry's inappropriate questions. Had warned Leah when no one else would. Was this Chris's subtle acknowledgment that Leah's concerns might hold validity?

"She's a natural in the water." Leah sipped her coffee, finding momentary sanctuary in their shared pride for Louise. "Ashley says she has excellent instincts."

Something softened in Chris's posture – not forgiveness exactly, but a temporary ceasefire in the territory of their daughter's accomplishments. "Like her mother." The words carried a hint of the tenderness that had been noticeably absent since last night.

Leah allowed herself to meet his eyes fully for the first time that morning. The hurt lingered there, mixed with confusion and that stubborn loyalty to family that both frustrated and endeared him to her. They stood in the kitchen they'd designed together, morning light illuminating the domestic landscape they'd built with such care, now threatened by forces neither fully understood.

"Chris, about last night—"

The sound of Louise's feet pattering down the hallway interrupted whatever fragile beginning Leah might have offered. Their daughter appeared in the doorway, hair tousled from sleep, elephant stuffed animal dragging behind her.

"Daddy! You're still here!" Louise launched herself at Chris's legs, her joy unaware of the delicate emotional threads stretching between her parents.

"Hey, sweet pea." Chris lifted her easily, his face transforming with genuine delight. "Just heading out to work. But I'll pick you up from swimming today."

"Promise? Ashley says I might get to jump in the deep end if I do good."

"Do well," Leah corrected gently, moving to pour Louise's juice. The familiar rhythm of parenting provided temporary shelter from the storm of their unresolved conflict.

"I promise." Chris pressed a kiss to Louise's forehead, then set her carefully in her usual chair. He moved toward the door, hesitating briefly before turning back. "I'll see you tonight."

The words carried multiple layers: acknowledgment that they needed to finish their conversation, recognition that the argument remained unresolved, perhaps even a tentative olive branch extended across the divide that had opened between them.

Leah nodded, a small gesture that somehow encompassed both acceptance and postponement. "Drive safely."

And then he was gone, the door closing with careful control rather than angry force – Chris, always mindful of Louise's watching eyes, maintaining appearances even in conflict. Leah turned to their daughter, summoning a brightness she didn't feel. "Pancakes this morning?"

Louise nodded enthusiastically, already pulling her coloring book from the kitchen drawer where they kept her breakfast activities. "With blueberry faces?"

"Absolutely."

As she mixed batter and heated the griddle, Leah's thoughts circled back to their argument. Chris wasn't entirely wrong – her experiences had taught her to look for hidden agendas, to question motives, to expect betrayal wrapped in smiles. Her father's calculated manipulations, Ryan's abandonment, even Kate's tragic loss – all had shaped her capacity for trust into something fragile and conditional.

But she wasn't wrong either. The surveillance photos hadn't materialized from paranoia. Terry's questions about Louise weren't imagined. The subtle campaign to document their failings was taking shape in church hallways and family gatherings, each seemingly innocent inquiry building a case against them.

The pancake batter sizzled as it hit the hot surface. Louise hummed tunelessly while coloring, her small world still intact despite the cracks spreading through the adult landscape around her. Leah arranged blueberries into a smiling face, the simple act of creating joy for her daughter momentarily eclipsing her fears.

The morning sunlight caught in Louise's curls, turning them to spun gold. She looked up, smile innocent of the shadows gathering at the edges of their family's happiness. "Can we have pancakes when Daddy gets home too? For dinner?"

"We'll see, sweet girl." Leah placed the plate before her daughter, the mundane promise somehow feeling like a declaration of faith – that there would be dinner, that Chris would return, that they would navigate these troubled waters together.

Louise stabbed her fork into the pancake's blueberry eye. "Aunt Terry says breakfast for dinner isn't proper."

The casual mention sent a chill through Leah that had nothing to do with the morning air. She kept her voice carefully neutral. "When did Aunt Terry tell you that?"

"At school." Louise shrugged, attention focused on drowning her pancake in syrup. "She brings me special snacks sometimes."

Leah's hands stilled on the counter. Terry at school? Without her knowledge? The implications unfurled like frost across glass – another boundary crossed, another sacred space invaded.

"Does Aunt Terry come to school often?" She fought to keep her voice light, unwilling to burden Louise with adult complications.

"Sometimes." Louise's answer carried the uncomplicated acceptance of a child who didn't yet understand the concept of surveillance. "She takes pictures of my art for Gram's refrigerator."

Pictures. Documentation. Evidence. The words lined up in Leah's mind like soldiers. Each innocent moment captured and transformed into ammunition. She turned to the sink, giving herself time to compose her expression before facing Louise again.

"That's nice of her." The words tasted like chalk. "Eat up, sweet pea. We need to get you dressed for school."

Later, after dropping Louise at preschool, Leah sat in her parked car, phone heavy in her hand. Chris should know about Terry's visits to the school. But after last night's argument, would he hear concern or simply more paranoia? Would he defend Terry's actions as innocent interest in Louise's education, or recognize the subtle invasion of their parental territory?

The text she finally composed aimed for neutral ground: *Terry's been visiting Louise at school. Bringing snacks, taking photos of her artwork. Did you know?*

His response came faster than expected: *She mentioned volunteering in the reading program. Didn't realize she was going during Louise's class time.*

Not quite acknowledgment, but not dismissal either. Leah studied the words, searching for subtext. At least he hadn't immediately defended Terry's actions or accused Leah of exaggerating. Small progress, perhaps.

She typed again: *Should we talk to the school about approved visitors?*

The response took longer this time: *Let me call her first. See what's going on.*

Disappointment settled like stone in Leah's stomach. Still trying to handle family matters internally. Still protecting Terry from consequences. Still reluctant to establish firm boundaries. She considered pushing harder, then decided against it. Last night's argument had taught her the danger of pressing too firmly against Chris's family loyalty.

Instead, she responded simply: *OK. See you tonight.*

She started the car, mind already planning her own approach. She would speak with Miss Andrews directly, establish clear guidelines about who could interact with Louise during school hours. If Chris wouldn't acknowledge his family's intrusion, Leah would do it herself and find ways to protect Louise. The realization settled with both weight and certainty – she was once again standing alone on the frontlines of Louise's protection, just as she had during those early days of single motherhood.

As she pulled away from the preschool, Leah caught sight of a familiar figure in her rearview mirror. Terry Henderson stood by the school entrance, phone raised as if taking a photo of Leah's departing car. The image sent ice through Leah's veins – not just surveillance of Louise now, but of her as well. Documentation extended to her every move, her comings and goings, perhaps even her conversations with teachers and staff.

The divide between her perspective and Chris's had never felt wider. Where she saw calculated invasion, he perceived family interest. Where she recognized patterns of control, he found expressions of love. How could they protect Louise when they couldn't even agree on the nature of the threat facing their family?

At the stop sign, Leah's phone pinged with another message from Chris: *I love you. We'll figure this out.*

Six simple words that somehow bridged the distance between them, if only momentarily. Not agreement, but commitment. Not understanding, but willingness to try. She touched the screen gently, as if connecting with him across the miles between them.

I love you too.

Three words that remained true despite their disagreement. Three words that might be enough to weather the storm gathering around them. Three words that carried both promise and plea – to listen, to see, to stand together when it mattered most.

2002

Twilight painted the living room in amber hues, each ray of fading sunlight illuminating dust motes that danced like suspended worries above six-year-old Chris. He sat cross-legged on the worn carpet, his small guitar cradled against his chest like a protective talisman. The instrument felt impossibly large in his hands, its frets stretching beyond the reach of his child-sized fingers, yet he persisted with the quiet determination that would later define his approach to love and music alike.

The worn chord sheet rested beside him, its edges soft from countless practice sessions. From the kitchen, adult voices carried the particular weight of financial anxiety—words like "final notice" and "bankruptcy" floating through the house like toxic smoke, poisoning the air he breathed without him fully understanding their meaning.

His father's palm struck the table with frustrated finality, the sound reverberating through Chris's small body like a physical blow. He instinctively curled around his guitar, the familiar wood and strings offering sanctuary against forces he couldn't name but could feel pressing against the edges of his world like gathering storm clouds.

The carpet beneath him held impressions of better times—circular depressions where the coffee table had once stood before being sold, rectangular shadows where the television had lived before disappearing one Tuesday while he was at school. These phantom spaces told the story of Johnson family life gradually stripped away, piece by piece, while he remained too young to understand the mathematics of loss.

"Hey, buddy." Tyler's voice cut through the oppressive atmosphere, warm and solid as an anchor. His older brother appeared in the doorway, seventeen years old and already carrying the weight of premature adulthood in his motor oil-stained work shirt. The familiar scent of the garage clung to him—grease and sweat and the particular metallic tang of machinery being coaxed back to life. "Practicing alone?"

Chris offered a small shrug, his throat too tight for words. The simple gesture contained multitudes—disappointment that their father no longer had time for music lessons, confusion about why their world had grown so heavy, the particular loneliness of a child trying to create beauty while chaos swirled around him.

"Mom said to," he finally managed.

Tyler crossed the room with careful steps, the floorboards creaking beneath his weight in a familiar percussion that had once comforted Chris but now seemed to echo with the hollowness of everything else that had changed. His brother reached for the lamp, bathing them in warm yellow light that pushed back the gathering shadows, creating a small circle of intimacy within the house's larger darkness.

"Show me what you've got." Tyler folded his long frame beside Chris, their knees almost touching in unconscious communion.

Chris bit his lower lip, anxiety manifesting in the small gesture. "Just 'Ode to Joy.'" The confession emerged whisper-soft, weighted with the knowledge that their father hadn't taught him anything new in weeks. The store consumed everything now—late nights calculating numbers that never added up, early mornings fielding calls from creditors whose voices carried the particular coldness of business conducted without sentiment.

Tyler settled cross-legged beside him, mirroring Chris's posture with the easy grace of someone who had always made himself available for his younger brother's needs. Their knees touched now, creating physical connection that anchored Chris against his floating anxieties.

"Let's hear it," Tyler said, his voice carrying genuine anticipation rather than the distracted approval Chris had grown accustomed to from harried adults.

Chris positioned his small fingers on the strings, his brow furrowing with concentration that aged his features beyond his six years. The melody emerged fragile but true, each note carefully placed like stepping stones across turbulent water. Beethoven's joy rendered in halting phrases by hands too small for the instrument they held, yet somehow managing to capture something essential—hope persisting despite circumstance, beauty insisting on its own existence regardless of context.

Tyler watched with the solemn focus of someone who understood that this moment carried weight beyond its apparent simplicity. The music filled the space between them, transforming their shared corner of the living room into something sacred, a chapel carved from chaos through the simple act of one brother listening while another played.

"That was perfect," Tyler said when the last note faded into silence.

"I made mistakes." Chris searched his brother's face for disappointment that never materialized, his need for approval as transparent as his musical aspirations.

"Everyone does." Tyler's response carried the wisdom of someone who had learned to find grace in imperfection. "The important thing is that you kept playing."

The kitchen door swung open with sudden violence, revealing Mary in the threshold. Dish towel twisted between her fingers like a rope of anxiety, her eyes carrying the particular redness that spoke of tears recently shed. Her gaze found Chris immediately, and he watched her expression transform with the lightning speed of maternal protection—worry melting into manufactured brightness, fear reshaping itself into forced cheer.

"Beautiful music, sweetheart," she managed, her voice only slightly strained around the edges.

The doorbell's chime cut through the moment, its cheerful two-note song incongruous against the household's underlying tension.

"That's Terry," Mary announced, smoothing her apron with nervous hands that refused to remain still. "Chris, show Tyler your LEGOs while I—"

But Terry's voice was already filling the house, carrying the particular authority she wielded like an inherited scepter. "Mary Henderson Johnson!" The full name rang out with both affection and command, establishing dominance before she had fully crossed the threshold.

She swept through the front door like a beneficent storm, her arms laden with casserole dishes that steamed with salvation. Behind her, four-year-old Kourtney struggled with a small paper bag, her presence adding brightness to the weighted atmosphere. Terry's arrival transformed the space instantaneously—her certainty pushing against the shadows of doubt, her practical solutions offering temporary refuge from the mathematics of failure.

"You look exhausted," Terry pronounced without preamble.. "Two Sundays missed at mass."

Mary's shoulders dropped incrementally, the weight of judgment settling across them like a familiar shawl. "You shouldn't have—"

74

"Family takes care of family." Terry deposited food on the table with movements that spoke of long practice in emergency intervention. Her orchestration was precise, purposeful, designed to restore order through the simple act of feeding people. "That's what we do."

Her gaze found Chris with his guitar, and her expression softened immediately into something approaching wonder. The transformation was remarkable—from general to godmother in the space of a heartbeat, authority melting into adoration.

"My talented godson!" She knelt beside him with surprising grace for someone of her sturdy build, her presence enveloping him in scents of cinnamon and vanilla, comfort distilled into olfactory memory. "I heard you from the driveway."

The praise warmed him like sunlight after endless rain, filling empty spaces inside his chest that he hadn't realized were waiting to be filled.

"Just 'Ode to Joy,'" he repeated, heat rising in his cheeks despite the unexpected pleasure of her attention.

"Just?" Terry's eyebrows rose in theatrical astonishment. "As if Beethoven were ordinary."

Her hand touched his cheek with cool certainty, the contact carrying promise and possibility in equal measure. This was Terry's particular gift—the ability to make ordinary things feel extraordinary through the simple application of focused attention.

"Sister Margaret needs performers for Christmas," she continued, her words opening vistas Chris had never considered. "The congregation should hear your gift."

The idea of performance terrified and thrilled him in equal measure. Mary would have asked his preference, negotiated with his anxiety, offered escape routes and alternatives. Terry simply knew what he needed, her certainty carving a path through his self-doubt.

"Wash up for dinner." She rose in one fluid motion, her presence already reshaping the evening's possibilities. "Kourtney brought cookies."

The kitchen transformed under Terry's command as if touched by magic wand rather than human will. Food appeared on the counters. Grocery bags emptied themselves into the refrigerator and pantry. Her certainty filled the room like rising water, buoying everyone who floated within its reach.

Tom entered from the garage, his shoulders stooped with invisible weight that seemed to settle more heavily each passing day. The garage had become his refuge, a place where broken things could sometimes be fixed, where his hands could still create solutions even if his business acumen had proven inadequate to larger challenges.

"Tom, sit." Terry's instruction brooked no argument as she pointed toward a chair with the authority of someone accustomed to being obeyed. "You're dead on your feet."

He obeyed without question, settling into the designated seat like water finding its level. Terry poured coffee into his favorite mug—the one with the faded logo from Johnson & Sons that she had somehow located amid the kitchen's reorganization. The gesture carried both comfort and painful reminder of what had been lost.

"Randy's friend at First National Bank called," she announced while arranging plates. "We can help until things stabilize."

The offer hung in the air, loaded with implications and conditions that wouldn't be named but were nonetheless present. Relief flickered across Mary's face like distant lightning—brief illumination followed by the return of familiar darkness.

"We don't need—" Mary began, but Terry's raised hand cut off the protestation.

"Don't be ridiculous." Her dismissal carried the weight of absolute certainty. "Pride doesn't feed children."

Terry's truth landed with devastating accuracy, stripping away pretense to reveal the reality they all lived with but refused to name directly. Mary's resistance crumbled like sand castle against incoming tide, her shoulders sagging with the relief of surrendering a burden too heavy to carry alone.

Chris watched this exchange with the particular clarity children bring to adult dynamics they don't fully understand but instinctively recognize as significant. The interplay of power and affection, of judgment and salvation, created patterns he would spend decades attempting to decode.

"Kourtney, set the table," Terry directed, her attention shifting seamlessly between adults and children. "Chris, help your cousin."

Kourtney nudged him toward the cabinet, her smile carrying conspiracy and shared understanding. They were allies in this adult world, united by their peripheral status and their instinctive recognition of safety in Terry's presence.

"Mommy made your favorite," she whispered, the secret shared like precious currency between them.

Terry's voice orchestrated the room's rhythm, everyone moving to her carefully conducted symphony. Chris and Kourtney placed forks beside plates with ceremonial gravity. Mary wiped counters that were already clean, the repetitive motion providing outlet for nervous energy. Tom stared into coffee gone cold, his silence suggesting agreement with unspoken assessments of his inadequacy.

"Some problems need practical solutions," Terry observed, placing food before Tom. "Tom's always been gentle. It's his nature."

Tom didn't contradict her analysis, his silence serving as confirmation of her evaluation. The gentle assessment contained both compassion and subtle condemnation—recognition of virtue that had proven insufficient to contemporary challenges.

"Johnson men feel deeply," Terry continued, her tone softening with something that might have been pity. "That's their gift. Also their burden."

Chris absorbed these words with the intensity of someone receiving prophecy about his own future. The categorization felt both comforting and constraining—an identity that explained his sensitivity while potentially limiting his possibilities.

After dinner, Terry claimed the sofa beside Chris, producing a package from her purse like a magician revealing the evening's final trick. Blue wrapping paper caught lamplight, transforming ordinary gift-giving into something approaching ceremony.

"For my favorite musician," she announced, her words conferring specialness that filled empty spaces in his chest.

Inside nestled a wooden metronome, its polished maple surface gleaming like precious metal in the warm light. Terry demonstrated its mechanism with reverent care, the steady tick-tock creating rhythmic certainty in a world that had grown unpredictable.

"My grandfather's, your great grandfather's" she explained, the revelation adding weight and history to the already precious gift. "Music requires discipline."

Chris traced the wood grain with fingers that recognized quality beyond his years, understanding intuitively that this represented more than mere tool—it was inheritance, expectation, promise all crystallized in polished hardwood.

"You're special, Chris," she continued, her voice dropping to levels that excluded other listeners. "I've always known it."

The metronome ticked between them with mechanical steadiness, its rhythm more reliable than business loans or financial security, more constant than the adult world's apparent determination to dissolve around him.

"Your parents love you," Terry's voice grew even softer, her words creating intimate space within the busy room. "But they don't always see what makes you exceptional."

She winked then, conspiracy glittering in her eyes like shared treasure. "That's why God gives children godmothers."

The evening continued around them—Terry and Kourtney eventually departing, leaving behind full stomachs and temporary peace, the metronome sitting on his nightstand like a silent sentinel. Chris lay awake listening to his parents' muffled conversation through thin walls, their voices carrying worry and calculation that seemed to go on forever.

But the metronome remained beside him, steady and certain and his. Reminder of Terry's absolute conviction that he was special, that his musical gift mattered even when everything else seemed to be falling apart. Her certainty made chaos feel manageable, transformed his father's failure into temporary setback rather than permanent defeat.

Years later, whenever doubts about Terry surfaced in his consciousness, Chris would remember this night. How she had arrived bearing solutions when his world was collapsing around him. How she had transformed bankruptcy into mere inconvenience through the simple application of casseroles and conviction. How she had created a cocoon of protection around him, shielding him from harsh truths about business failure and adult inadequacy that he was too young to process. How she had truly seen him when everyone else was consumed by crisis.

In those moments of childhood devastation, Terry had given him what his parents couldn't—not just comfort, but certainty. Not just love, but the specific recognition that he was chosen, special, worthy of attention and investment. She had become his anchor during the storm, his voice of conviction when everything else crumbled around him.

It would take decades and another woman's love to show him how protection could resemble control, how certainty could both illuminate and blind. How the gaps in his childhood understanding would later leave room for others to fill with their own narratives, their own interpretations of what family meant and who deserved to belong within its boundaries.

But tonight, as six-year-old Chris clutched Terry's gift and listened to the metronome's perfect time, she represented absolute safety. Her conviction became his comfort, her careful shielding of him from painful family history seeming like pure benediction rather than calculated control.

A gift he would carry into adulthood, even when—years later—that same certainty would turn against the woman he chose to love. Even when Terry's protection would reveal its hidden costs, its unspoken conditions, its demand for eternal gratitude expressed through unquestioning obedience.

The metronome kept perfect time, its rhythm as steady as Terry's love and just as impossible to escape.

Midnight had claimed their bedroom hours ago, but sleep eluded Leah. She lay still, listening to Chris's measured breathing beside her. The careful distance between their bodies marked unfamiliar territory. Their argument had left invisible borders—his side, her side—where once the boundary had been permeable.

Outside, rain began to fall. Not the dramatic downpour that might have matched their tension, but a gentle patter against the windowpanes. The sound filled their silence with its quiet rhythm.

Leah watched shadows shift across the ceiling. She remembered other nights when insomnia had claimed her—after Ryan's desertion, during those early months of single motherhood when terror and love had twined in her chest. Back then, she'd had only herself to rely on. Now the presence of someone who loved her made this sleeplessness sharper.

"You're awake."

Chris's voice startled her, though it came soft as breath. He hadn't turned toward her. His profile caught the diffused moonlight—the strong line of his jaw, the slight furrow between his brows.

"So are you," she whispered, suddenly afraid of full-voiced words.

He exhaled, a sound caught between resignation and longing. "I can't sleep when we're... like this."

The admission carried vulnerability she hadn't expected. Chris, who approached conflict with careful avoidance, whose gentleness sometimes masked the depth of his feeling—tonight he named the wound between them.

Leah's throat tightened. "I know," she managed. "I can't either."

The rain drummed more urgently now. Chris shifted slightly, his hand falling into the neutral territory between their bodies. An offering, not yet a touch.

"I keep thinking about what my mother would say," he murmured. "She'd tell us not to let the sun go down on our anger."

"It's been down for hours," Leah observed, a wistful smile touching her lips despite everything.

"Exactly." For the first time since climbing into bed, Chris turned toward her. The movement released the scent of his shampoo, familiar and dear. "We're failing at the oldest marriage advice in the book."

A small laugh escaped her, unexpected in its genuine warmth. "Your aunt Terry would have something to say about that too."

His expression darkened momentarily at the mention, then softened again. "Probably something about proper conflict resolution according to Henderson family tradition."

"Which would involve...?"

"The woman admitting she was wrong, of course."

Their eyes met in the darkness, shared understanding passing between them—how his words both acknowledged Terry's rigid worldview and subtly differentiated his own.

Chris's finger traced a pattern on the sheet between them. Not quite touching her yet, but narrowing the divide. "I don't want to believe they could be involved in this," he admitted, the words heavy with earlier conflict. "It feels like betrayal even considering it."

Leah watched his hand move—the same fingers that coaxed music from guitar strings, that braided Louise's hair with patient care. "I know," she said softly. "I see how much you love them. How much they matter."

His eyes sought hers, vulnerable in a way that made her chest ache. "But what if you're right?" The question emerged barely audible. "What if they're feeding information to Ryan's team? What if they're part of this... surveillance?"

The admission cost him. She saw it in the tension around his mouth, the way his shoulders curved inward against invisible weight.

"Then we'll face it," Leah said, her voice steadier than she felt. "Together."

Her hand moved across the cool sheet to cover his. The contact sparked between them—skin against skin, warmth against warmth.

"I'm sorry," Chris whispered. "Not for defending them. I can't help that part of me—the part that wants to believe the best." His fingers curled around hers, seeking anchor. "But I'm sorry for making you feel like your concerns didn't matter. Like your instincts weren't valid."

Leah's chest tightened. She'd expected him to apologize for the argument itself, not for the deeper wound beneath it—the dismissal that had left her feeling alone in her vigilance.

"I understand why it's hard to see," she said carefully. "They're your family. They've been there your whole life."

"So have their patterns." Chris's thumb traced circles on her palm. "Terry's control, my mother's silence... I've seen it before. With friends, with girlfriends." His eyes found hers in the darkness. "I just never wanted to connect those dots to what's happening now."

Rain pattered against the window. Somewhere in the house, an old beam settled with a soft groan—their home's way of reminding them of its presence.

"I'm scared, Chris." The admission emerged unbidden. "Not just of Ryan's legal team. Not just of the surveillance." Leah swallowed against the tightness in her throat. "I'm scared of losing what we've built. This family. This life."

His hand tightened around hers. "Never," he said fiercely. "Whatever happens with the lawyers, with custody hearings, with my family—what we have, the three of us, is real. Is solid."

She wanted to believe him. Wanted the certainty he offered. But Ryan's abandonment had taught her how easily promises shattered.

"You can't promise that," she whispered. "No one can."

Chris moved closer then, the remaining distance between them disappearing as he pulled her into his arms. His heartbeat steadied against her cheek, the rhythm she'd fallen asleep to countless nights.

"You're right," he murmured against her hair. "I can't promise what will happen. But I can promise who I'll be through whatever comes." His arms tightened around her. "I'll stand with you. I'll fight for Louise. I'll face whatever ugly truths we uncover—about Ryan, about my family, about myself."

The simplicity of his promise, stripped of impossible guarantees, reached deeper than grand declarations. Leah felt something unravel in her chest—not the complete release of her fear, but the beginning of shared burden.

"And I'll try to understand what this costs you," she whispered against his chest. "To question the family who raised you. Who shaped you."

His breath caught. "They did shape me. The good and the bad." His fingers traced the curve of her shoulder, gentle as rain against glass. "But you and Louise—you're reshaping me every day. Into someone stronger. Someone braver."

The confession hung between them, intimate as a shared breath. Outside, the rain continued its steady rhythm. Inside, something essential had been restored—not the innocent certainty they'd had before their first real conflict, but something deeper. A weathered connection.

"I love you," Leah whispered, the words simple but heavy with renewed conviction. "Through whatever comes."

"Through whatever comes," Chris echoed, his lips finding hers in the darkness.

Their kiss carried both apology and promise, tender and certain. When they finally drew apart, the invisible border that had divided their bed had dissolved. Chris's arms cradled her against his chest, her legs tangled with his in unconscious intimacy.

Louise's soft call broke through their reunion—a half-awake summons from her bedroom. Chris pressed his lips to Leah's forehead, a silent communication passing between them.

"I'll go," he murmured.

Leah watched him move through the darkness, his silhouette pausing at their bedroom door. He turned back toward her, his expression carrying a determination she hadn't seen before.

"Tomorrow," he said quietly, "we start making lists. Everyone who might have access to Louise. Every unusual question. Every unexpected appearance."

The promise caught her off guard—not just reconciliation, but alliance.

"Together," she agreed, the word carrying all she couldn't articulate—gratitude and relief and renewed certainty.

When Chris returned minutes later, Louise's stuffed elephant tucked under his arm, Leah had shifted to the center of their mattress, erasing the territories of their earlier discord. He slipped beneath the covers, his body naturally curving around hers, fitting together with the precision of instruments tuned to the same key.

Outside, the rain continued its patient percussion. Inside, two bodies found their familiar alignment, the rhythms of their breathing gradually synchronizing in the quiet dark.

Not perfect understanding. Not complete resolution. But a bridge built between words, strong enough to carry them toward morning.

CHAPTER 6

Declarations

G olden light filtered through the music room windows. Dust motes danced in the beams, catching fire as they drifted through sunshine. Chris sat on the piano bench, Louise cross-legged before him. Her small guitar rested against her knees, a quarter-sized instrument that still dwarfed her frame. Her dark curls caught the light, copper highlights revealing themselves as she bent over the frets.

"Try again," Chris urged, adjusting her fingers on the strings. "Remember what we talked about—gentle pressure."

"Like holding a butterfly?" Louise's brow furrowed.

"Exactly like that."

Outside, daffodils had pushed through soil still cold from winter. Birds returned with hesitant songs, their tentative notes mirroring the fragile hope taking root inside their home. The surveillance photos had been organized into careful files, their immediate threat contained but not eliminated.

Louise's tongue poked from the corner of her mouth. The chord emerged cleaner this time, vibrating through the quiet room.

"Perfect." Chris beamed with genuine pride. No polite pretense of accomplishment—real musical progress, note by note.

"You're developing calluses faster than I did at your age."

In the doorway, Leah leaned against the frame. Arms folded across her middle, she watched this tableau of connection. Her eyes softened at their matched expressions—Louise's determination mirroring Chris's focus when composing. Same furrow between the brows. Same slight head tilt.

Williams had filed preliminary responses to Wallace & Associates. The machinery of legal defense had been set in motion, grinding forward with methodical precision. Yet within these walls, on this ordinary Sunday, music still flowed between them.

"Mommy, listen!" Louise strummed with exaggerated flourish, face luminous.

"Beautiful, sweet girl." Leah entered the room with measured steps. Each movement careful, as if loud footfalls might shatter their reclaimed peace. "You're becoming quite the musician."

"Like Daddy," Louise declared. The word 'daddy' fell from her lips without hesitation or qualification. Simple truth in a child's voice.

Chris's fingers stilled on his own guitar. Something shifted in his expression—recognition blooming into certainty. Leah knew that look. She'd seen it the night he first said he loved her. The morning he proposed. The moment he saw her walking down the aisle.

It was the face of a man experiencing revelation.

"Daddy needs to talk with Mommy for a minute," he said, gently taking Louise's guitar. "Why don't you color that picture while we chat?"

Louise skipped to her art corner without protest. The transition revealed her security in their presence, her confidence in their return. Chris guided Leah toward the window seat, his hand pressed against the small of her back.

"What is it?" Leah settled beside him, body angled toward his. Their knees touched, a connection point that anchored her against his unusual intensity.

Sunlight caught in his eyelashes. It highlighted amber flecks in his brown eyes, transformed them to gold.

"I want to adopt Louise," he said without preamble. His words emerged with the certainty of long consideration rather than impulse. "Legally. Officially. I want her to have my last name."

The declaration hung between them. Weighty with implication. Unexpected in timing though not in sentiment.

Leah's breath caught. She'd known his devotion to Louise was absolute from their first meeting. But this formal commitment amid their growing legal complications felt both perfect and dangerous.

"Chris—" she began, uncertain whether to express joy or caution.

"I know," he interrupted, taking her hands in his. "I know it's complicated with Ryan challenging the termination agreement. I know it might antagonize him further." His thumbs traced circles on her palms, grounding them both. "But that's exactly why we should do this now. I need to be more than just her stepfather if we're heading into a custody battle."

Birds called to each other outside their window. A breeze stirred new leaves on the maple tree they'd planted last fall. Life continuing its cycle despite human complications.

Leah studied his face. She searched for any hesitation, any shadow of doubt suggesting reaction rather than resolution. She found none. Only the steady certainty that had first drawn her to him—quiet strength complementing her analytical approach to challenges.

"Are you sure?" Her question encompassed more than the adoption itself. "Your family might see this as—"

"As me claiming my daughter?" Chris finished, gentle firmness entering his tone. "Because that's what she is, Leah. Biology didn't make her mine, but every day since we met has." His gaze held absolute conviction. "Every nightmare soothed, every song taught, every scraped knee bandaged."

Louise hummed tunelessly from her art corner. Oblivious to the seismic shift occurring feet away. Sunlight caught her curls, turning them to burnished copper against the pale blue wall.

"Your aunt will see it differently," Leah said quietly, naming the elephant that had taken up residence in their relationship. "Terry will see it as me trapping you into responsibilities that aren't yours."

A muscle tightened in Chris's jaw—not anger at her assessment, but recognition of its accuracy. "Maybe it's time I stopped worrying about how Terry interprets my choices."

The declaration carried weight beyond its simple phrasing—a subtle shifting of allegiance from birth family to chosen family. Leah felt its significance like physical pressure against her heart.

"What about your mother?" She voiced her greater concern. Mary's gentler disapproval worried her more than Terry's volcanic objections.

"Mom loves Louise," Chris said with certainty, though something flickered in his expression. A recognition of complexities he'd previously avoided acknowledging. "She might worry about timing, about legal complications, but ultimately she wants what makes us happy."

Leah reached up to trace his jawline. The familiar terrain of his face transformed by this new resolve.

"You understand what you're taking on? Legally? Emotionally?"

"I do," he smiled, echoing their wedding vows. "I've been her father in every way that matters since the day we met. It's time the rest of the world recognized what we already know."

Louise looked up, sensing she was their conversation's subject. "Daddy? Is it guitar time again?"

"Not yet, sweet pea." Chris's voice carried tender affection. "Mommy and I are talking about something important."

Louise nodded solemnly. She accepted this delay with the security of a child who felt loved enough to endure temporary attention diversion. She returned to coloring, humming fragments of the melody they'd practiced.

"Yes," Leah said suddenly, the decision crystallizing within her. "Let's do it. Let's make it official."

The simple agreement released something in Chris—tension he'd carried without acknowledgment. Fear buried beneath casual certainty. His smile transformed his features with joy that couldn't be manufactured.

"We'll talk to Williams tomorrow." His mind already moved to practical planning. "Find out how to file while Ryan's challenge is pending."

Leah nodded. Her analytical mind sorted through legal implications, timelines, potential complications. But beneath these practical considerations, deeper certainty bloomed—recognition that this moment transcended procedure. It was Chris declaring his loyalties clearly, choosing their created family over external expectations.

The clock on the mantel chimed softly, reminding them of Sunday dinner at Terry's—a Henderson family tradition they'd skipped for two weeks, citing Louise's cold. The reprieve had ended with Terry's pointed text that morning: *Family belongs together, especially during challenging times. Dinner at 5.*

Chris's expression tightened momentarily. It was as if the symbolic intrusion of family obligation had arrived with perfect dramatic timing.

"We don't have to go," he offered, creating an escape neither quite believed possible.

"Yes, we do," Leah replied, rising with reluctant resignation. "But maybe not next week."

The subtle promise of boundaries hung between them. A silent agreement that something fundamental had shifted in their approach to the Henderson family orbit. Chris's decision to adopt Louise represented more than legal protection; it marked where accommodation would begin yielding to assertion.

As they prepared to leave, Chris caught Leah in a brief embrace by the door. His whispered words carried the weight of promise: "After tonight, we start telling them. My mother first, then the others. No more hiding what matters most."

Leah nodded against his shoulder. She breathed in his familiar scent—guitar strings and coffee and faint woodsy cologne. The decision had been made. Whatever storm followed would find them standing together, three souls bound by choice rather than obligation.

Louise skipped between them. Her hands reached for theirs automatically, forming their familiar three-person chain. Connected not by obligation or biology, but by countless moments of chosen love. Each small finger squeeze, each shared smile, each imperfect note practiced together had built something stronger than genetics.

Family, redefined.

Terry Henderson's dining room glowed with orchestrated warmth. Crystal glasses caught light from tapered candles. Family photographs observed from ornate frames—generations of Hendersons frozen in captured moments of coordinated happiness. The room itself served as a testament to Terry's commitment to tradition, to her vision of what family should look like, sound like, behave like.

The aroma of pot roast mingled with lemon furniture polish. Terry moved between kitchen and dining room, each step deliberate, each placement of serving dishes calculated. Her pearl necklace caught the light as she leaned to adjust a folded napkin, compensating with external perfection for her internal intellectual limitations.

"Louise, elbows off the table," Terry instructed, passing the bread basket with an authority entirely unearned by education or insight. "Young ladies keep their posture straight at dinner."

Chris watched his daughter—because that was how he now thought of her, with an ownership that transcended biology—dutifully adjust her position. Something tightened in his chest. Louise's spine straightened, her shoulders pulled back in conscious effort. The natural exuberance that filled their home seemed diminished here, contained within invisible boundaries of expectation.

Across the table, Kourtney nodded subtle approval at Louise's correction. Randy speared a potato, oblivious to the current of reshaping happening before their eyes. Only Mary, at the far end, showed a flicker of something—concern perhaps—before her expression returned to its habitual pleasant neutrality.

"So thoughtful of you both to join us," Terry continued, her tone striking the balance between welcome and reproach, wielding social niceties like weapons to compensate for her profound lack of genuine understanding. "We've missed you at family gatherings. Two Sundays without the complete circle feels... incomplete."

The bread basket passed between hands. Steam rose from serving dishes. An ordinary family dinner rendered extraordinary by currents of intention flowing beneath its surface.

"Louise's cold was quite persistent," Mary offered, her voice carrying hints of apology. "Better safe than sorry."

Terry's glance toward her sister carried sharp edges. Mary's fingers tightened briefly around her silverware before relaxing into submission. Chris had never noticed this silent exchange before—this subtle assertion of authority, this yielding to preserve peace.

"Well, we're all together now," Terry declared with the satisfied air of a general surveying assembled troops, her certainty inversely proportional to her actual comprehension. "As family should be during difficult times."

The reference to their "difficult times" hung in the air like a baited hook. Chris felt Leah tense beside him, her fork pausing momentarily above her plate. The surveillance photos remained unmentioned but present in every measured interaction, every careful phrase.

"Louise has started guitar lessons," Chris offered, deliberately steering toward safer waters. "She's showing real aptitude."

Terry beamed with affection. "Structure and creativity in perfect balance. That's what made Chris excel beyond simple talent."

The praise, familiar as his own heartbeat, no longer warmed Chris as it once had. Instead, he found himself noticing the subtle diminishment it contained—the implication that his artistic nature required Henderson correction to achieve proper form. Terry's simplified understanding of complex talents revealed itself in her reductive explanations.

"Louise has natural discipline," Leah observed quietly. "She practices without prompting."

Her voice carried no challenge, yet Terry's smile tightened imperceptibly. "Children thrive with consistent expectations. Clear boundaries."

The comment carried undertones Chris once would have missed entirely, his ear untrained for the subtle notes of criticism. Tonight, however, each word seemed to contain hidden chambers of meaning—the suggestion that Louise's life with Leah had lacked proper structure, that her current accomplishments must stem from Henderson influence rather than her own innate qualities or her mother's guidance.

"Some children are internally motivated," Mary suggested, her voice carrying the practiced neutrality of decades spent navigating her sister's certainties—certainties founded not on knowledge but on the rigidity that often masks intellectual insecurity. "Louise has always been remarkably self-directed for her age."

Terry's attention shifted to her sister with laser focus. "Nature versus nurture—the eternal debate. Though in my experience, proper nurturing can overcome almost any... inherited tendencies."

The irony of Terry invoking complex psychological concepts she barely comprehended hung in the air, unacknowledged by those accustomed to her pretense of expertise.

Chris set his fork down with deliberate care, the metal making a soft clink against fine china. The sound drew his aunt's attention immediately—any disruption to dining etiquette registering on her awareness like a wrong note in a familiar melody.

"Louise seems to have inherited her mother's focus," he said, the intentional praise of Leah's qualities carrying unmistakable significance. "Her ability to commit fully to what interests her."

Leah's hand found his beneath the table, a brief squeeze of gratitude for the small rebellion. Such moments had become their private language during family gatherings—tiny reassurances of alliance amid the crosscurrents of Henderson expectations.

"Speaking of focus," Terry pivoted smoothly, setting down her water glass. "I've been hearing concerning things about custody matters. These situations can become so complicated when biological parents have second thoughts."

Chris felt Leah's fingers tighten around his, though her expression remained carefully neutral. The casual reference to custody—as if Terry had insider knowledge—confirmed Leah's worst suspicions about information flowing between family members and outside parties.

"How interesting," Chris managed, fighting to keep his voice level. "What exactly have you been hearing?"

"Small communities," Terry dismissed with an elegant wave that betrayed her fundamental misunderstanding of both discretion and boundaries. "People talk. Concerns get shared. It's only natural when a child's wellbeing might be at stake."

Since when does Terry consider Louise's wellbeing? Chris thought, but maintained his careful composure.

"Louise, would you like to help me bring in dessert?" Mary interrupted, her intervention carrying the practiced grace of decades navigating Terry's conversational minefields. "I made that chocolate cake you love."

Louise looked to Leah for permission, receiving a slight nod before sliding from her chair. The child's careful observation of protocol—seeking maternal approval before accepting her grandmother's invitation—didn't escape Terry's notice.

"Such a considerate child," she observed once Louise had disappeared into the kitchen with Mary, her assessment built on platitudes rather than genuine child development knowledge. "Though sometimes too hesitant. Children need confidence to thrive in this world."

"Louise has plenty of confidence," Leah replied, her measured tone belying the tension visible in her shoulders. "She's simply been taught to respect boundaries."

"Of course," Terry agreed with practiced politeness. "Different parenting approaches for different... circumstances."

The conversation had entered dangerous territory, the subterranean currents of judgment now rippling closer to the surface. Chris felt something shift inside him—a tectonic plate of patience giving way to the pressure of accumulated slights, of veiled criticisms directed at the woman he loves, at the child they were raising together.

"Actually," he said, the word emerging with quiet certainty rather than defensive heat, "we've been talking about making our family more official. I'm planning to adopt Louise legally."

The announcement landed in the center of Terry's perfectly arranged table like an unexpected explosion. Silverware stilled against plates. Conversation suspended mid-breath. Even Randy, generally oblivious to interpersonal undercurrents, registered the seismic shift in atmosphere.

Terry recovered first, her fork placed alongside her plate in perfect horizontal alignment. "Chris," she began, using his name with gravity, "that seems like an extremely hasty decision given the current... legal uncertainties."

"Not hasty at all," Chris corrected gently. "I've been Louise's father in every way that matters. The legal part is just catching up to reality."

Kourtney exchanged glances with her husband, the silent communication carrying decades of Henderson family protocol. No direct disagreement with Terry, but no explicit support for Chris either—the careful neutrality of those who recognized shifting alliances but remained unwilling to choose sides.

"Have you consulted with a proper family attorney?" Terry pressed, her composure maintained through visible effort, cobbling together phrases she'd heard on daytime television legal dramas. "Adoption proceedings while custody challenges are pending—it's complicated territory."

"We have an appointment with Williams tomorrow," Leah supplied, her voice remarkably steady given the tension vibrating in the room. "She's been handling all the legal aspects."

"Williams," Terry repeated, the name carrying unmistakable dismissal. "Mary mentioned her. Rather... progressive in her approach to family law, I understand."

The characterization of their attorney—competent, direct, and unwilling to entertain Terry's subtle intrusions during their single meeting—carried clear disapproval. Chris recognized the pattern with newfound clarity: his aunt's systematic undermining of any professional whose education and expertise threatened her veneer of authority.

"She's excellent," Chris stated firmly. "Experienced with complex adoption proceedings."

"I'm simply concerned," Terry continued, leaning forward with practiced sincerity that masked a profound inability to grasp legal nuance, "about the impact on Louise if these proceedings become... serious. Children need stability, not legal battlegrounds."

The statement carried devastating irony given Terry's documented interference, her conversations about custody matters, her subtle campaign to build concern about Leah's parenting. Chris felt something crystallize within him—a clarity that had been building since the surveillance photos arrived.

"What Louise needs," he said with quiet authority, "is the security of knowing her family is legally recognized and protected. That the people who've been there for her everyday—who've braided her hair and soothed her nightmares and celebrated her accomplishments—are officially acknowledged as her parents."

Terry's mouth tightened into a thin line, the only visible crack in her composure. "Blood matters, Chris. Origin matters. You can't simply erase a child's heritage with legal paperwork."

The simplistic statement revealed her black-and-white thinking, her inability to grasp the complex interplay of nature, nurture, and chosen bonds that constitute true family.

The kitchen door swung open, Louise emerging with exaggerated care, balancing a small plate of cookies while Mary followed with the promised chocolate cake. The adults immediately shifted postures, adjusted expressions—the practiced metamorphosis of family conflict temporarily suspended in a child's presence.

"I helped put on the sprinkles," Louise announced proudly, her momentary joy untouched by the tension she'd narrowly missed.

"Beautiful job," Chris praised, genuine warmth breaking through the conflict-induced chill. "Very artistic arrangement."

Mary set the cake in the center of the table, her movements carrying the deliberate care of someone navigating an emotional minefield. "Desert, anyone?" she offered, the mundane question an attempt to restore normalcy to the fractured gathering.

"Yes, please," Terry replied, her composure fully restored behind the mask of gracious hostess. But as Mary moved to retrieve the desert tray, Terry added with casual calculation: "I was just expressing concern about Chris's plans to adopt Louise given the current legal situation."

The statement—deliberately introduced in Louise's presence—caused Mary to falter slightly, the desert tray tilting dangerously in her hand. Chris watched his mother's face transform, shock giving way to calculation, then to a careful neutrality that couldn't quite mask her discomfort.

"Perhaps that's a conversation for another time," Mary suggested, her glance toward Louise carrying unmistakable meaning.

But Terry had accomplished her goal—introducing the topic in the child's presence, ensuring it couldn't be fully addressed in the moment, yet planting seeds of uncertainty that would germinate in Louise's mind. Her tactical maneuver wasn't born of strategic brilliance but of the cunning that often accompanies intellectual limitation—a blunt instrument wielded without nuanced understanding of its consequences.

"What's 'adopt' mean?" Louise asked predictably, her fork suspended above her untouched cake.

The silence that followed felt leaden, pregnant with competing agendas and unspoken fears. Chris met Leah's eyes across the table, a moment of silent communication passing between them—not panic but shared resolve. This moment had arrived sooner than planned, forced by Terry's calculated indiscretion, but perhaps it was a gift in disguise. An opportunity to shape the narrative before others could distort it.

"It means," Chris said, turning to Louise with gentle directness, "that I would become your legal daddy, not just the daddy who loves you and lives with you. It means you could have my last name if you wanted. It means no one could ever question whether I'm really your father."

Louise considered this with the solemn concentration she brought to new concepts. "But you are my daddy," she stated, confusion creasing her brow. "You said families are made by love, not just blood."

"That's exactly right," Chris affirmed, his heart swelling with fierce pride at her perfect recall of their earlier conversations. "Adoption is just the way grown-ups make that official on paper."

Terry's silverware clinked against china—a subtle expression of disapproval at this simplified explanation that contradicted her rigid, unsophisticated understanding of family bonds. But Louise seemed satisfied, returning to her cake with the matter settled in her mind.

"Well," Terry pronounced with the air of someone graciously conceding a temporary defeat, though her facial expressions betrayed her limited comprehension of the nuanced discussion, "I'm sure you'll both consider all aspects carefully before proceeding. Family decisions deserve thorough reflection."

The statement, innocuous on its surface, carried unmistakable subtext: This conversation isn't over. My concerns remain valid. My influence will continue to be felt.

Chris met his aunt's gaze directly, allowing her to read the quiet determination in his expression. Whatever battle lines were being drawn tonight, he had chosen his position with absolute clarity. The family he was building with Leah and Louise now took precedence over the family that had shaped his childhood.

"More cake, anyone?" Mary offered, her voice carrying the slightly desperate quality of peace-makers everywhere.

The remainder of dinner unfolded with artificial pleasantness, conversation carefully steered toward neutral topics—church committee reports, Uncle Randy's golf game, Kourtney's new curtains. But beneath the surface, tectonic plates had shifted. Alliances had been declared. And in the center of Terry's perfectly arranged dining room, the battle for Louise's future had been joined in earnest.

Moonlight spilled across their bedroom floor, transforming the familiar landscape into something both intimate and alien. The drive home from Terry's had unfolded in weighted silence, Louise mercifully drifting to sleep in her car seat, sparing them the need for careful conversation in her presence.

"Well," Leah said softly, removing her earrings one at a time, "that went about as well as expected."

The understatement hung between them, heavy with the evening's unresolved tensions. Chris watched her reflection in the vanity mirror—the controlled movements, the subtle tightness around her mouth that betrayed contained emotion.

"I'm sorry," he offered, the inadequate words carrying the weight of deeper regret. "I didn't expect my announcement to create such... tension."

Leah set her earrings in their designated space. "Terry made her position very clear." She turned to face him directly, leaning against the vanity. "Blood matters. Origin matters. Legal paperwork can't erase heritage."

Terry's words from dinner landed between them with the same force they'd carried earlier.

"She questioned Williams' competence," he said, bitterness edging his voice. "Called her 'progressive' like it was an insult."

"She questioned everything," Leah corrected softly. "The timing. Our motivations. Whether the adoption serves Louise's interests or just our own."

A subtle distance opened between them. Chris pressed his fingers against the bridge of his nose, trying to hold competing truths in balance.

"I shouldn't have announced it like that," he said, regret coloring his tone. "In front of everyone. Without warning."

"Maybe," Leah conceded, moving to sit beside him on the bed's edge, her thigh pressing gently against his. "But it was honest. And sometimes honesty needs to be impulsive to break through years of careful calculation."

The observation struck home. Throughout his life, Chris had approached confrontation with measured deliberation, while Terry had orchestrated family dynamics with practiced skill, always anticipating his responses.

"We need to talk to Williams first thing tomorrow," he said. "Terry's reaction tonight—she's not going to just accept this."

Leah's fingers found his in the semi-darkness. "She made that clear when she talked about the 'legal uncertainties' and how this could impact Louise if proceedings become 'serious.'"

Terry's careful phrasing hung between them, each word laden with implied threat.

"She believes she's protecting me," Chris said quietly, still wrestling with the betrayal of his aunt's public opposition. "In her mind, that makes it justified."

Leah's gaze held his. "She believes Louise isn't really ours. That we're trying to 'erase her heritage' with legal documents."

Chris met her eyes directly. "Then we move forward," he said with quiet certainty. "With the adoption. With everything. We don't let her control our choices through doubt."

Relief flickered across Leah's features, followed quickly by pragmatic concern. "Williams said sixty days until the preliminary hearing. If we're going to do this, we need to be united. No second-guessing."

"No second-guessing," Chris agreed.

They sat in silence for a moment, the ambient sounds of their home creating a bubble of privacy. When Chris spoke again, his voice had softened.

"When I announced the adoption tonight," he said, "it wasn't impulsive, Leah. It wasn't a reaction to family pressure." He faced her then, needing her to see the truth in his expression. "It was recognition of what already exists. Louise is my daughter. Has been since that Sunday social at church when she was six months old, when her tiny fingers wrapped around my tie."

Leah's eyes softened with remembered tenderness. "She trusted you from the beginning. Children have instincts about people who will love them wholly, without reservation."

"I want to make it official," Chris continued, conviction strengthening his voice. "Not just for legal protection, though that matters. Not just to counter whatever objections Terry might raise, though that's part of it." He moved closer, kneeling before Leah. "I want the world to know that she is mine. That we're her family."

Leah's fingers traced the contours of his face. "Even if it means standing against your family? Against Terry's certainty that blood is what makes someone a 'real' parent?"

The question contained no manipulation, no ultimatum—only honest recognition of the choice that lay before him. Chris covered her hand with his own, turning to press a kiss against her palm.

"Especially then," he said with quiet certainty. "Because you and Louise are my family now. My first priority. My chosen home."

"And if Terry does more than just voice her disapproval?" Leah pressed gently. "If she actively opposes the adoption?"

Chris stood, pulling Leah up with him, gathering her into his arms. "Then we face it together. All three of us."

The declaration hung between them, weighty with promise. Outside their window, clouds drifted across the moon, momentarily dimming the silver light. When brightness returned, it revealed Leah's face transformed by the tenderness Chris had witnessed only in rare moments—when Louise accomplished something particularly challenging, when connections were made that transcended ordinary bonds.

"Then we'll face them together," she said simply.

Chris tightened his embrace, breathing in the familiar scent of her hair. The evening's confrontation at Terry's had clarified rather than complicated his path forward. Tomorrow would bring legal consultations, potential friction from Terry's corner, navigating the fallout from tonight's public declaration. But here, in the quiet certainty of their bedroom, the rightness of his decision settled around him.

"We should sleep," Leah suggested. "Tomorrow will demand clear thinking."

Chris nodded, beginning the familiar rhythm of their bedtime routine. As they moved through these domestic rituals—Leah washing her face, Chris setting the alarm, both checking on Louise before returning to their room—the ordinary nature of their actions contrasted sharply with the extraordinary decision that now shaped their path forward.

Later, as darkness gathered them close and sleep approached, Chris found himself thinking of Terry's words at dinner. The way she'd questioned everything—timing, motivation, permanence. The suggestion that they were trying to erase something fundamental about Louise's identity rather than claiming their place in it.

He turned toward Leah in the darkness, finding her hand beneath the covers. Their fingers interlaced.

"You know what?" Chris said softly. "Tonight clarified everything."

Leah shifted closer. "How so?"

"Because now I know exactly where we stand. No more wondering if Terry will come around, if the family will support this. We know. And we can stop hoping for their blessing and start building our case."

"Our family," Leah added.

"Our family," Chris agreed. "The one we're fighting for."

Whatever storms gathered on their horizon, they would weather them together. The family they had built was worth fighting for, worth standing against family disapproval to protect, worth whatever discomfort the coming days might bring.

As sleep finally claimed him, Chris carried one certainty into dreams: Terry's opposition had revealed where his family truly stood. But it had also revealed his own position—standing firmly beside Leah and Louise, ready to defend what they had built, regardless of who questioned their right to do so.

In the morning, they would call Williams. They would move forward with the adoption. They would show Terry and everyone else that the bonds they had forged were stronger than any argument about blood and heritage could break.

CHAPTER 7

Legal Maneuvers

M onday afternoon light sliced through venetian blinds, casting fractured shadows across Williams's conference table. Leah arranged the documents they'd prepared the night before – birth certificates, marriage license, financial statements. Everything needed to make official what Chris had declared to his family less than twenty-four hours ago.

"So you've decided to move forward," Williams said, settling into her chair. Not a question – she'd heard the determination in Chris's voice when he'd called first thing this morning.

"Absolutely." Chris leaned forward, his posture carrying none of the uncertainty that had marked their earlier meetings. "I announced it at Sunday dinner last night. There's no going back."

Williams raised an eyebrow. "How did the family take it?"

Leah and Chris exchanged glances, the memory of last night's confrontation still fresh.

"Mixed reactions," Leah said diplomatically. "Some family members have strong opinions about biological connections versus chosen bonds."

"That's common in these cases," Williams replied, making notes. "Family dynamics can complicate stepparent adoptions, especially when there's active opposition from relatives."

She spread several documents across the table. "Now, let's talk about the real complexities we're facing. Ryan's challenge to the termination agreement creates unusual legal terrain. We're essentially running two parallel cases – his attempt to restore his rights, and your petition to legally claim what's already yours."

"What does that mean for timing?" Chris asked.

"Normally, stepparent adoptions are straightforward," Williams explained. "File the petition, verify the biological parent's rights were properly terminated, brief hearing before a judge, and it's done within sixty to ninety days. But Ryan's challenge puts everything on hold."

"So we wait until his case resolves?" Leah asked, concern threading through her voice.

"No," Williams said firmly. "That would be a tactical mistake. We file now, aggressively. Filing establishes you as more than just a concerned stepfather, Chris. You become a legal party with standing in any proceedings involving Louise."

Chris straightened. "What does that mean practically?"

"It means you get a voice in every decision about Louise's welfare during this process. Ryan can't make unilateral choices about her education, medical care, or living arrangements without your input. More importantly, it forces the court to consider what's already established – your role as her father in every way that matters."

"And if Ryan's case succeeds?" Leah asked, voicing their deepest fear. "If he gets his rights restored?"

"Then we argue that overturning a stepparent adoption that's already been approved would be doubly disruptive to Louise," Williams said. "Courts hate undoing established legal relationships. But let's not get ahead of ourselves – termination of parental rights cases are notoriously difficult to overturn."

Leah pulled out the surveillance photos they'd received weeks ago. "Have there been any new developments with the surveillance situation?"

Williams reviewed the images they'd discussed before. "Continue documenting when and how you receive any new photos. Keep the envelopes, note dates and times. The pattern we're establishing shows escalating harassment that could work in our favor."

She flipped through the photos methodically. "Still just normal family activities. Their strategy seems to be documenting your daily life, hoping to find something they can twist."

"That's what worries us," Leah admitted. "Normal moments being presented as evidence against us."

"Which is why we need our own documentation," Williams said. "Counter their narrative with your own evidence of Louise's happiness and stability."

Williams pulled out a timeline chart, spreading it across the table. "Here's how this will likely unfold. We file your adoption petition today. Within forty-eight hours, Ryan's team will receive notice. They'll immediately request genetic testing to establish paternity – that's standard procedure and we can't oppose it."

"How long does that take?" Leah asked.

"Two weeks for results. Once paternity is confirmed, the dynamics shift. Ryan's challenge to the termination becomes stronger legally, but your adoption petition gains weight too – you're asking to adopt a child whose biological father chose to abandon her."

Chris's jaw tightened. "He didn't just abandon her. He actively chose not to be her father when it mattered most."

"Exactly the language we'll use," Williams agreed. "Wallace & Associates will frame it as a young man's mistake that he's now trying to correct. We frame it as calculated abandonment followed by opportunistic reappearance."

"What about our chances?" Leah asked. "Realistically?"

Williams considered carefully. "Ryan's hired top-tier representation. Wallace & Associates are expensive and effective, but they specialize in high-conflict divorces and corporate family disputes, not contested terminations. This isn't their strongest area."

"Is that good for us?" Chris asked.

"It means they'll rely on aggressive tactics rather than nuanced family law strategy," Williams explained. "They'll try to overwhelm rather than outmaneuver. We can use that against them."

Williams spread out the adoption petition forms. "I need you both to understand something. Once we file this, the stakes escalate dramatically. Ryan's team will scrutinize every aspect of your marriage, your parenting, your fitness to raise Louise. They'll interview neighbors, teachers, anyone who's observed your family."

"What are they looking for?" Leah asked.

"Anything that suggests instability or inadequate parenting. Arguments between you and Chris. Discipline issues with Louise. Financial stress. Social problems. They'll magnify minor concerns into major red flags."

"Let them look," Chris said, his voice carrying new steel. "Four years of daily fatherhood speaks louder than manufactured concerns."

"That's exactly the right attitude," Williams approved. "But we need to be proactive. Start documenting everything yourselves – Louise's school performance, medical records showing consistent care, photographs of normal family activities. Create your own narrative."

"We're already doing that," Leah said. "Every interaction with Louise, every sign of her happiness and security with us."

Williams nodded approvingly. "Good. Now, let's discuss strategy. The adoption petition serves multiple purposes beyond the obvious. It demonstrates commitment that predates Ryan's sudden interest. It shows Louise has an existing, stable parental relationship. Most importantly, it forces the court to consider disruption from Louise's perspective."

"How so?" Chris asked.

"If the court grants Ryan's termination challenge but denies your adoption, Louise loses the only father she's ever known without gaining any meaningful relationship with Ryan. If they approve your adoption but restore Ryan's rights, she has two legal fathers – an impossible situation requiring further litigation. The cleanest resolution is denying Ryan's petition and approving yours."

"You make it sound logical," Leah observed. "But family court isn't always logical."

"True," Williams conceded. "Which is why we need to prepare for every contingency. Character witnesses will be crucial. Who can testify about your relationship with Louise?"

"Her preschool teacher, Miss Andrews," Leah said immediately. "She's witnessed Chris with Louise countless times."

"Perfect. Anyone else?"

"Our pediatrician, Dr. Martinez. Chris has been to most of her appointments."

"Excellent. Medical professionals carry significant weight. What about family members?"

Chris and Leah exchanged glances. "My mother supports us," Chris said carefully. "But she avoids confrontation. I'm not sure she'd testify against other family members."

"We'll work with what we have," Williams said. "Sometimes family silence speaks as loudly as opposition."

She pointed to signature lines on the documents. "Are you ready to make this official?"

Chris reached for the pen without hesitation. "I've been ready since the night Louise first called me Daddy."

As he signed each page, Leah watched his face – the determined set of his jaw, the steady hand that had taught Louise to play guitar, the wedding ring that caught the afternoon light. This man who'd chosen their family over his own relatives' approval, who'd stood firm last night despite family pressure.

"Your turn," Williams said, sliding the papers to Leah.

Leah's signature joined Chris's with steady strokes, each letter an act of defiance against those who would tear their family apart. "What happens next?"

"I file these within the hour," Williams said, gathering the signed documents. "Ryan's team will receive notice within forty-eight hours. Expect them to accelerate their timeline – they'll want a hearing before your adoption gains momentum."

"How long before we know something?" Chris asked.

"Initial motions and responses take thirty to sixty days. The actual hearing could be three to six months out, depending on the court's schedule and how aggressively both sides push."

"That long?" Leah's voice carried exhaustion at the thought of months of uncertainty.

"Complex family cases take time," Williams said gently. "But remember – every day that passes is another day Louise remains securely in your home, another day of established routine and relationship."

Williams stood, organizing files with the efficiency of someone managing multiple family crises. "One more critical issue. Have you told Louise about any of this?"

Chris and Leah looked at each other. "Not yet," Leah admitted. "We wanted to file first, make it real."

"I strongly recommend telling her soon. Age-appropriate information, but the truth. Children absorb more than we realize, and she's better off hearing facts from you than creating her own explanations from overheard fragments."

"What should we say?" Leah asked.

"Keep it simple but honest. Someone who helped create her wants to meet her. Judges will decide what's best for everyone. You're working to keep your family together." Williams moved toward the door. "Most importantly, reassure her that whatever happens, your love for her never changes."

"Any other advice?" Chris asked as they prepared to leave.

Williams paused, her professional mask softening momentarily. "Trust your instincts. You know Louise better than anyone – better than Ryan, better than any court-appointed evaluator. That knowledge is your greatest strength."

In the elevator, silence settled between them, weighted with the magnitude of what they'd just set in motion. The building hummed around them, dozens of other legal battles proceeding simultaneously, other families fighting for their survival within the system's careful machinery.

"I keep thinking about Louise's reaction," Leah said finally. "How do we explain that someone wants to take her away from the only father she's ever known?"

"We don't frame it that way," Chris replied, his voice thoughtful. "We frame it as protecting our family from outside interference."

The elevator reached the lobby. Through the glass doors, they could see rain beginning to fall, late afternoon showers that would wash the streets clean and leave everything glistening.

"The papers are filed," Chris said as they stood at the threshold. "No turning back now."

"Good," Leah replied with surprising firmness. "I'm tired of being reactive. Time to go on the offensive."

They pushed through the doors into the rain, shoulders straight, documents tucked safely in Leah's bag. The legal machinery was now in motion – petitions filed, notices pending, battle lines drawn.

The Wallace & Associates building rose eighteen stories of steel and glass, reflecting afternoon clouds with cold indifference. Terry Henderson stood on the sidewalk, neck craned, cross pendant clutched between dampening fingers. Her Sunday shoes, rarely worn beyond church property, pinched against the unfamiliar terrain of downtown ambition.

She adjusted her blouse—the one with embroidered flowers she reserved for church council meetings. The fabric strained slightly across her shoulders, necessary armor for entering enemy territory, even when the enemy might become a temporary ally.

The revolving door trapped her momentarily. Terry pushed with excessive force, as though moral righteousness required physical demonstration. The security guard glanced up, then away. Another desperate civilian entering the machinery of family law.

The elevator ascended with the numbers illuminated in sequence. Terry rehearsed opening statements in her mind. Legal phrases gleaned from television procedurals collided with church committee assertions of authority.

The fourteenth floor reception area stretched before her in understated cream and mahogany. Leather-bound volumes lined built-in shelves, their gold lettering displaying terms Terry couldn't decipher from her position. The implicit knowledge contained behind those covers hung accusatory in climate-controlled air.

"May I help you?" The receptionist's perfect eyebrows arched with practiced neutrality.

Terry straightened her spine, adopting the posture she used when overruling budget concerns at church. "I have important information. For the Matthews case."

"Do you have an appointment with Attorney Wallace?"

"He'll want to see me." Terry's fingers smoothed non-existent wrinkles from her skirt. "I'm family. Of the child."

"Your name?"

"Theresa O'Donnell." She produced a church bulletin from her purse. "Vice President of St. Michael's Ladies' Auxiliary. Head of the Christmas charity committee three years running."

The receptionist accepted the bulletin with professionally concealed confusion, her manicured finger pressing an intercom button.

"Someone here regarding the Matthews case. A Ms. O'Donnell. Says she's family."

Terry settled into a leather chair that swallowed her modest height. Her eyes scanned the waiting area—legal journals arranged in perfect rows, their covers displaying terminology that swam before her eyes. She lifted a glossy publication, held it at reading distance in a performance of comprehension without substance.

"Ms. O'Donnell?" A voice from an interior hallway.

Attorney James Wallace extended his hand. His suit spoke of careful selection rather than off-the-rack necessity, his tie matching his pocket square.

Terry rose too quickly. The magazine slid from her lap to the floor.

"I was just reading about the—" She gestured toward the fallen publication. "The habeas courtship proceedings."

Wallace's expression revealed nothing as he retrieved the journal. "Fascinating topic." He glanced at the cover—an analysis of corporate tax law. "This way, please."

Terry followed him through hushed corridors lined with framed diplomas and tasteful abstracts. Each office they passed contained similar landscapes of success—mahogany desks, computer screens, bookended knowledge.

Wallace's office occupied a corner with windows on two walls revealing the city below. From this height, St. Michael's parish boundaries disappeared into meaningless geography.

"Please." Wallace indicated a chair positioned to maximize client intimidation.

Terry perched on its edge, her purse clutched against her lap like a shield. The crucifix embroidered on its canvas exterior faced outward—symbolic protection within secular territory.

"You mentioned you're family." Wallace settled behind his desk, the expanse of polished wood separating them like class distinctions.

"I'm Chris Johnson's aunt. His godmother." Terry's chin lifted slightly. "I helped raise him after his father's business failed."

"And your connection to the Matthews case?"

"That's why I'm here." Terry leaned forward, her voice dropping to conspiratorial levels. "My nephew is making a terrible mistake. He's planning to legally adopt that child."

"Louise Miller." Wallace supplied the name with professional neutrality.

"She's not really his." Terry's fingers twisted her cross pendant. "He married the mother barely a year ago. Now he wants to adopt her like she's his flesh and blood."

"I see." Wallace made a brief notation, his fountain pen moving across heavy stationery with practiced efficiency.

"Blood matters." Terry's voice carried the conviction of those who mistake simplicity for wisdom. "You can't just decide someone is family because you feel like it."

"And you believe this adoption would not be in Louise's best interest?"

"How could it be?" Terry's hands spread in unconscious supplication. "Her real father wants her back. Her biological father."

Wallace set his pen down carefully. "Ryan Matthews has indeed petitioned to have his termination of rights set aside. Though the legal hurdles are significant."

"That's why I came." Terry glanced toward the closed door as though expecting eavesdroppers. "I want to help you win."

"Help us win?"

"I know things." Terry's voice carried the same portentous quality she brought to prayer circle revelations. "About the mother. About Leah."

"What sort of things, Ms. O'Donnell?"

"She's not a good match for my nephew." Terry's certainty emerged undiluted by evidence. "Always thinks she knows better than everyone else."

"And her parenting of Louise?"

"She's very... controlling." Terry reached into her purse, extracting a small notebook with floral cover. "I've been keeping track."

The pages revealed Terry's rounded handwriting in dates, times, and observations transformed through her narrow perspective into evidence.

"June 12th. Louise not allowed second dessert despite church picnic special occasion." Terry read with grave significance. "July 8th. Bedtime enforced despite family gathering still ongoing. August 24th. Louise's art project modified by Leah before school submission."

Wallace studied her across the mahogany expanse, his gaze calculating something beyond Terry's awareness.

"I've been doing research." Terry continued, returning the notebook to her purse. "About adopting laws."

"Adoption statutes," Wallace corrected automatically.

"Right, exactly." Terry's dismissal revealed her pattern—rejection of correction as unnecessary complication. "I know it's hard to stop an adoption when both parents agree. But Leah is just forcing this to hurt Ryan."

"How did you learn about the adoption plans?"

"Chris announced it at Sunday dinner." Terry's mouth tightened at the memory. "Just sprung it on everyone. Completely disrespectful."

"And your goal in coming here today?"

"To protect my godson." Terry's voice carried absolute conviction beneath fractured reasoning. "Chris isn't thinking clearly. He's been manipulated by that woman."

"You're referring to his wife."

"She trapped him." Terry's certainty brooked no complexity. "Got pregnant by another man. Then found my sweet, sensitive nephew to raise her child."

Wallace made another notation, his pen scratching against paper.

"Leah Miller—Johnson now—is the daughter of John Miller." Terry pronounced the name with portentous weight. "His company destroyed my brother-in-law's business. Now she's trapped Chris. It's all connected."

Wallace's neutral expression never faltered, though something calculating entered his gaze.

"Tell me about the Miller connection."

"John Miller's company took over Johnson & Sons." Terry leaned forward, eager now. "Left my brother-in-law with nothing. The whole family suffered."

"And you believe Leah's relationship with your nephew..."

"Is revenge." Terry completed with triumphant certainty. "She's a Miller. They destroy Johnsons. It's what they do."

"You have evidence of this planning?"

"I know Miller tactics." Terry tapped her temple. "My sister's husband lost everything because of them. Now John Miller's daughter has my nephew under her spell."

Wallace's silence invited further revelation. Terry filled it with accumulated grievances.

"She moved into our town. Joined our church. Got close to Chris through the music program. It was all planned."

"Would you be willing to testify? To these concerns about the adoption?"

"Of course." Terry straightened in her chair. "I'm not afraid to stand up for what's right."

"And you have regular contact with Louise?"

"I'm her great-aunt." Pride infused the proclamation. "I see her at church. Family dinners. I've even visited her classroom."

"With permission?"

"I'm on the parish education committee." Terry waved away legal distinctions with bureaucratic credentials. "I visit all the children."

"Would you be willing to document your interactions with Louise moving forward? Note any concerns about her care or wellbeing?"

"I already do." Terry patted her purse where the floral notebook resided. "I've been keeping records for months."

"Excellent." Wallace reached for a business card. "We might need specific observations about Louise's relationship with her mother versus Chris."

"I can get pictures." Terry accepted the card with conspiratorial eagerness. "I have a new phone with an excellent camera."

"And your family's relationship with Chris and Leah?"

"My nephew Tyler sees through her." Terry's voice lowered again. "He's been investigating. Her history. Her father's business practices."

Wallace made a final notation before capping his pen. "Ms. O'Donnell, your information could be very helpful to our client's petition."

Pride straightened Terry's spine. Recognition from authority figures—especially educated males—represented rare currency in her circumscribed existence.

"I knew it would be." Self-satisfaction warmed her tone. "I understand these legal matters better than most people expect."

"Indeed." Wallace rose, signaling the meeting's conclusion. "We'll need to establish a discreet method of communication. Given your... personal connection to the situation."

"I understand discretion." Terry mispronounced with confident ignorance. "I run the prayer chain at St. Michael's. I know which information goes where."

"Perfect." Wallace extended his hand, the gesture conferring temporary equality across the mahogany divide. "One final question, Ms. O'Donnell."

Terry accepted his handshake with the gravity of treaty signatories.

"Does your nephew—Chris—know you're here today?"

Terry's expression revealed momentary uncertainty before righteousness reasserted itself.

"Some things are more important than temporary hurt feelings." Her voice carried the peculiar cruelty of those convinced of their own benevolence. "Sometimes we must protect people from themselves."

"Quite so." Wallace escorted her toward the door. "We'll be in touch."

The return journey through hushed corridors felt different to Terry. Her shoulders squared with newfound purpose. Each diploma they passed no longer intimidated but confirmed her new alliance with institutional authority.

"Ms. O'Donnell will be providing ongoing assistance with the Matthews case," Wallace informed his receptionist. "Please ensure her calls are put through promptly."

Terry's chest expanded with vindication. Her crusade legitimized by expensive surroundings and professional acknowledgment.

"I have names of character witnesses too." She opened her purse, extracting a handwritten list. "Church members who've seen how Leah separates Louise from proper family influences."

Wallace accepted the list with perfect professional courtesy. "Thorough indeed."

In the descending elevator, Terry composed text messages in her mind. Carefully worded updates for Tyler. Vague spiritualized assurances for her prayer circle. The language of righteousness cloaking actions that, examined directly, might reveal their true nature.

The lobby marble echoed beneath her sensible Sunday shoes. She passed the security desk with the confidence of those recently granted admission to higher circles.

Outside, afternoon sun illuminated the parish boundaries invisible from Wallace's windows. St. Michael's spire rose in the distance, its cross catching light like divine approval. Terry breathed deeply, savoring victory's particular sweetness.

She had acted to protect family. To preserve proper order. To save her godson from terrible mistake. The slight discomfort beneath her breastbone—something adjacent to shame but not quite reaching it—could be dismissed as indigestion.

Terry clutched her purse against her side. The notebook of observations pressed against her hip like a concealed weapon. Her cross pendant rested between collar bones, its silent witness to actions taken in its name.

The Wallace & Associates building reflected clouds in its glass exterior. The imposing structure now felt like an extension of Terry's influence rather than intimidating barrier. Her steps carried newfound purpose as she headed toward her car.

Some forms of betrayal wrapped themselves so thoroughly in protection's language that even perpetrators never recognized them for what they were.

The St. Michael's Parish recital had been advertised in the community bulletin Ryan still received. He told himself he was merely curious—a casual observation of the town where he'd once imagined building a life before ambition had redirected his trajectory toward Tesla and a future that had seemed so much larger than domestic routine.

The auditorium hummed with parental anticipation. Ryan chose a seat in the back row, anonymous among strangers. Around him, cameras emerged from purses and pockets, phones held aloft to document moments that would blur into the larger tapestry of childhood memory.

He hadn't planned to come. Had driven past the church twice before finally parking three blocks away. The program clutched in his hand listed Louise Miller among the beginner guitar students.

Louise Miller. Not Louise Matthews. Never Louise Matthews.

The stage remained empty, curtains drawn against light filtering through stained glass windows. Ryan's fingers worried the program's edges. The distance since signing those termination papers—through pregnancy he'd refused to witness, through birth he'd chosen to miss, through years of growth he'd deliberately ignored—had seemed like rational self-preservation. Now, sitting among parents who had earned their presence through daily devotion, that distance felt like amputation.

Miss Rodriguez appeared, announcing the first performers. Ryan's attention fragmented across the program until he found Louise's name—seventh in the lineup.

Six performances blurred past. Then Miss Rodriguez's voice cut through: "Our next performer is Louise Miller, who will be playing an original composition titled 'Daddy's Song,' taught to her by her father, Chris Johnson."

Her father. The words carried casual possession, as if Chris Johnson's claim required no qualification.

Louise walked onto the stage with confidence that stole Ryan's breath. She wore a purple dress, dark curls pulled back with clips that caught the stage lights, revealing a face that mirrored his mother's with unmistakable accuracy. The same delicate bone structure. The same serious expression when concentrating.

His daughter. Undeniably, genetically his daughter.

She carried a child-sized guitar with careful reverence. The instrument settled against her small frame with practiced ease, suggesting hours of instruction Ryan had never witnessed.

Behind her, Chris Johnson appeared from the wings. He crouched beside Louise with movements that spoke of intimate familiarity. His hand touched her shoulder briefly, and Louise looked up at him with complete trust.

The exchange lasted perhaps five seconds. Chris's whispered encouragement. Louise's small nod. The quick smile they shared before Chris retreated.

Five seconds that contained entire universes Ryan had never entered.

Louise's small fingers found the strings. The melody emerged with simplicity that somehow elevated it beyond mere beginner's exercise. Each note deliberate, carefully placed.

But it was her face that broke him. The concentration in the slight furrow between her brows. The unconscious way her lips moved, counting beats. The moment near the end when a small smile appeared—private satisfaction in her own accomplishment.

She was complete without him. Whole.

The song ended. Applause erupted, but Ryan heard only rushing in his ears. Louise bowed with childish grace, then looked toward the wings where Chris emerged. Her entire face transformed—joy unguarded and absolute. She ran to him with the confidence of someone who had never doubted her welcome, launching herself into arms that caught her with practiced ease.

Her small arms circled his neck. Even from the back row, Ryan could see her lips form words: "I did it, Daddy!"

Ryan's hands gripped the armrests. This should have been his moment. His arms. His ears receiving her joyful announcement.

Instead, he sat anonymous, a stranger bearing witness to a life proceeding beautifully without him.

California. His apartment overlooking the bay. That had been six months ago, before he'd handed in his resignation at Tesla, before he'd driven east toward a home he'd spent years avoiding.

The laptop screen had glowed in the darkness of his bedroom, two in the morning. Ryan's hands had trembled as he typed Leah's name into the search bar, something he'd done countless times before closing the browser in self-protective cowardice.

This time, he let the search complete.

Her profile appeared. The first image stopped his breath: Louise at three years old, paint-smeared and laughing, holding up artwork to the camera.

He'd scrolled through months of documentation. Louise's first day of preschool. Louise at a playground, airborne on a swing. Louise and Leah at the zoo, pressed against glass watching penguins. Each image a moment he'd missed.

Then he'd found the wedding photos.

Leah in a simple dress, flowers in her hair, happiness Ryan had never managed to give her. Chris Johnson beside her, looking at her with uncomplicated devotion. And Louise between them in a flower girl dress, holding both their hands, her smile unguarded and secure.

The caption: "We did it! Our little family is official."

Our little family.

Ryan had closed the laptop, then opened it again. Scrolled through the same photos, studying Louise's face for signs of absence, for evidence that she'd felt the hollow space where a biological father should have been.

He'd found none. Only joy. Security. Belonging.

The tears had started then, surprising him with their force. His shoulders shook with sobs he'd suppressed for years. He'd cried for the pregnancy he'd missed, for the birth he'd refused to attend, for the termination papers he'd signed with such relief, believing himself free when he'd actually been severing something essential.

Louise learning to walk, Chris's hands ready to catch her. Louise's second birthday, face covered in cake while Leah laughed. Louise and Chris at what appeared to be a music class, both holding small guitars, their postures mirroring each other.

Each image carved deeper. Not just grief, but recognition of his own foolishness. He'd believed career advancement and personal freedom were worthy trades for fatherhood. Had convinced himself that terminating his rights was responsible.

The photos revealed the lie.

Ryan had begun searching then. Termination of parental rights. Challenging voluntary termination. Restoration of parental rights. The legal phrases had filled his browser history through those sleepless California nights. Articles about precedent. Cases where biological parents had successfully petitioned courts. Success stories that felt like lifelines.

Wallace & Associates had appeared in multiple search results—a firm specializing in complex family law, with particular expertise in contested custody matters. Their website had showcased victories, testimonials from parents reunited with children through legal intervention.

Ryan had made the initial call himself, sitting in his Tesla in the parking garage of his apartment building, unable to bear having this conversation

121

inside walls that had witnessed his grief. The consultation had been clinical—Wallace asking questions about timeline, circumstances, Ryan's current stability and resources.

"These cases are challenging," Wallace had said, his voice carrying professional assessment rather than judgment. "But not impossible. Especially when the petitioner demonstrates genuine rehabilitation and changed circumstances."

That word—rehabilitation—had struck Ryan oddly, as if his choice to prioritize career had been pathology requiring treatment. But he'd accepted the framing. Had paid the retainer. Had authorized Wallace to begin preliminary investigation.

The final performance concluded. Parents filed toward the reception area. Ryan remained seated, unable to navigate the crowd that seemed to form an impenetrable barrier.

Through the auditorium doors, he watched Louise hold Chris's hand as they moved through the crowd, stopping to accept congratulations. Leah appeared, and the three of them formed a unit so natural that observers automatically made space, acknowledging their belonging.

His mother would have been there, had he not signed away his rights. Would have fussed over Louise's dress, documented every moment. His father would have offered measured praise.

Instead, the Matthews family's genetic legacy walked through a crowd of strangers, calling another man Daddy, building memories in which Ryan existed only as absence.

The grief that had driven him back from California began its transformation into something harder, more sustainable. He hadn't just abandoned her—he'd been replaced. Systematically displaced by someone who had recognized opportunity and claimed what Ryan had only temporarily set aside.

Ryan pulled out his phone, scrolling to the photos downloaded from Leah's Facebook. His daughter. In every image, undeniably his daughter, even as she lived a life that erased him completely.

The crowd in the parish hall thinned. Ryan watched Chris crouch to Louise's level, saying something that made her laugh. She ran ahead with unselfconscious energy, her purple dress bright against the subdued colors around her.

Ryan stood, legs uncertain as he navigated toward the exit. No one looked at him. No one acknowledged his presence. He was invisible here, a ghost haunting the periphery of a life that should have been his.

Outside, the air hit him with surprising intensity. His Tesla waited where he'd left it, its sleek lines speaking of success and achievement and the life he'd chosen over domestic routine. The car that had once represented freedom now felt like evidence of miscalculation.

He didn't start the engine immediately. Instead, he opened his phone's photo album, scrolling to the surveillance images Wallace's team had provided. Louise at the playground. Louise leaving school. Louise at her swim lessons.

These shouldn't be surveillance photos. They should be memories captured by a father present for ordinary moments.

Wallace had been clear about the challenges. Termination agreements were difficult to overturn. But not impossible. Not with the right strategy, the right witnesses, the right arguments about changed circumstances.

Ryan started the engine. The Tesla purred to life, a contrast to the human noise of families loading practical vehicles around him. He pulled away from the curb, leaving the church behind.

But the image remained—Louise's face transformed by joy, Chris's arms catching her, the casual "I did it, Daddy" that contained entire universes Ryan had never inhabited.

By the time Ryan reached his apartment—modest compared to California's luxury—he had fully committed to what needed to happen. This wasn't about redemption anymore. It was about restoration. About ensuring that genetic reality trumped emotional circumstance.

Louise was his daughter. The courts would recognize this truth. And once they did, Chris Johnson would become a footnote—a temporary placeholder in a narrative that rightfully belonged to Ryan Matthews.

That night, Ryan didn't dream of the daughter he'd signed away. He dreamed of the daughter he would reclaim, her face transformed from joy in someone else's arms to recognition in his.

The dream felt like prophecy. Like inevitability.

He woke determined, energized, certain of his path forward.

And entirely blind to the destruction such certainty would cause.

Mary's kitchen smelled of cinnamon and coming rain. Chris sat at the worn oak table where he'd eaten countless childhood breakfasts. Late afternoon light streamed through windows overlooking her garden, where spring plantings stood in neat rows alongside wild daisies she allowed to grow along the fence.

"More coffee?" Mary moved toward the pot without waiting for his answer.

Chris nodded, watching his mother's movements. The familiar rhythm of her hospitality offered temporary shelter from the conversation ahead. Since announcing his adoption plans at Terry's dinner three nights ago, he'd rehearsed this moment repeatedly.

"Mom." He wrapped his hands around the warm mug. "About Sunday night—"

"You surprised everyone." Mary's back remained turned as she wiped an already clean counter. "Terry hasn't stopped calling."

"I should have told you first."

Mary faced him then, her expression gentle. "You want to adopt Louise."

It wasn't a question. Mary had perfected the art of stating facts without revealing her position—a skill developed through decades of navigating between Terry's strong opinions and her husband's quieter convictions.

"I do." Chris met her eyes directly. "She's been my daughter in every way that matters since Leah and I started dating."

Mary's hands found her apron pocket. "You've been a wonderful father to her."

"But?" Chris prompted.

"No but." Mary settled across from him. "Just concerns about timing."

The unspoken hung between them. Through the window, clouds gathered above Mary's garden, bringing the scent of rain through the screen door.

"Williams says timing actually matters." Chris kept his voice steady. "Filing now shows commitment rather than reaction to Ryan's petition."

Mary's gaze drifted toward the refrigerator door where Louise's artwork hung—a family portrait showing three smiling figures before a house with musical notes floating from the chimney. The careful lettering beneath read: "My Family – Mommy, Daddy, Me."

"She sees herself as yours already." Mary's observation carried quiet warmth.

Chris smiled, gratitude filling his chest. "She draws my eyes in all her pictures."

"And your musical notation." Mary pointed to the chimney detail. "Family finds itself regardless of paperwork."

Lightning flashed beyond the window. The approaching storm had moved closer, dark clouds now overhead.

"Terry doesn't see it that way." Chris set down his mug carefully.

Mary's fingers found her wedding band, twisting it—an unconscious gesture Chris had observed throughout childhood whenever she felt conflicted.

"Your aunt believes in tradition." Mary's diplomatic phrasing revealed nothing of her own position. "Clear boundaries."

"Biology over choice." Chris didn't hide his disagreement.

Mary moved to the window. Rain had begun falling, fat drops creating dark spots on the garden path. "She worries about your heart."

"My heart is fully committed to Louise." The certainty in his voice filled the kitchen. "To Leah. To our family."

Mary remained at the window, her silhouette framed against the darkening sky. Something in her posture—a slight rounding of normally straight shoulders—suggested burdens beyond this conversation.

"Terry has been making calls." She spoke to the glass rather than her son. "To church members. About your announcement."

"Rallying opposition?" Chris felt frustration but no surprise. Terry's influence within St. Michael's parish extended through countless committees and prayer circles.

"Gathering prayers." Mary's diplomatic correction carried decades of practice. "For discernment."

Chris recognized the euphemism. Terry's "prayer circles" functioned as information networks, carefully crafted concerns disguised as spiritual support.

Thunder rolled overhead, closer now, directly above them.

"I need to check the garden doors." Mary moved suddenly toward the mudroom. "This storm looks serious."

Chris recognized the retreat—the familiar pattern of approach and withdrawal that characterized his mother's management of difficult truths. He waited as she disappeared, using the moment to gather his thoughts.

The kitchen walls held generations of family photographs. His graduation portrait hung beside Louise's preschool picture. The church bulletin board showed Terry's name heading three committee lists.

When Mary returned, her shoulders carried new tension. Water droplets clung to her sleeves where rain had caught her at the door.

"She means well." Mary offered the familiar defense, settling back at the table. "Terry has always felt responsible for your path."

"Louise is my daughter." Chris's voice carried quiet certainty. "Legal papers won't change that reality. They just protect it."

"I know." Mary's gaze returned to Louise's artwork.

Mary reached across the table, her garden-roughened fingers covering his. "Some bonds form instantly. Others need time."

The observation carried layers—acknowledgment of his connection to Louise alongside gentle reminder that others might require adjustment to this new family structure.

"Will you help Terry understand?" Chris asked. "What this means to us?"

Mary withdrew her hand. The question had pressed against boundaries she maintained carefully. "I can try."

The non-commitment hung between them. Chris recognized its familiar shape—his mother's lifelong pattern of promising effort without guaranteeing results, especially where Terry was concerned.

"That's all I ask." He accepted the compromise as he always had.

Mary rose again, but this time with purpose rather than retreat. She moved to a cabinet near the sink, reaching for something on the top shelf. When she returned to the table, she carried a small wooden box Chris had never seen before.

"This belonged to my grandmother." She placed it before him. The polished cherry wood gleamed in the stormy afternoon light. "She brought it from Ireland."

Chris recognized the redirection but allowed it. The weight in his mother's expression suggested this tangent carried purpose beyond evasion.

"Open it." Mary sat again, her hands folded tightly.

Inside the box nestled a delicate silver bracelet. Its filigree pattern caught the fading light, small Celtic knots connected in an endless circle.

"It's passed from mother to daughter." Mary's voice steadied. "Five generations now."

Chris touched the silver with reverent fingers. "It's beautiful."

"My grandmother gave it to my mother. My mother gave it to me." Mary reached for his hand. "I want you to have it for Louise."

The gift's significance struck him fully. Without words, Mary had acknowledged Louise as legitimate family—a daughter worthy of legacy regardless of biology. The bracelet represented what Mary couldn't verbalize directly—her blessing for the adoption, her recognition of Louise as a Johnson.

"Mom." Chris's throat tightened. "Thank you."

Mary's eyes filled with unshed tears. "Family is more than blood. I've always believed that."

The admission carried particular weight from a woman who had spent decades navigating her sister's more rigid definitions of family connection.

"The bracelet should be sized for her." Mary's practical observation broke the emotional moment. "When she's older."

Chris closed the box carefully. Its weight felt substantial in his palm—generations of women's lives contained in silver links.

"I'll keep it safe until she's ready." He pocketed the treasure, its presence against his chest both comfort and responsibility.

Mary walked him to the door. Rain continued against the windows. Water streamed from gutters in steady ribbons.

"Be patient with Terry." Mary's advice came as he stepped onto the porch. "She needs time to adjust to new ideas."

Chris hugged his mother briefly. "Time I can give. Louise's security I can't compromise."

Mary's arms tightened around him. The embrace carried what her words could not—love complicated by divided loyalties, support shadowed by lifelong patterns of accommodation. When she released him, her expression held pride mixed with worry.

"The bracelet belongs to Louise now." Mary's final statement carried quiet certainty. "Regardless of paperwork or court decisions."

Chris nodded, understanding the layers beneath her statement. In this one gesture, Mary had claimed Louise as family despite whatever objections might arise elsewhere.

He walked toward his car through sheets of rain. The wooden box pressed against his heart like a promise. Behind him, Mary stood in the doorway, her figure blurring in the downpour—a woman caught between courage and caution, between mother and sister, between voice and silence.

As he drove away, Chris felt both triumph and complexity settling in his chest. Mary had given Louise something precious, a tangible link to family history that transcended blood. But she had also shown him the careful dance required to maintain peace within a family where loyalty meant different things to different people.

The rain continued, washing the streets clean as he made his way home to tell Leah about this unexpected gift—and what it meant for their daughter's place in the Johnson family legacy.

CHAPTER 8

First Blood

The afternoon light streamed through the preschool classroom windows, illuminating Louise's artwork display. Chris stood before her family portrait—three figures holding hands before a house whose chimney released musical notes like visible melody.

What struck him most was how she had captured his posture: the slight forward lean he adopted when listening to her, head tilted as though her four-year-old observations required careful interpretation. The unconscious body language of someone who had learned that parenthood meant paying attention to the spaces between words.

"She's starting to use complementary colors intentionally," Leah murmured beside him, her voice carrying that particular softness it acquired when discussing Louise's development. Her hand brushed his elbow—an anchor touch, these gentle contacts that had become their wordless language of shared pride and protective vigilance.

The classroom hummed with parental voices, all carefully modulated to exhibition-appropriate levels. This was sacred space in the small universe of childhood—where finger paintings commanded the same reverent attention other cultures reserved for religious artifacts. Chris felt the familiar expansion in his chest, that sense of witnessing something miraculous unfolding under his daily care.

Louise materialized at his side with the fluid grace children possessed before self-consciousness taught them to move with purpose rather than joy. "Daddy, you have to see the music one!" Her small hand captured his larger one, tugging him toward another display with the urgency of a curator revealing her masterpiece.

The painting she presented showed his guitar rendered with remarkable attention to detail—each string a careful silver line, the sound hole depicted as a window into acoustic possibility. Around the instrument, she had painted what could only be described as visible melody: waves of color flowing outward like ripples on water disturbed by sound made tangible.

Chris knelt to her eye level, genuinely awed. "I can see the music moving, sweetheart."

Louise beamed, her face transforming with the particular radiance that came from having one's vision truly comprehended by someone whose opinion mattered above all others.

"Artistic talent must run in the family."

The voice cut through their moment like a scalpel finding the space between ribs. Chris felt his body register threat before his mind processed its source—primitive alarm systems activated by tone and timing, by the calculated nature of the interruption.

Ryan Matthews stood in the classroom doorway with the self-possessed presence of someone accustomed to making entrances. His blazer spoke of boardrooms and business lunches, the kind of carefully curated casualness that money could purchase. But it was his eyes that set off every paternal warning system Chris possessed—the way they moved across Louise's artwork with assessment that felt more acquisitive than appreciative.

"Ryan." Leah's voice emerged steady, though Chris felt the tremor that ran through her frame.

The classroom atmosphere shifted perceptibly, other conversations continuing unaware while the three adults created their own charged field of tension. Louise glanced between them with the confusion of someone who had walked into a conversation conducted in frequencies beyond her hearing.

Ryan crouched to Louise's level with movements that seemed rehearsed. "I've heard so much about your artwork, Louise. Even more impressive than I expected."

The casual use of her name struck Chris like fingernails against glass—this stranger presuming intimacy he had never earned, claiming knowledge he had never sought to gain through presence or patience.

Chris stepped closer to Louise, his hand finding her shoulder in a gesture that served dual purposes: comfort for her, restraint for himself. His daughter's solid warmth beneath his palm reminded him of what mattered most—her security in this moment, not his own desire to physically remove this threat from their sanctuary.

"We weren't expecting you here," Chris managed, proud of how level his voice sounded despite the volcanic pressure building beneath his ribcage.

"Dropping off paperwork for my cousin's son. Saw Louise's name on the roster." Ryan's explanation emerged with practiced ease. "Couldn't resist seeing her development firsthand."

The word 'development' hung in the air between them—clinical, possessive, suggesting ongoing observation Chris had never authorized. Louise shifted against his side, her child's intuition detecting undercurrents she couldn't name but instinctively recognized as disturbing to the peaceful world adults usually maintained around her.

"Such remarkable talent for her age," Ryan continued, his gaze moving between Louise and her artwork with calculating appreciation. "Creative genes must be particularly strong."

The emphasis on genetic inheritance struck Chris with devastating force. Each word carefully chosen to highlight biological connections while simultaneously diminishing the bonds forged through daily

133

presence—bedtime stories and bandaged knees, guitar lessons and midnight comfort, the thousand small acts that had woven their lives together.

"Louise works very hard at her art," Leah interjected, maternal protection wrapped in diplomatic phrasing. "Practice matters more than predisposition."

"Of course. Though natural ability provides foundation."

Louise's fingers found the fabric of Chris's shirt, clutching with unconscious desperation. Her small body had gone still in that particular way children adopted when adult emotions became too complex to navigate safely.

"Do you practice at home too?" Ryan addressed her directly.

"Daddy built me an art corner," Louise's response emerged tentative, uncertain. "With a real easel."

The word 'Daddy' seemed to reverberate through the space between them. Ryan's expression shifted almost imperceptibly—a tightening around his eyes that Chris recognized as the look of someone hearing their territory claimed by another.

"Daddy," Ryan repeated, testing the syllables. His gaze flicked to Chris with cold assessment.

Something fundamental crystallized in Chris's chest then—the recognition that this wasn't chance encounter but calculated campaign. Ryan wasn't here to admire artwork; he was here to establish presence, to begin inserting himself into Louise's consciousness as prelude to whatever legal machinery was already grinding forward in distant offices.

"We encourage all her interests," Chris replied, fighting to maintain composure while primitive protective instincts howled for more direct action.

"Stepping into such an important role," Ryan's tone carried clinical detachment that reduced years of devoted fatherhood to temporary intervention. "Very admirable."

Miss Andrews appeared then with educator's perfect timing, her professional instincts alerted by the shift in classroom atmosphere even casual observers could detect.

"Louise, would you help arrange the refreshment table?" The gentle redirection offered their daughter escape from tensions she couldn't understand but clearly felt pressing against her small world.

Louise hesitated, torn between obedience and inexplicable need to remain close to Chris's protective presence. She departed reluctantly after receiving Leah's encouraging nod.

The moment she moved beyond comfortable hearing range, the pretense of social nicety evaporated like morning mist under harsh sun.

"Why are you really here?" Leah's question carried controlled intensity.

"Louise's education matters to me," Ryan replied with practiced nonchalance. "Her wellbeing is important."

"After years of absence," Chris couldn't prevent the words from escaping.

"People change. Mature."

"You signed away your rights."

Ryan's smile held no warmth. "The courts will decide what's best for her."

The dismissal bell rang, its cheerful mechanical sound at odds with the tension that had transformed their exchange from chance meeting into declaration of war.

"This conversation will continue," Ryan stated with certainty that suggested predetermined outcomes.

"No," Chris replied quietly. "It won't."

Ryan departed with the same calculated efficiency that had marked his arrival, leaving Chris alone among children's artwork that had been transformed from celebration into battlefield. His hands trembled with suppressed adrenaline, his body slowly releasing tension that had coiled through his muscles like wire under stress.

When Leah and Louise rejoined him, their daughter chattering about cookies and color patterns, Chris felt the profound disorientation of someone who had just witnessed familiar territory become contested ground. Louise's innocence felt both precious and fragile now—something requiring protection against forces that seemed determined to shatter it for reasons she would never comprehend.

As they gathered her artwork and prepared to leave, Chris understood with crystalline clarity that their family's peaceful chapter had ended. Whatever came next would require different skills, different strategies, different strength than any he had previously needed to summon.

The war for his daughter's future had begun, fought not just in courtrooms but in moments like this—wherever love met calculation, wherever chosen bonds faced biological claims, wherever the complex architecture of family could be reduced to legal documentation and genetic proof.

Louise skipped between them toward the parking lot, her joy undiminished by adult complications she sensed but couldn't yet name. Her resilience both comforted and terrified him—this remarkable child who called him Daddy not because of paperwork but because of presence, not because of DNA but because of devotion freely given and gratefully received.

He would fight for her with everything he possessed. The certainty settled into his bones like bedrock, immovable and eternal.

Chlorine vapor hung thick in the air, mingling with echoing splashes and children's laughter. The natatorium's harsh fluorescent lights created a dreamlike quality to the afternoon, reflections dancing across the water's surface like fragmented memories. Leah sat on the hard metal bleacher, her notebook open but forgotten on her lap. She watched Louise glide through the water with unexpected grace, Ashley's patient guidance evident in each small improvement.

Something had shifted between them since their first encounter. The weight of their shared past still lingered, but it had transformed into a strange, tentative understanding. High school rivalries seemed impossibly distant now, buried beneath the more immediate concerns of motherhood and survival.

Leah checked her phone again. Three missed calls from Chris, each one increasing her unease. The custody situation was deteriorating faster than either of them had anticipated. Wallace & Associates' letter had contained surveillance photos so recent she could identify the clothes Louise had worn just last week.

Movement near the entrance caught her attention. A familiar silhouette appeared, then disappeared so quickly she questioned whether she'd seen it at all. Ryan? Her heart stuttered. She scanned the small crowd of parents, suddenly hyperaware of watchful eyes. Had Terry sent someone? Was someone documenting another "normal" family moment to be twisted into evidence?

Across the pool, Ashley blew her whistle to signal the end of class. Children scrambled from the water like small, excited seals, Louise among them. Her daughter's face broke into a beaming smile upon spotting Leah, washing away momentary concerns with the pure simplicity of her joy.

"Mommy! Did you see my backstroke? Ashley says I'm a natural!"

Leah knelt to wrap a towel around Louise's shivering shoulders. "I saw, sweetheart. You're amazing."

"Can I go change now? Marissa says they have hot chocolate in the lobby." Louise's eyes sparkled with the excitement of shared secrets with her new swim class friend.

"Five minutes, then meet me by the front desk." Leah watched her daughter skip toward the locker room, trailing water droplets. A familiar ache bloomed in her chest—the perpetual tension between protection and freedom that defined motherhood.

Ashley approached, clipboard in hand, professional demeanor firmly in place. But something in her expression seemed strained, her eyes darting toward the exit with unusual frequency.

"She's really progressing well," Ashley said, her voice pitched just loud enough to be heard over the ambient noise. "Her form is better than most kids twice her age."

"Thank you. She loves these lessons." Leah hesitated, sensing unspoken words hanging between them. "Everything okay?"

Ashley's professional facade cracked slightly. She glanced around before stepping closer. "Can you stay after? I need to talk to you. Without little ears."

The request carried unmistakable urgency that sent a cold chill through Leah's body. She nodded, sudden dread weighing her response. "Of course."

The café across from the rec center offered temporary sanctuary, its warmth and coffee aroma a stark contrast to the chemical-laden air they'd left behind. Leah had settled Louise at a table near the window with hot chocolate and a coloring book, positioned where she could keep her in sight while speaking privately with Ashley.

"I wasn't sure if I should say anything," Ashley began, wrapping her hands around her mug as if seeking warmth. "But after our conversation about Terry asking questions, something else happened."

Leah waited, tension climbing her spine.

"I recognized someone else watching Louise's class." Ashley's voice dropped lower. "Ryan Matthews."

The name struck like a physical blow. "Ryan?"

"Three times this past week. Always keeping his distance, watching." Ashley studied Leah's face with newfound empathy. "I remember you two from high school. Everyone thought you were close."

"We were friends back then," Leah corrected gently. "We didn't start dating until after graduation."

The clarification seemed inconsequential against the weight of what followed, yet Leah offered it automatically—a reflexive need for accuracy in a world increasingly distorted by others' interpretations.

"Has he approached Louise?" The question emerged barely above a whisper.

"No." Ashley's response came quick and firm. "I've been watching carefully. But yesterday he asked me questions about her schedule, tried to make it casual." Her mouth tightened. "Said he was her uncle, helping the family coordinate activities."

The lie sat heavy between them, its implications unfurling like poison. Leah's gaze darted to Louise, contentedly drawing elaborate patterns.

"A few weeks ago it was Terry, now Ryan." Leah's fingers curled around her mug. "There's a pattern forming."

"There's something I don't understand." Ashley hesitated, wrestling with the boundaries of their fragile new connection. "Why would your husband's aunt and your ex be working together?"

The moment hung suspended between them. Leah met Ashley's gaze directly, making a decision.

"Ryan isn't just my ex." The words emerged with practiced steadiness, though they still carried the weight of old wounds. "He's Louise's biological father."

Understanding dawned in Ashley's eyes, recontextualizing everything. "I had no idea."

"Junior year of college. Pre-med for me, engineering for him." Leah's fingers traced invisible patterns on the table's surface. "I discovered I was pregnant after we broke up. He made it clear he had no interest in fatherhood."

"God, Leah." The genuine sympathy in Ashley's voice carried none of the judgment Leah had feared.

"He signed away his rights before she was born." Leah's gaze drifted to Louise, who was adding blue swirls to her drawing. "I withdrew from school. Built a life for us. Then met Chris, who loved Louise from the moment he met her."

"And now Ryan wants back in," Ashley concluded, the pieces falling into place. "That's why he's watching. Why he's asking questions."

Leah nodded, years of emotions compressed into the simple gesture. "His lawyers sent paperwork challenging the termination agreement. Just before our wedding."

"And Terry might be helping him?" Ashley's brow furrowed with genuine confusion.

"Terry has very specific ideas about family." Leah's tone carried the weight of accumulated slights and subtle undermining. "In her world, biological connections outweigh everything else."

They sat in silence for a moment, the ambient café noise creating a bubble of privacy around their shared understanding. When Ashley spoke again, her voice had softened with something Leah hadn't expected—a vulnerability that transformed her entire demeanor.

"I owe you an apology." Ashley's eyes dropped to her coffee cup. "For high school. For all of it."

The unexpected shift caught Leah off-guard. "Ashley, that was years ago."

"It was cruel and completely unwarranted. You never did anything to me." Ashley shook her head, regret etching lines beside her mouth. "My father and your father were colleagues. Every time they got together, all I'd hear was how perfect Leah Miller was—straight As, star athlete, talented artist."

The revelation struck Leah with its stark simplicity. She had spent years wondering what she'd done to earn Ashley's animosity, searching her own actions for some unintentional slight or offense. The truth—that she had been a symbol rather than a person in Ashley's narrative—carried its own peculiar sadness.

"He'd come home from business dinners and ask why I couldn't make varsity starter like you." Ashley's voice carried the echo of old pain. "Why my grades weren't as high. Why I couldn't seem to excel at anything the way you did at everything."

"I had no idea." The words felt inadequate against the weight of what Ashley was sharing.

"How could you?" Ashley's smile held no joy. "I never gave you a chance to know me. It was easier to hate the idea of you than face my own insecurities."

The confession hung between them, transforming the space they occupied. Two women looking back at their younger selves with the clarity that only distance provides—seeing not just who they had been but why.

"I'm sorry about Kate, too." Ashley's voice softened further. "I heard about her passing. Leukemia, wasn't it?"

The mention of Kate's name sent a wave of grief crashing through Leah's chest—not the sharp, breathtaking agony of fresh loss, but the hollow ache of absence that never truly healed. In moments like this, facing unseen threats from multiple directions, Kate's steadfast loyalty felt impossibly distant.

"Stage four. It progressed so quickly." Leah swallowed against the tightness in her throat. "She was the only one who really knew me back then. Who saw past the perfect student everyone assumed I was."

"She defended you fiercely," Ashley acknowledged. "Even when I was at my worst."

"I miss her every day." The simple admission carried the weight of countless unshared moments. "But especially now, with everything happening with Ryan and Terry. Kate would have known exactly what to do."

Something shifted in Ashley's expression—resolve replacing reminiscence. "Look, I can't be Kate. No one can. But I can help."

"Why would you want to?" The question emerged unbidden, genuine in its confusion.

Ashley's gaze drifted toward the window briefly. "Because I know what it's like when people try to control your narrative. When they place expectations on you without considering who you really are." Her focus returned to Leah, determination evident in her straightened posture. "What they're doing to Louise—using a child as leverage in some twisted game—it's wrong."

The unexpected solidarity hit Leah with surprising force. She blinked rapidly against sudden moisture threatening her eyes.

"I'll keep documenting when Ryan comes to the lessons," Ashley said with quiet conviction. "Dates, times, what questions he asks—all without arousing suspicion." Her expression hardened with determination. "I can keep you updated regularly."

"You'd do that?" Leah couldn't mask her surprise.

"It's the least I can do." Ashley's posture straightened with newfound purpose. "Maybe it's time I used my father's obsession with meticulous record-keeping for something good for a change."

Leah felt a small smile form despite the weight of their conversation. "Thank you."

"Bring Louise to Saturday's advanced class. She's ready." Ashley stood, gathering her things. "And maybe someday we can grab coffee without a conspiracy to discuss."

The unexpected offer of friendship hung in the air between them. Leah nodded, warmth gathering beneath her breastbone despite the circumstances. "I'd like that."

As Ashley left, Louise bounded over, her drawing clutched proudly in small hands. "Look, Mommy! It's us swimming!"

The crayon figures showed two stick people in blue water, enormous smiles on their faces. No shadows lurked at the edges, no watchers documented their joy. Just pure happiness captured in waxy color.

"It's beautiful, sweetheart." Leah pulled her daughter close, breathing in the scent of chlorine and innocence, wondering how long either would last.

The parking lot had emptied considerably during their conversation, afternoon light fading toward evening. Leah helped Louise buckle into her booster seat, mind already planning her own approach.

She leaned against the car door, phone pressed to her ear, waiting for Chris to answer. The metal felt cold through her thin jacket, grounding her in physical sensation while her thoughts threatened to spiral.

"Hey." Chris's voice came through tinny and distant. "Sorry I missed your calls. Faculty meeting ran long."

"We need to talk." She kept her tone even, conscious of Louise watching from inside the car. "Ryan was at Louise's swim lesson today. And apparently, he's been there before."

The silence that followed carried weight, a tension she could almost see stretching between them. When Chris finally spoke, his voice had changed, something hard and unfamiliar edging his usually gentle tone.

"Tell me everything."

She relayed Ashley's information in clipped sentences, each revelation tightening the knot of anxiety between her shoulder blades. "She thinks there might be some connection between Ryan's sudden appearances and Terry's questions from a few weeks ago. Too many coincidences."

"The pattern keeps getting stronger." Chris's voice carried troubled recognition. "Terry's questions at the swim center, now Ryan showing up at Louise's activities. Either it's an incredible series of coincidences, or..."

He didn't finish the thought, but Leah heard what he couldn't say aloud—the growing possibility that his aunt was actively working against them.

"What are you thinking?" Leah asked quietly.

"I'm thinking it's time I had a direct conversation with Terry." His tone carried a determination she hadn't heard before. "If there's something going on, if she's involved somehow, maybe she'll tell me the truth if I ask her directly."

"And if she doesn't?" Leah glanced at Louise, who had become absorbed in a picture book, blissfully unaware of the adult conversation.

"Then we'll know where we stand." The steel in his voice surprised her. "I need to look her in the eye and ask her, Leah. I need to know if my own family is working against us."

Leah recognized the pain beneath his resolve—the cost of even considering such a betrayal. "Just be careful. If she is involved with Ryan's case..."

"I'll call Williams first thing tomorrow," Chris said. "Get her advice on how to handle this. But I can't keep wondering, keep seeing patterns and not knowing if they're real."

"I understand." She did, though the thought of him confronting Terry filled her with unease. "Whatever you learn, we'll face it together."

"Yes, we will." His voice softened momentarily before hardening with resolve. "I love you, Leah. And I won't let anyone tear our family apart—no matter who they are."

She ended the call and slipped into the driver's seat, forcing a smile for Louise's benefit. As they pulled away from the rec center, she couldn't shake the sensation of being watched, of eyes documenting their departure, their normalcy transformed into evidence for battles yet to come.

In the rearview mirror, she caught a glimpse of Ryan's car, parked at the far edge of the lot. He made no attempt to hide his presence now, his gaze following their departure with unsettling intensity.

Leah tightened her grip on the steering wheel, uncertainty gnawing at her. Tomorrow, Chris would seek answers from Terry. By evening, they might finally know if their worst suspicions were true—or if they were seeing conspiracies where only coincidences existed.

"Can we get ice cream?" Louise's voice broke through her thoughts, innocent and hopeful.

"Not today, sweetheart. We need to get home." Leah met her daughter's eyes in the rearview mirror, protecting her from the truth while wondering how long such shields could hold. "But how about we make cookies instead? Just the two of us."

Louise's excited agreement filled the car with momentary warmth, a small bubble of normalcy Leah would fight with everything she had to preserve. Behind them, the watchers documented this too, unaware that their targets had finally begun to see the pattern—and were preparing to test whether it was real.

Tomorrow would bring answers. Whether those answers brought relief or confirmed their worst fears remained to be seen.

CHAPTER 9

Boundaries Drawn

T he scent of fresh baking enveloped Chris as Terry opened her front
door. His aunt stood silhouetted against the warm interior light, a
wooden spoon still in hand. Perfect timing, as always. As if she'd been
watching through lace curtains for his arrival.

"Chris! What a wonderful surprise." She reached for him, arms extended.

He accepted her embrace with practiced motions. Her cardigan carried
traces of vanilla and the lavender sachet she kept in her dresser drawers. The
familiar scent triggered childhood memories—kitchen confidences over
fresh-baked cookies, whispered assurances that she understood him better
than his parents.

"We need to talk, Terry."

Something flickered across Terry's features—recognition,
perhaps—before her smile widened. "Of course, sweetheart. I just pulled
cookies from the oven."

Of course she had. The timing seemed suspicious, as if she anticipated
difficult conversations required sweetening. How many confrontations
throughout his childhood had been defused by still-warm cookies and
milk?

"About Louise," Chris continued, remaining in the doorway. "About boundaries."

Terry's wooden spoon paused mid-air. "Boundaries? What an odd word to use between family members."

"You've been visiting her swim instructor. Asking questions."

"Ashley Peterson?" Terry's laugh carried a note of dismissal. "I was simply showing interest in Louise's activities. Is that suddenly forbidden?"

Chris stepped into the house, the familiar hallway lined with family photographs suddenly feeling like evidence of surveillance rather than love. "You told her you were Louise's great-aunt. You asked about her schedule, her progress."

"I am her great-aunt. Through marriage, certainly, but—"

"You've never shown interest in her swim lessons before." Chris cut through her explanation. "And now you're suddenly there three times, asking detailed questions about when she attends and who brings her?"

Terry set down her wooden spoon with deliberate care. "I don't appreciate your tone, Christopher."

The use of his full name—her warning signal since childhood. But Chris was no longer seven years old, seeking her approval.

"And you've been visiting her at school," he continued. "Without telling us. Taking pictures of her artwork."

Terry's composure cracked slightly. "Those pictures were for your mother's refrigerator."

"Were they? Or were they for something else entirely?"

The question hung between them. Terry moved toward the kitchen, but Chris didn't follow.

"I'm trying to understand, Terry. Help me understand why you're suddenly so... invested in documenting Louise's daily life."

"Documenting?" Terry spun around, eyes flashing. "Is that what you think I'm doing?"

"What would you call it?"

Terry's hands found her cross pendant, clutching it like a shield. "Caring. Being a concerned family member."

"Concerned about what?"

The direct question seemed to catch Terry off-guard. She opened her mouth, closed it, then tried again. "About... about whether that child is receiving proper guidance."

"That child has a name. Louise. Your supposed great-niece."

"Don't twist my words."

"I'm not twisting anything. You just referred to my daughter as 'that child.'" Chris stepped closer. "The same daughter you claim to care so much about that you're monitoring her activities behind our backs."

Terry retreated toward the kitchen. "You're being ridiculous."

"Am I? Then explain it to me. Explain why Ashley Peterson felt uncomfortable enough about your questions to warn Leah. Explain why Louise mentions you visiting her school with 'special snacks' that we knew nothing about."

"I don't need permission to show interest in—"

"In what? In building a case?"

Terry's face registered genuine shock.

"A case? What are you talking about?"

"That's what this is about, isn't it?" Chris felt pieces clicking into place. "All this sudden interest. All these questions and photos and visits. You're gathering information."

"For whom?" Terry's voice rose, indignation replacing shock. "Who exactly do you think I'm reporting to?"

"I don't know, Terry. You tell me."

"That's the most ridiculous thing I've ever heard." Terry's laugh held a brittle edge. "You think I'm some kind of spy? In my own family?"

"Then explain the behavior."

"I don't have to explain showing love to my godchild to anyone. Not even you." Terry straightened, wounded righteousness replacing defensiveness. "The fact that you would even suggest such a thing..."

Chris watched her face carefully, searching for tells. But Terry's shock seemed genuine, her indignation real.

"People have been asking questions, Terry. About Louise. About our family."

"What people?"

"Ryan's legal team."

Terry's expression shifted to something more guarded. "What does that have to do with me?"

"Someone's been feeding them information. Someone with access to Louise's daily life."

"And you think it's me?" Terry pressed a hand to her chest, the gesture theatrical yet convincing. "Your own godmother?"

"I think someone in this family has been talking to them."

"Well, it certainly isn't me." Terry's denial came swift and absolute. "I've never spoken to any lawyers. I wouldn't know how to contact them if I wanted to."

Chris studied her face. The shock, the indignation—it all seemed authentic. But something nagged at him, an instinct that refused to quiet.

"Then why the sudden interest in Louise's activities? Why now?"

Terry's expression softened to something more familiar—the concerned aunt of his childhood. "Because I'm worried about you, Chris. About this whole situation."

"What situation?"

"This custody challenge. It's tearing you apart. I can see it." She moved closer, maternal instincts overriding his boundaries. "You barely sleep. Leah's constantly on edge. And poor Louise is caught in the middle."

"Louise is fine."

"Is she?" Terry's eyebrows rose. "Because when I've seen her lately, she seems... different. Quieter. More withdrawn."

"When have you seen her lately?" Chris asked, his voice sharpening. "Besides the swim center and school visits we just discussed?"

Terry faltered slightly. "Well, at church. Family dinners. I notice these things, Chris. I've been around children long enough to—"

"Her teacher hasn't mentioned any problems to us," Chris interrupted. "Neither has Ashley. If Louise was having trouble, don't you think they would have said something to her parents?"

The question hung in the air. Terry's face cycled through several expressions before settling on defensive concern.

"Perhaps they have and you just... haven't noticed. You've both been so stressed lately." Her voice carried a note of gentle condescension. "Sometimes when parents are overwhelmed, they miss the signs."

The implication stung—that he and Leah were too self-absorbed to notice their daughter's distress. But it also raised another question.

"And you've appointed yourself to fill that gap?" Chris asked. "By visiting her activities without our knowledge?"

"I was trying to help without adding to your burden." Terry's tone grew more defensive. "You're both dealing with so much already."

"By going behind our backs."

"By being discreet." Terry lifted her chin. "There's a difference."

"No, Terry. There isn't." Chris moved toward the door. "Not when it comes to my daughter."

"Our family," Terry corrected sharply. "She's part of our family too, whether you want to acknowledge it or not."

"Then act like family. Talk to us. Don't sneak around gathering information like some kind of detective."

Terry's face flushed. "I resent that characterization."

"Then stop giving me reasons to make it." Chris reached for the door handle. "No more surprise visits. No more questioning Louise's teachers or coaches without our permission. If you're concerned about something, you talk to us directly."

"And if you're too stressed to listen?" Terry's question carried a sharp edge. "Too defensive to hear valid concerns?"

"Then that's our problem to solve. Not yours to work around."

Terry followed him toward the hallway. "I've been part of this family before you were even born, Chris. I won't be dismissed like some stranger."

"I'm not dismissing you. I'm setting boundaries that should have been obvious from the beginning."

"After everything I've done for you—"

"This isn't about gratitude, Terry. This is about respect. For us as parents. For our decisions about Louise."

Terry's expression hardened. "Even when those decisions might not be in her best interest?"

"According to whom?" Chris turned back to face her fully. "You? Based on what expertise? What training in child development or family dynamics?"

The questions hit their mark. Terry's face colored with embarrassment and anger.

"I don't need a degree to recognize when a child is struggling."

"But you apparently need one to understand that her parents should be the first to know about it." Chris opened the door. "And the ones to decide how to handle it."

"You're making a mistake," Terry called after him as he walked toward his car.

"Maybe," Chris replied without turning around. "But it's mine to make."

He drove away with Terry's voice still echoing in his ears, her protests and justifications blending into white noise against his growing certainty. Something about her explanations didn't add up. Her knowledge of Louise's supposed behavioral changes. Her defensive responses when pressed for specifics.

Maybe he was seeing patterns that weren't there. Maybe stress was making him paranoid.

But maybe Terry wasn't being as honest as she claimed.

His phone buzzed with a text before he'd reached the next block: "I pray you'll reconsider before it's too late. Family unity has never been more important."

Chris deleted the message without responding and drove home, the taste of doubt bitter in his mouth.

The Henderson family home stood against the afternoon light, its Victorian gables and wraparound porch bearing witness to generations of family gatherings. Today, streamers draped across the banister announced another celebration, though the air inside carried currents far less festive than the decorations suggested.

Leah stood in the corner of the living room, a glass of untouched punch cooling in her palm as she observed the tableau before her. Chris had disappeared minutes ago to help his grandfather with something in the garage, leaving her momentarily stranded in this sea of familiar strangers. Her wedding ring caught the light as she adjusted her grip on the glass, still not quite accustomed to its weight after months of marriage.

"So you're the famous Leah," came a voice from her left, rich with what sounded like genuine warmth. "I've heard so much about you."

Sahara Johnson extended her hand, her smile reaching eyes that assessed with the sharpness of someone accustomed to reading facial micro-expressions in courtrooms. Her tailored pantsuit spoke of airports and conference rooms, of a life measured in billable hours and first-class upgrades.

"The mysterious sister-in-law," Leah replied, taking the offered hand. "Chris was starting to think you were mythical."

"Three cases back-to-back will do that." Sahara laughed with practiced ease. "Tyler keeps threatening to report me as a missing person."

Across the room, Terry's gaze flickered toward them, her conversation with Kourtney never faltering even as her attention split. Leah felt the familiar weight of observation settling across her shoulders, the constant awareness of being documented, assessed, found wanting in ways she couldn't quite identify.

"How are you finding married life?" Sahara asked, leaning against the wall beside Leah as if creating a temporary alliance in the crowded room. "I remember those early months—everything still shiny and new, before you discover he leaves wet towels on the bathroom floor."

"Chris is..." Leah paused, searching for words that wouldn't sound saccharine to this worldly woman who exuded competence and self-possession. "He's exactly who he presented himself to be. No false advertising."

Something passed across Sahara's features—curiosity, perhaps, or recognition of an unexpected depth. Before she could respond, Tyler appeared at his wife's elbow, his hand settling at the small of her back with possessive familiarity.

"I see you've met the newest Johnson," he said, his smile never quite reaching his eyes as they rested on Leah. "Mom's looking for you, babe. Something about the slideshow."

Sahara looked momentarily torn, professional courtesy warring with marital obligation. "We'll continue this later," she promised Leah, allowing herself to be guided away.

The study door remained partially open, just enough for Louise's small frame to press against the mahogany paneling and observe the adults who didn't know she was there. The heavy velvet curtains cast the room in shadow despite the afternoon light, lending a conspiratorial atmosphere to the gathering. Tyler stood by the fireplace, one hand gripping the mantel as if steadying himself. Sahara perched on the arm of a leather chair, her professional composure subtly altered in this private setting. Terry and Kourtney completed the circle, their expressions animated in ways Louise had never seen during family dinners.

"She was on track for med school, right? She must be intelligent," Sahara was saying, her tone carrying genuine curiosity.

"Not smart enough to avoid getting herself pregnant," Kourtney replied, her laugh brittle as thin ice. "Girls like that get pregnant on purpose. Trap men. It's a strategy."

Louise's brow furrowed. She recognized her mother as the subject of their conversation, though the undercurrents remained beyond her comprehension. She pressed smaller against the doorframe, instinct warning her to remain unseen.

"Did you see what she's wearing today?" Kourtney continued, her voice dropping to a stage whisper. "That department store dress with those shoes? It's like she's not even trying to fit in."

"And that voice," she added, mimicking in falsetto, "'Oh, Chris and I are so grateful for your support.' Please. She sounds like she's auditioning for a soap opera."

The laughter that followed carried edges sharp enough to cut. Louise's small hands pressed against the cool wood of the doorframe, something uncomfortable stirring in her chest.

"That poor girl doesn't even know who her real father is," Terry said, her voice carrying the particular tone of false concern she employed during prayer circles. "Living in confusion. It's borderline cruel, if you ask me."

"Real father?" The words slipped from Louise's lips in the barest whisper, confusion blooming across her features. In her understanding, Chris was her daddy—the only one she'd ever known, the one who braided her hair and taught her guitar. What did Terry mean?

"Ryan's been asking about her," Tyler added, his voice carrying authority. "Says she looks like his mother around the eyes."

"The whole thing is just sad," Kourtney sighed with theatrical compassion. "That child is going to grow up so confused. Probably end up with all kinds of issues."

Louise's chest tightened. The words themselves escaped her full understanding, but their tone—that she comprehended perfectly. The same tone used by preschool bullies who excluded others from games.

"And to think Chris wants to adopt her," Terry continued, her voice hardening. "Making it official when it's clearly just a ticking time bomb. That girl isn't a Johnson. Never will be."

The statement landed with devastating impact, even to Louise's young ears. Not a Johnson. Not family. Her small body tensed.

"Moving into our church community," Terry continued. "Getting close to Chris through the music program. Right after her father destroyed Tom's business. That's no coincidence."

"Well, Chris is old enough to make his own decisions about relationships," Sahara noted, her voice carrying professional detachment.

"You don't understand," Kourtney insisted. "Chris has always been... sensitive. Too trusting. Mom and I could see she had her claws in him the moment they met."

"But he seems happy with his marriage," Sahara said carefully.

"Happy?" Terry's laugh held venom. "You should have seen him yesterday when he came storming over, accusing me of interfering. That woman has him so twisted around, he can't see straight. She's drawing a wedge between him and his family, and he's too blind to notice."

"Maybe he's just protecting his wife," Sahara suggested.

"He's protecting a lie," Terry shot back. "And now she's got him ready to adopt another man's child while that child's real father wants her back."

Louise remained motionless in her hiding place, absorbing fragmented meanings from their tone rather than their words. All she understood with absolute clarity was that these people—family members who smiled at her mother at church—harbored a cold, sharp dislike beneath those gestures.

Mary called from the dining room, announcing dinner with a brightness that seemed deliberately timed. The family moved from their various conversations toward the dining room, where the large table had been arranged with seating cards. Leah found herself placed between Mary and an elderly great-aunt whose hearing difficulties made substantive conversation impossible. Chris's empty chair waited at the far end, Terry having orchestrated the seating to maximize distance between husband and wife.

"Leah, dear," Mary whispered as they settled into their places, "would you mind helping me with the gravy?"

The request offered momentary sanctuary from the watchful eyes of the Henderson contingent. Leah followed her mother-in-law to the kitchen, grateful for the temporary reprieve. As the kitchen door swung closed behind them, the dining room conversation shifted tone, voices lowering into the particular register of secrets being shared.

Louise, who had slipped away from the study unnoticed during the transition to dinner, found a new hiding place beneath the china cabinet in the dining room. From this vantage point, she could observe the adult table without detection.

The dining room hummed with conversation, plates of roast beef creating islands around which family politics navigated. Terry sat centered between Tyler and Sahara, her voice low but carrying.

"Of course, we were shocked when Chris announced the adoption," Terry was saying, fork poised above untouched dinner. "Such a whirlwind decision."

"They seem committed to each other," Sahara offered neutrally. "And Louise is absolutely delightful."

"Such a precious child," Terry agreed, the words dipped in something that tasted like vinegar beneath the sugar. "Though of course, not biologically Chris's. That makes things... complicated."

Tyler leaned forward. "Did you know her father is contesting the termination agreement? Wants custody back suddenly."

"After years of absence?" Sahara's surprise sounded genuine. "That's a difficult case to make."

"Money makes many things possible," Terry interjected. "And Ryan Matthews has plenty. His father was a judge, you know."

"I didn't realize you'd looked into Leah's past so thoroughly," Sahara remarked, something in her tone shifting toward caution.

Tyler's laugh carried no humor. "Not thoroughly enough, apparently. I hired someone to dig deeper after they got engaged. Too late to prevent anything, but—"

"Prevent?" Sahara interrupted. "That seems an unusual choice of word."

Terry's hand settled on Tyler's arm, a gesture of both restraint and solidarity. "What Tyler means is that we might have helped Chris see the situation more clearly before making such permanent decisions."

"The situation being?" Sahara prompted.

"Her father is John Miller," Tyler stated flatly. "Miller Financial. The company that systematically destroyed Johnson & Sons."

Silence spread outward from their corner of the table before family politeness smoothed it over.

"That can't be a coincidence," Terry continued. "Her suddenly appearing in our church, getting close to Chris through the music program."

"Chris is a full-grown adult," Sahara observed mildly. "He doesn't need supervision in his dating choices."

"You don't understand how these things work," Tyler's voice hardened. "Miller tactics are calculated. Patient. They destroy systematically."

"And you believe Leah is... what? Implementing some generational vendetta through marriage?" The skepticism in Sahara's tone was unmistakable.

"I don't know yet," Tyler admitted. "But I intend to find out before she does to Chris what her father did to our family."

"And now she's dragging our poor Chris into a custody battle," Terry added. "They've barely been married and it's already hitting rocky roads. One wonders how their marriage can possibly last."

"Such pessimism, Mom," Kourtney chided from further down the table, though her voice carried more amusement than reproach. "Usually you save the doom and gloom for after dessert."

"Not pessimism, dear. Realism." Terry's smile thinned. "Oh, you know what? I have an idea."

She rose with practiced grace, disappearing briefly into the kitchen before returning with two small glass jars that she set on the table.

"What's this now?" Tyler called from his seat, drawing the room's scattered conversations into focus.

"A little family tradition," Terry announced, though Louise had never witnessed such a ritual. "For when we need to mark our predictions."

With meticulous care, Terry produced two small labels, affixing them to the jars. Her handwriting spelled out "Less than 3 years" on one and "Less than 5 years" on the other.

"A friendly wager," she elaborated, setting a twenty-dollar bill in the second jar. "On how long Chris's and Leah's marriage will last, given the challenges they're about to face."

The silence that followed carried the particular quality of collective held breath. Then Michael laughed uncomfortably, breaking the tension.

"Always the optimist, aren't you, Terry?" He said, glancing toward the kitchen door with an apologetic wince.

"Just realistic, dear," Terry replied. "Now, who wants to place their bets?"

"This is inappropriate," Sahara said firmly, her professional composure cracking. "We're talking about real people. About Chris. About a marriage."

"Oh, lighten up," Kourtney waved dismissively. "It's just family fun."

"It's cruel," Sahara stood her ground. "What happens when they find out? What does this say about us as a family?"

"It's harmless," Tyler insisted, though he avoided his wife's gaze. "Just a little friendly wager between family members."

"There's nothing friendly about betting on someone's failure," Sahara's voice carried the authority of courtroom experience. "This is mean-spirited and divisive."

Terry's expression hardened. "I suppose some people understand family loyalty differently."

"Family loyalty would be supporting Chris's marriage, not gambling on its failure," Sahara shot back.

Despite her protests, family members approached the jars with varying degrees of enthusiasm and discomfort. Currency accumulated in both vessels, though the "Less than 3 years" jar filled more rapidly. Sahara remained seated, arms crossed, disapproval radiating from her posture.

"Sahara?" Terry prompted when Tyler's wife made no move to participate. "No predictions from our legal eagle?"

"I won't be part of this," Sahara said firmly. "And I think you should all reconsider."

Terry's smile never wavered. "How disappointing. I suppose not everyone appreciates family traditions."

Sahara watched the money accumulate in the jars, her mind racing. Had they done this when she married Tyler? Gathered in secret corners to place bets on how long the educated outsider would last in their insular family circle? The thought sat like ice in her stomach.

The dining room door swung open as Chris returned, his cheeks flushed from exertion, his smile fading as he registered the peculiar tableau. At the same moment, the kitchen door opened, bringing Leah and Mary back with fresh rolls.

"What did I miss?" Chris asked, the words falling into sudden, awkward silence.

Terry moved with practiced smoothness, sliding the jars beneath the table. "Just discussing the Thanksgiving committee, dear. Your timing is perfect—we're ready to serve dinner."

Louise watched this moment of deception with the clear-eyed perception children often bring to adult duplicity. She saw Terry hide the jars, saw the adults exchange knowing glances, saw her mother's face frozen in a smile that didn't match the tension visible in her shoulders.

As dinner began with forced normalcy, Chris found his way to the seat beside Leah, his hand finding hers beneath the table.

"Everything okay?" he whispered.

"Fine," she assured him. "Just another Sunday with the Johnsons."

Across the table, the glass jars remained hidden beneath Terry's chair, their presence like twin beacons of malice. Louise remained in her hiding place, her small world irrevocably altered by words spoken in shadowed rooms and actions performed in cruel ceremony.

The seeds had been planted—in those overheard words, in this witnessed ritual—seeds that would grow into questions too complex for her young mind to articulate but powerful enough to manifest in shifting behaviors, in nightmares, in sudden fears where confidence had once lived.

Terry caught Leah's gaze across the table, a smile curving her lips with the particular satisfaction of a predator who knows its prey is trapped but conscious. The jars beneath her chair clinked softly as she shifted.

Leah lifted her chin slightly, meeting that gaze without flinching. The battle lines had been drawn with glass containers and handwritten labels, with bills exchanged and predictions made. But the outcome remained unwritten, regardless of Terry's orchestration or the family's collective judgment.

Chris's fingers remained interlaced with Leah's beneath the white tablecloth, their connection hidden but no less real. In that touch, in the home they were building together, Leah found strength beyond the betting jars' prophecy.

Some wagers, after all, were destined to be lost by those who made them.

CHAPTER 10

Breathing Room

A fternoon light filtered through Attorney Williams's office windows, casting shadows across the polished desk. Leah tracked the light's movement, its slow migration marking time in this liminal space where futures hung in balance. The office smelled of leather-bound books and aging paper, with undertones of lemon furniture polish that couldn't quite mask the anxiety that had seeped into these walls over countless similar meetings.

She sensed Chris beside her, his breathing shallow. His right leg bounced in a subtle rhythm against the chair—a habit that had emerged after the Wallace & Associates letter, appearing whenever the custody dispute surfaced in conversation.

Williams cleared her throat, the sound cutting through the room.

"I have news." She lifted a document from her desk.

Leah's fingers curled into her palm. The small half-moons of her nails pressed white crescents into flesh. Chris's hand found hers, warm and solid.

"The judge has ruled on the emergency petition." Williams paused, her eyes moving between them.

Leah's chest tightened. The air felt suddenly thin.

"It's been denied." Williams allowed herself the smallest smile. "Judge Patel found Ryan's claim of 'changed circumstances' insufficient to warrant expedited proceedings."

The words hung in the air for a suspended moment.

"Denied?" Chris repeated, as if the word might dissolve if examined too closely.

Williams nodded. "Ryan's team pushed the narrative of his newfound stability and career success, but Patel wasn't convinced these constituted grounds for emergency review."

A rush of air escaped Leah's lungs. Her body seemed to remember breathing all at once. Chris's grip tightened on her hand, his palm suddenly damp against hers.

"So it's over?" The hope in her voice sounded foreign to her own ears. Too bright. Too fragile.

Williams set the paper down. "Not over. Delayed."

"How long?" Chris leaned forward.

"Sixty days minimum before the preliminary hearing."

Sixty days. The number expanded in Leah's mind. Two months of mornings with Louise. Pancake Sundays. Bedtime stories without the shadow of impending loss.

"God." Chris's voice broke on the word. "That's something."

It wasn't victory, but it was breath. Space. Room to stand up straight after weeks of bracing for impact.

"How did you manage it?" Leah asked.

Williams arranged papers on the desk. "Judge Patel takes a dim view of using 'changed circumstances' claims when the only thing that's changed is the petitioner's mind. Ryan's documentation of his new stability worked against him—it highlighted how long he's been absent."

The relief settled into Leah's bones like warmth after months of chill. She hadn't realized how rigid she'd been holding herself until now, when something in her core finally loosened.

"Thank you," she said. The words felt insufficient.

Williams nodded, acknowledgment without celebration. Her eyes flicked to another folder on her desk. The slight shift in her posture sent a whisper of warning through Leah's momentary calm.

"There is... another matter." Williams's voice took on a careful neutrality that made Leah's stomach tighten.

She slid a blue folder toward them. The tab read "ADOPTION PETITION - LOUISE MILLER."

Chris straightened. "The adoption paperwork?"

"Yes." Williams opened the folder. "There's been a development."

The tension crawled back into Leah's shoulders, reclaiming territory so briefly surrendered.

"What kind of development?" Her voice sounded thin.

"The court has placed your petition on administrative hold." Williams tapped a highlighted section of the document. "Standard procedure when custody is being contested."

The words fell like stones.

"But that's..." Chris started, then stopped. "You mean we can't move forward?"

"Not until Ryan's petition is resolved." Williams's tone remained level. "One case must conclude before the other can proceed."

Leah's throat constricted. "So the delay works against us here."

Williams nodded. "In this respect, yes."

The irony tasted bitter. The very reprieve they'd just celebrated now revealed its hidden cost.

"I don't understand," Chris said. "The custody challenge and adoption are separate issues."

"In practice, they're inextricably linked." Williams leaned back slightly. "No judge will rule on permanently altering parental rights while those rights are being actively contested."

Leah stared at the blue folder. An administrative hold. Such bloodless language for what felt like a knife twisting.

"This is exactly why we need the adoption finalized." The words tumbled out, sharper than she intended. "To protect her from this endless uncertainty."

Williams's expression softened, a rare crack in her professional facade. "I understand your frustration."

Chris's hand found her knee under the desk, a gentle pressure.

"What happens when Ryan's petition is resolved?" he asked. "Do we start over?"

A practical question. Something to grab onto while the floor seemed to shift beneath them.

"Your filing date remains the same," Williams assured them. "You won't lose your place. But until the custody matter is settled, everything stays on pause."

Leah closed her eyes. Pause. Another limbo. More waiting while Louise asked questions they couldn't fully answer.

Williams drew a breath, her fingers resting lightly on yet another folder. "I should mention that Ryan's team seems to be building something substantive."

A chill traced Leah's spine. "What do you mean?"

"They've indicated they're bringing forward witnesses." Williams's tone remained carefully neutral. "People who claim to have relevant observations about Louise's current living situation."

Chris's posture stiffened. "What kind of witnesses?"

"They haven't disclosed specifics yet." Williams's gaze held a measured warning. "But the language in their filing suggests people with regular access to Louise. People who might be considered credible observers."

The implication hung in the air, unspoken but palpable. People close to them. People they trusted.

"Is that normal?" Leah asked. "To not disclose who's testifying?"

"At this stage, yes." Williams closed the folder with a soft finality. "They'll have to provide a witness list later, but right now, they're playing their cards close."

The air in the office felt suddenly too dense, too close. Leah's mind raced through possibilities, cataloging every interaction, every church event, every family gathering where watchful eyes might have been collecting ammunition.

"So where does this leave us?" Chris's voice had hardened.

"With time," Williams said. "Sixty days to prepare our response. To gather our own witnesses."

Leah thought of Louise's preschool teacher. Ashley from swim class. People who saw the reality, not whatever narrative was being constructed against them.

"We'll need character witnesses," Williams continued. "People outside the immediate family who can speak to your parenting and Louise's well-being."

The task stretched before them like a mountain. More people to involve. More explaining. More exposing their private life to scrutiny.

"This isn't fair to Louise," Leah said. "She shouldn't have to prove she belongs in her own home."

Williams's expression held genuine sympathy. "I know. The system isn't designed for fairness. It's designed for process."

"And children get caught in the machinery." Bitterness edged her words.

"Yes." Williams didn't offer false comfort. "They do."

The brutal honesty was strangely reassuring. No platitudes.

"So we have breathing room with the custody hearing," Chris summarized. "But the adoption is stalled, and someone is actively working against us."

"That's accurate." Williams gathered the folders into a neat stack. "I suggest using this time to document daily life with Louise. Keep records of school events, doctor visits, activities. Build a paper trail of normalcy."

Such a strange directive. Document love. Prove belonging. Turn the ordinary rhythms of family life into evidence.

"We'll do that," Chris agreed.

Leah nodded, but her mind had already jumped ahead to the morning, to Louise's questions about visiting Grandma Mary, to the church picnic next weekend where watchful eyes would be evaluating, perhaps collecting moments to be twisted into something unrecognizable.

Williams stood. The meeting had reached its natural conclusion.

"Thank you," Chris said, rising. "For the news about the delay. That's something, at least."

"It is," Williams agreed. "Use the time well."

The attorney's handshake was firm, her gaze direct. Leah felt the weight of her unspoken message. Sixty days wasn't just breathing room. It was preparation time for the real battle ahead.

In the hallway, the fluorescent lights cast harsh shadows. Leah's heels clicked against marble floors, the sound unnaturally loud in the hushed corridor.

Chris pressed the elevator button. His profile looked carved from stone.

"You okay?" she asked, though the answer was obvious.

He shook his head once, a tight movement. The elevator arrived with a soft chime. They stepped inside, and the doors closed, sealing them in momentary privacy.

"We need to find out who these witnesses might be." His voice was quiet, controlled. "Someone close to us is watching, reporting back."

Leah studied his face in the muted elevator light, searching for acknowledgment of what she already knew with bone-deep certainty. "It's Terry, Chris. You know it is."

A small muscle tightened at the corner of his jaw. "I just spoke with her. I looked her in the eye when she promised she wouldn't interfere."

"And you believed her?" The question emerged softer than she intended, bereft of accusation and heavy with resigned understanding.

Chris pressed his fingers against the bridge of his nose. "I have to believe she wouldn't deliberately lie to my face. Not about something this important."

The elevator descended, each floor marker illuminating briefly before surrendering to darkness. Leah felt the mechanical journey mirrored their conversation—moments of clarity quickly swallowed by familiar shadows.

"Terry has strong opinions about family," Chris continued. "She oversteps boundaries. She says things she shouldn't. But actively working with Ryan's legal team? That's different. That's..."

"Betrayal," Leah finished when he couldn't.

He nodded, the simple gesture carrying the weight of his reluctance to name what lived in the space between knowledge and acknowledgment.

"Who else could these witnesses be but your family?" Leah asked. "Who else has regular access to Louise? Who else has been taking photos, asking questions, showing up at her school?"

Chris stared at the illuminated floor numbers, each digit counting down toward a confrontation he'd spent a lifetime avoiding. "I don't know. But Terry gave me her word."

The words carried no conviction, only the echo of childhood faith in a figure whose approval had once defined his world. Leah recognized the cost of this desperate clinging to trust.

"She believes she's protecting you," Leah said gently. "In her mind, that makes it justified."

Chris turned to her then, his eyes carrying vulnerability she rarely witnessed. "If you're right..." He couldn't finish the thought.

"Then we face it together," she said, completing what he couldn't articulate.

The elevator reached the lobby. Before the doors opened, Chris squeezed her fingers.

"Sixty days," he said, the timeframe transformed into both promise and preparation.

The doors slid apart, exposing them once more to the world beyond. A world where victory and defeat had become impossible to distinguish, where even breathing room came with hidden costs, where the hardest betrayals came wrapped in the language of love and protection.

Leah stepped forward, still holding his hand. Sixty days. They had sixty days.

Leah sat in her car, engine silent, fingers curled around the legal papers she'd retrieved from Attorney Williams's office. The custody delay. The adoption hold. The clinical language of legal process that couldn't capture what was truly at stake.

Rain pattered against the windshield, mirroring the weight pressing against her chest. Sixty days until the hearing. Sixty days of uncertainty while somewhere, Ryan prepared his case. Gathered his witnesses. Built his narrative.

She closed her eyes, letting her head rest against the seat. The memory rose unbidden, crystalline in its clarity despite the year that had passed. The hospital room. The beeping monitors. The night that had changed everything.

One year earlier

The hospital room pulsed with fluorescent certainty. Lights that never dimmed, never softened, the kind that revealed every fear etched across Leah's face as she watched Louise's small chest rise and fall with labored effort. Three hours in the emergency room had crystallized into this private space with its relentless monitoring equipment, antiseptic walls, and the terrible beeping that measured her daughter's struggle against the pneumonia that had ambushed them with such terrifying swiftness.

The fever had spiked past 104 by the time they reached the hospital. Louise's normally rosy cheeks had taken on a frightening pallor beneath the flush of fever, her breathing ragged and shallow. Now, oxygen flowed through a nasal cannula, the clear tubing looking impossibly large against her tiny features.

"Mommy?" Louise's voice emerged papery and thin, a ghost of her usual exuberance. Her eyes, a reflection of Leah's own, carried questions she couldn't answer.

"I'm here, sweet girl." Leah moved closer, her fingers finding Louise's hand, scorching with fever despite the cooling blanket. "The medicine will help soon."

Outside, darkness pressed against the small window. Seven o'clock. Well past Louise's usual bedtime, but sleep remained a distant country across a border of rattling breaths and medication.

The door opened. Dr. Wilson entered with quiet efficiency. Her face revealed nothing as she checked the monitors and took Louise's temperature again.

"102.8," she noted, her tone carefully neutral.

Leah nodded, her medical training surfacing through layers of maternal fear. Bacterial pneumonia. Consolidation in the lungs. Broad-spectrum antibiotics fighting invisible invaders. The data fell into analytical patterns in her mind, even as her heart raced with primal terror.

"The ceftriaxone should show greater efficacy after the second dose," she stated, clinging to clinical language like a life raft amid emotional turbulence. "Has the chest x-ray shown the extent of the consolidation?"

Dr. Wilson seemed to recognize the dual nature of her question, both medical professional and terrified mother coexisting in the same trembling frame. "Lower left lobe primarily, with some infiltrates in the right. The oxygen support is precautionary while the antibiotics work."

Louise's eyelids fluttered as the doctor used her stethoscope, listening to the congested battlefield her lungs had become. The small movement, just the opening and closing of eyes, seemed to require monumental effort.

"I'm sure you know bacterial pneumonia responds well to the treatment protocol we've initiated," Dr. Wilson added, her words acknowledging Leah's abandoned medical career with subtle respect. "But the first twenty-four hours are always the most challenging."

The monitors continued their electronic vigilance. Beep. Beep. Beep. Each sound marking the distance between crisis and safety.

"I'll be back to check on her in an hour." Dr. Wilson's hand touched Leah's shoulder briefly. "Try to rest if you can. This might be a long night."

The door closed with a soft click. Leah sank into the chair beside the bed, exhaustion settling into her bones like an old friend. Her phone buzzed. Kate's third message in an hour. Updates requested. Concern radiating through digital space.

Louise's eyelids drooped. The medication made her drowsy despite her labored breathing. Her small fingers remained curled around Leah's with surprising strength given her condition.

"I've got you." Leah whispered the words like a prayer. "I'm not going anywhere."

She'd made the same promise in the delivery room thirty months ago. The same vow when Ryan signed the termination papers without a backward glance. A promise easier to keep than to believe in, sometimes.

A soft knock broke the room's rhythm. The door opened, revealing not the expected nurse but Chris. He stood in the threshold, guitar case in one hand, his face mapped with concern.

"Chris?" Leah straightened in surprise. "The children's showcase—"

"Doesn't matter." He entered the room, setting his guitar in the corner. His eyes went immediately to Louise, cataloging her condition before turning back to Leah. "Kate called. Said you needed backup."

The simple words cracked something in Leah's chest. Backup. Not obligation. Not duty. Just presence. Freely given.

"You didn't have to—" She started, then stopped at his expression.

"Yes, I did." Chris pulled a second chair beside hers. "How is she?"

"Bacterial pneumonia." The diagnosis emerged with the precise clinical detachment she'd cultivated during her truncated medical education. "Infiltrates in both lungs, primarily the lower left lobe. Resisting antipyretics but responding to oxygen support."

The medical terminology flowed easily, creating momentary distance from the terrible reality, this was Louise, not some anonymous case study. Her daughter, not a clinical exercise.

Chris nodded, absorbing the information without visible alarm, though she noted how his fingers tightened on the chair's arm. His other hand found Leah's, warm and solid against her cold fingers.

The room's harsh lighting seemed to soften with his presence. The monitors' beeping receded slightly in Leah's awareness, replaced by the comfort of shared vigilance.

"You should be at the school." Guilt threaded through her voice. "Those children were counting on your performance."

Chris shook his head. His thumb traced circles on her palm. "Jim stepped in. The kids will be fine."

"You've been planning that showcase for months."

"Some things matter more." His gaze returned to Louise, then back to Leah. "Some people matter more."

The simplicity of his certainty struck Leah with physical force. Months of tentative dating after a year of friendship. Louise had come to know him first as Mr. Chris from music class, then Mommy's friend, and now simply Chris, a fixture in their weekend routines, their Tuesday night dinners, their gradually expanding life.

Louise stirred slightly. Her eyes opened, finding Chris through the haze of fever and medication.

"Hey, Sunshine." His voice softened to the tone he reserved for her alone. "Nice elephant pajamas."

A ghost of a smile appeared on Louise's dry lips. Her free hand reached toward him, fingers opening and closing in silent request.

Chris captured her small hand in his. "I brought my guitar too." He reached for the guitar case with his free arm. "Maybe some music will help you feel better."

Louise's eyes brightened slightly at the sight of the familiar instrument.

"Music later," a nurse said, entering to check Louise's IV antibiotics. "Medicine first."

Chris stood, moving to make room. "We'll be right outside, Sunshine."

Louise's fingers tightened around his. Panic flashed across her fever-bright face.

"Stay," she pleaded, the simple word carrying her desperation.

Chris looked to the nurse, who nodded permission. "I'll stay right here," he promised. "Just moving to the foot of the bed so the nurse can help you."

In the hallway afterward, Leah leaned against the wall. Fluorescent lights buzzed overhead, casting shadows across the commercial artwork hanging at measured intervals.

"The showcase was tonight," she said quietly. "Your first as music director."

Chris stood beside her, shoulders against the same wall. Their arms touched lightly.

"I called Jim from the car. He understands."

"These children have been practicing for months." The words carried the weight of expectations abandoned. She knew that weight intimately, had carried it since withdrawing from med school during pregnancy.

"It was never a question," he said simply. "Where I needed to be tonight."

Not just where Leah needed him. Where Louise needed him. The distinction mattered, illuminated something Leah had sensed but not fully recognized until this moment.

"You didn't have to come." She needed to be sure, needed to hear his reasons directly.

Chris turned to face her fully. The hallway's harsh lighting caught the exhaustion in his eyes, the worry lines that matched her own.

"Yes, I did." His certainty remained unshaken. "You're not doing this alone anymore, Leah. Not if I have anything to say about it."

Something shifted in her chest, a recognition of what stood before her. Not just a boyfriend. Not just a man who tolerated her daughter. Something far more profound.

Dr. Wilson emerged from checking on another patient before Leah could respond. "The radiologist noted possible pleural involvement on the latest films. I'm modifying the antibiotic protocol as a precaution."

Leah's medical knowledge translated the information immediately, anxiety rising at the implications. "Pleural effusion?" Her abandoned training supplied the concern before she could filter it through maternal composure.

"Minor, if present at all," Dr. Wilson assured her. "But I prefer to adjust treatment proactively rather than reactively."

Chris listened to their exchange, his expression revealing recognition of the medical terminology without full comprehension. He asked practical questions about timeline, about what to watch for, about how they could best support Louise through the night.

"Are you family?" Dr. Wilson glanced between them, noting different last names on Leah's paperwork.

"Yes," Chris answered without hesitation. No qualification. No explanation. Simply truth.

They returned to find Louise drowsy from medication but breathing slightly easier. The nurse adjusted the oxygen flow before departing.

"Owie?" Louise asked, her limited vocabulary reduced further by fever and fatigue. Her small hand reached toward her chest, communicating what words couldn't.

Chris settled back into the chair beside her bed. "Your lungs have some germs inside." He kept his explanation simple for her two-year-old understanding. "The doctors are giving you medicine to make them go away."

"Stay?" She reached for him again, eyes wide with plea.

"All night," he promised. "We both will."

Louise's gaze traveled to the guitar case in the corner. "Music?" The word emerged in a hopeful whisper.

"Of course." Chris smiled. "Would you like that?"

Louise nodded, the movement slight but definitive.

Chris retrieved the guitar, settling it on his lap with practiced ease. His fingers found chords, soft and melodic.

"This is a special song," he explained, voice gentle. "For brave girls who need to rest and heal."

The music filled the sterile room, transforming it. The monitors still beeped, the oxygen still hissed, but these mechanical sounds became merely percussion beneath Chris's melody. He sang softly, a tune he'd composed specifically for Louise during their Sunday music sessions.

Leah watched her daughter's eyes grow heavy, the tension easing from her small body as the music worked magic medicines couldn't touch. Chris's voice wrapped around them both like a blanket, offering security within these uncertain walls.

When Louise finally drifted to sleep, her breathing still labored but more regular, Chris set the guitar aside. His hand found Leah's again in the quiet darkness.

"Thank you," she whispered. The words felt inadequate against what he'd given tonight.

"No thanks needed." His voice remained low, mindful of Louise's sleep. "This is where I belong."

The certainty in his statement washed over her. Months of cautiously building something together. Such a short time to create something so solid.

"The showcase—" she began again.

"—doesn't matter," he finished. "Not compared to this."

The night stretched before them. Leah reclined her chair slightly, preparing for uncomfortable vigilance. Chris did the same, their shoulders touching in the dim room.

"You should sleep," he said. "I'll watch the monitors."

"I can't." She glanced at Louise's small form, the oxygen cannula looking alien against her flushed face. "I keep thinking I should have recognized the symptoms sooner. My medical training, it should have been useful."

"You got her help exactly when she needed it." His hand squeezed hers. "You're her mother first, Leah. Not her doctor."

The words touched places inside her that hadn't realized their emptiness until this moment. Louise had only known one parent. Leah had carried every decision, every worry, every middle-of-the-night fever alone. Until now.

"I've always done this solo." The admission emerged in darkness, easier to voice without full light. "Even with Kate's help, the responsibility was all mine."

"Not anymore." Simple words. Profound promise.

Chris turned in the dim light, his eyes finding hers. "I love you, Leah." His voice carried quiet certainty. "I love you both, so much. And we're going to get through this. All of it. Together."

The words hung in the room's darkness, not just comfort, but truth. Leah felt tears well, the emotional dam finally breaking under the weight of his unwavering presence.

"I love you too," she whispered back, the words carrying all she couldn't fully articulate, gratitude, wonder, fierce attachment. "More than I thought possible."

His arms encircled her, pulling her against his chest as best the awkward hospital chairs allowed. His heartbeat steady beneath her ear, a counterpoint to the medical monitors tracking Louise's vital signs.

"Rest," he murmured against her hair. "I've got you both."

Sleep claimed Louise completely. The medication and music had done their work. Her breathing remained labored but stable, the monitors tracking her progress in green digital readouts.

Around midnight, a nurse came to check vitals. Louise's temperature had spiked again: 103.4. The nurse added another medication to her IV, her efficiency tinged with concern.

"The fever's cycling," Leah noted, clinical assessment battling maternal fear. "Has Dr. Wilson ordered cultures for resistant strains?"

The nurse's eyes reflected recognition of a fellow medical professional. "Full panel, results pending. We're covering all bases until we identify the specific pathogen."

This exchange, this small return to medical territory, steadied Leah momentarily. The familiar language provided illusory control in a situation where she had none.

"Call immediately if her breathing becomes more labored," the nurse instructed before leaving.

Chris moved aside during the nurse's visit but didn't leave. His presence remained constant, watchful without hovering.

"You should stretch your legs," he told Leah after the nurse departed. "I'll stay with her."

"I don't want to leave her—"

"Just to the hallway and back," he encouraged gently. "Five minutes. You need to move."

Reluctantly, Leah stood. Her back protested hours in the uncomfortable chair. "Five minutes," she agreed. "Call if anything changes."

The hallway's emptiness provided momentary solitude. Leah paced the short corridor, working circulation back into stiff limbs. Through the small window in Louise's door, she could see Chris leaning forward, speaking softly to her daughter who had awakened briefly.

Something about the tableau struck her with unexpected force. Chris, guitar forgotten, focused entirely on Louise's comfort. His hand smoothed her curls back from her forehead, the gesture one Leah recognized from her own repertoire of parental comfort.

She couldn't hear their words through the door. Didn't need to. The connection visible through glass told its own story, one of care that transcended obligation, of love freely given without condition.

When she reentered, Louise had fallen back asleep. Chris looked up, offering a tired smile.

"She woke up worried you were gone," he explained. "I told her you were just stretching your legs."

"Thank you." Leah settled back into her chair. "For everything tonight."

"Always." The word carried weight beyond its syllables.

They fell into companionable silence. The room's darkness wrapped around them, creating intimacy within institutional walls. Sometime after two, exhaustion claimed Leah despite her resistance. Her head drooped against Chris's shoulder, sleep arriving in fragments between anxious waking.

A small sound roused her from half-sleep. Louise's monitor beeped with a different tone. Her temperature had spiked again, and her oxygen levels had dipped.

Instantly alert, Leah straightened. Chris was already on his feet, pressing the call button.

"Mommy?" Louise's voice emerged panicked and raspy. Her breathing had worsened again, each inhale a visible struggle.

"I'm here, baby." Leah moved to the bedside, heart racing. The medical part of her brain cataloged symptoms with detached precision, increased respiratory rate, intercostal retractions, nasal flaring, while her maternal instincts screamed with primitive fear. "Help is coming."

The night nurse entered, assessing the situation with practiced efficiency. She checked Louise's vitals, her expression tightening.

"104.2," she confirmed. "I'll page the doctor immediately."

Terror gripped Leah's chest. Louise's eyes were wide with fear, her small body tensed with the effort of breathing, her skin radiating heat like a furnace.

"It's okay," Chris moved beside them both. His voice remained steady despite the fear Leah saw in his eyes. "Remember how we breathe during singing practice? In through your nose, slow and steady."

Louise's gaze fixed on him, desperate for anchor amid rising panic.

"Like this." Chris demonstrated, exaggerating the calm inhale. "One, two, three. Then out. One, two, three."

Incredibly, Louise followed his lead. Her breathing remained labored but slowed slightly, panic receding as she focused on his counting.

"That's it, Sunshine." Encouragement flowed through his words. "You've got this. In—one, two, three. Out—one, two, three."

Dr. Wilson arrived, moving swiftly to examine Louise. Chris stepped back, giving space while maintaining the counting rhythm Louise now followed with fierce concentration.

"We need to change antibiotics," Dr. Wilson decided after checking Louise's lungs. "The cultures show resistance to the initial treatment. And add cooling measures. The infection is fighting back harder than we anticipated."

The next hour blurred into medical intervention. New medication administered. Ice packs applied to Louise's overheated body. Oxygen levels monitored. Her small form battling invisible invaders while machines tracked her progress in digital readouts.

Leah's medical knowledge both helped and hindered, she understood each intervention's purpose, recognized each value on the monitors, but this clinical awareness provided no comfort against the primal fear of watching her child struggle.

Through it all, Chris remained. When Leah's strength faltered, his voice continued the steady counting. When Louise's fear peaked, his hand provided anchor alongside Leah's. His presence never wavered, never diminished.

Finally, the crisis passed. Louise's breathing eased as the new medication took effect. Her temperature dropped to 102.8, still high but moving in the right direction. The monitors returned to their steady, less urgent rhythm.

"She's stabilizing," Dr. Wilson confirmed. "The new antibiotic appears to be effective against the resistant strain."

Exhaustion crashed over Leah in waves. The adrenaline that had sustained her ebbed, leaving trembling in its wake.

"You should sit," Chris guided her gently to the chair. "Before you fall."

Louise watched them both with heavy-lidded eyes. The medication made her drowsy, but fear kept her fighting sleep.

"Rest, sweet girl," Leah encouraged. "We'll be right here."

"Promise?" The word emerged small and scratchy from her raw throat.

"Promise." Leah stroked her daughter's hand. "Both of us."

Louise's gaze moved to Chris, seeking confirmation.

"Right here all night," he assured her. "Me and my guitar."

Louise's eyes began to close, then opened again with sudden urgency. "Daddy?"

The word hung in the room's darkness. Simple. Profound. Spoken with such natural certainty it momentarily stopped time.

Chris's hand stilled on Louise's. His eyes met Leah's across the hospital bed, shock and wonder reflected between them.

"Yes, Sunshine?" His voice emerged rough with emotion.

"Stay." Louise's fingers curled around his. "Don't go."

"I won't." The promise carried weight beyond its simplicity. "Not ever."

Louise nodded once, satisfied with his answer. Sleep claimed her properly this time, medication and security working together to ease her into healing rest.

In the quiet that followed, Leah stared at her daughter's sleeping face, then at Chris. The word echoed between them. Daddy. Not a title granted through paperwork or biology. A recognition of something already true, already lived.

"She's never—" Leah began.

"I know." Chris's eyes shone with moisture in the dim room.

Morning arrived in pale strips of light through hospital blinds. Louise's fever had continued its slow retreat through the night. Her breathing had steadied, though the congestion in her lungs would take days to fully clear.

Dr. Wilson arrived with the morning shift, examining Louise with careful thoroughness.

"Much improved," she pronounced. "The cultures confirm sensitivity to the new antibiotic regimen. We'll keep her through another night for observation and to continue IV therapy, but I believe we've turned the corner."

Louise had awakened hungry, a good sign. She consumed half a container of apple juice before falling back asleep, her body demanding rest to continue healing.

In the room's corner, Chris packed his guitar carefully in its case. His movements were slow with exhaustion, but his face carried peace beneath the fatigue.

"You could go home," Leah suggested. "Get some real sleep. I'll call if anything changes."

Chris shook his head. "I told her I'd stay."

The simple words carried the weight of promise kept. Of commitment not easily broken.

"About what she called you..." Leah began carefully. "She was sick, feverish. If it makes you uncomfortable—"

"It doesn't." Chris set the guitar case down, turning to face her fully. "Unless it bothers you."

Leah studied him, this man who'd abandoned career opportunity without hesitation, who'd counted breaths through the night's darkest hours, who'd promised to stay and meant it.

"It doesn't," she answered honestly. "It feels right."

Something settled between them, an understanding deeper than the many months they'd been dating, than the life they'd been slowly building. A recognition of truth that had been quietly growing all along.

"I love her," Chris said simply. "Not because she's yours. Because she's herself. Because she's Louise."

The distinction mattered. Illuminated everything that made this different from obligation or conditional acceptance.

"I know." Leah's throat tightened with emotion. "She knows too. Has known maybe before either of us really did."

The windshield wipers dragged Leah back to the present. Rain continued its steady rhythm against the car, the sound no longer matching the tears that had begun to slide down her cheeks.

One year since that night in the hospital. One year since Louise first called Chris "Daddy" in fever-bright certainty. And now, Ryan's attempt to reclaim what he had so easily discarded threatened everything they'd built.

But the memory carried strength as well as vulnerability. That night had revealed what truly mattered, not legal paperwork, not biological connection, but chosen love. Steadfast presence. The family they had created through daily acts of care and commitment.

Leah wiped away her tears and started the car. Williams had said to document everything, every moment that showed the reality of their family. The paperwork from the meeting lay beside her, its clinical language unable to capture what she had just relived.

But she knew now, with renewed clarity, exactly what they were fighting for. Not just against Ryan, but for the truth Louise had named in that hospital room a year ago.

The truth they lived every day.

The family they had chosen. The bond they had built. The love that had claimed them all, paperwork or not.

CHAPTER 11

Shattered Silence

The silence in Chris's home studio felt heavy with unspoken confrontation. Tyler's car had pulled into the driveway just as Chris was putting away his guitar from an afternoon lesson, the unexpected arrival immediately shifting the atmosphere. Chris adjusted the guitar on its stand, fingers lingering on the polished wood as if drawing strength from the instrument that had always understood him better than his own blood.

Tyler stood with his back to the room, studying the wall of family photographs. His tailored suit jacket hung across shoulders that had carried familial responsibility. The fabric alone represented more than Chris's monthly mortgage payment—a silent testament to the divergent paths their lives had taken.

"Nice setup you've got here." Tyler's voice filled the sound-treated space. "Still teaching at the school?"

"And private lessons." Chris gestured toward the student guitars lined against the wall. "Business is good."

Tyler's reflection appeared in the window glass, his expression unreadable in the late afternoon light. For just a moment, Chris glimpsed something unguarded—concern, perhaps, or judgment masked as concern—before his brother turned away from the window.

"How long are you in town?" Chris asked.

"Just tonight." Tyler turned finally. "Meetings tomorrow in Chicago."

The practiced small talk stretched between them. Brothers separated by eleven years, by vastly different memories of the same family collapse, by opposing interpretations of loyalty and protection. Chris studied the stranger wearing his brother's face, searching for traces of the eighteen-year-old who had departed for college when Chris was only seven.

"Drink?" Chris offered, moving toward the small refrigerator.

Tyler shook his head. "This isn't a social call."

"I figured." Chris straightened. "Terry called you."

"Mom did." Tyler's mouth tightened. "Said you're planning to adopt Louise."

Chris nodded. "The paperwork's filed."

"While her biological father is fighting for custody?" Tyler's eyebrows rose. "Bold move, little brother."

The diminutive landed with particular weight, positioning Chris precisely where Tyler had always seen him—as the baby who needed protection from his own decisions.

"It's the right thing for Louise." Chris kept his voice measured. "For our family."

"That's what I'm here about." Tyler moved to the center of the room. "Family."

Something in his tone raised the fine hairs on Chris's neck.

"I've been doing some digging." Tyler reached into his breast pocket, extracting a slim folder. "About the Millers."

Chris stared at the folder. "Digging?"

"Background research." Tyler extended the folder. "Professional investigation."

"You hired someone to investigate my wife's family?" The words escaped barely controlled.

"I hired someone to protect our family." Tyler's correction came swift and absolute. "There are things you need to know, Chris."

Chris didn't reach for the folder. "Like what?"

"Like the fact that your wife's father systematically destroyed Dad's business." Tyler placed the folder on the keyboard stand. "Like the suspicious timing of her appearance in your life."

"I already know all this." Chris fought to keep his voice level. "We resolved it before the wedding."

Tyler's expression flickered—surprise briefly displacing certainty. "What are you talking about?"

"John Miller." Chris held his brother's gaze. "Leah found documents in her father's office when helping him move. She brought them to me."

"And you what—forgave and forgot?" Disbelief colored Tyler's voice.

"We talked to Dad and Mom." Chris moved closer to the windows. "John even apologized to them directly."

"And that makes it okay?" Tyler's voice rose slightly. "Sorry I destroyed your family business, let's be in-laws now?"

"It was over twenty years ago, Tyler." Chris turned back to face his brother. "Dad's moved on. Mom's moved on."

"Easy for them to say." Tyler's jaw tightened. "They weren't the ones who had to watch Dad fall apart. Who had to step up at eighteen."

There it was—the core of Tyler's self-appointed guardianship. The mantle of responsibility he'd shouldered when their father's business collapsed.

"I know what you did for our family." Chris softened his tone. "But this vendetta against the Millers—it's not healthy."

"It's not a vendetta." Tyler's denial emerged with particular vehemence. "It's pattern recognition. Miller destroyed our father's business. Now his daughter has inserted herself into your life, and suddenly you're fighting a custody battle for her child."

Chris studied his brother's face, searching for traces of the teenager who had left home when Chris was still building with Legos. All he found was the carefully constructed identity Tyler had built from the ashes of their father's failure.

"Is that really how you see Leah?" Chris asked quietly. "As some kind of infiltrator?"

"I see her as John Miller's daughter." Tyler's gaze remained unwavering. "The apple doesn't fall far from the tree."

"You don't know her." Chris moved toward his guitar, needing something solid and familiar. "You've barely spent time with her. Or with Louise."

"I know enough." Tyler tapped the folder. "I know she got pregnant by another man, then found herself a replacement father."

The words landed like physical blows. Chris's fingers curled into fists at his sides.

"You've crossed a line, Tyler."

"Have I? Or am I just saying what everyone's thinking?" Tyler moved closer. "That child has a biological father who wants her back. What gives you the right to insert yourself?"

"The right?" Chris's voice lowered. "Years of bedtime stories. Years of bandaging scraped knees. Years of being there every single day since she was six months old."

"Playing house doesn't change biology." Tyler's words carried particular cruelty. "Blood matters, Chris. You can't simply erase her heritage."

190

In that frozen moment, Chris recognized the echo of Terry's influence in his brother's certainty.

"Louise calls me Daddy because I am her father." Chris's voice steadied. "Not because of legal papers. Not because of marriage. Because I've earned it, every day."

"You're not thinking clearly." Tyler's expression softened to something more dangerous—pity wrapped in fraternal concern. "You've always been the emotional one. The sensitive artist. I'm asking you to think logically for once."

"Don't do that." Chris stepped back. "Don't reduce my life choices to artistic temperament."

"Then prove me wrong." Tyler spread his hands. "Give me one logical reason why this adoption makes sense while her biological father is fighting to be in her life."

"Because Ryan Matthews signed away his rights before she was born." The words emerged clipped. "Because he wanted nothing to do with her."

"People make mistakes." Tyler shrugged. "He's trying to correct his now."

Something in his brother's tone shifted the atmosphere in the room.

"How would you know what Ryan's trying to do?" Chris asked carefully.

Tyler hesitated, the pause microscopic yet revealing.

"You've talked to him." The realization crystallized in Chris's mind. "You've actually been in contact with Ryan."

"I've had a few conversations." Tyler didn't attempt denial. "Professional curiosity."

"Professional curiosity?" Chris echoed. "He's trying to take my daughter, and you're having friendly chats?"

"Your daughter?" Tyler's eyebrows rose. "That's exactly my point, Chris. She's not biologically yours."

"Get out." The words emerged from some ancient place inside Chris.

"I'm trying to help you." Tyler held his ground. "Before you get hurt worse than Dad did. Before Louise gets caught in the middle of something ugly."

"Louise already has a father." Chris moved to the door, holding it open. "She doesn't need Ryan Matthews sweeping in after years of absence. And I don't need my brother undermining my family."

"You're making a mistake." Tyler remained rooted. "Ryan has resources. Connections. His father was a judge, for God's sake."

"And that makes him more deserving?" Chris shook his head. "Money and connections trump actually raising her?"

"The courts look at stability." Tyler's tone shifted to something almost clinical. "Financial security. Extended family. Future opportunities."

The calculated evaluation hit Chris with sudden clarity. "You're not just talking to Ryan. You're advising him."

Tyler's silence confirmed everything.

"My God." Chris's voice hollowed. "You're actually helping him build a case against us."

"I'm helping ensure Louise ends up where she belongs." Tyler's expression hardened. "With her biological family."

"She is with her family." Chris's voice fractured. "Me. Leah. The people who've been there every day of her life."

"Biology isn't something you can simply ignore." Tyler moved closer. "It's in her DNA, Chris. Her identity. Her future health history. These things matter."

"You know what matters more?" Chris held his ground. "Being there. Every boring Tuesday night. Every stomach flu at 3 a.m. Every nightmare and spelling test and scraped knee."

"You've always been the emotional one." Tyler sighed. "Dad was the same way. Heart over head."

"And look where your head has taken you." Chris gestured toward his brother. "Betraying your own family to help a stranger."

"I'm trying to protect you." Frustration fractured Tyler's composed exterior. "From making irreversible mistakes. From legal battles you can't win."

"And it never occurred to you that I might know what I'm doing?" Chris asked quietly. "That I actually understand my own heart better than you do?"

For the first time, uncertainty flickered across Tyler's face.

"You don't see the pattern." Tyler's voice lowered. "You're too close."

"There is no pattern." Chris's patience frayed completely. "Just a man who wants to be a father to the child he loves. And another man who suddenly wants to claim rights he signed away years ago."

"It's more complicated than that." Tyler reached for the folder again. "The timing of Leah entering your life—"

"Was chance." Chris cut him off. "Or fate. Or God. Pick whatever explanation helps you sleep at night, but stop trying to make my wife into some kind of villain."

"You really believe she just happened to join your church?" Tyler pressed. "Get close to you through the music program? Right in the same town where her father once destroyed our family business?"

"Yes." Chris met his brother's gaze without wavering. "Because I was there. I lived it. While you were building your career across the country, I was falling in love. I was becoming a father."

"You really love her." Tyler's observation emerged as realization. "The child."

"Her name is Louise." Chris's voice gentled. "And yes, with everything I am."

Tyler moved to the window, staring out at the yard where afternoon shadows stretched across the grass. "Ryan seems sincere. About wanting to make things right."

"After years of absence?" Chris shook his head. "Convenient timing, just as Louise is old enough to be interesting. Just as we're building a stable life."

"People change." Tyler remained facing the window. "Have second thoughts. Regrets."

"And their regrets should trump our reality?" Chris asked. "Louise's stability?"

"The courts will decide what's best for her." Tyler's shoulders stiffened. "That's what the system is for."

"The system isn't designed for situations like this." Chris moved to stand beside his brother. "It can't measure love, or commitment, or the thousand little moments that make a family."

"I can't support this adoption." Tyler finally turned to face Chris. "I won't testify against Ryan."

The statement hung between them, final and irrevocable.

"I'm not asking you to." Chris met his brother's gaze. "But I am asking you to stop actively working against us."

"I'm trying to protect this family." Tyler's certainty remained unshaken.

"No." Chris shook his head slowly. "You're trying to protect your idea of what family should be. Blood and DNA and biology."

"That's what family is." Tyler insisted.

"It's part of it." Chris conceded. "But it's not everything. Not even the most important part."

"I hope you know what you're doing." Tyler reached for his coat. "When this goes to court, when the lawyers start digging through everyone's past..."

"I do." Chris stood firm. "Because Louise is worth fighting for. Worth standing up to Ryan, to Terry, even to you."

Tyler paused at the door. For a moment, Chris glimpsed something familiar in his brother's eyes—the echo of protection that had once been selfless before calcifying into control.

"Be careful, Chris." Tyler's warning carried genuine concern. "Family conflicts leave scars that never fully heal."

"I know." Chris didn't move toward him. "I'm looking at one right now."

Tyler nodded once, then he was gone. The front door closed with quiet finality.

Chris stood alone in his studio, surrounded by instruments and family photographs. He reached for his guitar, fingers finding chords without conscious intention. The melody that emerged was something new—not the gentle compositions he created for Louise, but something with edges, with tension, with resolution still seeking form.

Outside, Tyler's car started. Headlights swept across the yard, then disappeared down the street. Between brothers, something had broken tonight. But within Chris, something had crystallized—certainty bright and sharp as diamond.

His fingers moved across guitar strings, shaping the melody into something that carried both loss and determination. Tomorrow would bring its own battles—legal documents, family tensions, preparations for whatever Ryan might attempt next.

But tonight, in his studio, with music flowing from his hands, Chris had found the answer to Tyler's challenge. Family wasn't just blood. It was chosen, built, sustained through daily acts of love. And for that understanding, he would fight with everything he had.

Chris found his mother kneeling among her roses, silver hair pulled back as she worked with focused intent. The late afternoon light caught the careful architecture of her garden—decades of patient cultivation creating beauty from stubborn earth. She hadn't noticed him yet, and he hesitated at the garden gate, unsure how to begin the conversation that had driven him here after Tyler's devastating visit.

"Mom?"

Mary glanced up, her face immediately registering concern at his expression. The trowel in her hand stilled against the dark soil. "Chris. You look like you're carrying the weight of the world."

"Tyler came to see me last night." The words tumbled out as he pushed through the gate, each step heavy with the burden of family fractures.

Mary's hands went still. "About Louise's adoption?"

"About everything." Chris crossed the path to where she knelt. "He's been talking to Ryan. Advising him. Helping him build a case against us."

The admission hung between them like smoke from a distant fire—something that had been burning for weeks, finally visible.

Mary set down her trowel with deliberate care. "I was afraid it might come to this."

"You knew?" The question escaped sharper than he intended.

"I suspected." Mary's voice carried the weariness of someone who had been watching storm clouds gather. "Your aunt has been making calls. Terry's never been good at keeping secrets when she believes she's on a righteous mission."

Chris studied his mother's face, noting the new lines around her eyes, the careful way she chose her words. "And you've just been watching it happen?"

Mary stood slowly, brushing earth from her hands with movements that spoke of internal struggle. "I've been wrestling with my conscience, if you must know. Wondering how much loyalty I owe to my sister versus how much I owe to what's right."

Something in her tone made Chris look at her more carefully. Gone was the diplomatic neutrality he'd expected. Instead, he saw something he'd rarely witnessed—his mother's will, sharpened to a fine edge.

"What do you mean?"

Mary moved toward her garden shed, her steps measured but purposeful. "Terry has been documenting things. Taking pictures of Louise at school without asking. Making notes about your family like she's conducting some kind of investigation."

"How do you know this?"

"Because she can't help herself." Mary emerged with a small notebook, its cover worn from handling. "She showed me some of her 'evidence' last Sunday. Wanted my opinion on whether Louise seemed 'unstable' in your care."

The words landed like stones thrown into still water, creating ripples of disbelief. Chris felt something cold settle in his chest.

Mary opened the notebook, revealing pages of her own careful handwriting. "I started keeping track after that. Every inappropriate comment. Every boundary she's crossed. Every time she's used Louise as ammunition for her theories about blood and belonging."

Chris stared at the notebook, recognizing his mother's precise script documenting a pattern of betrayal he'd been too close to see clearly. "You've been gathering evidence against your own sister."

"I've been protecting my granddaughter." Mary's voice carried a strength Chris had heard before, but never directed toward family conflict. "Some battles choose us, Chris. This one chose you, but it chose me too."

The weight of that statement settled between them. Mary had always been the family's peacekeeper, the one who smoothed over conflicts and found middle ground. To see her taking sides felt both remarkable and heartbreaking.

"This is extensive," Chris said, scanning the dated entries. Each one revealed another layer of Terry's calculated interference.

"Terry crossed a line when she started involving Louise directly." Mary closed the notebook, holding it against her chest like a shield. "When she began asking that child questions about who her 'real daddy' is. When she started making Louise doubt her place in our family."

"You witnessed that?"

Mary's expression darkened with remembered pain. "Last Sunday at church. Terry cornering Louise by the fellowship hall kitchen, asking if she understood the difference between daddies who share blood and daddies who just live in the same house."

"God." Chris felt rage kindle in his chest, hot and immediate.

"Louise looked so confused, so hurt." Mary's voice trembled slightly. "I intervened, but the damage was already done. That little girl shouldn't have to defend her family's legitimacy to adults who claim to love her."

Chris sank onto the garden bench, overwhelmed by the scope of what his mother was revealing. The afternoon light had grown softer, casting long shadows across the carefully tended rows. Everything felt different now—not just the conversation, but his understanding of where the battle lines had been drawn.

"What are you planning to do with all this?"

"Whatever it takes to protect Louise." Mary sat beside him, the notebook resting between them like a promise. "Support you and Leah completely. Testify if necessary. Show the court what Terry's really been doing."

"She's your sister." The words carried all the complexity of family loyalty, the bonds that transcended logic and often defied justice.

"And Louise is the future." Mary's gaze drifted toward the house where she'd raised her own children, where Louise now played and laughed and felt safe. "I won't sacrifice that child's happiness to preserve my sister's pride."

They sat in silence as evening approached, the weight of Mary's decision settling around them like gathering dusk. Chris felt something shift in his understanding of courage—not the dramatic gestures of movies, but this quiet determination to choose love over loyalty, truth over comfort.

"Tyler thinks I'm being naive," Chris said finally. "That Ryan has legitimate rights I'm trying to deny."

"Tyler has been angry for twenty years." Mary's assessment carried the weight of maternal observation. "Your father's business failure, his sense that the world treated our family unfairly—it's shaped everything he sees. Now he's found someone to blame and someone to rescue. It makes him feel useful."

"And you don't think Leah manipulated her way into our lives?"

"I think Leah found her way to love." Mary's voice softened with something that sounded like wonder. "And Chris, in thirty years of watching relationships, I've learned to tell the difference between calculation and genuine affection. What you two have, what you've built with Louise—that's real family. The kind that forms not from obligation but from choice."

Chris studied his mother's profile in the fading light, seeing strength he'd somehow missed before. "What changed your mind? About staying neutral?"

Mary turned to face him fully. "Watching Louise's face when Terry started talking about 'biological connections' and 'real families.' That little girl didn't understand all the words, but she understood the judgment. She understood that people she trusted were questioning whether she belonged."

The image pierced Chris with its clarity—Louise's confusion transforming into hurt, then withdrawal. All those changes in her artwork, her growing silence, suddenly made terrible sense.

"Terry believes she's protecting family traditions."

"Terry believes a lot of things that sound righteous but feel cruel." Mary's voice hardened again. "She's convinced herself that causing pain now will prevent greater pain later. That questioning Louise's security is somehow protecting her future."

"What should I tell Leah?"

Mary stood, decision radiating from her posture like heat from summer pavement. "Tell her she has an ally. Tell her that when this goes to court, she won't be fighting alone. Tell her that sometimes the strongest families are the ones that have to defend their right to exist."

Chris rose, moving toward his mother with gratitude that felt too large for words. When he embraced her, he felt the solid strength that had anchored his childhood, now redirected toward protecting his daughter's future.

"Thank you," he whispered against her shoulder. "For choosing us."

"Don't thank me yet." Mary pulled back to meet his eyes, and he saw in them the same fierce protectiveness he'd discovered in himself the night Louise first called him Daddy. "Thank me when we've won. When Louise is legally your daughter and this nightmare is over."

"The notebook—"

"Stays with me." Mary's grip on it tightened. "I'm not done collecting evidence. Terry's getting bolder, which means she's getting careless. By the time this reaches court, I'll have everything we need."

As Chris walked back to his car, the evening air cool against his skin, he felt something fundamental had shifted. Not just in his relationship with his mother, but in his understanding of what family meant. Mary had chosen justice over blood, future over past, love over loyalty.

For the first time since Tyler's visit, he felt hope—not just for their legal case, but for the deeper truth that families weren't just born but built, not just inherited but earned, one difficult choice at a time.

Behind him, Mary returned to her roses, but her movements carried new purpose. She was no longer just tending her garden—she was cultivating something stronger, more essential. A fortress of truth around the family that mattered most.

CHAPTER 12

Shadows in Crayon

Ryan paced the length of Wallace & Associates' conference room, his reflection fragmenting across the city skyline. The denied petition lay centered on the polished table like a funeral announcement.

Sixty days. The words had hollowed him from within.

Sixty more days of Louise calling another man "Daddy."

"This judge has a history of caution in custody cases," James Wallace said, entering with two junior associates. "Emergency hearings are rarely granted without evidence of imminent harm."

Ryan turned, jaw rigid. "My daughter not knowing her real father is harm."

Wallace placed his leather portfolio on the table. The two associates—a woman with copper hair twisted into a severe knot, and a younger man whose suit still carried the stiffness of recent purchase—arranged themselves like sentinels.

"Sixty days gives us time to strengthen our position," Wallace said.

Ryan's laugh held no humor. "Strengthen? Chris files an adoption petition the moment I challenge the termination. Now we're told to wait while he tries to erase me legally."

The associates exchanged glances, a silent communication that prickled Ryan's awareness. Something unspoken hovered in the air between them.

"What?" Ryan demanded.

Wallace gestured toward a chair. "You should sit, Ryan. We have developments."

Ryan remained standing. "What kind of developments?"

"The kind that could change everything," Wallace said. "Three weeks ago, a woman named Terry O'Donnell came to our offices."

"Who?"

"Chris Johnson's aunt. His mother's younger sister."

Ryan's head snapped up. "His aunt came to you?"

"She strongly opposes this adoption," Wallace said. "And she's been documenting what she considers concerning behavior."

The female associate opened a slate-gray folder. "She's been keeping detailed records for months. Dates, times, observations about Louise's care and the family dynamics."

Ryan stilled. The conference room seemed to contract around him.

"Chris's aunt is gathering evidence against him?"

"She believes she's protecting Chris from making a terrible mistake," Wallace said. "Terry sees herself as the family's voice of reason, though her approach is... let's say unsophisticated."

The younger associate consulted his notes. "She's been visiting Louise at school without the parents' knowledge. Taking photographs of the child's artwork. Questioning swim instructors about Louise's behavior and schedule."

Ryan sank into the leather chair, the magnitude of this revelation washing over him. "She's been conducting surveillance?"

"More like amateur detective work," the female associate said with barely concealed disdain. "But thorough in its own way. She's documented incidents that she believes show poor parenting judgment."

Wallace leaned forward. "Terry has very specific ideas about family structure and bloodlines. In her mind, biology trumps everything else. She sees your petition as an opportunity to restore proper order."

"Do you believe her concerns are legitimate?"

"Terry O'Donnell is not exactly a sophisticated observer," Wallace said carefully. "Her education is limited, her understanding of child development rudimentary. But she's sincere in her convictions, which makes her potentially effective on a witness stand."

The female associate nodded. "Juries relate to concerned family members, even if their methods are questionable. Sometimes especially then—it suggests genuine worry rather than calculated testimony."

"What exactly is she offering?"

Wallace opened another folder. "Detailed logs of what she considers inappropriate incidents. Photos of Louise's artwork showing concerning themes. Documentation of the child asking questions about family identity."

"And she's willing to testify?"

"Eagerly," Wallace confirmed. "She believes she's saving Chris from himself and protecting Louise from an unstable situation."

Ryan stood, needing movement. "This feels like I'm being handed a gift I didn't earn."

"Family dynamics are complex," Wallace said. "Terry has her own motivations that align with your interests."

"There's something else," the younger associate said. "We understand you've been in contact with Chris's older brother?"

Ryan nodded. "Tyler Johnson. We've had a few conversations."

"He reached out to you directly?" the female associate asked.

"Professional curiosity, he said. He's been investigating Leah's background independently." Ryan's expression darkened. "He hired a private investigator to look into her family connections."

Wallace made a note. "What's Tyler's position on the adoption?"

"He thinks Chris is making an emotional mistake. Something about Leah's father having destroyed their family business years ago." Ryan shrugged. "Tyler seems to think there's some calculated revenge element to their relationship."

"Interesting theory," Wallace said. "Though difficult to prove. Still, having Chris's own brother expressing doubts about the adoption could be valuable."

"Tyler didn't offer to testify," Ryan clarified. "He just... shared his concerns about Chris's judgment."

"Sometimes family members who won't actively support still won't actively oppose," the female associate observed. "Silence can be telling in court."

Wallace leaned back. "Between Terry's documentation and Tyler's obvious reservations, we're painting a picture of a family divided about this adoption. That creates reasonable doubt about whether it truly serves Louise's interests."

"And Terry is definitely willing to go on record?"

"She's practically chomping at the bit," Wallace said. "The woman has appointed herself as some sort of family guardian. She genuinely believes she's protecting everyone involved."

The female associate opened her laptop. "We should coordinate Terry's testimony carefully. Her... enthusiasm could work against us if she comes across as vindictive rather than concerned."

"What do you mean?"

"Terry O'Donnell is not a subtle person," Wallace explained. "She tends toward dramatic pronouncements and absolute statements. We'll need to coach her on how to present her observations without sounding petty or jealous."

"Is she petty or jealous?"

The associates exchanged another glance.

"She's complicated," the female associate said diplomatically. "Methodical enough to write things down, but her emotional investment in the outcome could undermine her credibility if we're not careful."

"The key is framing her testimony around child welfare rather than family politics," Wallace said. "Let her present the facts she's observed and let the court draw conclusions."

Ryan moved to the windows, the city stretching below. "What does this mean for my challenge to the termination agreement?"

"It transforms everything," Wallace said. "Instead of just arguing that you've changed and want to be involved, we can argue that Louise's current environment isn't as stable as it appears. That even family members have concerns."

"And the adoption petition?"

"With a family member testifying against it, questioning the decision-making process? It becomes much harder for a judge to approve permanently severing your rights while simultaneously granting Chris's petition."

Ryan pressed his palms against the cool glass. "So we use Terry's observations."

"We present all relevant testimony to the court," Wallace corrected. "Including testimony from family members who question this adoption."

The younger associate straightened his papers. "How should we handle coordination with Mrs. O'Donnell?"

"Very carefully," Wallace said. "She's useful, but she needs significant guidance. Her instincts aren't sophisticated, and her execution can be... problematic."

"Meaning?"

"She tends to overstate everything," the female associate explained. "Every minor incident becomes 'deeply concerning' or 'highly inappropriate.' She lacks the nuance to distinguish between actual problems and personal grievances."

Wallace stood. "I'll schedule a meeting with Terry for next week. We'll review her documentation and prepare her testimony. The goal is to present her as a concerned family member, not someone with limited understanding making dramatic accusations."

"And Tyler?"

"We leave that door open. If he becomes more cooperative, excellent. If not, we have what we need from Terry."

The conference room had grown darker. Ryan felt energy returning, the hopelessness of the denied emergency petition replaced by tactical opportunity.

"We're done with half measures," Ryan said.

The words hung in the air. A vow. A threshold crossed.

Wallace closed his portfolio. "So we're proceeding with Terry's cooperation?"

Ryan didn't hesitate this time. "Yes. Set up the meeting. Let's see exactly what Chris's own family is willing to say about this adoption."

"Excellent," Wallace said, standing. "We'll move quickly on all fronts."

The associates gathered their materials, the machinery of legal battle shifting into higher gear. Ryan remained seated as they filed out, leaving him alone with Wallace.

"Ryan," the attorney said, his voice losing some of its professional detachment. "Terry O'Donnell is... earnest in her convictions. But she's also not particularly sophisticated. Once we bring her testimony into this, we're relying on someone whose understanding of family dynamics is fairly black and white."

"Is that a problem?"

"It could be an advantage," Wallace said carefully. "Simple, heartfelt concerns often resonate with juries. But we need to manage her carefully. She could just as easily hurt our case if she appears vindictive or small-minded."

Ryan gathered his materials and slipped them into his briefcase. "As long as she's honest about what she's observed."

"Oh, she'll be honest," Wallace assured him. "Perhaps too honest. That's what we need to work on."

The elevator descended. Ryan straightened his tie, his reflection hardening into something more confident.

Terry O'Donnell might not be sophisticated, but her documentation could be devastating. And sometimes the most effective weapons were the simplest ones.

The doors opened to the marble lobby. Ryan stepped out, shoulders squared, briefcase swinging with purpose.

Behind him, the machinery he had set in motion continued its relentless forward movement, now powered by an unexpected ally whose very limitations might prove to be strengths.

Victory felt within reach for the first time since this began.

Miss Andrews arranged Louise's drawings across her desk in chronological order. The earliest artwork showed vibrant family portraits—three smiling figures before a house with musical notes floating from windows—but the progression told a different story. Recent drawings had grown monochromatic, the bright colors replaced by blacks and grays. The most recent showed a small figure alone beneath a dark sky, raindrops falling like tears around her.

The transformation wasn't sudden but gradual—a slow dimming of light. Louise had stopped raising her hand during morning circle. She refused to sing during music time. Yesterday, she sat alone during lunch, shoulders curved inward like protective wings.

Miss Andrews had learned to read children through subtle shifts. A new hesitation in their voices. Changes in their artwork. Withdrawal from friends. These small signals often spoke volumes about upheavals at home.

Louise's signals screamed in darkness.

The intercom buzzed. "Mr. and Mrs. Johnson have arrived."

Miss Andrews gathered the drawings into their progression from light to shadow. The evidence would speak for itself.

Leah's knuckles whitened around her coffee cup. Fluorescent lights cast everyone in unflattering pallor, turning Miss Andrews' concerned expression ghostly. On the table between them, Louise's artwork told a story that made her stomach clench.

"When did you first notice the change?" Chris asked, voice steady despite the tension visible in his jaw.

Miss Andrews pointed to a drawing from weeks ago. "This was the first shift. The house has no windows, though her previous drawings always showed open windows with music notes."

Leah studied the progression. Houses without windows. Trees without leaves. Skies darkening. Colors fading from vibrant primaries to blacks and grays. The family portrait now showed a small figure standing apart, a question mark floating above her head.

"Has Louise mentioned anything bothering her?" Miss Andrews asked.

"She's been quieter," Chris admitted. "We attributed it to being tired. The custody situation has disrupted her routine."

Leah couldn't take her eyes off the drawings. "She's started asking questions about family. Who belongs to whom. Why some children live with grandparents."

"This one especially concerns me." Miss Andrews slid forward yesterday's drawing. Louise had pressed her crayon hard enough to tear the paper. Rain fell in black streaks. The small figure stood alone, faceless beneath the deluge. "Has she experienced any significant changes? Family events? Conversations she might have overheard?"

The question hung between them. Leah's mind raced backward through recent weeks. The family dinner at Terry's. The growing tension with Tyler. Ryan's appearance at school.

"We've tried to shield her," Chris said.

"Children absorb more than we realize," Miss Andrews replied. "They may not understand the content of adult conversations, but they comprehend the emotional undercurrents with remarkable accuracy."

She gathered the drawings into a folder. "I'm not suggesting anything specific has happened. But this dramatic shift in self-expression indicates Louise is processing something significant. Something she lacks the vocabulary to articulate."

Leah swallowed against the tightness in her throat. "What should we do?"

"Create opportunities for her to talk. Use art, play, storytelling—whatever gives her a safe way to express herself." Miss Andrews handed them the folder. "Most importantly, listen without immediately reassuring.

Sometimes our rush to fix things prevents children from fully expressing their fears."

The bell rang, signaling the end of day.

"I've kept Louise in the classroom," Miss Andrews said. "I thought you might want to collect her directly."

Leah clutched the folder to her chest like armor. Chris's hand found the small of her back as they moved through the hallway, past bright bulletin boards that suddenly seemed to mock their daughter's darkening world.

Louise sat at her desk, head bent over a blank piece of paper. The classroom stood empty except for a teaching assistant sorting books nearby.

"Sunshine," Chris called softly. "Time to go home."

Louise looked up, her face revealing nothing—no joy, no relief, none of the usual exuberance. She gathered her things with mechanical care.

"What were you drawing?" Leah asked, crouching to her daughter's eye level.

Louise shrugged, folding the blank paper with deliberate creases. "Nothing."

The single word fell between them like a stone.

In the car, Louise stared out the window. Her small fingers traced raindrops as they raced down the glass. Her reflection showed eyes too solemn for a four-year-old, mouth set in a straight line that belonged on a much older face.

"Would you like music?" Chris asked.

Louise shook her head.

"How about ice cream?" Leah tried.

Another head shake.

They exchanged glances in the rearview mirror. This silent child was a stranger wearing their daughter's face.

At home, Louise went straight to her room. No request for a snack. No questions about dinner. No desire to practice guitar with Chris.

"I'll start dinner," Leah whispered. "Maybe you can check on her?"

Chris nodded, already moving toward Louise's room. The folder of drawings sat on the kitchen counter, its presence accusing.

Leah moved through dinner preparations on autopilot, mind racing through recent weeks. The family gathering at Terry's. Ryan's appearance at school. The growing tension with Tyler. How much had Louise witnessed? What fragments of adult conflict had she absorbed?

When Chris returned to the kitchen, his face told her everything.

"She's coloring," he said. "Asked to be alone."

"Did she say anything?"

"She said she's fine. Just tired." He ran a hand through his hair. "I've never seen her like this, Leah. It's like someone switched off her light."

The pasta water boiled over, sizzling against the stovetop. Like all the unsaid things between them, it demanded immediate attention.

Bedtime routines unfolded – bath without splashing, teeth brushed without songs, story time without interruptions. Each deviation from normal added weight to the stone in Leah's stomach.

Louise sat in bed, hair still damp from her bath, Bear Elephant clutched against her chest. The stuffed animal had been her first gift from Leah after learning of her pregnancy—a promise made before birth, kept through every night since.

"Would you like a different story?" Leah asked, setting aside the unfinished book.

Louise shook her head, fingers working at the elephant's worn ear.

"Something's bothering you," Chris said, sitting at the foot of her bed. "You can tell us anything, Sunshine. Even hard things. Even scary things."

"Even angry things," Leah added.

Louise's fingers stilled on the elephant's ear. She offered a small shrug, eyes fixed on the elephant's face rather than meeting their gaze.

"What are you feeling?" Leah tried again.

Louise looked between them, something troubled flickering in her dark eyes. "About daddies."

The word hung in the air, small and enormous simultaneously.

Chris's body tensed, though his face remained carefully neutral. "What about daddies?"

"Aunt Terry said you're not my real daddy." The words tumbled out in a rush, as if she'd been holding them inside for too long. "But you ARE my daddy. So what does that mean?"

The room seemed to tilt. Leah fought for breath against the sudden vise around her chest.

"I was hiding when they talked," Louise continued, voice dropping to a whisper. "They said words I don't know. Like...bio-logical. And custody." Her face scrunched with confusion. "Are you pretend?"

"Oh, sweetheart." Leah moved to cradle her daughter, but Louise shrank back.

"I don't understand," Louise said, tears beginning to well in her eyes. "You're my daddy. You live here and you read stories and you teach me guitar. How are you not real?"

Chris reached for Louise with trembling hands. "I am your real daddy, Sunshine. I'm not pretend, and I'm not going anywhere."

"Then why did Aunt Terry say that?" Louise's chin quivered. "She said there's another daddy somewhere else. But I don't want another daddy. I want you."

"You don't have to have another daddy," Leah said firmly, gathering Louise into her arms despite her initial resistance. "We're your family."

"But what did those words mean?" Louise looked up at Chris with wide, fearful eyes. "Will I have to go away?"

"No," Chris said, his voice hoarse with emotion. "You're not going anywhere. You're our daughter, and we're your parents."

Louise's breathing slowed, her small body relaxing against Leah's chest. "I was scared," she whispered. "I didn't know what Aunt Terry meant, but it sounded bad."

"Aunt Terry used confusing grown-up words," Chris said gently. "Words that scared you when you didn't need to be scared."

"Will you stay?" Louise murmured, exhaustion finally overtaking her.

"All night if you want," Leah promised.

They sat in silence as Louise's breathing deepened into sleep. Neither moved, as if the slightest shift might shatter this fragile moment of truth.

Wind rattled the kitchen windows. Outside, leaves swirled across their yard in miniature cyclones. Leah watched their chaotic dance, mind racing ahead to necessary actions.

"We need to restrict access," she said. "No more unsupervised time with Terry. No more family dinners. No more church events where she might corner Louise."

Chris nodded, jaw set in the same determined line that had appeared when Ryan confronted them at school. "I'll call my mother tonight. This changes everything."

"Will she believe us?"

"She already knows." Chris's voice carried bitter acknowledgment. "She's been documenting Terry's behavior, witnessed her asking Louise those questions about 'real daddies' at church last Sunday. Mom's been quietly gathering evidence for us."

Leah felt a flicker of hope. "Then she'll help us stop this?"

Chris ran a hand through his hair, frustration evident in every line of his body. "She's been helping by taking notes, staying silent while she collects documentation. But now..." He gestured toward Louise's drawings scattered across the counter. "Terry's escalated beyond what documentation can protect against."

"What do you mean?"

"I need to ask her to do something she's never done in her entire life." Chris's voice carried the weight of impossible requests. "Confront Terry directly. Stand up to her. Tell her to stop interfering with our family."

The magnitude of what he was asking settled between them. Leah had witnessed the dynamic between the sisters—Mary's lifetime of diplomatic silence against Terry's domineering certainty.

"She's never confronted Terry about anything. Terry's been the family authority since they were children. Mom has spent sixty years avoiding direct conflict with her sister."

"And now you're going to ask her to draw a line in the sand."

Chris looked at Louise's artwork again—the progression from light to shadow, from security to confusion. "Documentation isn't protection anymore. Terry isn't just observing—she's actively poisoning Louise's sense of security." His voice hardened with resolution. "I need my mother to choose a side publicly. To tell Terry she won't tolerate this behavior anymore."

"That could destroy their relationship."

"Terry already destroyed it the moment she used Louise as a weapon." Chris's jaw tightened. "Mom just hasn't admitted it yet."

Leah studied his profile in the kitchen's warm light, seeing the determination that had emerged since becoming Louise's father. "What if she can't do it? What if asking her to confront Terry is asking too much?"

"Then we'll know where we truly stand." Chris's voice carried painful acceptance. "And we'll protect Louise ourselves, with or without family support."

The kitchen clock continued its steady rhythm, counting down the hours until morning brought necessary confrontations. Chris reached for his phone, thumb hovering over his mother's contact.

"I should call her now," he said. "Before I lose my nerve. Before another day passes with Louise carrying this confusion."

"What will you tell her?"

Chris looked at the scattered drawings one more time—evidence of his daughter's fracturing world rendered in crayon and heartbreak. "That quiet support isn't enough anymore. That Louise needs her grandmother to find the courage she's never had to show." His finger pressed the call button. "That sometimes protecting family means standing up to family."

CHAPTER 13

When Silence Breaks

The drive home from Mary's house felt endless. Chris gripped the steering wheel, his knuckles white against the dark leather. Beside him, Leah stared through the passenger window at streets that blurred past like watercolor paintings in rain, each traffic light another moment to replay their mother-in-law's devastating retreat.

"She had everything documented," Chris said, his voice carrying the hollow resonance of betrayal. "Pages of notes about Terry's behavior. Evidence of every boundary crossed, every inappropriate comment."

Leah traced raindrops on the window, each path mirroring the tears she refused to shed. "But when you asked her to actually confront Terry..."

"She folded." Chris shook his head, frustration bleeding through his controlled tone. "Just like always. The moment it required backbone instead of quiet observation, she retreated into her shell."

They had gone to Mary's hoping for an ally willing to stand up to Terry's interference. Instead, they'd watched Chris's mother transform before their eyes—from determined grandmother protecting Louise to the familiar peacekeeper who'd spent a lifetime avoiding confrontation with her sister.

"What exactly did she say again?" Leah asked, though she'd witnessed the painful conversation.

"That she needed time to think about the right approach. That maybe there was a gentler way to handle Terry without causing family division." Chris's laugh held no humor. "She kept saying she understood our concerns but didn't want to destroy her relationship with Terry over what she called 'misunderstandings.'"

"Misunderstandings?" Leah's voice sharpened with disbelief. "Terry told Louise you weren't her real father. She's been documenting our family like we're criminal suspects. What part of that is misunderstood?"

"That's exactly what I said. But Mom just kept wringing her hands, talking about family harmony and giving Terry the benefit of the doubt." Chris turned into their driveway, the familiar sight of home offering no comfort. "She has good intentions, but when it comes to actually standing up to Terry..."

"She becomes a turtle," Leah finished. "All the courage disappears the moment real action is required instead of passive documentation."

The car rolled to a stop. The engine's cessation left them suspended in silence, neither willing to disrupt the momentary sanctuary of shared disappointment.

Mrs. Abernathy met them at the door, Louise's favorite babysitter with her crown of silver hair and gentle manner. "She asked for you three times before finally surrendering to sleep," she said, gathering her knitting. "Wouldn't have her usual story. Just kept asking when you'd be home, whether you were talking to Grandma Mary about Aunt Terry."

The words landed between them like small, devastating explosions. Louise had been tracking their movements, understanding far more than they'd realized about the adult conflicts swirling around her small world.

Chris paid Mrs. Abernathy while Leah moved toward Louise's room. The hallway stretched before her, each step requiring deliberate intention. Louise lay curled into herself, a small crescent moon of vulnerability beneath cloud-patterned sheets. Bear Elephant remained clutched against her chest, a talisman against nightmares both sleeping and waking.

"Mommy?" Louise's voice emerged from sleep's borderlands, fragile and undefended.

"I'm here, sweet girl." Leah sat on the bed's edge, pressing her lips to Louise's temple where pulse and thought converged beneath translucent skin. "Just checking on you."

"Did you see Grandma Mary?" Louise's eyes remained closed, but tension threaded through her small frame.

"Yes," Leah managed. "Everything's fine. Go back to sleep."

"Will Aunt Terry still say mean things?" The question emerged without preamble, revealing the hidden architecture of Louise's anxieties.

Something cold and sharp pierced Leah's chest—the realization that Louise had been carrying this specific worry, cataloguing potential threats, mapping the changing landscape of their family's fracturing alliances.

"We'll talk tomorrow," Leah whispered, continuing the rhythmic stroking of Louise's hair. "Sleep now."

Louise's breathing eventually slowed, but her fingers maintained their grip on Bear Elephant. Even in unconsciousness, her body remembered to hold fast to whatever security remained.

Chris appeared in the doorway, his silhouette familiar against the hall light. Leah rose without a word and followed him out, their movements choreographed by years of shared parenthood and growing desperation.

"Mrs. Abernathy said she wouldn't nap today," Chris said as they moved toward the kitchen. "Kept asking when we'd be back, whether we were going to fix things with Terry."

"She's mapping the conflict," Leah said, her voice catching on something jagged in her throat. "Creating contingencies. Trying to understand who might disappear next from her world."

The kitchen felt different now, transformed by the weight of Louise's drawings from school that sat on the counter like evidence of wounds too deep to heal with simple reassurances. Chris reached for her, his hand extending across the distance she'd maintained since leaving Mary's garden.

"Leah—"

"I need a minute." She stepped back, away from comfort that might dissolve her remaining composure. "Just one minute to process this."

The bathroom door closed behind her with a soft click that belied the finality of her retreat. Cold tile pressed against her feet, its unyielding surface a counterpoint to her internal dissolving. The mirror offered a stranger wearing her face: hollow-eyed, pale, features arranged in careful approximation of strength that couldn't quite disguise the fractures beneath.

Leah turned on the shower, letting water create white noise to mask whatever sounds might escape her. She sank to the floor, back against the tub's cold porcelain, her body curling forward until her forehead touched her knees, completing a circuit of defeat.

The shower's steady rhythm created a private soundscape, a sanctuary for breaking apart. Steam gathered around her in gentle conspiracy, obscuring the room's hard edges. Within this temporary refuge, her defenses began to disintegrate piece by piece.

Louise's artwork from school seemed to pulse with accusation from her bag, abandoned beside the sink. Leah reached for it with trembling hands, spreading the pages across the bathroom floor where they formed a narrative more honest than any words could convey.

Dark crayon pressed hard enough to tear paper. Rain falling like tears from storm clouds. Small figures alone beneath threatening skies. The progression of darkness across weeks of drawings created a chronicle of Louise's interior landscape, one Leah had refused to fully read until this devastating moment.

Legal documents from their meeting with Williams mocked her from beside the artwork. Victory on paper. Sixty-day delay. Procedural wins that meant nothing against Louise's fractured smile and whispered questions about "real" family, about belonging, about whether the only father she'd ever known might somehow be taken away.

Something essential collapsed within Leah's chest. The first sob broke through without permission, raw and desperate. The second followed with the momentum of inevitability. Then a flood she couldn't contain: grief and terror and fury converging into a single overwhelming current that swept away every careful barrier she'd constructed.

Her body shook with the force of her surrender. Every fear she'd held tight since the first Wallace & Associates letter. Every rage she'd swallowed since Ryan's calculated appearance at school. Every despair she'd denied since Terry's venomous whispers reached Louise's innocent ears and planted seeds of doubt about her place in their family.

The bathroom floor felt like the bottom of an ocean, pressure crushing her from all directions. She couldn't breathe, couldn't think beyond the images scattered around her—Louise's artwork telling a story of security slowly dissolving, of a child trying to understand why the adults who claimed to love her were suddenly speaking in riddles about blood and belonging.

"I can't—" The words emerged broken, fractured by sobs that seemed to originate from somewhere deeper than her lungs. "I thought we could protect her. I thought love would be enough."

The door opened without a knock. Chris knelt beside her on the bathroom floor, gathering her against his chest while water drummed against the shower door like rain against windows during storms that threatened everything fragile.

"Look at her drawings," Leah gasped, gesturing toward the scattered pages with hands that shook like leaves in wind. "We're losing her, Chris. Piece by piece, day by day, we're watching our daughter disappear."

Chris reached for the nearest drawing—a stick figure girl surrounded by question marks, no ground beneath her feet, dark sky pressing down like judgment. His own breathing became labored as the full impact of Louise's deteriorating emotional state hit him anew.

"I don't recognize her anymore," Leah continued, her voice raw with accumulated pain. "No singing in the car. No silly jokes during dinner. No spontaneous hugs or requests for extra bedtime stories. Just questions about Terry and daddies and who she belongs to, as if belonging could be revoked like a library card."

The metaphor struck them both silent. Chris stroked her hair while his own eyes filled with moisture that caught the bathroom's harsh light.

"She asked me yesterday if you were pretend," Leah whispered, the confession extracted like a splinter from infected flesh. "A four-year-old child asking if her father is real or imaginary because adults she trusts have been planting doubt like poison in her mind."

"God." Chris's voice cracked on the single word.

"And when we ask for help from your family..." Leah's composure shattered completely. "Your mother documents everything but won't act when action is needed. Tyler actively works against us like we're the enemy. Terry systematically destroys Louise's sense of security while claiming to protect family values."

"We're winning the legal battles and losing the war that matters most," Leah said, tapping the drawing with one finger. "Right here, in her heart, in her understanding of who she is and where she belongs."

Chris set the artwork down with the reverence of someone handling evidence of wounds too deep to heal with bandages and time. "What are you saying?"

Leah's spine straightened against the tub, gathering scattered fragments of composure amid her surrender. "I'm saying we can't shield her from this anymore. The questions she's asking, the fear in her drawings—she knows something is threatening her security. She's creating her own explanations in the absence of truth, and those explanations are more terrifying than reality."

Chris's expression shifted, understanding forming beneath the surface of his features. "You think we should tell her. About Ryan. About the custody case."

"Not everything," Leah said, wiping her face with the back of her hand. "But something true. Something that gives her words for what she's feeling instead of leaving her to imagine monsters she can't name."

They moved to the bedroom eventually, carrying Louise's drawings and the weight of this new understanding. The familiar rituals of preparing for sleep—teeth brushed, faces washed, the choreography of long intimacy—provided thin comfort against the night's revelations.

In the gentle lamp light, they sat on the bed's edge, Louise's artwork spread between them like tarot cards revealing an unwelcome future.

"What would we even say?" Chris asked, his voice hoarse with emotion. "How do you explain a custody battle to a child who should be worried about nothing more complex than learning to tie her shoes?"

Leah turned toward him, her body seeking the familiar geography of his shoulder, the hollow where her head had rested through countless difficult nights. "I don't know. But she's already creating her own story from fragments she's overheard. From Terry's cruel half-truths and whispered adult conversations that stop when she enters rooms."

"She's too young," Chris said, giving voice to his deepest fear.

"And yet she's living it regardless," Leah replied. "Whether we give her words or not, she's experiencing the consequences of adult decisions. The difference is whether she understands what's happening or continues imagining threats we can't even begin to address."

They lay in darkness, processing the magnitude of what it meant to introduce such adult complexities into their daughter's still-forming understanding of the world. The house settled around them with familiar sounds, but nothing felt familiar anymore—not their roles as parents, not their ability to protect, not their faith that love and presence could overcome legal challenges and family betrayal.

"I've spent years trying to protect her from painful truths," Leah admitted, the confession emerging easier in darkness. "First that her biological father chose career over fatherhood. Then that there are people who value blood over bonds, DNA over devotion."

"Now she's creating her own explanations," Chris said. "Drawn in crayon and question marks, rendered in shadows and rain."

"What would we tell her when she asks if she'll have to go with him?" The question emerged as barely more than a whisper, giving voice to the fear that lived in the marrow of their bones.

Chris's arm tightened around her waist, a physical manifestation of his refusal to surrender that possibility. "We tell her we're fighting with everything we have to keep our family together. That judges listen to what's best for children, and we believe being with us is what's best for her."

"And when she asks why Terry said you're not her real father?"

"I tell her that being a real parent means showing up every day," Chris's voice grew stronger with each word. "Reading bedtime stories and teaching guitar chords and bandaging knees and celebrating triumphs. That family is built through love and choice and presence, not just biology."

A car passed on their street, headlights momentarily sweeping across their ceiling before returning them to intimate darkness. Leah traced patterns on Chris's arm, her fingertips following familiar contours that had become geography she could navigate without sight.

"The hearing is in weeks, not months," she said, the countdown a constant presence in her consciousness. "She should hear the truth from us before then. Before something happens at school or church that we can't control or explain away."

"Tomorrow," Chris said, certainty replacing the uncertainty that had plagued him for weeks. "We'll find the right words tomorrow."

"Together," Leah agreed, the word carrying all the weight and lightness of their shared commitment.

The decision settled between them like dawn breaking over landscape previously shrouded in darkness. Not hope exactly, but purpose. Direction. A strategy that didn't depend on Mary's backbone or Terry's conscience or anyone else's courage but their own.

Outside their window, clouds shifted to reveal stars—pinpricks of light persistent against vast darkness. Inside, two people bound by choice rather than obligation continued crafting a plan to preserve what they had built, each decision a small constellation in the larger universe of their commitment to Louise, to each other, to the family they had created through daily acts of love and presence.

Sleep approached slowly, finding less resistance than it had in weeks. Their bodies remained intertwined, physical proximity maintaining connection even as consciousness began to fade. Tomorrow would demand strength and vulnerability in equal measure. Tonight offered respite, communion, the gathering of resources for battles ahead.

The last thought Leah registered before surrendering to sleep was not of fear but of determination. They would tell Louise the truth. Would face whatever came together. Would fight with everything they had, armed now with honesty instead of protection, transparency instead of concealment.

Their broken places had formed new edges—sharper, more defined, better equipped for the war ahead.

Morning light spilled across the kitchen table, fracturing into prisms where it caught the edge of a water glass. It painted Louise's dark curls with copper highlights, transforming ordinary breakfast rituals into something almost sacred. She sat with Bear Elephant propped against the syrup bottle, a silent sentinel against invisible fears. Her small fingers traced patterns only she could see across the wooden tabletop, working through anxieties she lacked words to name.

Chris stood at the stove, muscles tense beneath forced casualness. He flipped another pancake, attempting shapes from their private mythology: elephants with trunks like question marks, giraffes with impossibly long necks, wobbly approximations of rabbits. His hands moved with careful attention, though his mind occupied distant territory, rehearsing words that refused to arrange themselves into appropriate comfort.

"More juice?" Leah's voice carried the deliberately light tone adults adopt when navigating emotional minefields.

Louise shook her head, eyes narrowing slightly. She studied her parents with the particular intensity children reserve for adults who aren't fooling anyone. "You both look weird."

"Weird?" Chris turned from the stove, spatula suspended mid-air.

"Like when Miss Andrews talks about serious things." Louise pulled Bear Elephant closer, small fingers curling into his worn fur. "All smiley but with worried eyes."

Leah's gaze met Chris's across the kitchen's expanse. The carefully scripted introduction they'd practiced in whispers at dawn dissolved against their daughter's perception. Some truths could not be softened with rehearsal.

Chris placed a misshapen pancake on Louise's plate. "This one's supposed to be a lion." The admission carried subtle apology, not just for the pancake's failed artistry.

"It looks more like a potato." Louise poked it with her fork, suspicion momentarily replaced by the honest evaluation only children provide.

The unexpected observation startled a genuine laugh from both adults. Tension broke like thin ice underfoot, reminding them of the resilient child at the center of their careful navigation.

"We do want to talk about something important," Leah said, sliding into the chair beside Louise. Her hand hovered near her daughter's arm, not quite touching, as if uncertain whether contact would comfort or constrain. "Something we should have explained before."

Louise set down her fork with deliberate care. Her small shoulders squared with determination that mirrored Chris's stance before difficult conversations. "About Aunt Terry?"

"Partly." Chris joined them at the table, abandoning the remaining pancake batter. "Remember how you asked about what makes someone a real daddy?"

Louise nodded, her fingers finding Bear Elephant's paw. "Aunt Terry said you weren't my real daddy."

The borrowed phrase hung between them, adult language in a child's voice, its clinical terminology incongruous with the stuffed animal clutched in small hands.

Chris reached across the table. His hand, callused from guitar strings, enveloped Louise's smaller one. "You know how sometimes when you help me bake cookies, we need different ingredients to make something new?"

Another nod, more tentative this time, wariness evident in the slight tilt of her head.

"Well, making a baby is kind of like that too. It takes a little piece from a mommy and a little piece from a daddy, and they mix together to start making a baby."

Louise's brow furrowed, creating tiny valleys of concentration. "Like when we put flour and eggs together?"

"Similar." Chris smiled, genuine warmth breaking through his anxiety. "The daddy who gave his piece to help start you wasn't me. It was someone named Ryan."

Louise's eyes widened, recognition flickering across her features. "Ryan? Was he the man at my school? The one looking at my pictures?"

The unexpected connection jolted Leah from careful script to unplanned territory. Her fingers pressed against the table's edge, seeking stability. "You remember him?"

Louise nodded, her lower lip caught between her teeth. "He talked to me when you were getting my coat." Her gaze shifted to Chris, confusion evident in the small furrow between her brows. "But I didn't like him much. He smelled funny."

"Funny how?" Leah asked, curious despite herself.

"Like Grandpa Tom's shaving cream, but too much." Louise wrinkled her nose. "And he asked weird questions."

Chris and Leah exchanged glances, another piece falling into place. Ryan's interaction with Louise had been more intrusive than they'd realized.

"Yes, that was Ryan," Leah confirmed, her voice steadier than the trembling in her chest would suggest. "He's connected to you because he helped make you. But Chris became your daddy by being here every day."

Louise's gaze dropped to her pancake, fork abandoned as she poked the misshapen lion-potato with absolute focus. "Did Ryan not want to be my daddy before?"

The question pierced Leah's carefully constructed explanation. Direct. Unavoidable. The truth they'd hoped to soften with metaphor.

"When you were still growing inside me, Ryan wasn't ready to be a father." Leah measured each word, balancing honesty against protection. "He signed papers saying he didn't want to be your daddy."

"Why does he want me now?" Louise looked up, her question carrying the innocent perplexity of a child unable to comprehend adult inconstancy.

"Sometimes grown-ups change their minds," Chris said carefully. "He's talking to people called lawyers and judges about it."

"That's why Aunt Terry said those things," Leah added, her hand finally settling on Louise's arm. "About blood and being a real Johnson."

Louise abandoned all pretense of breakfast. She pulled Bear Elephant fully into her lap, an instinctive gathering of allies. "Is Ryan going to take me away?"

The question they'd dreaded most, delivered with the devastating directness only children possess.

"No." Chris's voice carried absolute certainty despite the doubts that had kept both adults awake for weeks. "We won't let that happen."

"But he might want to meet you," Leah added, her hand joining Chris's around Louise's. Three sets of fingers interlaced across the breakfast table, a physical manifestation of their unity. "The judges will decide what happens next."

Louise's gaze traveled to the family photos lining the wall. Her eyes lingered on one from her third birthday: Chris with her on his shoulders, both their faces caught mid-laugh, Leah looking up at them with unguarded love.

"Will I have to call him Daddy too?" Her voice had shrunk.

"No, sweetheart." Leah squeezed Louise's hand. "You decide what feels right to you."

Louise looked straight at Chris, her dark eyes holding his with an intensity that belied her age. "But you're my daddy." The declaration emerged with childlike ferocity, the 'but' carrying all her confusion, fear, and certainty.

The simple statement struck Chris with physical force. His eyes glistened in the morning light, hands tightening around the smaller ones they held. "That's right, Sunshine. I'll always be your daddy."

"No matter what happens with Ryan or the judges or anyone else," Leah added, her voice steady despite the tremor in her fingers.

Louise studied their faces, something shifting in her expression. The tightness around her eyes eased, like sunshine breaking through storm clouds.

"Is that why my tummy hurt at night?" She patted Bear Elephant's head as if consoling a friend sharing her concerns. "Because I heard grown-up whispers about a different daddy?"

Leah's breath caught. The description so viscerally accurate it stopped her heart for one beat, then restarted it with painful clarity.

"That's exactly it," Chris said, his thumb tracing small circles on Louise's palm. "Worries can feel that way when we don't understand them."

"Did Miss Andrews show you my pictures?" Louise asked, her expression suggesting she'd stumbled upon a connection between school and home that surprised her.

Leah nodded. "Miss Andrews was concerned about you. She thought you might be worried about something."

Louise slid from her chair, the movement carrying purpose rather than retreat. She walked to the counter where her art supplies waited, placed there the night before with deliberate hope. Her small fingers sorted through crayons with care that belied her age.

"Can I draw now?" She selected bright green. Yellow. Purple. Colors absent from her recent artwork.

"Of course." Leah cleared space at the table, relief coursing through her at this simple request. "Finish your pancake first?"

Louise returned to her seat. She cut the misshapen lion into triangles, approaching breakfast with newfound determination. "Aunt Terry said mean things about you too, Mommy."

Leah's hands stilled in the act of gathering syrupy plates. "What things, sweet girl?"

"That you tricked Daddy." Louise speared a pancake triangle, her focus on the food allowing the difficult words to emerge. "That you weren't a real Johnson either."

Chris's jaw tightened, a muscle working beneath the skin. "Aunt Terry was wrong to say those things."

"Especially where you could hear them," Leah added.

"They didn't know I was there," Louise explained, her voice dropping to a conspiratorial whisper. "I was hiding in the big cabinet with the fancy plates. Aunt Terry was talking to Aunt Kourtney and Uncle Tyler."

The revelation sent a chill through Leah's spine—her daughter concealed in darkness, absorbing toxic words like poison. Chris's hand clenched around his coffee mug, knuckles whitening.

Louise chewed thoughtfully, processing with methodical consideration. "Grandma Mary wasn't there."

Leah and Chris exchanged glances, this clarification adding another layer to their understanding. Not just Terry's cruelty, but Louise's careful cataloging of who said what, who was present, who might have intervened.

"Families are complicated sometimes," Chris said, his words carrying the weight of recent confrontations. "Even grown-ups disagree about important things."

"Like what makes a real family?" Louise asked, the question emerging with simple profundity.

The question hung suspended in morning light. Innocent yet devastating in its accuracy.

Chris leaned forward, elbows on the table in a way they usually discouraged. "What do you think makes a real family, Sunshine?"

Louise considered this with solemn concentration, her fork abandoned beside the half-eaten pancake. "People who love you even when you're cranky. Who know about monsters under beds and how to fix broken toys." She paused, then added with four-year-old logic, "And who make the best pancake animals, even when they look like potatoes."

Something loosened in Leah's chest. A knot unraveling after weeks of tightening. Her daughter's wisdom cutting through adult complications with devastating accuracy.

"That's exactly right." Chris's voice carried quiet wonder, his gaze fixed on his daughter's face as if seeing her anew. "That's what real family means."

Louise finished her pancake with renewed purpose. She reached for her crayons, arranging them in order. Green first. The color of growing things.

"Can I draw our family?" She smoothed white paper with her palm. "The real one?"

"I'd like that very much." Leah's voice caught on unexpected emotion.

They sat in companionable silence. Louise's crayon moved with focused intensity. Green became grass beneath three figures holding hands. Yellow sunshine blazed above. No storm clouds. No question marks about belonging.

Chris rose to clear breakfast dishes. His hand brushed Leah's shoulder in passing, a silent acknowledgment of victory, however temporary. Their strategy had worked. Truth, carefully offered, had dissolved fears that protection had only magnified.

"Look." Louise held up her drawing with pride that had been absent for weeks. "It's us at the park."

Three figures stood beneath a crayon sun. The smallest between two larger ones, all hands connected. No division lines. No shadowed faces. Just three people and a small brown bear with disproportionately large ears.

"You put Bear Elephant in our family picture." Chris smiled, returning to the table.

"He's family too." Louise stated this as self-evident fact, her expression suggesting the adults might be slow to grasp obvious truths. "He keeps secrets and scares away bad dreams. Plus, he's really good at listening."

Leah studied the drawing with reverence. The bright colors. The connected hands. The return of joy absent from Louise's artwork for weeks.

"Can we put this on the refrigerator?" Leah asked. "Right where everyone can see it?"

Louise nodded, adding one final touch – musical notes floating in the air. Their family ritual captured in crayon.

Leah secured the drawing with alphabet magnets, her fingers lingering on the edges. The refrigerator gallery now showed their family's journey: older drawings where Louise first called Chris "Daddy," holiday memories, and now this bright reclamation of security.

"I got another question." Louise retrieved Bear Elephant from her chair, clutching him against her chest. "Will Ryan try to take me to his house?"

The directness caught them off-guard again. Their daughter's ability to articulate her deepest fears felt both gift and heartbreak.

Leah knelt to Louise's level, bringing their eyes into alignment. "We're doing everything we can to make sure that doesn't happen."

"The judges listen to what's best for children," Chris added, joining them on the kitchen floor. "And we believe being with us is what's best for you."

"I think so too." Louise nodded with serious conviction. "Ryan doesn't know about monster-check or how I like my sandwiches cut in triangles not squares. And he probably doesn't know Bear Elephant's real name."

"What's Bear Elephant's real name?" Chris asked, playing along.

"Sir Elephant Bear the Third," Louise announced with the gravity of someone revealing state secrets. "But only family gets to know that."

The observation, so childlike yet profound, cracked something open in Leah's chest. Relief poured through the fissure. Their daughter understood. In her own way, she comprehended what truly mattered in parenthood.

"Would you like to practice guitar today?" Chris asked, his voice lighter than it had been in weeks. "We could work on that new song."

Louise's face transformed. The shadow that had haunted her features dissolved like morning mist. "The one about sunshine?"

"That's the one." Chris touched her nose gently. "Your special song."

Louise spun toward her room, Bear Elephant clutched against her chest. "I'll get my guitar! The little one with the purple stickers!"

Her footsteps pattered up the stairs. Energy restored. Movement fluid again after weeks of careful navigation.

Leah leaned against Chris. Their bodies aligned with familiar ease, fitting together in the geography of shared burden. "That went better than I expected."

"She's stronger than we realized." Chris's arm circled Leah's waist. "Wiser too."

"We should have trusted her with the truth sooner." Regret tinged Leah's words.

"We did what seemed right then." Chris pressed his lips to her temple. "And now we know better."

Louise's laughter drifted down the stairs. The sound carried notes they hadn't heard in weeks—unguarded joy, security reclaimed through honesty rather than protection.

Louise appeared in the doorway, her small guitar slung across her body with serious intent. "Ready, Daddy!"

Chris squeezed Leah's hand once before moving toward their daughter.

Leah watched them go. Listened as guitar strings came to life under their hands. The melody rose and fell, father and daughter creating harmony in the face of potential discord.

For now, at least, truth had conquered fear. Their strategy had worked. Louise's laughter filled their home again.

The phone rang. Atty. Williams flashed on the caller ID.

Leah let it go to voicemail.

Today belonged to guitar songs and crayon drawings. To their family, reclaiming joy one honest conversation at a time.

To truth that had surprisingly, if only temporarily, worked.

CHAPTER 14

When Love Becomes Surveillance

The house felt different now—lighter somehow, as if honesty had lifted invisible weight from familiar walls. Leah lingered in the doorway of the music room, watching Chris and Louise hunched over their guitars. Afternoon sunlight spilled through windows, transforming ordinary instruments into vessels of gold. Louise's tongue poked from the corner of her mouth, the exact habit Chris displayed when tackling difficult compositions.

"That's it!" Chris's voice lifted with genuine pride. "Perfect G chord."

Louise's face brightened. The smile reached her eyes in ways Leah hadn't witnessed in too long. Gone were the shadows that had haunted their daughter's expressions, replaced by the unguarded joy they'd feared might never return.

We did the right thing, Leah thought to herself.

The weight that had crushed her that night in the bathroom, collapsed on the floor surrounded by Louise's darkening artwork, had lifted. In its place bloomed cautious hope. Their decision to tell Louise the truth about Ryan had worked. Miss Andrews had called to report "remarkable improvement" at school—raising her hand during circle time, playing with friends again, even volunteering for the class puppet show.

She leaned against Chris's side, her small body fitting against him with natural ease. No hesitation. No questions about belonging. Just the unthinking confidence of a child secure in her place.

The doorbell's chime fractured their moment.

"I'll get it," Leah offered.

She moved through the hall, trailing her fingers along the wall as if to maintain connection with the sanctuary behind her. A delivery courier waited on the porch, holding an oversized manila envelope.

"Delivery for Leah Johnson? Signature required."

The heavy cream paper bore the Wallace & Associates letterhead.

Leah carried the envelope to the kitchen, her fingers numb against its smooth surface. She spread its contents across the counter. Photographs slid across granite in a damning cascade.

Louise in the swing at the park, tears streaming down her face. The image conveniently omitted the moments before, when she'd fallen from the monkey bars and Chris had picked her up, brushed her off, helped her process her fear.

Louise at church, face distorted mid-tantrum. The camera had captured the moment perfectly, erasing the context—her rising fever that had reached 102° by bedtime, the gentle way they'd taken her home to rest.

Louise at school, sitting alone during lunch. The isolation frozen in time, with no follow-up image of her rejoining friends after finishing her apple.

Each photograph carried a timestamp and brief notation: "Child displaying signs of emotional distress," "Social isolation observed," "Inconsistent parenting approach."

"What is it?" Chris asked from the doorway.

His question hung between them. The joy from moments before had vanished, replaced by the familiar weight of impending conflict.

Leah pushed the photographs toward him. "Wallace & Associates. They've been watching her."

Chris's face hardened as he moved through the images. His finger lingered on the deliberately cropped art class photo. "They manipulated this. I was in that drawing. I saw it when we picked her up."

"They're building a case that she's unhappy," Leah whispered, glancing toward the music room where Louise remained with her guitar. "That we're causing her emotional distress."

A note slipped from the envelope's interior pocket. Typed on firm letterhead, its message read: *"A preview of evidence to be presented regarding minor child's emotional wellbeing. This is standard discovery procedure as we prepare for proceedings."*

The clinical language didn't disguise what this really was. Chris recognized it immediately—not legal courtesy, but intimidation wrapped in professional letterhead.

"This is psychological warfare," Chris said, jaw clenched. "They're not sharing evidence—they're trying to break us down before we even get to court."

Leah swept the photographs together with trembling fingers. "The church tantrum—that was her fever starting. We took her home immediately."

"And this one—" Chris tapped Louise looking tearful in their front yard. "This was when that neighbor's dog got loose. She was fine minutes later."

"They're documenting everything without context," Leah said, her voice fracturing around the edges. "Creating a narrative of a troubled child."

Leah stared at the photographs, recognizing professional-grade psychological warfare when she saw it. Wallace & Associates played at a level that made Williams's conventional legal approach feel almost quaint.

Dad would know how to counter this. The thought surfaced before she could stop it. John Miller had spent decades advising clients through hostile business situations—he'd understand Ryan's financial strategy and legal maneuvering because he'd guided others through similar battles.

Her hand moved toward her phone, then retreated. No. She'd left that world behind for good reason. Calling him would mean admitting she needed tactics she'd spent years condemning, would mean exposing Chris and Louise to her father's particular brand of strategic calculation.

They would handle this themselves. Somehow.

The temporary victory of recent weeks dissolved beneath her fingers. The sense of accomplishment that had carried her through days of renewed hope shrank against this new assault. She could see the strategy clearly now—Ryan's legal team wasn't just building a case, they were launching a campaign designed to make them surrender before the battle even began.

The doorbell rang again.

Leah stiffened, half-expecting more legal documents, more evidence of invasion. Her hand pressed flat against the counter, steadying herself before moving toward the door.

Terry stood on their porch.

Her expression arranged itself in practiced concern, eyebrows drawn together, mouth curved in sympathetic lines that never reached her eyes. She wore her church committee outfit—beige cardigan with embroidered flowers, sensible pumps, cross pendant hanging at her throat.

"Mary mentioned Louise wasn't well." Terry held out a container. "Brought cookies."

The timing confirmed everything. This wasn't coincidence—it was reconnaissance.

"She's fine," Leah said, not stepping aside to invite her in. "Just practicing guitar with Chris."

"Oh." Disappointment flickered across Terry's features before disappearing behind renewed concern. "I thought she might need cheering up. I brought cookies."

She extended a container of perfectly arranged chocolate chip cookies, Louise's favorite.

"That's thoughtful. But we're having a family afternoon."

Terry's smile tightened. "That's why I'm here. Louise, with all this uncertainty..."

From inside came the sound of Louise's laughter, bright and unrestrained. Terry's head tilted slightly, as if this evidence of happiness contradicted her prepared narrative.

"Louise?" Terry called past Leah. "It's Aunt Terry! I've brought your favorite cookies!"

"We're in the middle of something," Leah said, shifting to block the doorway more completely.

But Louise had heard. She appeared in the hallway, guitar still hanging from her small shoulders by its strap. "Aunt Terry?"

Her voice carried none of the unguarded joy it had held moments before, only wary assessment. The transformation cut through Leah with painful clarity. Their daughter had learned to be cautious in Terry's presence.

"There's my sweet girl!" Terry exclaimed, pushing slightly past Leah's boundary. "I've missed you at church activities! Are you feeling better?"

Louise looked to Leah, then past her to where Chris had appeared. The silent communication between them—parent to child—carried the weight of their recent honest conversation.

"I'm learning guitar," Louise said finally, her voice measured in ways no four-year-old's should be. "With Daddy!"

The emphasis on the final word wasn't subtle. Terry's smile flickered momentarily.

"How wonderful," she said, voice honey-sweet but eyes watchful. "And how are you feeling about everything? Your mommy and daddy told me you've been having some... concerns?"

The question hung between them, deliberately crafted to extract something usable. Something that could be twisted into evidence. Leah realized with growing alarm that Terry wasn't here out of family concern—she was here gathering intelligence, just like those photographs.

Before Leah could intervene, Louise stepped forward. Her expression carried the particular solemnity children adopt when addressing matters they recognize as important.

"I'm okay now," she stated with surprising clarity. "Mommy and Daddy told me about Ryan. That he's connected by blood but Daddy is connected by love. And love is more important."

Terry's expression shifted microscopically, satisfaction at extracting useful information warring with disappointment at its content.

"They told you about Ryan?" Terry asked, voice dripping with manufactured concern. "That must have been very confusing for you, sweetheart."

"Not really," Louise shrugged with the beautiful simplicity of childhood. "It's like when we make cookies. You need different parts to make something good."

"What an... interesting way to explain things," Terry said, her gaze sliding accusingly toward Leah. "I wonder if others would find that age-appropriate."

The threat, thinly veiled, landed exactly as intended. Leah felt the victory of recent weeks crumbling beneath this new assault. Their honesty, their hard-won family understanding, was being transformed into a weapon before her eyes.

"I think we'll need to continue this another time," Chris said, stepping forward to place a protective hand on Louise's shoulder. "We're in the middle of a lesson."

"Of course," Terry retreated with practiced dignity. "I completely understand. Family time is precious..." Her pause carried deliberate weight. "...especially when circumstances are so uncertain."

The door closed on Terry's departing figure. The sound echoed through their entryway like a prison gate sealing shut.

Leah gathered the scattered photographs with unsteady hands. Their temporary triumph dissolved into bitter uncertainty. The honesty that had seemed to heal Louise had also created new vulnerabilities—every word, every explanation, every moment of family healing now transformed into potential ammunition.

"She's going to use this against us," Leah whispered, holding up the Wallace & Associates letter. "Document what we told Louise and find a way to make it sound inappropriate."

Chris moved to the refrigerator. He gathered Louise's drawings, the bright family portraits she'd created since their honest conversation. "These tell the true story," he said, voice steady despite the fear evident in his eyes. "She's healing, not breaking."

"But will a judge see that?" Leah asked, the question hanging between them as Louise disappeared back into the music room.

The soft sounds of her guitar drifted through their home, halting but determined notes strung together with stubborn hope. The melody provided counterpoint to the evidence spread across their kitchen counter.

"They're not just watching," Chris said, his finger tracing one particularly egregious cropped photograph. "They're manufacturing a crisis. Making it look like we're the problem when we're the ones who've been honest with her."

"Every moment of our lives is being documented and twisted," Leah said, gesturing toward the surveillance photos. "They're turning normal parenting challenges into evidence of instability."

"We have our own evidence," Chris said, tapping the folder of Louise's artwork. "Her teachers, her improvements at school, her own words."

"Her words that Terry just documented," Leah countered, palm pressing against her forehead. "Words that could become 'evidence of parental alienation' or 'age-inappropriate discussions' if someone wanted to twist them that way."

Louise appeared in the doorway, guitar abandoned. "Is Aunt Terry mad at me?"

The question struck with innocent precision. Leah knelt to her level, careful to keep her expression neutral. "No, sweet girl. Why do you ask?"

"She looked mad when I talked about Ryan." Louise's perception remained unclouded by adult rationalizations. "Her eyes got tight like when Miss Andrews doesn't like an answer."

Chris joined them, creating a protective circle around their daughter. "You didn't do anything wrong. You told the truth."

"Is the truth bad?" Louise asked.

The question contained such profound simplicity that it momentarily silenced both adults. In its wake hung the central paradox of their situation—truth that had healed their daughter now threatened her security.

"No," Leah said finally. "The truth is never bad. But sometimes people try to make it sound different than it is."

Louise nodded, accepting this with the particular wisdom children sometimes display. "Like when Tommy said I pushed him but I just bumped him by accident."

"Exactly like that," Chris agreed.

Louise studied their faces with careful attention. "Are you scared?"

Another direct question that pierced their careful parental shields. Leah exchanged glances with Chris, silent communication passing between them.

"A little," Chris admitted. "But being scared doesn't mean we stop doing what's right."

"Like when I was scared of the deep end but tried anyway?"

"Yup!" Leah confirmed, smoothing Louise's hair back from her forehead. "Being brave isn't about not feeling scared. It's about doing things even when they're scary."

Louise nodded, considering this with serious concentration. Then, with the remarkable resilience of childhood, her mood shifted. "Can we finish our song now?"

"Absolutely," Chris said, relief threading through his voice at this evidence of their daughter's unbroken spirit. "Why don't you go set up the music stands?"

As Louise disappeared back into the music room, Leah gathered the photographs from Wallace & Associates. She slid them back into their envelope with decisive movements.

"We did the right thing," she said, voice steady despite the doubt churning beneath her certainty. "Even if they try to use it against us."

Chris nodded, collecting Louise's drawings into a folder—documentation of their own to counter the manipulated narrative being constructed against them. "Her artwork alone shows the difference. Before, everything was dark. Now there's color again."

"And if a judge doesn't see it?" Leah asked, giving voice to the fear that had lodged between her ribs.

"Then we keep fighting," Chris said, simple certainty replacing his earlier doubt. "We keep telling the truth. We keep being her parents."

From the music room came the sound of Louise humming, a spontaneous melody that carried none of the darkness that had haunted her before. The evidence of her healing spirit provided momentary comfort against the gathering threats.

Their accomplishment remained real. Their doubt, equally so. Victory and vulnerability had become inseparable companions in their journey forward.

Leah placed her hand over the Wallace & Associates envelope. "I want to burn these."

"I know," Chris agreed. "But we need to show Williams. Document their harassment."

The truth of his assessment didn't lessen its bitterness. Leah nodded, shoulders straightening with renewed resolve. "They won't stop, will they?"

"No," Chris said, certainty hardening his voice. "But neither will we."

The battle had merely entered a new phase—one where their greatest strength, their honesty with Louise, was being weaponized against them. But as Louise's voice drifted from the music room, bright with renewed confidence, they knew they had made the right choice.

The Wallace & Associates building gleamed with corporate authority against the sky, its glass façade reflecting clouds with cold indifference. Terry O'Donnell smoothed her floral cardigan, the one reserved for church committee meetings, and clutched her cross pendant as she entered the revolving door for the second time. The marble lobby still intimidated her, each polished surface a reminder of worlds beyond her comprehension.

The fourteenth floor conference room held different energy today—not just Wallace's controlled confidence, but the presence of someone new. Ryan Matthews rose as she entered, his tailored suit and engineering background immediately cataloging her as useful despite obvious limitations.

"Ms. O'Donnell." Wallace's introduction carried professional warmth. "This is Ryan Matthews, Louise's father."

Their handshake lingered as assessment passed between them. Ryan saw provincial dress and eager righteousness. Terry saw the sophisticated success Chris deserved to understand—not the manipulative woman who'd ensnared him with pregnancy and family drama.

"Thank you for your concern about Louise," Ryan said, his voice carrying practiced sympathy that didn't quite reach his calculating eyes.

Terry straightened in her chair, mission crystallizing. "I'm doing what's right for the family. Chris has been drawn into something that isn't his fault."

Ryan's eyebrows lifted fractionally. This wasn't the family conspiracy he'd anticipated, but something more complex—protective instincts misdirected toward him rather than against him.

"Tell me about your recent observations," Wallace prompted, opening his legal pad with methodical movements.

Terry extracted her floral notebook, pages filled with careful documentation. "They've been filling Louise's head with confusing ideas. About different types of fathers, about choosing family over blood." Her voice dropped with disapproval. "Making a four-year-old process adult concepts she can't understand."

"What exactly did Louise say?" Ryan leaned forward, genuine curiosity replacing his initial skepticism.

"That you're connected by blood but Chris is connected by love. That both matter, but one earned its place." Terry's repetition carried theatrical concern. "No child should have to navigate such complexity."

Wallace made notes with practiced efficiency. "Age-inappropriate discussions of family structure could constitute psychological manipulation."

Ryan studied Terry's earnest expression, recognizing something useful despite her obvious intellectual limitations. Her genuine concern for Chris provided cover for motivations that might otherwise seem calculated.

"You believe Leah orchestrated this approach?" Ryan asked carefully.

"Of course." Terry's certainty carried years of family management. "She's always been too clever for her own good. Using pregnancy to trap Chris into raising another man's child, then manipulating Louise to ensure her position."

The crude assessment struck Ryan with unexpected force. His engineering mind automatically processed the systematic nature of Terry's accusations, but something deeper recoiled from hearing his daughter reduced to strategic asset in adult warfare.

"Chris isn't the problem," Terry continued, warming to her theme. "He's a good boy who's been taken advantage of by someone who understands exactly how to exploit his kindness."

Ryan felt pieces falling into place—not the family conspiracy he'd imagined, but something more personally useful. Terry's protective instincts toward Chris could provide cover for legal strategies that might otherwise appear calculating.

"What kind of evidence have you documented?" Wallace asked, his pen poised above yellow legal paper.

Terry flipped through notebook pages with obvious pride. "I visited them just yesterday. Louise was confused about family structure, parroting complex explanations she clearly didn't understand." Her voice gained momentum. "When I asked how she was feeling about everything, she recited this rehearsed response about blood versus love connections. It was clearly coached."

Ryan scanned Terry's notes, recognizing the importance of fresh documentation. A witness this incapable of sophisticated deception would be difficult to discredit.

"These observations are quite detailed," Ryan said, though he privately winced at the spelling errors and elementary analysis.

"I've been very careful," Terry replied with satisfaction. "Someone needed to pay attention while Chris was being blinded by manipulation."

Wallace gathered the notebook, already calculating how Terry's testimony could be positioned. "Your community standing and family connections establish credibility that opposing counsel can't easily challenge."

Ryan felt strategy crystallizing despite his reservations about Terry's methods. Her obvious limitations would actually strengthen their case—judges trusted witnesses who seemed incapable of calculation.

"The child used some analogy about making cookies," Terry continued, consulting her notes. "Saying you need different parts to make something good. When I questioned whether this was age-appropriate, Leah and Chris immediately shut down the conversation."

"Defensive behavior," Wallace observed, making additional notes.

"Very defensive," Terry agreed. "Chris insisted they were in the middle of a lesson and needed to continue another time. But I could see Louise was troubled by having to explain such adult concepts."

Ryan absorbed this information, though something about Terry's interpretation felt slightly off. The cookie analogy sounded like something a child might naturally create, not necessarily coached manipulation.

"Will you provide formal testimony?" Wallace asked. "Your observations about Louise's behavioral changes could be crucial evidence."

Terry nodded enthusiastically. "I'd do anything to protect Chris from making a permanent mistake he'd regret forever."

The phrase hung between them, revealing the heart of Terry's motivation. Not malice toward Louise, but misguided protection of Chris disguised as concern for biological relationships.

Ryan studied her across the mahogany table, recognizing both opportunity and danger. Terry's genuine feelings for Chris would make her testimony more compelling, but her intellectual limitations could easily be exposed under cross-examination.

"We appreciate your willingness to help," Ryan said finally, though uncertainty colored his voice.

Terry beamed with validation, straightening in her chair like a child praised for good behavior. "Chris will understand someday that everything I did was to save him from repeating his father's mistakes."

The meeting concluded with strategic efficiency, but Ryan carried reservations that felt increasingly significant. Terry's help came with complications he was only beginning to understand—her protective instincts could serve his case, but they also revealed motivations that made him question his own.

The elevator descended fourteen floors. Terry watched numbers illuminate in reverse sequence. Her missionary work completed. Evidence delivered to those with power to restore proper order.

In the lobby, light streamed through glass doors. Saint Michael's spire visible in the distance. Terry moved toward it with renewed purpose. Each step carrying the weight of righteousness satisfied. Of moral authority exercised in defense of proper family.

Behind her, in the corner conference room, Ryan remained at the window. The signed affidavits lay on the table behind him. His reflection stared back at him from the glass.

"Are we doing the right thing?" he asked Wallace, who arranged documents.

"We're doing the necessary thing," Wallace replied. His distinction carried practical weight. "To win."

Ryan nodded once. The moment of doubt dissolved like morning fog. The path forward crystallized with renewed clarity.

Justice and victory had become indistinguishable. The end justifying increasingly questionable means.

Louise deserved her real father. Whatever it cost. In family peace. In moral certainty.

In what remained of his better self.

CHAPTER 15

The Currency of Betrayal

Several weeks had passed since the night Leah and Chris had sat with Louise and explained the truth about Ryan, their words careful and measured, seasoned with age-appropriate honesty. The kitchen felt peaceful again—their daughter's laughter had returned to its natural rhythm, her artwork blooming with color where shadows had once dominated. The refrigerator door displayed this progression in crayon and construction paper, a gallery of emotional recovery.

Evening light slipped through the kitchen windows, casting their family dinner in warm tones. Louise twirled pasta around her fork with intense concentration, her brow furrowed in the same way Chris's did when he composed music. Sauce dotted her chin as she worked through the architectural challenge of a particularly long strand of spaghetti.

Leah watched her daughter with the mixture of wonder and vigilance that had become her emotional baseline—gratitude for each ordinary moment shadowed by knowledge of how fragile such peace could be.

"What does betting mean?" Louise set down her fork.

Leah's hand froze. "Where did you hear that?"

"Grandma Emma's party."

Chris glanced at Leah across the table, caution evident in his expression.

"What happened at the party?" he asked, voice carefully controlled.

"Aunt Terry had these special jars." Louise resumed twirling her spaghetti, interest already drifting. "People were putting money in them and little pieces of paper."

The kitchen clock seemed to tick more loudly in the sudden tension. Leah set down her water glass with deliberate care.

"What kind of jars?" Leah asked, each word shaped with neutral calm.

"Just glass ones." Louise took another bite, sauce smearing across her cheek. "People wrote their names on the papers and put them inside with the money."

Chris's fingers tightened around his fork. "Did anyone say what they were for?"

Louise considered this with dreamy distraction. "Something about you guys. Uncle Tyler laughed. Aunt Kourtney too." She reached for her milk, oblivious to the impact of her words. "What does betting mean? Is it a grown-up game?"

Leah breathed carefully, each inhalation a conscious act of control. She wiped sauce from Louise's chin with a napkin, the gentle maternal gesture contrasting with the rage building beneath her composure.

"People guess what might happen," Leah said. "For money."

Louise nodded, absorbing this explanation with pragmatic acceptance. "Oh. Like when Tommy says he'll give me his cookies if I can climb higher than him at recess?"

"Something like that," Leah agreed, grateful for the innocent comparison.

Chris set his fork down deliberately. "Do you remember anything else about the jars, Sunshine? What people were saying about them?"

Louise speared another meatball before answering. "Just that Aunt Terry hid them when you and Mommy came back in the room."

The revelation twisted deeper. Leah swallowed against the bitterness rising in her throat.

"I followed her," Louise continued with casual honesty. "She put them in Grandma Emma's garage behind the other glasses. On the high shelf with the fancy cups nobody uses."

Chris's knuckles whitened around his water glass. "Why did she hide them?"

Louise asked with genuine curiosity.

The innocent question demanded an answer that preserved childhood while acknowledging truth—the impossible balance they'd navigated for weeks.

"Sometimes grown-ups don't want other grown-ups to know what games they're playing," Chris said, each syllable measured carefully.

Louise nodded, accepting this explanation with beautiful simplicity. "Can I have ice cream now?"

The ordinary request anchored them back to the present moment. Leah rose, grateful for the excuse to turn away, to hide the tears threatening at the corners of her eyes.

"Of course, sweet girl. Vanilla or chocolate?"

"Both?" Louise's hopeful question drew a genuine laugh from Chris despite everything.

"Just this once," he agreed, ruffling her hair with deliberate gentleness.

While Louise ate her dessert, they maintained the performance of normalcy—simple questions about preschool friends, weekend plans, the practiced routine of family life continuing while beneath the surface, understanding shifted and realigned.

Later, after teeth were brushed and bedtime stories read, Louise drifted to sleep clutching Bear Elephant. Chris and Leah stood in the hallway outside her room, the dim nightlight casting their shadows large against the wall.

Chris pressed his forehead against the wall, eyes closed. His shoulders trembled with rage he couldn't express while Louise slept nearby.

"Our family," he whispered, voice cracking. "My family did this."

Leah moved behind him, her palm settling between his shoulder blades. She felt the knots of tension beneath her fingers, muscles coiled tight with betrayal.

"Come here," she whispered, turning him toward her.

His eyes held grief deeper than anger—the particular pain of someone losing childhood certainties about love and loyalty. She cradled his face between her palms, thumbs brushing across cheekbones that had sharpened with stress.

"Jars with money." His voice emerged hollow with disbelief. "Secret betting games they hid from us. At a family gathering while we were there."

"While smiling to our faces," Leah finished. "While holding our daughter."

They moved toward the kitchen, now transformed into a space for reckoning. Leah leaned against the counter, arms wrapped around herself against an internal chill. Chris paced in tight circles, restless movement of a man whose understanding of family had collapsed.

"It wasn't enough to whisper behind our backs," he said finally. "They made it into entertainment. With actual money."

"What are you going to do?" Leah asked, though she sensed his internal struggle.

Chris turned to her suddenly, his expression raw with remorse. "You saw this coming. You tried to tell me. About Terry. About all of them."

Leah remained silent, allowing him space to continue.

"I kept making excuses. Kept dismissing your concerns. Believing they wouldn't go that far." He ran his hand through his hair in frustration. "I'm sorry, Leah. I should have trusted what you saw."

"You wanted to believe in them," she said—not absolution, but acknowledgment. "They're your family."

"No." He shook his head with certainty. "You and Louise are my family. The one I chose. The one that matters."

Leah crossed the kitchen, stepping into his space. Her arms circled his waist, head resting against his chest where his heartbeat carried fear and anger in equal measure.

"Part of me hopes it's not what we think," he confessed. "That Louise misunderstood. That there's some innocent explanation for jars with money and names." He exhaled shakily. "But why hide them when we entered the room? Why keep secrets unless they knew it would hurt us?"

"I know," she whispered. "But whatever it is, we face it together."

He held her tighter, as if physical connection might anchor them both against emotional undertow. "We need to find those jars."

"You believe her about where they're hidden?"

"Louise remembers everything." Chris's voice steadied, finding strength in practical action. "Down to which shelf they're on."

Leah looked up at him, her gaze unwavering. "What are you planning to do?"

"Get evidence." His voice hardened with purpose. "Then decide who in my family deserves to remain in our lives."

She nodded, her own decision forming in perfect harmony with his. "Tomorrow?"

"Tomorrow." Chris pressed his lips to her forehead. "We face this together."

They stood in their kitchen, the remains of dinner still on the table between them. Family photographs watched from the walls, frozen moments of joy now complicated by new understanding. Louise's artwork hung from the refrigerator in bright defiance of darkness—crayon figures holding hands beneath an enormous sun, the world as she believed it should be.

Outside, night gathered into fullness. Inside, in the quiet kitchen, Chris and Leah held each other, gathering strength for tomorrow's revelation, bodies aligned against whatever would come.

The kitchen clock ticked steadily forward, counting down the hours until morning would deliver truth hidden behind unused glasses, on high shelves, in places they were never meant to find.

Sunday afternoon light filtered through the stained glass panel in Grandma Emma's front door, casting fragments of cobalt and amber across the worn welcome mat. Chris paused on the threshold, his finger hovering above the doorbell as if touching it might complete an electrical circuit of painful revelation. In his jacket pocket, the small silver pocket watch he'd brought along sat heavy against his thigh—a prop in this necessary theater, a tangible excuse that might keep his voice steady when everything else threatened to tremble.

"Are you sure about this?" Leah asked, the question carrying all the weight of decisions that can never be unmade.

Chris studied the familiar grain of the wooden door, mapping its knots and whorls as if they might reveal some hidden truth about the family that dwelled behind it. "No," he admitted, the single syllable containing multitudes of doubt. "But I need to know."

Leah's hand found his, her fingers cool against his palm. The simple contact anchored him momentarily, a lifeline in the gathering tempest of uncertainty. "Whatever we find, we find together."

The doorbell's chime echoed through the house, three musical notes that had announced his arrival since childhood visits when this Victorian with its gingerbread trim and wraparound porch had represented sanctuary, unconditional welcome, the very definition of family. Now those same notes carried a question he never thought he'd need to ask: Who among those he loved had wagered on his failure?

Footsteps approached from within, the familiar cadence of his grandfather's gait. The door swung open, revealing Billy Henderson's weathered face, eyes crinkling with genuine pleasure that Chris now studied with newfound suspicion, searching for inauthenticity where he had once assumed only truth.

"Well now," he exclaimed, "this is a surprise!" He stepped back, gesturing them inside with the expansive welcome that had characterized his relationship with the world for decades. "Emma! Look who's come to visit!"

Chris crossed the threshold, the familiar scent of cinnamon and furniture polish wrapping around him like a childhood memory resurrected. The dissonance struck with physical force—how could this space, these people, remain so utterly unchanged while his understanding of family unraveled thread by thread?

"I was just telling Leah I think I left my grandfather's pocket watch in the garage during the party a few weeks ago," he explained, the rehearsed fiction emerging more naturally than he had feared. "I didn't notice until this morning when I was looking for it."

Billy clapped him on the shoulder, the gesture carrying decades of casual affection that Chris now received with unsettling ambivalence. "Always leaving things behind," he chuckled. "Just like when you were ten and forgot your baseball mitt here every other Tuesday."

Emma appeared from the kitchen, flour dusting her apron, her silver hair arranged in the same bob she'd worn for decades. "Chris! Leah! What a lovely surprise." She wiped her hands, leaving ghost-white fingerprints across the blue fabric. "I'm just putting together an apple cobbler. You'll stay for some when it's done?"

The invitation hung between them, innocent and weighted simultaneously. Chris felt Leah's subtle pressure against his side, a physical reminder of their purpose. "We can't stay long," he managed, "but maybe just a quick piece?"

"The watch should be in the garage," he added, gesturing vaguely toward the side door. "Mind if I go look for it? I'm pretty sure I set it down on the workbench when I was helping Grandpa with the lawn chairs."

Emma waved him toward the mudroom. "Of course, dear. You know where everything is. Billy, why don't you help him look while I get Leah some tea?"

Chris caught Leah's eye, a moment of silent communication passing between them—she would manage the kitchen conversation while he investigated the garage. The unspoken coordination of partners navigating treacherous emotional terrain together.

The mudroom stood as transitional space between house and garage, a liminal territory where rubber boots awaited garden work and old jackets hung with patient permanence. Chris paused at the garage door, his grandfather's presence behind him suddenly overwhelming.

"You seem tense, son," Billy observed, his perception unclouded by age. "Everything alright with you and Leah?"

The question carried no judgment, only the gentle concern that had characterized Billy's approach to family matters throughout Chris's life. For a moment, Chris considered unburdening himself, laying the whole sordid betting jar revelation at his grandfather's feet, asking directly for confirmation or denial of his involvement.

Instead, he forced a smile that didn't quite reach his eyes. "Just the usual stress. The custody hearing's coming up soon."

Billy nodded, understanding darkening his gaze. "That is difficult business. But you've got solid ground to stand on—being there every day counts for more than biology in the eyes of any sensible judge."

The garage door opened to reveal the familiar landscape of Billy's organization: garden implements hanging on labeled hooks, holiday decorations in clear plastic bins, the workbench where he had taught Chris how to measure twice and cut once, how patience transformed raw materials into something both beautiful and useful.

"Now, where did you say you left it?" Billy asked as they moved toward the workbench.

Chris's eyes tracked to the high shelves along the back wall, the place Louise had described with such detail. There, behind the crystal punch bowl and champagne coupes, he could just make out the curved edges of glass jars positioned exactly as his daughter had reported. The confirmation sent a wave of nausea through him, despite having steeled himself for this possibility.

"I think it was over here," Chris replied, moving toward the workbench, away from those damning jars. He reached into his pocket, fingers closing around the silver pocket watch he'd brought for this charade. "I was helping you set up the extra chairs, remember? I must have set it down..."

The phone rang from inside the house, its shrill demand piercing the garage's contemplative quiet. Billy glanced toward the door, clearly torn between helping Chris and answering the call.

"That'll be your Uncle Randy about the church committee," Billy sighed, his expression apologetic. "Emma can't hear worth a damn anymore. Would you mind if I grab that? You know the garage better than most—if it's here, you'll find it."

Relief washed through Chris at this unexpected opportunity. "Go ahead," he encouraged, keeping his voice casual. "I'll keep looking. It has to be here somewhere."

Billy nodded gratefully. "Check that upper shelf too, if you don't find it on the bench. Sometimes things migrate in here." He moved toward the door. "Won't be but a minute."

The moment the door closed behind his grandfather, Chris moved with quiet urgency toward the step ladder. The aluminum rungs creaked slightly beneath his weight as he climbed, each step bringing him closer to confirmation he both dreaded and needed. At eye level with the shelf, he could see exactly what Louise had described—two Mason jars partially concealed behind seldom-used serving pieces, their paper labels bearing Terry's unmistakable handwriting.

With careful movements, he eased the first jar forward. "Less than 3 years" proclaimed the label, the prediction itself a paper cut across his heart. Inside, folded slips nestled among currency—twenties, tens, fives, the denominations themselves a casual cruelty. With trembling fingers, he lifted the lid.

He extracted the first slip and unfolded it. Kourtney's looping script filled the small square: "$20 - Less than 3 years. There's no way this marriage survives the custody battle."

The words blurred momentarily as his eyes filled with unexpected moisture. He blinked it away, reaching for another slip. Uncle Randy's block capitals: "$30 - Less than 3 years. Being generous considering he's saddled with another man's child."

Each revelation struck with physical force, each familiar handwriting a separate wound. He reached deeper, fingers closing around a larger denomination—a fifty folded with precise corners. He opened it to find Tyler's distinctive sharp angles: "$50 - Less than 3 years. The adoption attempt proves desperation."

The cruelty lay in the casual certainty, the confidence with which they'd wagered on his failure, on Louise's displacement, on the destruction of the family he'd built through daily acts of love and presence.

Time contracted around him as he methodically examined each slip, taking photos for evidence, creating a mental catalog of betrayal. From the house came the murmur of Billy's voice on the phone, each second of his absence precious. Chris reached for the second jar—"Less than 5 years"—and quickly examined its contents. More slips, more currency, more familiar names and handwriting predicting slightly longer but equally certain failure.

What pierced deepest was what he didn't find—Emma and Billy's names appeared on no betting slip, nor did he see his parents, Susan and Tom Johnson. These absences formed a fragile constellation of loyalty amid a galaxy of betrayal, four stars still shining in what had become an otherwise darkened sky of family connection.

Footsteps approached from the house. Chris took final photos and hastily replaced the lids, sliding the jars back to their original positions. He descended the ladder with practiced quiet, his heart hammering against his ribs with such force he feared it might be audible.

By the time Billy pushed open the door, Chris had positioned himself by the workbench, the silver pocket watch now visible among scattered washers and screws.

"Sorry about that," Billy said, rejoining him. "Randy's in a state about the church fundraiser. These committee people, I swear they think the world will end if we don't have enough prizes for the raffle."

"Found it," Chris announced, voice steadier than he expected as he lifted the watch. "It was right here all along, just hidden under some workshop odds and ends."

Billy smiled, relief softening his weathered features. "Your grandmother would have had my hide if we'd lost another family heirloom. She still hasn't forgiven me for that missing silver serving spoon from her mother's set."

Chris pocketed the timepiece, its weight nothing compared to the knowledge now pressing against his chest. "I should let Leah know we can go. She's probably ready to head out."

As they walked back toward the house, Billy's hand settled on Chris's shoulder, the weight both familiar and suddenly strange. "Everything alright, son? You seem distant today."

The concern in his grandfather's eyes momentarily pierced Chris's protective detachment. The question hovered between them—the opportunity to confront, to demand answers, to ask directly if Billy knew about Mason jars filled with wagers on his grandson's failing marriage.

Instead, Chris smiled with careful emptiness. "Just tired. The custody situation takes a lot out of us."

Billy nodded, acceptance settling across his features. "You're doing right by that little girl. Standing up for what matters. Your grandmother and I are proud of you, Chris. Never doubt that."

The words sparked an unexpected flash of pain beneath Chris's ribs—the confirmation that his grandparents, at least, remained untainted by the betting scheme. The relief of their innocence, alongside his parents', created a small territory of trust he could still inhabit within the now-foreign landscape of family.

They returned to the kitchen where Emma was pressing a container of cookies into Leah's hands despite her polite protests. "For Louise," Emma insisted. "I know these are her favorites."

Leah caught Chris's eye across the sunny kitchen, her raised eyebrow a silent question: *Did you find them?* His slight nod confirmed what Louise had reported, while the subtle gesture of four fingers against his thigh communicated something else—four family members not implicated. Their silent language had evolved to encompass even this unforeseen complexity.

"Found the watch," Chris announced, patting his pocket. "Right where I thought, just hidden under some workshop odds and ends."

"Wonderful!" Emma exclaimed. "Now, are you sure you can't stay for cobbler? It'll be out of the oven in fifteen minutes."

"We really should get going," Leah interjected, her voice carrying the perfect balance of regret and determination. "We promised Louise park time this afternoon."

The goodbyes unfolded with practiced normalcy—Emma's insistence on additional cookies, Billy's firm handshake and shoulder clasp, promises to visit again soon that Chris delivered with hollow certainty. The wooden porch steps creaked beneath their feet as they descended, the sound unchanged from Chris's childhood visits yet somehow altered by new context, by his shifting understanding of the family mythology that had shaped his entire identity.

They walked toward their car in silence, each step carrying them farther from what had once represented unconditional belonging, each molecule of distance between house and body representing Chris's emotional separation from the family narrative he'd believed unquestionable.

In the car, he didn't immediately start the engine. His hands rested on the steering wheel, knuckles whitening with the force of his grip. "I saw inside them," he said finally, voice hollow with confirmation. "The betting slips. The money. Everything Louise said was true."

Leah's hand settled on his forearm, her touch both anchor and acknowledgment. "How bad?"

"Kourtney. Randy. Tyler. Sarah. Almost everyone," Chris said, each name another small laceration across his heart. He swallowed hard before adding, "But not my grandparents. Not my parents. Their names weren't on any of the slips."

"That's something, at least," Leah offered, her fingers tracing small circles against his jacket sleeve. "Four connections that might remain intact."

Chris stared through the windshield at his grandparents' house—the white clapboard and gingerbread trim now seeming less like architectural details and more like deliberate disguise, a façade concealing uglier truths that existed just beyond view. The porch where he'd spent countless evenings listening to his grandfather's stories. Memories now cast in different light by what lurked in Mason jars on high shelves.

"I took some pictures, but I still need to document everything I saw," he said suddenly, determination hardening his voice. "While it's still fresh—names, amounts, exactly what they wrote."

"We will," Leah assured him, her nature finding footholds amid emotional devastation. "When we get home, we'll record everything we know."

Chris started the engine, each movement carrying new purpose despite the weight of betrayal pressing against his chest. Emma's Victorian diminished in the rearview mirror, its familiar shape transforming into something smaller, less significant with each yard of distance. The white clapboard catching afternoon sunlight like a promise his family had failed to keep, the wraparound porch empty of the welcome it had once seemed to offer.

"I always thought family was this unbreakable thing," Chris said quietly, eyes fixed on the road ahead. "This foundation you could count on when everything else failed." He glanced briefly at Leah, his expression transformed by painful clarity. "But that's not what I had. It's what we're building."

Leah's hand found his across the console, their fingers interlacing with practiced ease. "We'll get through this," she assured him. "We'll figure out how to move forward."

The car turned onto their street, their own house appearing at the end of the block—modest compared to his grandparents' Victorian, but solid in its foundations, authentic in its welcome. Louise would be waiting with Mrs. Abernathy, her favorite babysitter, probably working on the fairy garden they'd started the previous weekend.

"I choose this," Chris said as they pulled into their driveway. "I choose you. I choose Louise. Every day."

Leah's fingers tightened around his, the pressure carrying acknowledgment of what they had confirmed and what remained to be processed—that family was not inheritance but creation, not blood but choice, not certainty but daily commitment to withstand whatever storm gathered at their horizon.

Behind them, leaves danced across the driveway in gentle spirals, indifferent to human betrayals, to jars filled with cruel wagers, to the recalibration of an entire understanding of family. Nature's persistence offered its own comfort—life continuing beyond broken trust, beyond shattered illusions, beyond the complex pain of discovering that those who claimed to love you had secretly wagered on your suffering.

The future remained unwritten, uncalculated, unwagered upon—theirs to claim with each step forward, each boundary established, each day chosen anew.

Night had settled over their bedroom with the particular stillness that followed Louise's bedtime—the careful quiet of parents navigating around sleeping children. Lamplight pooled across familiar surfaces in warm circles, transforming their sanctuary into something that felt both safe and fragile.

Chris sat on the edge of their bed, still dressed despite the late hour. His tie hung loose around his neck, a noose half-removed. The betting jar evidence lay documented in his neat handwriting on the legal pad beside him. Names. Amounts. Cruel predictions rendered in familiar handwriting.

Leah emerged from Louise's room, closing the door with careful silence. She studied him from the doorway, recognizing the particular stillness of someone holding themselves together through sheer will.

"You're allowed to fall apart," she said quietly, crossing to sit beside him.

"I know." His voice emerged steady despite the tremor in his hands. "I'm fine."

Chris stood and moved to the window. His reflection stared back at him, ghostly and translucent against the night beyond. The careful control he'd maintained since leaving his grandparents' house was finally beginning to crack.

Leah watched him, waiting. She'd learned over their years together that some pain needed to surface on its own timeline, that pushing would only drive it deeper.

"I keep seeing their handwriting," Chris said finally, his finger pressed hard against the window glass. "Uncle Randy's block letters. Kourtney's loops. Each one a person I've known my entire life, and they..." His voice caught. "They wagered money on our failure."

"I know," Leah said, giving him space to process.

"Louise." He whispered her name like a prayer. "They reduced her to a burden. A reason to bet against us." His control fractured. "My family—the people who were supposed to love her—they turned her existence into entertainment."

The raw honesty broke something open between them. Leah moved to him without thinking, her arms circling his waist. His body remained rigid for one breath, two, before collapsing against her, his face buried against her neck.

"They're supposed to be family," he whispered against her skin, the words muffled by emotion and fabric. "That word meant something to me. Safety. Belonging. Foundation."

Each phrase emerged with increasing rawness, the careful barriers falling away to reveal the wounded child beneath—the boy who had believed family meant unconditional love, discovering that foundation had been built on quicksand.

Leah held him tighter, feeling the tremors running through his body as years of accumulated trust shattered. This wasn't about being right or wrong anymore. This was grief for something irretrievably lost.

"What hurts most," Chris said, his voice breaking completely now, "is that some part of me still wants to make excuses for them. To find a way to understand why they would do this." He pulled back enough to meet her eyes. "How broken am I that I'm still trying to protect the people who betrayed us?"

"You're not broken," Leah said firmly, her palms framing his face. "You're loyal. There's a difference."

"Loyalty to people who don't deserve it feels like stupidity."

"It feels like love," she corrected gently. "The kind that doesn't turn off just because it should."

Chris closed his eyes, leaning into her touch. His hands found her waist, holding on like she was the only solid thing in a world that had tilted sideways. "I don't know who I am without believing my family is good."

The confession hung between them, raw and devastating. Leah understood—she'd faced similar reckoning five years ago when Ryan's betrayal had forced her to rebuild her entire understanding of love and trust.

"You're the man who chose to be Louise's father when you didn't have to," she said, her thumbs brushing across his cheekbones. "The man who learned her middle-of-the-night fears and her favorite breakfast and the exact pressure of holding her hand that makes her feel safe. That's who you are. Not who they failed to be."

Something in her words reached him. His breathing began to slow, the trembling subsiding into exhausted stillness. He opened his eyes, and in them she saw not just pain but the beginning of acceptance—that grief and love could coexist, that some losses couldn't be fixed.

"I need to let them go," he whispered. "Not all of them. But the idea of them. The family I thought I had."

"Yes," Leah agreed simply.

"I don't know how."

"You start by feeling it." She guided him back to their bed, settling beside him in the small island of light from the bedside lamp. "All of it. The betrayal. The grief. The loss of certainty."

Chris's forehead came to rest against hers. "I'm scared of what comes after."

"What comes after," Leah said, her hand finding his, "is us. The family we've built through daily choice rather than obligation."

She shifted, turning to face him fully. "Before I got pregnant with Louise, I had such clear dreams about the perfect family I wanted someday. A loving husband, children, a home filled with warmth—the complete opposite of my parents' cold, achievement-focused household."

Chris listened, sensing she was offering him something important.

"Then everything fell apart. Ryan's infidelity. The breakup. Finding out I was pregnant when medical school was so close." Her voice softened with remembered pain. "When Ryan made it clear he wanted nothing to do with us, I had to redefine everything I thought family meant."

"How did you do it?" Chris asked.

"One day at a time. Building something new with each bedtime story, each scraped knee bandaged, each moment I chose to be fully present when it would have been easier to collapse." Her eyes held his. "Family isn't what happens to you. It's what you build deliberately, through daily choices and conscious presence."

"Like us," Chris said.

"Exactly like us." She pulled him closer. "What we have isn't accidental. It's not circumstance or biology or tradition. It's something we choose every single day."

The simplicity of this truth seemed to reach him. His shoulders relaxed, the tension he'd carried since discovering those betting jars finally easing beneath her words.

"I choose you," he said, the declaration carrying renewed commitment. "I choose Louise. Every morning when I wake up and every night before I sleep."

"We choose you back," she whispered. "Every day."

Chris pulled her against him, his need for physical connection overtaking words. Their lips met with the particular hunger that follows survival, relief transforming into something deeper, more primal.

"I needed this," he confessed when they parted. "To remember what's real."

"This is real," Leah whispered, her hands moving to the buttons of his shirt. "Us. Louise. What we've built together. Not the betting jars. Not their betrayal."

He helped her remove his shirt, then hers, their movements carrying the practiced intimacy of people who had mapped each other's bodies through years of shared nights. But tonight felt different—not just desire but desperation to affirm their connection, to prove through touch what words couldn't fully express.

They moved together with increasing urgency, grief transforming into the fierce need to celebrate what remained rather than mourn what was lost. His hands knew her body, her responses, the exact points where pleasure bloomed into something transcendent. She knew his rhythms, his needs, the way his breathing changed when control began to slip.

When release came, it felt like exorcism—years of accumulated pain finding outlet through shared pleasure, bodies affirming what betrayal had tried to demolish. They lay tangled together afterward, breathing synchronized, hearts beating variations on the same essential rhythm.

"Thank you," Chris whispered into the darkness, his arms tightening around her. "For being my foundation when everything else crumbled."

Leah pressed a kiss to his shoulder. "That's what we do. We hold each other up when the ground shakes."

Outside their window, the neighborhood slept in suburban tranquility. Inside their bedroom, two people held each other against whatever morning would bring—understanding that some losses couldn't be fixed, but that love could survive them.

Chris's breathing deepened toward sleep, his body finally surrendering to exhaustion. Leah remained awake a while longer, her hand resting over his heart, feeling its steady rhythm that had become her favorite lullaby.

Tomorrow they would begin the work of rebuilding boundaries, of deciding which family relationships could be salvaged and which needed to be released. But tonight, they simply held each other in their darkened bedroom, proving through presence that what they'd built together was stronger than what others had tried to destroy.

The betting jars couldn't touch this. The betrayal couldn't diminish it. Whatever came next, they would face it as they always had—together, choosing each other, building their family through daily acts of love that transcended biology or tradition or anyone else's expectations.

That was enough. It had to be enough.

And in the sacred darkness of their bedroom, wrapped in each other's arms, it was.

CHAPTER 16

What Science Can't Measure

The testing facility lobby gleamed with antiseptic brightness, its sterile whiteness reminiscent of places where hope came to surrender. Leah tightened her grip on Louise's small hand, transmitting her anxiety through the connection that had sustained them both since before birth.

"Mommy, you're squeezing too hard," Louise whispered, her dark eyes lifting with that peculiar wisdom children possess when adults begin to fracture.

Leah released her grip with an apologetic smile. The intake desk loomed ahead, all Formica and merciless fluorescence, staffed by a woman in blue scrubs who checked names against a screen without bothering to look up.

"Miller-Johnson?" The receptionist's voice carried no recognition of the lives being processed through this clinical machinery.

Forms appeared on a clipboard, standard paperwork transformed into instruments of betrayal. When Leah wrote Louise's name, her pen faltered over "Father's Name," the empty space mocking everything she'd built.

"What are we doing here, Mommy?" Louise asked, leaning warmly against Leah's side.

It was the question Leah had rehearsed answers for during sleepless hours before dawn, had hoped somehow to avoid altogether.

"Remember how we talked about Ryan, the man connected to you by blood?" Leah kept her voice steady, a feat requiring every measure of control she possessed. "Today the doctors need to check that connection."

"With science?" Louise's eyes widened with the fascination children reserve for important-sounding concepts.

"Yes, with science."

The memory descended without permission—not a bathroom with a pregnancy test as she'd sometimes told others to simplify her story, but Nurse Thompson's office at the university clinic. The gentle way the older woman had rested her hand on Leah's knee as she delivered the news that had altered everything. "The blood work confirms it, dear. You're about sixteen weeks along." Four months after discovering Ryan's betrayal, four months during which she'd attributed the fatigue and nausea to grief and pre-med stress.

A technician directed them to a small examination room, its walls lined with generic artwork selected for its total absence of emotional content. The space smelled of rubbing alcohol and latex, a cocktail transporting Leah back to university labs where organic matter was reduced to component parts, analyzed and categorized.

"The process is simple," the technician explained, her voice matching the room's atmosphere—cool, efficient, distant. "We'll take a cheek swab from inside the child's mouth, no pain involved."

"What's that?" Louise pointed at the packaged swab, her curiosity undiminished by the clinical setting.

"It's like a little brush," the technician explained with a professional smile. "Just a quick swipe inside your cheek to collect some cells."

"Will it hurt?"

"Not at all."

Lies wrapped in clinical reassurance. This process would hurt—not physically, but in ways the technician couldn't comprehend. Each step reopened wounds Leah had cauterized years ago with determination and love.

"Mommy?" Louise tugged at Leah's sleeve. "Why do they need all these science things? Is Ryan lost?"

The question pierced Leah's heart with unexpected force. Lost. What a perfect word for the man who had abandoned them both.

"No, sweet girl," Leah knelt to Louise's level. "It's just a way grown-ups confirm things they already know."

"Like when Miss Andrews checks our math even though we already did it?"

"Something like that."

The door opened without warning. A second technician appeared. "Mrs. Johnson? Could you step outside for a moment?"

Cold dread pooled in Leah's stomach. "Why?"

"There's been a request from the other party."

The other party. Such a sterile phrase for the man who had walked away from his own child before she drew her first breath.

"I'll stay with Louise," the first technician assured her. "This will only take a minute."

The hallway waited, antiseptic and unforgiving. Leah stepped out reluctantly, every maternal instinct screaming against leaving Louise alone.

And there stood Ryan Matthews—older than when he'd signed the termination papers without a second glance. His tailored suit conveyed the success he'd chosen over fatherhood, his Italian shoes the tangible rewards of priorities that had never included them.

"Leah," he said, her name in his mouth sounding wrong somehow.

"What do you want?"

Ryan glanced at the closed door. "I wanted to see her."

"That wasn't our agreement."

"The agreement is being challenged."

Fluorescent lights buzzed overhead, each second stretching impossibly as they stood in this sterile no-man's-land between past and present.

"I've changed," Ryan said, voice dropping lower as though sharing a confession. "I know I made terrible mistakes—all of them—and I've had to live with the consequences."

His eyes searched hers with an intensity that stirred unwelcome memories of a time when she'd believed in his sincerity. "What happened between us—the way I betrayed your trust—it's haunted me."

"Save it," Leah cut him off, her voice a blade forged in years of single motherhood and midnight doubts. "Your guilt isn't my responsibility."

"I'm not asking for forgiveness," Ryan insisted, taking a half-step closer. "But I need you to know that the person I was then—the one who cheated on you, who walked away—that's not who I am now."

"Convenient timing for your transformation. Years after the difficult part of parenting has been handled by someone else."

"I deserve that," he acknowledged, running a hand through his hair in a gesture so familiar it made her stomach clench. "But Louise deserves to know her father—her real father."

"Biology doesn't make you a father," Leah stated with quiet conviction born of witnessing Chris's daily devotion.

"The courts disagree."

"I think about you. Every day. What I threw away—"

"Don't." Leah's voice went cold. "You signed those papers without a second thought."

"And I've regretted it every day since."

"Regret doesn't raise a child at 3 A.M. when she's burning with fever," Leah responded. "It doesn't sing her to sleep or teach her to tie her shoes."

The door opened behind them. "All done!" Louise announced triumphantly. "The lady gave me a sticker too!"

Ryan's expression transformed at the sight of her, hunger and recognition flashing across his features in rapid succession. Leah moved instinctively between them, but Louise had already noticed the stranger's presence.

"Mommy, that's the man from my school," she observed with the unfiltered directness of childhood. "The one who looked at my pictures."

Ryan smiled, his professional charm sliding into place. "Hello, Louise."

Panic flared in Leah's chest. This encounter violated everything they'd arranged through their lawyers—no direct contact, no unmonitored interactions.

"We need to go," Leah insisted, taking Louise's hand.

"But the lady said I get juice after," Louise protested, pointing toward a small refreshment area. "She said it's a reward for being brave."

"We'll get juice somewhere else," Leah promised, already calculating the fastest route to the exit.

Ryan knelt to Louise's level, his expensive suit creasing as he positioned himself eye-to-eye with the child he'd abandoned. "You were very brave today."

"It was just a cotton stick," Louise shrugged with casual bravado. "Not scary at all."

Leah pulled her daughter closer. "Ryan, this isn't appropriate."

"I just want to talk to her for a minute."

"Through our lawyers. That was the agreement."

Louise looked between them, confusion clouding her expression as she sensed the tension crackling in the adult atmosphere. "Are you mad at each other?"

The innocent question crystallized everything wrong with this situation. Leah made a decision then, one that would have consequences she couldn't yet foresee.

"Louise, this is Ryan," she explained with careful simplicity. "The man we talked about."

Louise studied Ryan with renewed interest. "Oh. The one who wasn't ready to be a daddy when I was in your tummy."

Ryan's face paled slightly, unprepared for such direct understanding from a four-year-old.

"That's right," Leah confirmed. "And we need to go now."

"But he's here," Louise observed with the linear logic of childhood. "Does that mean he's ready now?"

The question hung between them, too simple and too devastating.

"That's what the judge will help decide," Leah answered, the most honest response she could offer.

Ryan stood, something shifting in his expression as determination replaced momentary uncertainty. The businessman reclaimed ground from the briefly exposed human beneath.

"Leah," he said, his voice just low enough that Louise couldn't hear, "we could work this out between us, for her sake, for all our sakes."

The suggestion carried insidious intimacy, as if they shared some secret bond that transcended his betrayal and abandonment.

"There is no 'us,'" she replied with quiet finality. "Not anymore."

"I'll see you at the hearing."

"Not before then," Leah countered, guiding Louise toward the exit.

"Is Ryan a good person?" Louise asked as they reached the car.

Leah fastened her daughter's seatbelt, buying precious seconds to formulate an answer that would honor truth without causing harm.

"People are complicated," she said finally. "Even good people make mistakes."

"Like when I broke your vase?"

"Something like that. But bigger."

Louise nodded with solemn understanding. "Will I have to live with him instead of you and Daddy?"

The question Leah had dreaded most, the fear that lived in her marrow.

"No, sweet girl," the promise emerged before she could stop it. "You'll always live with us."

As she started the car, Leah recognized her error—the absolute certainty she couldn't guarantee, the promise that might prove impossible to keep if the legal system valued biology over bonding.

The choice that might backfire later.

Louise hummed quietly in the backseat, the testing facility already receding in her awareness. But for Leah, the white building diminishing in the rearview mirror represented everything still at risk—the family she'd built through determination and love, the bonds that transcended biology's simple blueprints.

The Copper Kettle café buzzed with mid-afternoon energy, a sanctuary of warmth against the world beyond its windows. Ashley stirred her latte, one eye on her practice schedules, the other on the door. The weekend swim meet required planning—class assignments, lane distributions, parent volunteer coordination—but her mind kept drifting to Louise's determined little face as she'd mastered the backstroke that morning.

Her phone chimed, another email from the recreation director requesting budget justifications. Ashley sighed and returned to her spreadsheets. The coffee shop's warmth enveloped her, scents of espresso and cinnamon providing momentary shelter from administrative burdens that threatened to consume her afternoon.

The bell above the door jingled.

Ashley glanced up from habit, then froze. Terry Henderson stood in the entrance, shaking droplets from her umbrella. Her eyes swept the café with that same evaluating gaze Ashley had observed at Louise's swim lessons—cataloging, assessing, gathering information.

Ashley lowered her head, instinct urging her to avoid detection. She slid deeper into her corner booth, grateful for the partial wall screening her from the entrance. Her pulse quickened, a primitive warning system activated by the appearance of someone she'd watched operate with such deliberate intent.

Terry moved to a table near the window, her back straight as a committee chairwoman awaiting subordinates. Her floral cardigan and sensible pumps broadcast respectability, church-committee authority wrapped in grandmotherly camouflage that fooled only those who hadn't witnessed her in action.

The door chimed again.

Ashley's breath caught. Ryan Matthews entered, smoothing his cashmere coat with manicured hands. The same confident smile that had charmed teachers in high school. The same assessing eyes that evaluated everyone as either useful or irrelevant.

But something was different today. His movements carried an edge of urgency that hadn't been there before, a tension in his shoulders that spoke of someone running out of time and options.

Terry waved him over. Ryan joined her without the unhurried confidence Ashley had seen at the elementary school. He dropped into the chair across from Terry with visible frustration barely contained beneath his professional veneer.

Ashley's coffee cooled untouched before her. She angled her laptop screen to shield her face, creating a barrier between herself and their awareness. The meeting here, just days before the hearing, sent ice spreading through her veins. Why weren't they at Wallace & Associates? Why the informal setting?

Her hand moved to her phone without conscious decision. She opened the recording app, angled it above her laptop screen where it could capture audio. The action felt both significant and necessary—documenting what instinct told her was important, even if she didn't yet understand why.

"Thank you for meeting me on short notice," Terry said, her voice carrying across the café's afternoon lull. "I wanted to touch base before the hearing."

"Wallace needs something concrete," Ryan said, his voice tight with frustration. "Something recent that shows current concerns about Louise's environment. The older observations are helpful, but we need fresh evidence."

Terry's fingers worked nervously around her coffee cup. "Well, I've continued documenting what I can observe. There was that incident where Louise used the cookie analogy to explain family structure—"

"You already told me about that." Ryan's interruption carried impatience. "What else? Recent observations? New incidents?"

The silence stretched. Ashley watched understanding dawn across Ryan's face—the realization that this meeting wasn't going to deliver what he'd hoped for.

"They've stopped coming to family gatherings," Terry admitted, her voice defensive. "After Chris found out about... after certain family tensions became apparent, they haven't attended Sunday dinners. They're not at church anymore. Louise isn't at the family picnics or birthday parties."

"So you have nothing new." Ryan's words landed flat, accusatory.

"It's not that I have nothing," Terry bristled. "It's that they've deliberately isolated themselves. Which in itself could be seen as concerning behavior—"

"We can't testify about what we *can't* observe," Ryan cut her off. "Wallace wants documented incidents. Recent ones. Things that show the current environment is problematic."

Terry straightened in her chair, her voice taking on the defensive tone of someone whose usefulness was being questioned. "I've done everything I could. I documented every concern I had access to. But they've shut me out completely. Mary won't even return my calls."

Ryan rubbed his face with both hands, the gesture revealing exhaustion beneath his engineered composure. "Then we work with what we have. Your earlier observations. The documented behavioral changes." He paused, seeming to search for something concrete. "Wallace says those observations are valuable. They establish patterns."

"I should go," Ryan said abruptly, checking his watch. "Wallace wants to review my testimony this afternoon."

"Monday," Terry said, as if confirming a battle date. "I'll be there. And Ryan, whatever happens, remember that we're doing this for Louise. To give her access to her real family."

Ryan nodded, but Ashley caught the flicker of doubt in his expression—brief and quickly suppressed, but present nonetheless. He gathered his coat and left without the confident stride she'd observed before. This was a man whose strategy was unraveling, held together only by momentum and stubborn refusal to accept defeat.

After Ryan left, Terry remained at the table for several minutes, staring into her coffee with an expression that suggested she was trying to convince herself of certainties that felt increasingly fragile. Finally, she rose and departed, leaving behind only the lingering scent of her floral perfume and the weight of a conspiracy that was crumbling under its own inadequacy.

Ashley sat motionless as the door closed behind Terry, her phone still recording until she was certain they were truly gone. The café resumed its ordinary rhythm around her: baristas called orders, customers tapped keyboards, the world continued its rotation seemingly unchanged by the conversation she'd just documented.

But Ashley's phone screen glowed with evidence. Not the coordinated conspiracy she'd expected to capture, but something perhaps more damning—the desperation of a case falling apart, held together by witnesses with nothing new to offer and a man who couldn't admit he was fighting a battle already lost.

Her finger hovered over Leah's contact information. Their former rivalry seemed childish now, rendered insignificant by what she'd just witnessed—the systematic attempt to dismantle a family, even as that attempt revealed itself to be built on nothing more substantial than old grievances and wishful thinking.

Ashley pressed "call" before doubt could reestablish its grip. Three rings, then Leah's voice answered, cautious but open.

"Leah, it's Ashley." Her voice emerged steadier than expected. "I just witnessed something you need to know about before Monday's hearing."

The words bridged decades of misunderstanding in an instant.

"Ryan and Terry just met at the Copper Kettle. They were planning testimony, but..." Ashley paused, choosing her words carefully. "It's falling apart, Leah. Ryan's desperate for new evidence, and Terry has nothing to give him. Their entire case seems to be built on old observations and family drama."

She took a breath. "And I recorded everything."

Chris's hands tightened on the steering wheel as they turned onto Fifth Street, the late afternoon sun casting long shadows across the dashboard.

Beside him, Leah stared out the passenger window with the particular stillness of someone whose mind was racing through calculations too complex to share aloud.

"We'll get through this," Chris said quietly, though the words felt inadequate against the weight of what waited in Williams' office—final preparations for a custody hearing that could reshape their entire world.

Leah's phone buzzed, Ashley's name flashing across the screen. She glanced at Chris before answering, confusion flickering across her features. "Ashley? Is everything okay with—"

"I need to talk to you," Ashley's voice cut through the car's speakers, urgent but controlled. "About Ryan. I witnessed something today that you need to know about before Monday's hearing."

Chris pulled into a parking spot outside Williams' office building but didn't kill the engine. The car idled in place as Ashley continued, her words tumbling out with the particular intensity of someone who understood the magnitude of what they'd witnessed.

"I was at the Copper Kettle this afternoon working on swim schedules. Ryan and Terry showed up—together, Leah. They sat close enough that I could hear their conversation, and..." She paused, drawing breath. "I recorded it. The whole thing."

Leah's breath caught. "You recorded them?"

"Every word. Ryan was pushing Terry for fresh evidence, anything recent he could use at the hearing. She kept saying she has nothing new because you've been avoiding family gatherings." Ashley's voice carried both anger and vindication. "It wasn't casual conversation—they were strategizing. Coordinating their testimony. She was literally telling him about incidents she'd documented for his case."

Chris felt something cold spreading through his chest.

"I'm sending you the file now," Ashley continued. "But I wanted you to know before you went into your meeting. This wasn't Terry being a concerned aunt—this was conspiracy. She admitted she's been documenting your family specifically to help Ryan's custody case."

The audio file arrived with a soft chime. Leah stared at her phone screen where the waveform appeared like evidence of something they'd suspected but hadn't been able to prove.

"Thank you," Leah whispered, her voice thick with emotion she couldn't quite name. "Ashley, I don't even know what to say."

"You don't have to say anything. Just use it." Ashley's response carried fierce protectiveness. "Louise deserves better than adults who play games with her security. I'll testify if you need me to—about what I saw, why I recorded it, all of it."

The call ended, leaving them sitting in the parked car with the audio file that could transform everything. Chris stared through the windshield at Williams' office building, processing the magnitude of what they'd just received.

"She recorded them," he said finally, his voice hollow with disbelief. "Terry and Ryan. Actually coordinating testimony."

Leah's hands trembled slightly as she gripped her phone. "Terry's been working with him all along. Not just sharing concerns—actively collaborating to build his case against us."

"We should listen to it," Leah said quietly, though her finger hovered over the play button without pressing it.

"No." Chris's response surprised them both. "Not here. Not alone. Williams needs to hear this with us—she'll know how to use it, what it means legally."

Leah nodded slowly, recognizing the wisdom in waiting. They sat in silence for a long moment, letting the reality of what they now possessed settle around them like armor they hadn't known they needed.

"This proves it wasn't just misguided concern," Leah said finally. "Terry hasn't been a worried family member sharing observations. She's been an active participant in Ryan's campaign."

"Gathering intelligence," Chris added, his voice carrying bitter recognition. "Documenting our family. Strategizing with his lawyers. All while claiming to love us."

The weight of that betrayal pressed against his chest, but underneath it ran something unexpected—relief. They weren't crazy for suspecting Terry's involvement. They weren't paranoid for questioning her motivations. The conspiracy they'd sensed had been real all along, and now they had proof.

"We should go in," Leah said, though neither of them moved immediately. "Williams is waiting."

Chris reached for her hand across the console, their fingers intertwining with practiced intimacy. "Are you ready for this? For what happens when we use this recording against her?"

"She chose this," Leah replied, her voice carrying quiet conviction. "We didn't make her collaborate with Ryan. She did that while claiming to protect you."

They gathered their things and stepped out into the afternoon air. As they crossed the parking lot toward Williams' office building, Chris felt the weight of the recording like a talisman against all the calculated cruelty they'd endured. Ashley's simple act of documentation had given them something precious—proof that their instincts about Terry's betrayal had been accurate all along.

Williams' conference room held its familiar gravity—mahogany table polished to mirror shine, leather chairs arranged for serious conversation, afternoon light filtered through blinds that cast everything in strategic shadow. Elizabeth Williams rose as they entered, her professional composure shifting immediately as she read the urgency in their expressions.

"What's happened?" she asked, gesturing them toward seats while her eyes tracked between their faces with practiced assessment.

"Ashley Peterson just called," Leah said, settling into her chair with careful deliberation. "She was at a café this afternoon when Ryan and Terry showed up. She overheard their entire conversation—and recorded it."

Williams' expression sharpened instantly, professional instincts activated. "Recorded them? In a public space?"

"The Copper Kettle," Chris confirmed. "They sat close enough for her to hear everything. She said they were coordinating testimony, discussing strategy for the hearing."

"Ashley described it as conspiracy rather than casual conversation," Leah added, pulling out her phone. "Terry was telling Ryan about incidents she'd documented specifically for his custody case. She admitted she has nothing recent because we've been avoiding family gatherings."

Williams reached for her legal pad with decisive movements. "I need to hear this recording. Now."

Leah placed her phone on the conference table. "Ashley said she'd testify if we need her to—about what she witnessed, why she felt compelled to record it."

"Play it," Williams said, pen already poised above paper.

Chris pressed play, and the recording filled the conference room with devastating clarity. The background noise of the café—clinking dishes, muffled conversations, the hiss of the espresso machine—couldn't obscure the voices that mattered. Ryan's frustration bled through as he pressed Terry for recent evidence. Her defensive responses revealed the systematic nature of their coordination, each exchange building a picture of conspiracy that went far beyond concerned family member sharing observations.

Williams' pen moved rapidly across paper as she documented key phrases, her expression transforming from professional focus to grim satisfaction. When the recording ended, she set down her pen with deliberate precision.

"This changes everything," she said, the words carrying weight beyond simple statement.

"How?" Leah asked, though strategic possibilities were already assembling in her mind.

Williams leaned back in her chair, her fingers steepled as she processed implications. "Terry's testimony strategy has been built on appearing as an objective family member simply sharing honest concerns. This recording destroys that narrative completely."

She stood, pacing the conference room with restless energy. "When Terry takes the stand claiming to be a worried great-aunt, we introduce this. We show Judge Erikson that her 'observations' weren't organic family concern—they were coordinated testimony designed to support Ryan's custody claim."

"Is it admissible?" Chris asked, his musician's precision making him cautious about evidence that seemed too perfect.

"Absolutely." Williams' response carried absolute certainty. "Public café. No reasonable expectation of privacy. Ashley was positioned where she could naturally overhear the conversation. She documented what was said in a public space—there's no wiretapping violation, no illegal surveillance. It's completely admissible."

Chris felt something loosening in his chest—not relief exactly, but recognition that they finally had proof of what they'd always known. Terry's campaign against their family hadn't been misguided love. It had been calculated collaboration with lawyers trying to steal their daughter.

"The recording also reveals Ryan's desperation," Williams continued, making rapid notes. "He needs fresh evidence. He's frustrated that Terry can't provide it because you've protected yourselves through reasonable boundaries. That desperation undermines his entire 'concerned father' narrative."

"So we use this during Terry's cross-examination," Leah said, understanding crystallizing.

"Exactly. We let her present herself as objective observer, let her describe her concerns about Louise's wellbeing." Williams' smile carried predatory satisfaction. "Then we play the recording. The contrast between her claimed neutrality and her actual coordination with Ryan's legal team will devastate her credibility."

Chris absorbed this with growing appreciation for how completely the recording would undermine Terry's testimony. Not just contradicting her words but revealing the calculated nature of everything she'd done while claiming family concern.

"There's another element here," Williams said, consulting her notes. "Terry complains that you've isolated yourselves from family gatherings, but she frames it as concerning behavior rather than reasonable response to betrayal. That framing reveals her lack of self-awareness."

"She doesn't see her own role in forcing our boundaries," Leah observed.

"Which makes her testimony even less credible," Williams agreed. "Judge Erikson will see someone so convinced of her righteousness that she can't recognize how her own actions drove you away. Combined with the betting jars, it paints a picture of systematic family sabotage disguised as concern."

Chris felt validation mixing with the anger that had been building since Ashley's call. They hadn't been paranoid. They hadn't overreacted by creating distance from family. Terry's betrayal had been exactly as deep as they'd feared—maybe deeper.

"Ashley's willing to provide context," Leah said. "To testify about witnessing the meeting, about why she felt compelled to record it."

"That strengthens it even more," Williams replied. "An objective third party who observed their behavior and recognized it as problematic enough to document. Her testimony will frame the recording properly for Judge Erikson."

Williams returned to her seat, organizing her notes with practiced efficiency. "This recording, combined with the betting jars, reveals a pattern. Not isolated incidents but systematic campaign. Ryan identifying vulnerabilities, Terry providing intelligence, Wallace & Associates coordinating the attack."

The comprehensive nature of their strategy became visible through Williams' analysis. They weren't just defending against individual threats—they could demonstrate the coordinated psychological warfare that had been waged against their family for months.

"We present this pattern to Judge Erikson," Williams continued, "and we show that Ryan's petition isn't about reconnecting with his daughter. It's about systematic manipulation using family members as weapons while claiming Louise's best interests."

Chris felt preparation replacing the defensive anxiety that had characterized recent months. For so long they'd been reacting to attacks from unpredictable angles. Now they had evidence that would let them take the offensive.

"What do you need from us before Monday?" Williams asked, shifting to practical implementation.

"Our IT specialist can clean up the audio," she continued before they could respond. "Remove background noise, enhance the voices, make sure every word is clearly audible for the court. But even the raw recording is powerful—its imperfect quality actually adds authenticity."

"How long will that take?" Chris asked.

"A few hours, maybe less. I'll have him work on it tonight." Williams made additional notes. "We'll have both versions ready—the original and the enhanced version. Judge Erikson can hear how clear their coordination was even through café background noise."

Leah nodded, understanding that the recording's amateur quality somehow strengthened rather than weakened its impact. This wasn't manufactured evidence but honest documentation of conspiracy caught in the act.

"I need you both prepared for Monday," Williams said, her tone shifting to something more serious. "When we introduce this recording, Terry will likely have an emotional reaction. She may try to justify her actions, claim misunderstanding, position herself as the victim of our interpretation."

"Let her try," Chris said quietly. "I'm done protecting someone who's spent months actively trying to destroy my family."

Williams studied his face, seeing the transformation from defensive father to someone ready to fight rather than merely endure.

"Good! Then we're ready," Williams said, gathering her materials with satisfaction. "Monday, we show Judge Erikson exactly what kind of campaign Ryan Matthews has been running—using his own collaborators' words against them."

As they prepared to leave, Chris felt the weight of what they now possessed. Not just evidence but vindication. Not just proof but justice finally within reach.

"Thank you," he said to Williams. "For knowing how to use this."

"Thank you for trusting me," Williams replied. "And thank Ashley. She gave us exactly what we needed."

They walked to their car through evening shadows, the office building's glass facade reflecting early stars. Chris held Leah's hand, their connection carrying both relief and recognition that Monday would bring reckoning.

"We finally have proof," Leah said quietly as they reached the car. "Of everything they've been doing."

Chris pulled her close, breathing in the familiar scent of her hair. They stood together in the parking lot as evening deepened around them. The recording existed. The truth was documented. And for the first time since Ryan's custody petition arrived, they had weapons that matched the systematic attack they'd been enduring.

"Let's go home," Leah said finally. "Louise will be wondering where we are."

They drove through familiar streets toward the house where their daughter waited, carrying proof that sometimes justice arrived through unexpected allies, through simple acts of courage, through the decision to document truth when faced with calculated deception.

Monday's hearing would reveal exactly how much Ashley's recording had changed everything.

Terry's bedroom held decades of accumulated order—photographs arranged by year, books alphabetized, jewelry hierarchically organized. The floral notebook lay open on her nightstand, its hardcover binding announcing the seriousness of intent behind months of documented observations.

Tomorrow morning, Judge Erikson would validate what she'd seen. Tomorrow, Chris would finally understand.

She adjusted her reading glasses, reviewing the afternoon's final entry:

Church picnic - Louise withdrawn. Asked to leave early, citing "tummy ache" though playing energetically moments before. Leah's immediate departure without consulting Chris. Pattern of control?

The observation felt significant, though a small voice whispered that children's stomachaches rarely evidenced parental manipulation. Terry silenced it. Individual incidents might seem innocent, but patterns revealed truth.

She turned back several pages:

Louise asks about "different kinds of daddies." Age-inappropriate discussion.

Louise's artwork increasingly dark. Teacher concerned (overheard in fellowship hall).

Each entry had seemed crucial when recorded. Strung together, they formed a narrative any reasonable person would recognize as troubling. Yet when she'd explained this to Mary, her sister had responded with that particular expression—the one suggesting Terry was overreacting, seeing problems where none existed.

Mary doesn't understand. She never has.

Mary had always been the softer sister, prioritizing feelings over facts. Someone needed to maintain clarity, and that responsibility had always fallen to Terry.

Her hand moved to the envelope tucked between pages—photographs from Wallace's investigator. Louise crying at the park. Louise withdrawn at school. Each image captured what she'd been documenting, visual evidence that her concerns weren't overreach but legitimate observation.

She studied the crying photograph, Louise's tear-streaked face frozen mid-fall. The context—Chris catching her, comfort working within minutes—felt less important than the captured moment itself.

Except she wasn't unstable. The tears were from the fall. And Chris's comfort worked because he's been her father for years.

Terry's jaw tightened. She flipped to a fresh page, needing to clarify before tomorrow's testimony:

My role: observe and document because someone must protect Chris from repeating his father's mistakes. Tom's business collapsed because he trusted wrong people. Chris is doing the same—trusting Leah Miller despite her family's history of—

Her pen hovered. Despite her family's history of what? Business acumen? Strategic thinking? The ability to build successful enterprises while Tom's ventures crumbled?

Despite her family's history of destroying ours.

But even written, the justification felt thin, stretched across a framework no longer quite supporting its weight. John Miller hadn't destroyed Tom's business—market forces, poor decisions, stubborn refusal to adapt had done that. Everyone knew it, even if no one said it aloud.

Terry closed the notebook sharply. She was allowing doubt when she needed certainty. Tomorrow required confidence, not second-guessing.

She moved to her closet, selecting the navy suit with pearl buttons—authoritative but approachable. The outfit of someone who could be trusted with difficult truths.

Her reflection showed a woman who had spent decades making herself indispensable. After Chris's father's business collapsed, she'd ensured bills got paid, managed the household budget, made certain Chris and Tyler had stability despite their parents' emotional withdrawal. She'd earned the right to be protective.

You earned the right to be controlling. There's a difference.

"I'm protecting him," she said aloud, needing conviction. "Someone has to."

But memory surfaced unbidden: Chris as a young boy, his face pale with confusion when creditors called, when childhood's careful world fractured to reveal adult failures he wasn't equipped to understand. She'd shielded him from those harsh realities. Kept that promise through illnesses and heartbreaks, through college struggles and career uncertainties.

The problem was that Chris no longer needed protection. He'd built a life, chosen a family, created stability independent of her vigilant oversight. Acknowledging that meant accepting her role—the identity she'd constructed across decades—was no longer necessary.

I'm still necessary. I'm the only one who sees clearly.

Tomorrow she would testify about patterns, about systematic manipulation. Ryan's lawyer had been clear: stick to observations, express concern, maintain objectivity while revealing troubling truth.

She'd practiced a dozen times: *"It breaks my heart to be here, Your Honor, but I love my nephew too much to remain silent when I see patterns that concern me."*

Reluctant but resolved. Pained but principled.

The betting jars flickered through her mind—those Mason jars hidden at Emma's house, filled with predictions about Chris's marriage failing. Standing alone in her ordered bedroom, Terry allowed herself to acknowledge what she'd refused to admit even to Ryan: the jars hadn't been harmless entertainment.

They'd been documentation of her certainty made manifest. Physical proof she wasn't the only one who saw the inevitable collapse. If others agreed, it validated her observations, transformed interference into wisdom. She needed Chris's marriage to fail because she needed to be right—needed to prove decades of vigilant protection hadn't been control masquerading as love, but genuine wisdom only she possessed.

And when the marriage survives? When your predictions prove wrong?

Then she would have been wrong about everything. The observations, the patterns, her role as protector. She would have sacrificed her relationship with Chris, exposed herself to his anger and Mary's disappointment, all for nothing.

The thought was intolerable.

Her phone buzzed: *Final prep call at 8am tomorrow. Everything on track.*

Everything on track. The phrase settled in her stomach like something cold and foreign.

Terry closed the notebook and placed it in her purse, each movement deliberate, ceremonial. She'd chosen this path. Collaborated with Ryan's legal team, shared family information, documented moments now evidence in a custody case. Doubt was no longer an option—the machinery was in motion, and her role as key witness demanded unwavering conviction.

Tomorrow she would testify with the certainty that had sustained her through months of careful observation. Tomorrow Judge Erikson would hear the truth only she had been brave enough to document.

Tomorrow everything would be vindicated.

She turned off her lamp and settled into bed, the navy suit hanging in the closet like armor waiting for battle. Sleep came slowly, punctuated by rehearsed phrases and imagined validation, her mind cycling through testimony that would prove she'd been right all along.

The notebook remained in her purse, pages filled with observations that felt increasingly like confessions she wasn't ready to read.

CHAPTER 17

When Masks Fall

The family courtroom held a particular gravity that made breathing difficult. Morning light filtered through high windows, casting everything in stark relief—the polished wood bench where Judge Erikson would preside, the two tables positioned like opposing armies, the gallery where family and observers would bear witness to the dismantling or preservation of a family unit.

Judge Erikson entered with measured pace. His silver temples caught the filtered sunlight as he settled behind the bench, reading glasses perched on his nose with scholarly authority. The traditional black robe emphasized the weight of his position, the gravity of what would unfold here.

Ryan Matthews entered first, flanked by his legal team from Wallace & Associates. His tailored suit conveyed confidence earned through engineering success, though something in his eyes darted nervously as he took his seat. James Wallace moved with the predatory grace of someone who had argued hundreds of custody cases, his portfolio containing documents that would either legitimize or destroy Ryan's fatherhood claim.

Chris and Leah arrived moments later, hands clasped with the unconscious intimacy of people who had weathered storms together. Their entrance drew subtle reactions from the gallery—Emma and Billy Henderson's supportive smiles, Tyler's calculating assessment, Kourtney's carefully neutral expression.

Chris felt his pulse quicken as they took their seats, the familiar weight of Leah's palm against his own suddenly amplified by the formal setting. Years of intimate knowledge—how she pressed her thumb against his when anxious, how her breath quickened almost imperceptibly when threatened—translated into immediate understanding in this moment. They were venturing into a battle for their family's very existence.

Mary Johnson sat in the front row behind Chris's table, her husband Tom beside her. Their presence offered quiet strength that filled the space differently than others. Mary's fingers worked the handle of her purse with controlled tension, each small movement betraying the anxiety she tried to contain. Tom's weathered hands rested steady on his knees, offering silent support through their motionless presence.

"All rise," the bailiff intoned.

Judge Erikson surveyed the assembled parties with practiced neutrality. "We are here to hear the petition of Ryan Matthews to challenge the voluntary termination of his parental rights regarding minor child Louise Danielle Miller. Mr. Wallace, you may proceed with your opening statement."

James Wallace rose with theatrical deliberation, adjusting his tie with the unconscious gesture of a man preparing for battle.

"Your Honor," he began, his voice resonating through the small courtroom, "we ask not for the impossible—time travel—but for the logical. A child needs her father. Not a substitute. Not a replacement. But the man whose blood courses through her veins, whose lineage shapes her identity, whose very genetic blueprint determines not just her eye color but potentially her health history, her predispositions, her inheritance of a medical past this court must consider."

He paced before the bench, each word calculated for maximum impact. Leah's fingers tightened around Chris's, her medical training automatically dissecting Wallace's rhetoric. The invocation of genetic inheritance struck particularly sharp—her abandoned medical career suddenly weaponized as evidence of biological imperatives she'd chosen to transcend.

"Five years ago, Ryan Matthews made a decision born of youth and fear. He signed away his rights believing it was best for all involved. But circumstances change. People mature. The law recognizes this through provisions for reinstating parental rights when changed circumstances warrant."

Wallace turned to face the courtroom, his gaze sweeping over Chris and Leah with studied compassion that rang false to those who truly knew the game being played.

"Mr. Matthews has transformed his life. He owns a successful consulting firm. He has a stable home environment. He has, most importantly, the capacity for love that every child deserves from their biological parent. Meanwhile, this court must examine whether the current environment, while perhaps well-intentioned, truly serves Louise's best interests."

The opening statement landed with measured impact. Ryan sat straighter, color returning to his face as hope kindled visibly in his expression. Across the aisle, Chris's jaw tightened, his hand finding Leah's and gripping with unconscious force.

"Thank you, Mr. Wallace," Judge Erikson said, making notations on his pad. "Ms. Williams, your opening statement."

Elizabeth Williams stood with less theatrical flourish but equal purpose. Her charcoal suit and sensible heels made a different kind of statement—one of competence over performance, substance over style.

"Your Honor," she began, her voice steady and clear, "Mr. Wallace speaks of blood, but parenting flows through presence, patience, and unconditional love. Biology creates potential. Love creates family."

She turned toward Louise's empty chair—the court had wisely decided the proceedings were not age-appropriate for a young child's attendance.

"For four years and five months, Chris Johnson has been the only father Louise has known. Not because of circumstance or accident, but because of daily choice. Every bedtime story. Every scraped knee bandaged. Every nightmare soothed. Every small triumph celebrated. These moments don't require DNA analysis—they require devotion."

Williams moved to her table, her movements economical and purposeful. Chris straightened almost imperceptibly, drawing strength from her words that validated everything he'd chosen over biological imperative.

"This court will hear testimony about abandonment versus redemption. But we ask you to listen carefully to what abandonment truly means. It began not with the signing of legal documents, but with the conscious choice to emotionally withdraw from responsibility. The termination papers merely formalized a decision Mr. Matthews had already made in his heart."

She fixed her gaze on the judge. "Today's hearing isn't about denying a biological connection. It's about validating the family that has sustained this child through every milestone of her life. The family that didn't require a court order to love her."

Mary's eyes met Chris's across the courtroom. The communication was instant, maternal—pride mixed with protective concern. Her slight nod conveyed more than words could express in this formal setting.

As Williams returned to her seat, Leah's breath released in a shuddering exhale. Chris felt the tension in her shoulders ease fractionally—their lawyer had captured precisely what they needed the court to understand.

"Mr. Wallace," Judge Erikson prompted, "you may call your first witness."

"The defense calls Dr. Melissa Kennedy, expert in child psychology and attachment theory."

Dr. Kennedy took the stand with academic authority. Her credentials sounded impressive—PhD in developmental psychology, published research on parent-child attachment, consultant for family courts nationwide.

"Dr. Kennedy, in your professional opinion, how important is biological connection to a child's emotional development?"

"Research consistently demonstrates that children benefit from knowing and having relationships with both biological parents when possible," Dr. Kennedy stated with scholarly confidence. "The biological connection provides not just genetic continuity but psychological grounding in identity formation."

Leah felt the blood drain from her face. Her abandoned medical studies provided enough knowledge to recognize the oversimplification, but the expert testimony carried weight that would be difficult to counter.

The testimony continued, painting pictures of children who successfully maintained multiple parent figures, emphasizing the unique role of biological ties in identity formation. Each scholarly statement added another brick to Wallace's carefully constructed argument.

Williams' cross-examination focused on exposing the theoretical nature of the testimony.

"Dr. Kennedy, have you personally interviewed Louise?"

"No, I have not."

"Have you interviewed Mr. Johnson or Ms. Miller?"

"I reviewed psychological profiles provided by Mr. Matthews' legal team."

"Profiles compiled by whom exactly?"

"I believe they were prepared by the legal team's researchers."

"So your expert opinion is based on secondhand information prepared by advocates for one side?"

"My opinion is based on established research in the field—"

"Research about children in general, not about this specific child and her specific circumstances?"

"Correct, but the principles apply—"

"Thank you, Dr. Kennedy. No further questions."

Wallace called several church members who testified about Louise's "changes" since learning about Ryan. Their observations, carefully curated, suggested instability without directly attacking Chris or Leah's parenting. Each witness described moments of withdrawn behavior, artwork that seemed darker, questions about family structure that concerned them. The testimony accumulated like snowfall—individually insignificant, collectively creating an impression of troubling patterns.

During the brief recess, Chris and Leah remained in their seats, processing the weight of testimony that had transformed innocent moments into evidence against them. Leah's hand found his knee beneath the table, her touch grounding them both.

"Ms. Williams," Judge Erikson said as court reconvened, "you may proceed."

"Thank you, Your Honor. The plaintiff calls Susan Anderson."

Susan entered with quiet dignity. Her silver hair, styled simply, framed a face etched with both grief and resilience. She moved to the witness stand without theatrical flourish.

"Ms. Anderson, please describe your relationship to the parties involved."

Susan's shoulders straightened slightly, her gaze drifting briefly to Leah before returning to the judge. "My late daughter Kate and Leah were best friends since kindergarten. When I lost Kate to leukemia, the void was..." Her voice wavered momentarily, then steadied. "Leah became the daughter who remained."

The courtroom air thickened with the weight of this shared history. Ryan shifted uncomfortably in his seat.

"Kate was with Leah through every early doctor's appointment, every midnight worry," Susan continued. "She was in the delivery room when Louise was born—holding Leah's hand while Ryan remained completely unaware."

Her words painted a devastating picture of Ryan's calculated abandonment—from infidelity to immediate rejection of responsibility to signing termination papers without hesitation.

"When Leah told Ryan about the pregnancy, his response was immediate. He wanted no part of it. When Leah refused to consider termination, Ryan simply walked away. No discussion of support, no consideration of alternatives. That's when Leah contacted me for legal referrals. I recommended Ms. Williams. Within a week, the voluntary termination of parental rights was drafted. Ryan signed immediately upon receiving it with no questions and no hesitation."

Ryan visibly paled, his carefully constructed narrative unraveling.

Miss Andrews followed, providing professional assessment of Louise's emotional journey.

"Initially, there was marked psychological regression," Miss Andrews testified. "Her artwork became darker, her social interactions decreased. However," she emphasized, "once her parents addressed the situation honestly and age-appropriately, Louise's recovery was remarkable. Within two weeks, she was participating fully in classroom activities again."

Ashley Peterson testified next, describing Louise's swimming confidence and Ryan's calculated appearance at the recreation center.

"I observe their interactions regularly," Ashley explained. "Chris knows her fears about deep water, celebrates her small victories, corrects her technique with patience. Louise calls him 'Daddy' without prompting—it's completely natural."

The testimony continued building their case, each witness adding layers of evidence that Chris had earned his role through presence, not claimed it through biology.

"Mr. Wallace, your next witness?" Judge Erikson prompted.

"The defense calls Terry O'Donnell."

The courtroom's energy shifted as Terry rose from the gallery. Her floral cardigan and pearl necklace created an image of wholesome traditionalism.

301

She moved toward the witness stand with the measured steps of a woman who had spent decades commanding church committees.

Leah's throat constricted. Chris's fingers twitched against the legal pad before him, recognizing the subtle movement as tension manifesting through muscle and bone.

"Ms. O'Donnell, please state your relationship to the minor child."

"I'm Louise's great-aunt. My nephew, Chris, married her mother." Terry's voice projected with perfect modulation. "I've known Louise since Chris and Leah announced their engagement."

Wallace approached with calculated friendliness, his demeanor suggesting he was merely facilitating a concerned relative's honest observations.

"Ms. O'Donnell, as a family member who has observed Louise regularly, can you describe your concerns about her wellbeing?"

Terry's shoulders straightened, her expression settling into lines of practiced concern. "Of course. I love my nephew dearly, and I want what's best for Louise. That's why I've been so troubled by what I've witnessed. The child is bright and sweet, but clearly struggling with confusion about her family structure. I've witnessed crying at church events, increasing withdrawal from family gatherings, artwork that's become progressively darker in subject matter."

Wallace nodded encouragingly. "Can you provide specific examples?"

"At the church picnic several weeks ago, I overheard Louise tell another child that her daddy 'isn't her real daddy.' She seemed confused, almost distressed about it." Terry's voice carried calculated concern. "It breaks my heart to see such confusion in a child so young. And yes, I've seen drawings that concerned me greatly—dark clouds, rain-soaked figures, houses without windows. The kind of imagery that suggests a child processing significant emotional distress."

Wallace approached with a manila folder. "Your Honor, I'd like to enter as Exhibit A—Louise's recent artwork, displaying signs of emotional distress."

The drawings emerged—powerful images that, stripped of context and the subsequent recovery Miss Andrews had testified about, appeared damning. Judge Erikson examined them with practiced neutrality, but concern flickered across his features.

"Ms. O'Donnell," Wallace continued, "in your observation as a concerned family member, how would you describe the family dynamics?"

"Complicated," Terry said with seeming reluctance. "Chris is a good man—I helped raise him, and I love him dearly. But I worry he's been drawn into a situation that's beyond his capacity to handle. Louise needs stability, and what I've observed is increasing uncertainty about her place in the family."

The testimony continued with Wallace extracting carefully curated observations that painted a picture of instability without directly attacking Chris or Leah's character. Each question was designed to present Terry as nothing more than a loving great-aunt sharing honest concerns about a child's wellbeing.

"No further questions, Your Honor," Wallace said finally, returning to his seat with visible satisfaction.

Judge Erikson looked up from his notes. "Ms. Williams, you may cross-examine the witness."

Williams rose slowly, her movements carrying the confidence of someone about to deploy a prepared strategy.

"Thank you, Your Honor." Williams approached Terry with measured steps. "Ms. O'Donnell, you've presented yourself as a concerned family member simply sharing honest observations about Louise's wellbeing."

"That's correct."

"And these observations were made purely out of love for Louise and concern for her emotional state?"

"Absolutely."

Williams moved to her table, lifting a document folder with deliberate precision. "Your Honor, I'd like to introduce Exhibit B—evidence that speaks to the actual motivations behind Ms. O'Donnell's testimony."

She distributed packets containing photographs. Chris felt his pulse quicken—the moment they'd discussed was arriving.

"These photographs document betting jars discovered at the Henderson family residence. They contain actual money and written predictions about how long Chris and Leah's marriage will last."

Terry's entire body tensed, color draining from her face as understanding struck with devastating clarity. All those times she'd assured herself this was harmless family entertainment, just innocent wagering on what everyone expected would happen anyway. The jars had been hidden carefully, visited only when she needed to document something new. How had they been found?

Mary gasped audibly, her hand flying to her mouth as the true extent of her sister's deception laid bare before the court. Tom's arm immediately circled her shoulders, but his own face had darkened with barely contained rage. This wasn't just family disapproval—this was calculated cruelty transformed into cash incentive.

"These jars were found by Chris Johnson following a conversation with Louise, in which their four-year-old daughter asked what 'betting' meant after overhearing family discussions." Williams paused, letting the implication sink in. "The slips of paper bear the names of several family members, including Ms. O'Donnell's prediction."

She held up a photocopy of one slip, enlarged for the court to see clearly. "'Less than 3 years. Chris is saddled with another man's child.'"

The words echoed through the courtroom like a physical blow. Chris felt Leah's sharp intake of breath, her body trembling slightly against his. Their daughter, their beloved daughter, reduced to a burden in someone's gambling ledger.

"Ms. O'Donnell," Williams continued, "Did you facilitate this betting game and asked family members to place bets on when Chris and Leah's marriage would fail?"

Terry's mouth opened and closed wordlessly. Her carefully constructed persona of concerned relative was crumbling in real time.

"I... it was just... it wasn't serious—"

"Not serious?" Williams' voice sharpened. "You wagered money on the failure of your nephew's marriage. You reduced his stepdaughter to a burden. And you did this while presenting yourself as a loving, concerned family member."

"Objection," Wallace attempted, rising from his seat. "Counsel is badgering the witness—"

"Overruled," Judge Erikson said, his expression having transformed from professional neutrality to something harder, more judgmental. "The witness will answer the question."

Terry's hands gripped the witness stand railing, knuckles white. "It was meant as... we didn't think..."

"You didn't think Chris and Leah would find out," Williams supplied. "But they did. Because Louise, the child you claim to be so concerned about, overheard adult conversations about these betting jars and asked her parents what 'betting' meant."

The courtroom had gone completely silent except for Terry's labored breathing. Even the court reporter's fingers had stilled on the keys, everyone transfixed by the systematic demolition of Terry's credibility.

"Ms. O'Donnell, you testified earlier that you've been documenting Louise's behavioral changes out of concern for her wellbeing. Is that correct?"

"Yes," Terry managed.

"And did you discuss these concerns first with Chris and Leah before documenting them?"

"I felt an obligation to protect Louise—"

"That's not what I asked," Williams interrupted sharply. "Did you discuss your concerns with Louise's parents before documenting them for potential legal proceedings?"

"No, but—"

"Thank you. Now, I have additional evidence regarding the coordination of your testimony." Williams produced a tablet from her table. "Your Honor, with the court's permission, I'd like to play a recording made by Ms. Ashley Peterson, who observed and documented a meeting between Ms. O'Donnell and Mr. Matthews at the Copper Kettle café."

"Objection!" Wallace was on his feet immediately. "We had no notice of this evidence—"

"The recording was made in a public establishment with no expectation of privacy," Williams countered calmly. "Ms. Peterson will testify to its authenticity if required. The recording is relevant to establishing Ms. O'Donnell's actual motivations for her testimony here today."

Judge Erikson considered briefly, his gaze moving between the lawyers before settling on Terry's pale face. "I'll allow it. Proceed."

Williams pressed play on the tablet. The audio quality was slightly muffled—café background noise, the hiss of an espresso machine, fragments of other conversations—but Terry's voice came through with damning clarity:

"Well, I've continued documenting what I can observe. There was that incident where Louise used the cookie analogy to explain family structure—"

Ryan's voice, tense and frustrated: *"You already told me about that. What else? Recent observations? New incidents?"*

"They've stopped coming to family gatherings. After Chris found out about... after certain family tensions became apparent, they haven't attended Sunday dinners. They're not at church anymore. Louise isn't at the family picnics or birthday parties."

"So you have nothing new."

"It's not that I have nothing. It's that they've deliberately isolated themselves. Which in itself could be seen as concerning behavior—"

"We can't testify about what we can't observe. Wallace wants documented incidents. Recent ones."

When the audio ended, the courtroom sat in stunned silence. Terry's face had gone from pale to ashen, her entire body rigid with the horror of hearing her own words played back as evidence of conspiracy.

"Ms. O'Donnell," Williams said quietly, the deadly calm of her voice more devastating than any shout, "that recording reveals that you've been coordinating with Mr. Matthews and his legal team, actively strategizing about how to build their custody case against Chris and Leah. Is that correct?"

Terry couldn't contain herself any longer. She half-rose from her seat, her voice carrying across the stunned courtroom with desperate urgency:

"Chris, please! It was just a friendly family wager. Nothing serious! You have to understand—I would never actually hurt you. I was trying to protect you!"

"Ms. O'Donnell!" Judge Erikson's gavel came down sharply, the sound like a gunshot in the silent courtroom. "You are out of order. Sit down immediately and wait for counsel to finish her cross-examination."

But Terry persisted, desperation overriding courtroom protocol and any remaining sense of self-preservation. She moved toward the edge of the witness stand, her hands reaching out in pleading gesture, ignoring the judge's warning and the bailiff who had started to move toward her.

"I've always protected you, Chris. Always! Since you were a boy, since your father lost everything. I couldn't let you make another mistake—"

The courtroom had descended into chaos, voices rising, family members choosing sides with visible allegiance shifts. Emma and Billy retreated from Terry, their faces masks of shock and disappointment. Kourtney avoided everyone's eyes, her own name likely among those in the betting jars.

Judge Erikson's gavel came down repeatedly, the sharp reports demanding order. "This court will come to order! Ms. O'Donnell, you will sit down immediately, or I will hold you in contempt!"

Terry finally seemed to register where she was, what she'd done. She stumbled back to her seat in the witness stand, her legs barely supporting her weight as the reality of her complete implosion penetrated her defensive rationalizations.

"Order! ORDER in this court!" Judge Erikson's voice thundered through the space. "Bailiff!"

The bailiff moved forward with professional efficiency, positioning himself near the witness stand to ensure no further outbursts disrupted the proceedings.

Judge Erikson waited until order was restored before addressing Williams. "Counsel, do you have any further questions for this witness?"

"Just one, Your Honor." Williams' voice carried the calm of someone who had achieved complete victory. "Ms. O'Donnell, given what this court has just witnessed, would you like to revise your earlier testimony about being motivated purely by concern for Louise's wellbeing?"

Terry couldn't even lift her head. "No further comment," she whispered.

"No further questions, Your Honor." Williams returned to her seat, leaving Terry's credibility in complete ruins.

"The witness is excused," Judge Erikson said, his tone carrying unmistakable disgust.

Terry rose on shaking legs and made her way back to the gallery, though the space around her had cleared as if her betrayal was contagious. Even Mary couldn't look at her sister, her arm firmly linked with Tom's as they created a protective barrier.

During closing arguments, Wallace attempted damage control, but the betting jars and recorded conspiracy had fundamentally altered the courtroom's emotional landscape. His professional demeanor couldn't mask the impact of Terry's outburst or the documented evidence of family members literally profiting from anticipated divorce.

"Your Honor, despite the unfortunate revelations about family dynamics, the core issue remains unchanged. Ryan Matthews is Louise's biological father. He seeks to exercise rights that the law recognizes can be reinstated under changed circumstances. The betting jars, while distasteful, don't negate his biological connection to his daughter."

Williams' closing was surgical in its precision: "Your Honor, this court has witnessed not a father seeking connection, but an engineer executing a calculated campaign. The betting jars prove family members viewed this child's stability as entertainment. The café recording proves strategic coordination with witnesses who presented themselves as objective. This is not a father seeking to reconnect—this is systematic manipulation using family dysfunction as ammunition. Mr. Matthews had rights—he voluntarily terminated them. He had opportunities—he squandered them. What he seeks now is not fatherhood but absolution for abandonment. This court should not reward his campaign of systematic family destruction."

Judge Erikson removed his glasses with deliberate slowness, the gesture suggesting his mind was made up. The courtroom held its collective breath as he organized his notes.

"This court will issue a comprehensive written decision within ten days addressing all matters raised in these proceedings." He paused, his gaze moving between the two tables with judicial gravity. "However, I am prepared to rule from the bench on the emergency stay requested by Mr. Matthews."

He fixed Ryan with a stern gaze. "Your petition came with a request for immediate visitation. This court denies that request. The evidence suggests your campaign, aided by family members who wagered on this child's family failing, has manufactured rather than prevented distress. Any contact will remain supervised and limited until final determination."

Ryan's face darkened, his hands gripping the table's edge until his knuckles turned white. The legal defeat had been total, humiliating, public.

"This court is adjourned."

As the room erupted into movement, Terry made one last desperate attempt to reach Chris. She pushed through the crowd, ignoring Mary's protective stance, her eyes fixed on her nephew with pleading intensity.

"Chris, please. Just talk to me. Let me explain—"

But Chris turned away without acknowledgment, his arm circling Leah and guiding her toward the exit. The message was clear: some betrayals could not be explained away, some trust once broken could not be easily mended.

Outside the courtroom, the world continued its normal rhythm while theirs had been forever altered. Chris and Leah stood on the courthouse steps, processing victory that tasted of relief, triumph shadowed by family devastation but vindication of everything they'd fought to protect.

"Daddy! Mommy!" Louise's voice carried across the plaza as she ran from the babysitter, her joy untouched by the battle waged for her future.

Chris scooped her up, his anger dissolving instantly into fierce protectiveness. Her small arms circled his neck, and in that moment, he knew with absolute certainty: they would survive this. The family they'd chosen was stronger than any that had rejected them.

But as he carried Louise to their car, his eyes caught movement across the parking lot. Ryan stood beside his vehicle, his gaze fixed on them with an intensity that spoke of unfinished business. Terry hovered nearby, clearly attempting some form of reconciliation. Ryan's dismissive gesture sent her reeling, his attention never wavering from Chris.

The legal war had a clear victor, though Judge Erikson's final ruling would come within ten days. But the look in Ryan's eyes promised that legal defeat might not be the end of their troubles.

Inside their car, Louise chattered happily about her morning adventures. Leah's hand found Chris's on the gear shift, fingers interweaving with silent communication: they'd faced the storm together. Whatever came next, they would weather that too.

310

Behind them, Terry finally accepted Ryan's rejection. Her crusade to "protect" Chris had demolished the relationships she'd claimed to cherish. The betting jars, once hidden symbols of certainty, now stood as permanent testament to the price of playing God with other people's happiness.

As Chris drove away, his daughter's laughter filled the interior space. The courthouse diminished in the rearview mirror, but Ryan's figure remained visible, watching, planning. The custody hearing had exposed the conspiracy against their family, but it had also revealed depths of betrayal that would take time to process and heal from.

Some wars, Chris realized, left scars even in victory. But as Louise's voice sang out with joy, he knew they had protected what mattered most—her security, her happiness, her family.

The house welcomed them with silent understanding. Darkness had fallen hours ago, but someone, Mrs. Abernathy, perhaps, had left a lamp burning in the entryway. Its gentle glow transformed familiar corridors into sanctuaries of warmth after the battlefield of the courtroom.

Louise had fallen asleep in the car, her energy finally depleted after celebrating their return with unrestrained joy. The simple happiness of a child unaware of how close her world had come to fracturing beneath her feet. Chris carried her carefully up the stairs, her small form nestled against his chest, dark curls spilling over his arm.

Leah followed, fingers trailing along the wall's familiar texture. The day's victory clung to her like courthouse dust, not quite settled into reality. The betting jars. The recordings. Terry's desperate face as everything collapsed. The memories fought for dominance, threatening to invade even this sacred space.

By silent agreement, they tucked Louise into bed together. Chris smoothed her favorite quilt while Leah arranged Bear Elephant in his rightful place beside her pillow. Their daughter's sleep remained untroubled by procedural victories or family betrayals. Her world remained intact, protected by their silence in the face of Terry's cruelty, by their honesty when truth became necessary.

"We won," Chris whispered as they closed Louise's door, the words carrying both triumph and disbelief. The hallway light transformed his face, highlighting the exhaustion etched into lines around his eyes, yet unable to dim the quiet elation beneath.

Leah nodded, her throat suddenly tight. "For now."

Downstairs, they moved through familiar rituals that suddenly felt new again. Chris uncorked a bottle of wine saved for special occasions. Leah lit candles across their living room. Neither spoke much, the silence between them comfortable with shared understanding. Their bodies gravitated toward each other across ordinary spaces—hand brushing arm, shoulder leaning briefly against shoulder, eyes meeting in communion more profound than words.

"To family," Chris said finally, raising his glass. The crystal caught candlelight, transforming ordinary glass into something precious.

"To chosen family," Leah amended, her glass meeting his with gentle percussion.

The wine spread warmth through her body, muscles gradually releasing tension held for too many weeks. She settled beside him on the couch, their thighs touching with comfortable intimacy. Louise's artwork decorated the coffee table—bright scenes created since their honest conversation, evidence of healing that no court could fully appreciate.

"I keep seeing his face," Chris admitted, fingers tracing the wine glass's stem. "Ryan's eyes when the judge denied his petition. Something dangerous there."

"Not tonight," Leah whispered, setting down her glass. "He doesn't get to live here too."

She reached for him with deliberate intention, fingers threading through his hair. His response was immediate—arms circling her waist, drawing her closer with gentle insistence. Their lips met with the particular hunger that follows survival, relief transforming into something deeper, more primal.

"I was so afraid," he murmured against her neck, the confession emerging only now in safety. "That somehow biology would trump everything we've built."

Leah drew back, framing his face between her palms. "Nothing trumps this," she said, eyes holding his with fierce certainty. "Nothing trumps what we've chosen every day since we met."

His hands moved along her spine with practiced familiarity, each vertebra known territory mapped through countless nights. Yet tonight carried something different—the particular intimacy that follows shared battle, vulnerability laid bare and accepted without judgment.

"Take me upstairs," she whispered, the words carrying transparent intention.

The bedroom welcomed them like old friends. Moonlight spilled through half-drawn curtains, painting silver paths across familiar terrain. They undressed each other with deliberate care, fingers lingering over exposed skin, reaffirming existence through touch. Each moment unfolded with measured grace, the hurricane of the courtroom transformed into gentle tide pulling them toward shared horizon.

His hands trembled slightly as they traced the familiar geography of her body. Fingertips mapped constellations across skin that had become both known territory and perpetual revelation. The courtroom's clinical dissection of their family bonds—reduced to legal terminology and biological definitions—dissolved in the honest truth of touch. Here lay evidence no lawyer could present, no witness could testify to—the silent language they'd crafted through years of chosen intimacy.

"I need you," Leah whispered, the simple phrase carrying layers of meaning beyond physical desire. Need as recognition. Need as choice. Need as deliberate selection of this man who had chosen fatherhood not through biological imperative but through daily acts of love.

Chris's eyes held hers as he lowered her to their bed. The mattress received her with the familiar depression of countless nights—the topography of their shared history. His weight above her provided counterbalance to the day's weightlessness, where their family had been suspended between legal definitions and judicial determinations.

"You have me," he answered, his voice carrying the roughened edges of emotion too complex for courtroom expression. "Always."

Their bodies connected with the precision of instruments tuned to the same key. Familiar rhythms accelerated by the day's threats, deepened by the recognition of what they had nearly lost, transformed by the knowledge of what they'd fought to preserve. The courthouse's harsh fluorescent reality gave way to the candlelit truth of their bedroom—the space where they had constructed family through choice rather than obligation.

Leah's fingers pressed against the muscles of his back, feeling the tension of weeks finally releasing beneath her touch. Each point of contact between their bodies represented defiance against those who would reduce their connection to legal terminology or biological coincidence. Their shared breath created counterpoint to the day's sterile proceedings, their synchronizing heartbeats offering evidence no paternity test could measure.

Outside, rain began to fall, its gentle percussion against the roof providing soundtrack to their movements. Inside, they created sanctuary from storm, shelter against judgment, protection from the cold calculations of custody determinations.

Her hands cradled his face, forcing him to meet her gaze. In the dim light, his eyes revealed what he'd concealed in the courtroom—the wound of family betrayal, the determination to protect what mattered most, the fierce love that had transformed him from Louise's mother's boyfriend to her father in every way that mattered.

Their bodies moved with increasing urgency, need accelerating into necessity, desire transformed into the particular hunger that follows near-loss. Each touch reaffirmed existence. Each connection repaired what legal proceedings had threatened to fracture.

The moonlight cast their shadows on bedroom walls, merged silhouettes inseparable from each other. They moved together with the practiced harmony of those who had chosen each other repeatedly, daily, across years of shared challenges. This wasn't merely physical connection but deliberate reconstruction of the bonds Terry's betting jars and Ryan's paternity claims had attempted to dismantle.

Their breathing synchronized as they approached the edge together. The boundary between separate consciousness dissolved, replaced by the particular unity that transcends biological definitions or legal categorizations. In these moments, they existed beyond the court's jurisdiction, beyond scientific testing, beyond the limited understanding that reduced family to DNA or paperwork.

Release came like emotional tsunami, washing away courtroom debris and family betrayals. The moment suspended them together in perfect counterpoint to the day's separation—unified rather than divided, connected rather than categorized, whole rather than fractured.

Afterward, wrapped in sheets carrying their mingled scent, Chris traced constellations across her bare shoulder. Leah's head rested against his chest, her ear pressed to the steady drumbeat that had become her most trusted lullaby.

"Tomorrow we start over," he said, the vibration of his voice resonating where skin met skin. "Just us. No Terry. No Ryan. No betting jars."

Leah nodded, her fingers finding the familiar territory of his collarbone. "Just family," she agreed. "The one we've built."

"I mean what I said in court," he whispered into the darkness. "Every day, I choose her. I choose you."

"I know," Leah murmured, her fingers tracing the calluses on his fingertips, marks of countless guitar lessons, of patient teaching, of choosing music as language when words failed. "I never doubted."

He pulled her closer, their bodies aligning with practiced ease. The courtroom's clinical dissection of family bonds—biological versus chosen, genetic versus cultivated—dissolved in the simple truth of their physical connection. Here lay evidence no paternity test could challenge, no legal brief could diminish, no family betting jar could undermine.

Outside their window, stars continued their ancient patterns, indifferent to human victories or defeats. Inside, in the sanctuary they'd created through choice rather than obligation, two bodies remained intertwined—battle-worn but undefeated, marked by betrayal but not defined by it.

The night enfolded them in temporary peace. Tomorrow would bring new challenges, Ryan's unspoken threats, family bonds requiring redefinition. But tonight belonged to them alone, to skin against skin, to whispered affirmations, to the small sacred space they'd carved from chaos.

As sleep claimed them, their bodies remained connected, hands intertwined, breath synchronized, hearts beating variations on the same essential rhythm. Not perfect, not untouched by storm, but standing.

Together.

CHAPTER 18

The Price of Thirty Seconds

Sunlight streamed through the kitchen windows, painting golden rectangles across scattered party supplies. Three weeks had passed since Judge Erikson's ruling, and their house had settled into something approaching peace. Leah spread rainbow streamers across the granite counter while Chris sorted through the guest list, his fingers hesitating over certain names with familiar weight.

The refrigerator door served as gallery for Louise's recent artwork—a progression that told its own story of healing. The dark, rain-soaked figures from months ago had given way to explosions of color, family portraits where stick figures held hands beneath enormous suns.

"Mommy, can we hang my rainbow one in the living room?" Louise bounced into the kitchen, her latest creation clutched in both hands. The watercolor piece showed their family as a garden—three flowers growing together with roots tangled beneath the soil, surrounded by butterflies that looked more like cheerful blobs but carried her unmistakable joy.

"Absolutely," Leah smiled. "Miss Andrews said that one was her favorite."

The call from the school had come yesterday—Louise's artwork selected for the district showcase, one of only five chosen. Miss Andrews had called it "remarkable emotional depth for someone so young."

"Is everyone coming to my party?" Louise asked, settling onto her stool.

"Most everyone," Chris said carefully, studying the invitation list.

His grandparents' names went into the "yes" pile without hesitation. His parents too—solid anchors in the storm. But the next name made his hand pause. Uncle Randy, who had wagered thirty dollars with the notation "generous considering he's saddled with another man's child."

"Is Aunt Terry coming?"

The question struck like a carefully aimed dart. Leah's hands stilled on the streamers.

"Things are complicated right now, sweet girl," Leah answered with practiced calm.

Louise's face scrunched with confusion. "But she always comes to parties."

"Sometimes grown-ups disagree about important things," Chris said, his voice rougher than intended.

His phone buzzed. A text from his mother: *Your dad and I can't wait to celebrate Louise's art achievement. So proud of all of you.*

Relief flooded through him. Another text appeared—this one making his jaw clench: *Please let me explain. I never meant to hurt anyone. - Terry*

He deleted it without responding, though his finger trembled against the screen.

"Daddy?" Louise climbed into his lap, her small hands framing his face. "Are you sad about my party?"

The innocent question shattered his careful composure. He pulled her close, breathing in the strawberry scent of her shampoo. "No, Sunshine.

I'm so proud of you. Your art teacher said you're one of the best in the whole district."

"All the districts?" Louise's eyes widened.

"Every single one."

Leah's phone rang—Williams' name flashing. She answered on speaker.

"I have good news," Williams said without preamble. "The adoption finalization hearing is scheduled. Judge Erikson's office called—you're on the docket for next week."

Chris looked up sharply, hope and caution warring in his expression. After months of Ryan's custody petition holding everything in limbo, the path forward had finally cleared.

"Next week," he repeated, testing the words.

"Wednesday morning, nine AM. It's a formality at this point—Judge Erikson already indicated his approval during the custody hearing. This makes it official."

Leah felt tears threatening. "Thank you."

"You've earned this," Williams replied warmly. "I'll send the details this afternoon."

The call ended, leaving them sitting in profound silence. Mary knocked softly at the door before entering, her arms full of supplies. "I brought things for the party. Decorations, snacks, everything I could think of."

Louise squealed, launching herself at her grandmother. Mary's face softened, the weight of recent weeks briefly lifted by small arms circling her waist.

"Grandma Mary! I won the art contest! My pictures are going to be in the big showcase!"

"I know, sweetheart. I'm so proud of you."

Chris studied his mother, searching for signs of divided loyalty. The betting jars had shattered his ability to trust family instincts—everyone required scrutiny now.

Mary caught his assessment, pain flickering across her features. She straightened after Louise skipped away. "We need to talk."

They moved to the living room while Louise returned to her artwork.

"I didn't know about the betting jars," Mary began. "If I had—"

"Would you have stopped her?" Chris interrupted.

Mary's silence stretched too long. "I don't know," she finally admitted. "But I'm choosing now. Your side. Louise's side. Whatever it costs."

"It might cost everything," Chris warned. "Terry won't forgive what she'll see as betrayal."

"Then that's her choice." Mary's voice carried unexpected steel. "I've already lost too much by avoiding hard decisions."

The afternoon progressed with party preparations taking shape. Streamers hung in rainbow progression. Art supplies arranged for guests who might want to create. Display easels positioned throughout the house.

"This is going to be wonderful," Leah said, surveying their work.

Chris wrapped his arm around her waist. "She deserves this. Pure celebration without the shadow of legal battles."

"We all deserve this," Leah corrected. "Peace. The chance to just be a family."

Mary watched them from across the room, relief and hope replacing the grief that had characterized recent weeks. "I'm proud of you both. For not letting them break you."

"They came close," Chris admitted.

Louise's voice drifted from the kitchen, singing to herself with unselfconscious joy. The melody carried perfect contentment—soundtrack of childhood unmarred by adult complications.

"One more week," Chris said, pulling Leah closer. "One more week until the adoption becomes final."

"Don't jinx it," Leah whispered, though she smiled.

As evening settled over their home, they allowed themselves to hope that the worst had passed. That Louise's artwork would be celebrated rather than scrutinized. That her party would be joyful rather than surveilled. That their family's security was real rather than temporary reprieve.

The invitation list lay completed on the kitchen counter—names sorted into categories of trust and distance, relationships recalibrated against new understanding. Some bonds had been severed. Others had been strengthened through loyalty tested under fire.

Outside their windows, evening progressed toward dusk. Inside, a family rebuilt itself through careful attention to what mattered—not victory over enemies, but preservation of love that had survived systematic attempts at destruction.

Louise's laughter rang out as she discovered a new color combination. Mary helped Leah hang streamers while Chris reviewed the guest list one final time, ensuring only those who could genuinely celebrate would witness Louise's joy.

The party would be perfect. Small, intimate, focused entirely on a little girl whose artwork had become both weapon and testimony, evidence and healing.

But tonight, they planned a celebration unmarred by fear. Tonight, Louise's artwork blazed across their refrigerator. Tonight, the adoption papers moved steadily toward finalization. Tonight, they were simply a family preparing to honor their daughter's talent.

Tomorrow would bring whatever challenges it required. But tonight belonged to hope, to healing, to the peace that came from believing love could survive anything—even the systematic destruction attempted by those who claimed to be family.

Rainbow streamers hung like cheerful banners from the ceiling, their vibrant colors catching the afternoon sunlight streaming through the kitchen windows. The air smelled of chocolate cake and fresh-cut grass, punctuated by the sweet laughter of children who remained blissfully unaware of adult complications swirling around them.

Chris stood guard by the front gate, his tall frame casting a shadow across the driveway as his eyes swept the street with intensity. Every car that passed sent electricity through his nervous system, his hands unconsciously flexing and releasing as tension coiled through his shoulders. Leah had laughed at his vigilance that morning, calling him overprotective, but now he scanned faces like someone protecting precious cargo.

"Daddy, come see!" Louise called from the bounce house, her dress sparkling in the sunlight as she jumped with pure joy. Her dark curls caught the light, creating a halo effect around her beaming face that made Chris's chest tighten with fierce protectiveness.

"Coming, Sunshine," Chris forced his shoulders to relax, pushing down the coiled tension that had become his constant companion since the custody hearing. This was Louise's day, her moment of celebration for being selected for the district art showcase, and nothing would be allowed to spoil it.

Mary and Tom Johnson moved around the picnic table with determined normalcy, arranging gift bags with focused attention that spoke of people maintaining cheerful facades. Their presence anchored him—family who had chosen sides when choosing became necessary. Tom's weathered hands carefully straightened each bag while Mary fussed over party favors, both filling potential silence with cheerful chatter that held anxiety at bay.

Susan Anderson emerged from the kitchen carrying homemade ice cream, three flavors she'd spent the morning preparing. Her silver hair caught the breeze as she moved with confidence earned through becoming Louise's chosen grandmother by heart rather than genetics.

Leah's phone buzzed in her pocket. She glanced at the screen—her mother's name flashing. She stepped away from the celebration's center, answering with a smile that Chris could hear in her voice even from across the yard.

"Hi, Mom... Yes, we're celebrating right now... She's over the moon about the art showcase... I know, only five students chosen from the entire district..." Leah's voice softened. "Thank you. And yes, the hearing went better than we could have hoped... No, they're still back east... Just Dad nearby now, which has been... surprisingly helpful, actually."

She listened for a moment, her expression warming. "I'll tell her you're proud of her. She'd love that... We'll send photos... Love you too."

Leah ended the call and returned to Chris's side, a small smile playing at her lips despite the tension of the day. "Mom sends her congratulations to Louise. And to us, for the hearing."

Chris squeezed her hand, grateful for the reminder that family could exist in different forms, across distances, through phone calls that bridged the miles between Leah's past and their present.

"Chris, relax," Leah whispered, her hand finding his forearm, warm fingers pressing against tense muscle. "You're scaring the other parents with that stare."

Her familiar scent wrapped around him like a gentle reminder of what mattered most. He breathed deeply, trying to absorb her calm, but the vigilance remained like a fever he couldn't shake.

"I can't shake the feeling that something's about to go wrong," he admitted quietly.

"We won, Chris. It's over."

She was right, of course. The custody hearing victory should have brought peace. Instead, it had amplified his protective instincts to painful intensity.

A black sedan with tinted windows pulled up across the street. Chris's entire body went rigid, his frame straightening as every instinct screamed danger. The car sat there, engine running, windows too dark to see inside, but somehow radiating menace.

"Chris," Leah's voice carried a warning note. "Don't let paranoia steal this moment from Louise."

The sedan's door opened, and Ryan Matthews stepped out onto the asphalt. Time seemed to crystallize—Ryan's confident stride as he surveyed their domestic sanctuary, the assessment in his eyes as he took in the celebration with calculating gaze.

"Call the police," Chris said, his voice dropping to deadly calm.

"He's not doing anything illegal," Leah replied, though her face had drained of color. "Not yet."

Ryan approached the front gate with calculated casualness, his movements deliberate as he carried a silver-wrapped present. His smile was sharp enough to cut glass, the kind of expression that looked friendly from a distance but revealed its predatory nature up close.

"Hello, Leah," Ryan's voice carried through the chain-link barrier. "Chris." The greeting held just enough civility to seem reasonable while carrying undertones of ownership and challenge.

Other parents began to notice the commotion, their animated conversations faltering as they sensed the shift in atmosphere. Children continued playing with oblivious joy, but the adults developed that stillness that animals display when predators enter their territory.

"You need to leave," Chris stated with finality, his hand remaining firmly on the gate's latch. "Now."

"It's Louise's celebration," Ryan replied, holding up the wrapped box. "I brought her a gift. Surely even you can't object to that."

The casual dismissal hit Chris like a physical blow, his role as Louise's father reduced to an inconvenience to be brushed aside.

"You have no right to be here," Leah said, stepping closer to Chris until their shoulders touched. "The court order was very specific about no contact."

"I'm not asking for visitation. I'm simply delivering a gift. A five-minute interaction, completely public, with dozens of witnesses."

Louise spotted the commotion from the bounce house, her small face lighting up with innocent recognition. "It's the man from school! Mommy, it's Ryan!" Her voice carried across the yard with the clarity of a child who saw the world in simple terms.

Her innocent acknowledgment sent ice through Chris's veins while other parents turned to stare. Whispered conversations began to ripple through the gathering.

"Louise, stay in the bounce house," Leah called, her voice strained with the effort of maintaining false cheer. "Keep playing with your friends."

"But he brought me a present," Louise protested, bouncing higher to see over the adult heads that had formed a barrier.

Ryan's smile widened with satisfaction. He had accomplished exactly what he'd come for—Louise's attention, a public scene, and the perfect positioning of himself as the gift-bearing father being denied access.

"Just leave the present by the gate," Chris said through clenched teeth. "Then get in your car and drive away."

"I'd prefer to give it to her personally," Ryan replied smoothly. "After all, that's what any loving father would want to do."

Mary Johnson appeared beside them, her usually gentle face hardened into protective lines. "Is there a problem here?"

"No problem at all," Ryan said, turning his charm on Louise's grandmother. "Just a father bringing his daughter a gift. Though some people seem to think that's inappropriate."

The subtle emphasis painted Chris and Leah as the unreasonable parties while positioning himself as the wronged father simply trying to celebrate his child's achievement.

"You forfeited that privilege years ago," Leah said, her voice carrying the accumulated rage of years spent building a family while he pursued career advancement.

Ryan's mask slipped momentarily as calculation replaced charm. "People change, Leah. People grow. People recognize their mistakes and work to correct them." His pause was deliberate. "Though I suppose some people prefer to cling to comfortable arrangements rather than face difficult truths."

The comment carried barbed implications about their marriage, suggesting it was built on convenience rather than genuine love. Chris felt the tension in Leah's body through their connected shoulders.

"What's that supposed to mean?" Chris stepped closer to the gate, his imposing frame casting Ryan into shadow.

"Nothing at all," Ryan replied with false innocence, though his eyes glittered with satisfaction at having drawn a reaction. "Just observing that Louise deserves to understand her true family history. Her real heritage."

Other parents were openly staring now, some pulling out phones to record what was clearly becoming a confrontational scene. The celebration had transformed into unwilling theater.

"Like how you climbed into Jessica Fitzgerald's bed while I was carrying Louise?" Leah shot back, her composure finally cracking. "While I dealt with morning sickness and doctor appointments and preparing for our daughter's birth without any support from the man who was supposed to love us?"

The reference to his infidelity and abandonment hung in the air like poison gas, causing several nearby parents to exchange shocked glances.

"Ancient history," Ryan recovered quickly. "What matters now is Louise's future and ensuring she has access to her rightful place."

"Her place is with us," Chris stated with absolute certainty. "The family that's been there for her since birth."

"Is it though?" Ryan's voice dropped to a more intimate register. "How long do you think this little arrangement will last when Louise gets old enough to understand what really happened? When she realizes her mother trapped you into raising another man's child?"

The words hit Chris like physical blows, each syllable designed to wound multiple targets simultaneously. The suggestion that Leah had manipulated him, that Louise was a burden he'd been tricked into accepting, that their family was built on deception rather than love.

"That's enough," Leah whispered, her face flushing with rage and humiliation.

"Tell me, Chris," Ryan continued with surgical precision, "what do you think will happen when Louise starts asking the hard questions? When she wonders why her real father wasn't allowed to be part of her life? When she realizes you're just the man her mother settled for because she needed someone—anyone—to help raise her mistake?"

The casual cruelty of reducing Louise to a "mistake" combined with the implication that Chris was merely a convenient placeholder sent molten rage coursing through his bloodstream. His vision began to narrow as protective instincts overrode rational thought.

"Do you honestly think," Ryan pressed on, "that a brilliant little girl like Louise won't eventually figure out that her mother used you? That you're nothing more than a substitute father who was desperate enough to take on another man's responsibility?"

The systematic dismantling of everything Chris held sacred—his role as Louise's father, his marriage to Leah, his worth as a man—was delivered with precision designed to maximize damage while maintaining plausible deniability to the watching audience.

The word *mistake* hung in the air like poison gas. Around them, parents were pulling out phones, recording what was clearly becoming confrontation.

"You son of a—" Chris started forward.

"Chris, don't!" Leah grabbed his arm, but he was already moving.

His control didn't shatter so much as evaporate. One moment he was standing at the gate, the next his body was vaulting the chain-link barrier with fluid violence that came from somewhere primal and unstoppable. Years of suppressed rage erupted through his muscles with devastating force.

Ryan stumbled backward, genuine surprise replacing his calculated confidence. His expensive shoes found no purchase on the damp grass as Chris closed the distance between them in two powerful strides.

Chris's first punch came from his shoulder, his entire body weight behind the swing. His fist connected with Ryan's jaw with a sound like a baseball bat hitting leather—a solid, meaty *crack* that sent shock waves up Chris's arm. The impact snapped Ryan's head sideways with such force that spittle flew from his mouth in a crimson spray.

Ryan's knees buckled. He tried to catch himself, hands grasping at air, but Chris was already following through. His left hand grabbed a fistful of Ryan's expensive suit jacket, the fabric bunching in his grip as he steadied his target. His right fist drove upward into Ryan's solar plexus with piston-like precision.

The air exploded from Ryan's lungs in a wet, desperate *whoosh*. His mouth opened in a perfect O of shocked pain, eyes bulging as his diaphragm spasmed. Chris felt the give of soft tissue beneath his knuckles, the way Ryan's body folded around the impact like paper crumpling.

"You pathetic piece of shit," Chris snarled, his voice unrecognizable—something feral and ancient rising from depths he'd never known existed.

Ryan tried to double over, but Chris's grip on his jacket kept him upright like a puppet on strings. Chris's fist found his face again—a crushing blow to the cheekbone that split skin and sent blood spraying across perfectly manicured grass. The impact made a sound like a raw steak being slapped against marble, wet and final.

Children shrieked. Parents scattered, gathering their offspring while uncertain whether to intervene or flee. The bounce house deflated with a long, dying wheeze as someone hit the emergency cutoff, adding its collapse to the chaos of celebration becoming violence.

Ryan swung wildly, his fist grazing Chris's temple with enough force to send white sparks across his vision. The punch was desperate rather than calculated, panic rather than technique, but it connected. Pain bloomed sharp and immediate behind Chris's left eye.

The hit only fed his rage. Chris released Ryan's jacket and drove both hands into his chest with the force of a linebacker making a tackle. Ryan flew backward, his feet leaving the ground entirely before he crashed through the gift table. Susan's ice cream containers exploded on impact, vanilla and strawberry bleeding into the grass in swirls of white and pink. Glass shattered as serving dishes hit the ground, crystal fragments catching sunlight like scattered diamonds.

Ryan's shoulders hit first, then his head snapped back against the table's collapsing legs with a hollow *thunk* that made several onlookers gasp. But Chris was already on him, his knees hitting the ground on either side of Ryan's chest.

Chris's fist came down like a hammer. Once. Twice. The first punch split Ryan's lip wide open, blood welling immediately and spilling down his chin. The second caught him on the bridge of his nose with a sickening *crunch* of cartilage compressing. Not broken—Chris's musician hands instinctively pulled the punch at the last microsecond—but enough to send blood streaming from both nostrils.

"Daddy, stop!" Louise's voice cut through the red haze like a blade made of pure sound.

Chris froze with his hands wrapped around Ryan's throat, his daughter's distress finally penetrating the primitive rage that had consumed him. Louise stood at the edge of where the bounce house had been, tears streaming down her face, her purple dress seeming to wilt with her emotional devastation.

Ryan seized the moment of hesitation, his hands clawing at Chris's face. Manicured fingernails raked across Chris's cheek, drawing three parallel lines of fire from temple to jawbone. The sharp sting brought Chris fully back to himself.

He released Ryan's throat and stumbled backward, his chest heaving. His right hand throbbed, knuckles already swelling and split where skin had caught on Ryan's teeth. Blood—his own and Ryan's—painted his hands in abstract patterns.

Ryan collapsed to his knees in the trampled grass, gasping for breath. His face was a ruin—left eye already swelling shut, blood streaming from his nose and split lip, a purple bruise blooming across his cheekbone like some grotesque flower. His designer suit hung in tatters, the jacket torn at one shoulder, white shirt spotted with crimson.

"You see?" Ryan managed to gasp out to the gathered crowd, his voice thick with blood and calculation despite his battered state. "This is the man raising my daughter. This is what Louise witnesses."

The performance was breathtaking. Even beaten and bloodied, sprawled in melted ice cream and broken glass, he was crafting narrative. Every labored breath was staged for the audience of parents whose phones had captured Chris's loss of control.

Chris struggled to process what he'd done, adrenaline beginning to ebb and leave him shaking. Around them, parents held phones that had documented every punch, every moment of violence—digital evidence that would spread through social media within hours.

"This is what desperation looks like," Ryan continued, using the overturned table to pull himself upright. His legs trembled, and he nearly fell before catching himself. "A man who knows he has no legitimate claim resorting to violence when confronted with simple truth."

"You started this," Leah protested, moving to Chris's side. "You came here uninvited. You said those horrible things—"

"I brought a gift to my daughter," Ryan replied with manufactured innocence, dabbing blood from his nose with his sleeve. "He attacked me without any physical provocation whatsoever."

The lie hung in the air, protected by selective truth. The phones had captured the assault but not the psychological torture that preceded it.

Louise ran to Chris despite having witnessed his violent outburst, her small arms circling his waist. "Daddy, are you hurt?"

The question cracked something fundamental in his chest. He knelt to her level, ignoring the pain in his ribs and the burning shame of what he'd done in front of her. "I'm okay, Sunshine," he whispered, though he was anything but okay.

"Why did you hit him?" Louise asked, confusion clouding her features. "He just brought me a present."

The question he couldn't answer without destroying her innocence hung between them. Police sirens wailed in the distance, growing louder.

"I need to go," Ryan announced, picking up his fallen gift with theatrical care. Blood dripped from his chin onto the silver wrapping. "Before this situation deteriorates further."

He approached Louise with calculated gentleness despite his obvious pain, kneeling to her level. "Congratulations, sweetheart. I'm sorry your special day got disrupted by adult problems."

The subtle blame was perfectly crafted. Louise accepted the damaged present with reluctant politeness, her eyes wide and uncertain.

"Maybe we can celebrate properly sometime soon," Ryan continued, meeting Chris's eyes over Louise's head. "When things are calmer."

The implication was clear—this incident would be weaponized. Ryan's legal team would paint Chris as violent, uncontrolled, dangerous.

Ryan limped toward his car, his movements stiff and pained but functional. The police arrived just as his sedan disappeared around the corner, two officers approaching with professional caution as parents pointed toward Chris.

"Sir, we need you to put your hands behind your back," the first officer commanded.

The handcuffs closed around Chris's wrists as Louise screamed and tried to grab his legs. Her cries of "Don't take my daddy!" shattered what remained of his composure.

"It's okay, Sunshine," Chris called as they led him toward the patrol car. "Mommy will explain everything. I'll be home soon."

But even as he said the words, he knew they might be lies. The video evidence of his assault would be difficult to explain, and Ryan's team would use it to reopen the custody case with devastating effectiveness.

The patrol car door slammed shut. Through bulletproof glass, Chris watched Louise's celebration dissolve into chaos. Parents gathered their children and departed with uncomfortable haste, rainbow streamers trampled into grass, joy replaced by trauma that would mark this day in his daughter's memory forever.

Ryan's sedan was long gone, but Chris could imagine him already calling Wallace & Associates, already crafting the narrative. The custody battle they'd thought was over had just been reignited, and this time Chris had provided all the ammunition they needed.

As the police car pulled away from the wreckage of Louise's art celebration, Chris caught one final glimpse of his daughter in Leah's arms, both of them crying. The game had changed completely, and he had fallen into the trap Ryan had carefully constructed.

Violence was harder to explain than abandonment. In losing control for thirty seconds, Chris had potentially lost everything that mattered most—his daughter, his family, his future.

Behind them, chocolate cake sat untouched on the kitchen counter, celebration that had become nightmare none of them would ever forget.

CHAPTER 19

The Miller in Her

C hocolate cake sat abandoned on the kitchen counter. Outside, rainbow streamers hung torn from tree branches, fluttering in the evening breeze like prayers no one would answer.

Leah sat on the front steps, Louise's small body pressed against her chest. Her daughter's celebration dress had grass stains across the sequined fabric. Dried tears created salt tracks down cheeks still flushed from crying.

"When is Daddy coming home?" Louise asked for the seventh time, her voice small and lost.

Leah's throat closed around words that wouldn't form. How could she explain bail hearings to a young child? How could she describe assault charges to someone who still believed in the goodness of celebrations?

"Soon, baby girl." The lie tasted like copper pennies. "Soon."

Melting ice cream bled vanilla and strawberry into the grass where Susan's homemade containers had overturned. The sticky sweetness drew flies that buzzed with manic energy around the celebration's corpse.

Louise clutched Ryan's silver-wrapped present against her stomach. The paper was torn, stained with grass and something that might have been blood. She hadn't opened it yet. Hadn't asked to.

"Why did Daddy hurt that man?"

The question pierced what remained of Leah's composure. Her medical training supplied clinical terms—acute stress reaction, fight-or-flight response, temporary loss of impulse control. None of them helped.

"Sometimes grown-ups make mistakes when they're scared."

"Was Daddy scared of Ryan?"

Scared. The word felt insufficient. Chris had been protecting them with the primitive instinct of a father defending his family. But try explaining that to police officers. Try explaining that to a judge.

Leah's phone buzzed against the concrete step. Another voicemail. The seventh since Chris's arrest. She didn't need to listen to know what they contained—concerned neighbors, cancelled playdates, whispered questions about violence and stability.

Mary and Tom had left hours ago, their faces etched with shock and something that looked like shame. Even they couldn't defend what Chris had done.

"Mommy, my tummy hurts."

Louise's confession broke through Leah's spiraling thoughts. She pressed her palm against her daughter's forehead, checking for fever with automatic habit. Normal temperature. But trauma manifested in countless ways.

"Let's get you inside."

The living room felt like a crime scene. Gift bags scattered across hardwood floors. Decorations trampled and torn. The bounce house deflated in the backyard like a collapsed lung.

Louise's friends had fled with their parents, wide-eyed children pulled away from the wreckage of what should have been a celebration. Some parents had apologized. Others had simply loaded their children into minivans and driven away without backward glances.

The phone rang. Williams' name flashed on the screen.

"Not now," Leah whispered, declining the call.

It rang again immediately. She turned it off.

Louise sat on the couch, still clutching Ryan's gift. Her small fingers traced the torn edges of silver paper without opening it. Something in her posture, the careful stillness, the guarded expression, reminded Leah of herself at that age. Learning that adults weren't always safe. That family could fracture without warning.

"Are you hungry?" Leah asked, though the thought of food made her stomach clench.

Louise shook her head. Her dark eyes held questions too complex for her vocabulary. Why had her celebration become a nightmare? Why had her father's hands turned violent? Why did safety feel so fragile?

The doorbell rang. Leah's entire body tensed, fight-or-flight response activated by the simple sound. Through the peephole, she saw Mrs. Chen from down the street, holding a casserole dish with apologetic shoulders.

Leah didn't answer. Couldn't face another well-meaning neighbor with careful questions and worried glances.

The house felt smaller with Chris gone. His absence occupied space like a physical presence, highlighting every corner where his laugh usually echoed, every surface where his coffee cup normally rested.

Louise finally spoke, her voice barely audible. "Is Daddy going to jail?"

The question hit like a physical blow. Leah's knees buckled slightly as she sank onto the couch beside her daughter. Her medical school training had included courses on childhood trauma. She knew the statistics about family violence, about children who witnessed domestic abuse.

But this was different. Chris wasn't an abuser. He was a man pushed beyond breaking point by deliberate cruelty.

"I don't know, sweetheart."

Honesty felt brutal. But Louise had already seen too much deception. Had already learned that adults could smile while hiding terrible truths.

"I'm scared," Louise whispered.

"Me too."

They sat together on the couch, Louise's small body tucked against Leah's side. The silence stretched between them, heavy with unspoken fears. Gradually, Louise's breathing began to slow, exhaustion finally claiming her after hours of sustained emotional upheaval. Her head grew heavier against Leah's shoulder, the tension in her small muscles releasing as sleep offered merciful escape.

Within minutes, she had surrendered completely, her face smoothed of worry, one hand still loosely holding the edge of Leah's shirt. Leah carefully shifted, lowering Louise until she lay fully on the couch. She retrieved the soft throw blanket from the armchair and tucked it around her daughter's sleeping form, smoothing dark curls back from her forehead with infinite tenderness.

Automatic timers activated security lights across the neighborhood, illuminating ordinary homes where ordinary families ate dinner and helped with homework and maintained the illusion that life was predictable.

The phone buzzed with text messages. Leah glimpsed fragments on the lock screen—Williams demanding to know about bail arrangements, Mary offering to bring dinner, Ashley asking if they needed anything.

Everyone wanting to help. No one understanding that help felt impossible when your entire world had collapsed.

Louise's breathing deepened toward sleep. Exhaustion finally claiming her after hours of sustained trauma.

Leah carried her upstairs, each step feeling like climbing mountains. Louise's room remained untouched by the day's destruction—bright sheets and stuffed animals arranged exactly as they'd been that morning when celebration excitement filled the space.

She tucked Louise under covers that smelled like lavender fabric softener and childhood innocence. Bear Elephant assumed his protective position beside her pillow.

"Sweet dreams, baby girl."

But Leah knew the dreams wouldn't be sweet. That nightmares would feature handcuffs and blood and the sound of her father being taken away.

Downstairs, the kitchen felt like an archaeological site. Celebration cake with melting frosting. Dirty dishes stacked in the sink. Evidence of joy transformed into monuments of destruction.

Leah's phone buzzed again. This time she answered without checking the caller ID.

"What?" The word emerged harsher than intended.

"Leah?" Williams' voice carried professional concern. "We need to discuss bail arrangements."

"Not tonight."

"The arraignment is tomorrow morning. We need to—"

"I said not tonight." Leah ended the call, her finger stabbing the screen with unnecessary force.

It rang again immediately. Williams, persistent as always.

Leah answered with fury building in her chest. "Can't you understand that my daughter is traumatized and my husband is in jail and I can't think about legal strategy right now?"

"I understand you're upset—"

"Upset?" Leah's voice rose despite Louise sleeping upstairs. "Upset doesn't begin to cover this. My family has been destroyed. My daughter's innocence is gone. Everything we built has been demolished by thirty seconds of violence."

"Which is exactly why we need to plan—"

Leah hung up. Turned off the phone. Threw it across the kitchen where it skittered across linoleum and came to rest against the refrigerator.

Silence returned. But it felt different now. Heavy with the weight of decisions unmade and options unexplored.

She opened the refrigerator and stared at celebration cake remains. At juice boxes Louise would never finish. At the normal detritus of family life that now felt like museum pieces from a civilization that no longer existed.

The wine bottle from their celebration after the custody hearing sat on the counter, half-empty. She poured the remainder into a coffee mug and drank it like medicine. It tasted like victory that had curdled into defeat.

Ryan had won. Not through legal maneuvering or expert testimony, but through the simple strategy of pushing Chris beyond his breaking point. Violence was harder to explain than abandonment. Harder to justify than surveillance or family betrayal.

The adoption petition was dead. Chris would likely lose his teaching job. They'd be lucky if Louise wasn't removed from their home entirely.

Leah finished the wine and poured another glass from a different bottle. Then another. The alcohol provided temporary buffer against the sharp edges of reality.

But even drunk, her mind continued working. Analyzing. Calculating. Looking for angles and opportunities in the wreckage of their life.

She retrieved her phone from across the kitchen. The screen had cracked when it hit the floor, spider-web fractures distorting the display. But it still functioned.

Her contacts list scrolled past familiar names—Williams, Mary, Ashley, Susan. People who meant well but lacked the resources for the kind of fight this had become.

Her finger hesitated over another name. One she hadn't called since the wedding. One that represented complicated history and uncomfortable truths.

John Miller.

Her father's contact information stared back at her through cracked glass. The man who had built a successful business through strategic thinking and calculated risk. Who understood that sometimes winning required methods that made others uncomfortable.

She'd sworn never to become like him. Never to use manipulation and power as primary tools. But desperate times demanded desperate measures.

Louise needed protection. Chris needed defense. Their family needed weapons that Williams couldn't provide through standard legal channels.

Leah's thumb hovered over the call button. Once she made this choice, there would be no going back. She'd be asking John Miller to go to war. And wars always had casualties.

But Ryan had already drawn first blood. Had already proven that he would use any tactic, exploit any weakness, cause any amount of collateral damage to claim what he considered his property.

Time to fight fire with fire.

She pressed call before courage could abandon her. The phone rang once. Twice.

"Leah?" Her father's voice carried surprise and immediate concern. "It's late. Is everything alright?"

"No," she said, her voice steady despite everything. "Nothing is alright. And I need your help."

"I need your help." The words hung in the digital silence between them, each syllable carrying the weight of months since their last real conversation.

John Miller's voice sharpened with paternal concern. "Ryan Matthews."

Not a question. A statement that confirmed what Leah had momentarily forgotten—her father missed nothing. Had probably been tracking the custody case from the moment it began.

"He engineered Chris's arrest tonight. Provoked him into violence at Louise's art celebration." Leah found herself pacing the kitchen, her bare feet silent against cold linoleum. The wine had burned away, replaced by crystalline focus that reminded her why she'd once been pre-med.

"Tell me what happened." John's tone shifted, not just listening but gathering intelligence.

Leah recounted the evening with clinical detail—the district showcase selection that should have been pure celebration, Ryan's calculated appearance with a gift, the systematic provocation designed to destroy Chris's control in front of witnesses and cameras.

"He called Louise a mistake," she said, her voice hollow. "Reduced her to a burden designed to make Chris snap. And it worked."

Papers rustled on his end. "Video evidence?"

"Multiple angles. Parents with their phones out. Ryan's legal team will paint Chris as violent and unfit." She paused. "We need to change the game."

"Now you're thinking like a Miller."

The observation should have stung. Instead, it felt like coming home to a language she'd tried to forget but never lost. The syntax of strategy. The grammar of victory.

"What do you know about Wallace & Associates?" she asked.

"Expensive. Effective. Ethically flexible." More paper sounds. "I'll reach out to my contacts and provide a full analysis. Financial backing, client history, vulnerabilities."

Leah's pulse quickened. Information was currency. Knowledge was weapon. "Ryan's funding this somehow. Engineering consultants don't typically afford firms like Wallace."

"Leave that to me." The phrase carried decades of corporate warfare. "No one launches this kind of campaign without leaving footprints. I'll find them."

"Dad." The word emerged before she could stop it, cracking through her composure. "I swore I'd never become like you. Never use people as chess pieces."

"Sometimes the choice isn't whether to play the game. It's whether to win." His voice gentled with something that might have been understanding. "You're protecting your child. That changes everything."

Louise's sleeping face appeared in her mind. Dark curls spread across mermaid pillowcases. Small fingers still clutched around a damaged present. The image crystallized her resolve.

"What do I need to do?"

"Stop playing defense," John said, his voice taking on the particular edge she remembered from childhood—the tone he used when explaining business strategy at the dinner table. "Your lawyer has been reacting to Ryan's moves. That's appropriate for legal counsel, but it's not how you win wars. You need to identify his vulnerabilities and apply pressure where he can't defend."

"What vulnerabilities?" Leah asked, her mind already shifting into the analytical mode her father was invoking.

"Start with his funding source. Someone is bankrolling Wallace & Associates' fees. Find out who and why, and you'll understand what leverage points exist." He paused. "Ryan's an engineer, not a strategist. He's following his legal team's playbook, which means he's predictable. But more importantly, whoever is funding him has expectations. Disappoint those expectations enough, and the money disappears."

The approach felt different from anything Williams had suggested. Not documenting for court, but finding the infrastructure supporting Ryan's campaign and dismantling it.

"The Miller family." Leah tested the words, feeling their weight. She'd spent years keeping distance from that legacy. Tonight, she'd claim it as armor.

"Your siblings are resources too. Bryan's and Grace's connections. We've been waiting for you to ask."

The casual mention of reinforcements made her knees weak with relief. She wasn't alone. Had never been alone. Had chosen independence over obligation, but family remained family.

"I'll call them if I need to." Decision crystallized with each word. "After I get Chris out."

"Good." A pause. "Leah, I need to know—how far are you willing to go with this?"

The question hung between them, weighted with implications she understood too well. Her father was asking not about legal strategy but about moral boundaries. How much of his methods was she willing to adopt? How far would she push to protect her family?

"I want to destroy him." The admission emerged raw, unfiltered by the careful control she'd maintained all evening. "I want Ryan Matthews to lose everything. His reputation, his consulting firm, his father's respect. I want him to understand what it feels like to have someone systematically dismantle your entire life while claiming it's for your own good."

Silence stretched across the line. Not disapproval, but consideration.

"That's anger talking," John said finally, his voice carrying unexpected gentleness. "And anger makes us do things we'll regret forever."

Leah felt tears threatening, hot and bitter behind her eyes. "He traumatized my daughter at her art celebration. He engineered assault in front of children. He's spent months trying to steal our family—"

"I know." Her father's interruption was soft but firm. "And we'll make sure he can't hurt Louise again. But there's a difference between protecting your family and becoming the kind of person who destroys others out of rage."

The distinction cut through her fury like cold water. Leah pressed her palm against the counter, steadying herself against the realization that she'd been inches away from asking her father to wage the kind of psychological warfare that had defined his business career—effective, ruthless, devastating.

"Get some sleep," John continued. "I know that sounds impossible right now, but you need to be clear-headed for what comes next. I'll make arrangements for Chris's bail first thing in the morning. I'll coordinate with Williams to handle everything."

"You will?" The relief was immediate, overwhelming.

"Of course!" His tone carried absolute certainty. "We'll get Chris out."

Leah felt something loosening in her chest. Chris wouldn't spend days in that cell. The immediate crisis had a solution.

"And I'll come by in the morning," John added. "Before things get started. We'll talk through strategy when you've had some rest."

She understood what he wasn't saying directly—that the rage consuming her would lead to decisions that served her need for vengeance rather than Louise's need for stability. That becoming her father's daughter meant understanding when to deploy his methods and when to reject them.

"Thank you," she whispered. "For everything. For understanding what I need and what I don't."

"You're my daughter. Of course I understand." His voice carried warmth she'd forgotten existed beneath his corporate exterior. "Now get some sleep. Tomorrow we start protecting your family the right way."

The call ended, leaving Leah alone with the knowledge that help was coming. Not just legal assistance or strategic advice, but actual protection—the kind her father's resources could provide when deployed with care rather than cruelty.

She moved to the window, studying her reflection in the darkened glass. The woman looking back bore little resemblance to the girl who had told Ryan about her pregnancy with quiet dignity. This woman had learned that love sometimes required strategic thinking, that protection occasionally demanded calculated response, that fighting for family meant choosing effectiveness over purity.

But she'd also learned, and was still learning, that there was a difference between her father's methods and her father's ruthlessness. She could be strategic like him without being cruel. She could protect her family without destroying others for the satisfaction of revenge.

The wine bottle sat empty on the counter, evidence of the evening's attempt to numb pain that couldn't be drowned. But tomorrow morning, John Miller would arrive with the resources needed to mount a real defense. And Chris would come home to the family worth fighting for.

Tomorrow would bring bail hearings and strategy sessions and the beginning of real defense against Ryan's campaign. But tonight, she simply stood at her kitchen window, processing the magnitude of having asked for help and receiving not just assistance but understanding—that anger needed wisdom, that fury required temperance, that protecting those you love sometimes meant protecting them from your own worst impulses.

Louise stirred upstairs, her small voice calling for water. Leah moved automatically, leaving her reflection behind as she climbed the stairs toward her daughter's room. The mother her child needed wasn't the vengeful destroyer she'd been becoming. It was someone who could fight without losing herself in the process.

And tomorrow, with her father's help, she would learn to be exactly that.

The phone line went dead, leaving John Miller alone with the echo of his daughter's voice and the rage building in his chest like pressure in a sealed vessel. He sat in his home office—not the corporate fortress downtown, but the smaller sanctuary Claire had helped him design after the divorce, walls lined with photographs that marked his slow transformation from ruthless businessman to something approaching human.

His hand remained frozen around the phone, knuckles white with restraint. The evening had settled into that particular stillness that amplified thought, made internal voices impossible to ignore.

Louise's art celebration. Ryan engineered assault at a child's art celebration.

The words replayed with each heartbeat, stoking fury that felt both foreign and terrifyingly familiar. This was the old John Miller awakening, the man who had built his success by identifying enemies and systematically dismantling everything they valued. The man who had understood that true power came not from winning battles but from ensuring your opponent never recovered enough to fight again.

His other hand formed a fist against the desk's polished surface. Ryan Matthews had touched his granddaughter. Had traumatized a young child to gain legal advantage. Had provoked Chris into violence while children scattered in fear, then used that manufactured crisis as ammunition in his custody campaign.

The mental catalog of responses assembled itself with practiced ease. Ryan's consulting firm depended on reputation—a carefully placed word to the right clients could poison that well permanently. His professional network was surprisingly thin—isolating him further would be simple. The engineering community was smaller than most people realized, and John Miller's reach extended into territories Ryan couldn't imagine.

I could destroy him.

The thought arrived with seductive clarity. One morning of phone calls, a few conversations with people who owed him favors, and Ryan Matthews would find his world contracting. His clients would receive anonymous concerns about his stability. His professional references would be quietly undermined. His consulting practice would wither before he understood what was happening.

John's pulse accelerated as the strategy refined itself. He knew how to weaponize reputation, how to turn someone's greatest strengths into fatal vulnerabilities. Ryan's engineering background could be reframed as obsessive behavior. His determination could become dangerous fixation. His abandonment could be painted as something far more sinister than simple cowardice.

And he would never know it was me.

The beauty of it was its invisibility. Ryan would watch his world collapse while searching for enemies in all the wrong places. He'd suspect Chris and Leah, or perhaps other business competitors. He'd never trace the careful destruction back to a grandfather protecting his family.

John rose from his desk, pacing to the window. His reflection stared back at him—silver-haired, successful, dangerous in ways that boardrooms and courtrooms couldn't fully contain. This was who he'd been before Claire's intervention had forced him to examine the cost of his victories.

How many families did I destroy exactly like this? How many Ryan Matthews did I create—men so desperate to prove their worth that they'd hurt innocent people?

The question landed like cold water on flames. His hands pressed against the window's cool glass, steadying himself against the vertigo of moral reckoning. He was thinking about Louise's trauma, using it as justification for the same systematic destruction he'd inflicted before. The same tactics that had driven competitors to bankruptcy, destroyed careers, shattered families who had the misfortune of standing between him and whatever he'd decided to claim as his own.

Claire's voice echoed from memory—not their divorce conversation, but something she'd said months later when he'd tried to explain his methods: *"You were so busy winning that you forgot to ask whether your victories were worth what they cost everyone else. Including you."*

He'd dismissed it then as bitter recrimination from someone who couldn't understand business realities. But standing here now, John recognized the terrible truth: he'd been exactly like Ryan Matthews. Different circumstances, different stakes, but the same fundamental wound—the desperate need to prove worth through conquest, to validate existence through domination, to silence inner doubt by destroying anyone who reminded him of his own vulnerability.

You can't right a wrong with another wrong.

The phrase surfaced from somewhere deep, perhaps something Claire had said, or maybe something he'd read during the months of therapy after the divorce when he'd been forced to confront what his business brilliance had actually created: a legacy of damage, a trail of broken people, a life that looked successful from the outside while feeling hollow at its core.

John moved back to his desk, sinking into the leather chair that had witnessed countless planning sessions. But tonight's strategy needed to be different. Not destruction for its own sake, not revenge disguised as protection, but genuine defense that served Louise's wellbeing rather than his own need to prove he could still wage effective war.

There has to be another way.

He opened his laptop, the screen's glow casting blue light across his features as his mind shifted gears. Ryan wasn't the real problem—he was a symptom. A desperate man making terrible choices, enabled by a legal system that treated children as property to be claimed and a law firm that specialized in exactly this kind of psychological warfare.

Wallace & Associates. The name alone carried reputation in family law circles—not admiration, but wary respect for their effectiveness. They were the firm you hired when winning mattered more than ethics, when you needed custody cases fought with corporate merger ruthlessness. Their track record was impressive, their methods often questionable, their clients typically wealthy individuals willing to pay premium rates for results that conventional legal approaches couldn't deliver.

That's the real weak point.

Understanding crystallized with the particular clarity that had built his success. Ryan was just the latest client in Wallace & Associates' machine. Eliminate him and the machine would find another desperate parent to exploit. But examine the machine itself, understand its actual vulnerabilities, and you could potentially dismantle the entire operation.

It reminded him of something Leah used to do as a child—that block-stacking game where you removed pieces until the whole structure collapsed. She'd been fascinated by it, understanding instinctively that everyone focused on the top blocks, the visible pieces. But the real vulnerability was always in the foundation. Remove the right supporting piece and everything above it came tumbling down.

John reached for his phone, scrolling through contacts accumulated over decades of business. Not the violent options his rage had initially demanded, but information specialists who understood how to map organizational structure, find financial vulnerabilities, trace connections that revealed systemic weakness rather than individual failure.

The first call went to Marcus Chen, who had retired from corporate intelligence but still maintained connections John could only imagine. Marcus answered on the second ring, his voice carrying the particular wariness of someone who recognized John Miller's number.

"This better be important," Marcus said without preamble. "I'm retired, remember?"

"I need information," John replied, his tone carrying none of the demanding edge that had characterized their previous professional relationship. "Not corporate espionage. Family matter."

The distinction seemed to penetrate Marcus's defenses. "Family?"

"My granddaughter. She's being targeted by a custody case that's really psychological warfare." John paused, choosing his next words carefully. "I need to understand the infrastructure supporting the attack, not because I want to destroy it for satisfaction, but because I need to know how to protect a young child."

The silence stretched long enough that John wondered if Marcus would refuse. Then: "Send me the details. No promises, but I'll look."

The second call went to Patricia Morales, who had spent years as a paralegal before becoming a legal consultant specializing in attorney misconduct investigations. Her reputation was built on careful documentation rather than sensational exposures, the patient dismantling of legal practices that crossed ethical lines while maintaining plausible deniability.

"Wallace & Associates," John said after brief pleasantries. "Family law division. I need to understand their operational methods, funding sources, case patterns. Everything you can find that's a matter of public record."

"That's a big firm," Patricia replied cautiously. "What's your interest?"

"They're representing someone trying to traumatize my granddaughter for legal advantage. I'm not looking to destroy them—I'm looking to understand if there's a systemic problem that needs addressing through proper channels."

"Proper channels," Patricia repeated, skepticism evident. "Since when does John Miller worry about proper channels?"

"Since I decided I wanted to be someone my granddaughter could be proud of knowing." The admission cost him something, but it carried the weight of truth. "I can help dismantle a problematic legal practice, or I can become the kind of grandfather who teaches a young child that power justifies any action. I'm trying to choose differently than I have before."

The third call went to his accountant—not for personal matters, but because Sarah Brennan had a particular talent for following money trails that revealed organizational vulnerabilities. If Wallace & Associates had financial pressure points, Sarah would find them within the bounds of legal investigation.

"I need a financial analysis," John said. "Nothing illegal, just public records, professional assessments, the kind of research that would inform whether a firm has systemic issues beyond individual case ethics."

Each call ended with the same understanding: information gathering, not warfare. Documentation that could support legitimate challenges rather than manufactured destruction. The distinction felt foreign to the old John Miller, but essential to whoever he was becoming.

He leaned back in his chair as the last call concluded. The rage that had driven him to imagine Ryan's systematic destruction had cooled into something more sustainable—not vengeance, but protection. Not conquest, but genuine defense of people he loved.

This is what changed men do.

The thought arrived without the bitter self-recrimination that had characterized his early attempts at reformation. He was learning, however slowly, that strength could be directed toward building rather than destroying. That business acumen could serve creation rather than annihilation. That loving his daughter and granddaughter meant choosing their long-term wellbeing over his short-term satisfaction.

But even as he made this choice, John recognized that information itself was power—and power, once gathered, could be wielded in ways that blurred the line between protection and revenge. The contacts he'd just activated would return with intelligence that could be used ethically or destructively depending on his choices in moments yet to come.

The test isn't gathering the information. It's what I do with it once I have it.

He closed his laptop, the office settling into darkness around him. Tomorrow would bring the first reports from his contacts. Within days, he would understand Wallace & Associates' vulnerabilities, Ryan's actual resources, the structural weaknesses that could potentially end this campaign without requiring him to become the monster he'd spent years trying to outgrow.

The phone sat silent on his desk, waiting. And John Miller, ruthless businessman turned reluctant penitent, found himself hoping that whatever his contacts discovered would offer a path forward that served justice without requiring him to sacrifice the slow, difficult growth of becoming someone worthy of his granddaughter's trust.

CHAPTER 20

When Walls Close In

H ours had passed since the art celebration assault, since handcuffs had clicked around his wrists while Louise screamed for her daddy. The holding cell breathed disinfectant and broken dreams. Each inhalation burned Chris's throat, the chemical sting mixing with something deeper, more visceral. The metallic taste of his own failure.

Fluorescent tubes hummed their mechanical dirge overhead. The light fell in harsh rectangles across concrete walls, carving shadows that seemed to shift and writhe. Like the guilt eating through his chest.

The metal bench pressed into his spine through county-issued cotton. Each ridge of his vertebrae found purchase against unforgiving steel. Physical pain anchored him to this moment, this place, this catastrophic reality he'd authored with his own hands.

Louise's face.

The image slammed into him again. Her expression in that split second when understanding dawned. When her daddy, the man who sang her to sleep, who kissed scraped knees, who taught her that hands were for creating music, became something else entirely.

Something monstrous.

351

Her artwork had been selected for the district showcase—only five students chosen. She'd been so proud, her smile bright enough to light the entire celebration. Instead, she got handcuffs clicking around her father's wrists.

"Daddy, don't go!"

The words ricocheted off concrete walls, each echo a fresh blade sliding between his ribs. Her voice, high and desperate, had followed him into the patrol car. Would follow him into whatever came next.

Chris pressed his palms against his temples. The pressure brought momentary relief, like holding broken pieces together through sheer force of will. But his skull couldn't contain what lived inside it now. The moment. The choice. The thirty seconds that had rewritten everything.

Ryan's face, split lip weeping red. The crunch of cartilage beneath his knuckles. The savage satisfaction that had bloomed in his chest like some prehistoric flower, beautiful and terrible.

I am capable of this.

The realization hollowed him out. Somewhere beneath his gentle exterior, behind years of choosing peace over conflict, lived something that could destroy. Something that could traumatize the one person he'd sworn to protect above all others.

His hands trembled in his lap. The same hands that had guided Louise's fingers across guitar strings. That had become weapons in the space between one heartbeat and the next.

The cell door's electronic lock hummed. Keys jangled against polyester, authority made audible. Chris didn't lift his head. He deserved this concrete cage, these steel bars. Deserved the particular stench of institutional failure that clung to everything here.

"Johnson, you've got a visitor."

The guard's voice carried the boredom of someone who processed human wreckage for a living. Chris remained motionless, studying the patterns his tears had made on the concrete floor. Salt stains like accusations.

"I said you've got a visitor. Your lawyer."

No one should see me like this.

But his body moved without conscious decision. Muscle memory of compliance, trained by years of choosing the path of least resistance. His legs carried him forward while his mind remained trapped in that moment of impact. Knuckles meeting flesh. Louise's scream.

The hallway stretched endlessly. Each step echoed in the institutional silence, bouncing off cinder block walls painted the color of old sickness. Other cells held other failures, other moments when good people discovered their capacity for destruction.

The visitation room reeked of industrial cleaning solution and desperation. Bulletproof glass bisected the space like a physical manifestation of separation, of before and after. On one side sat the people who belonged in the world. On the other, those who had forfeited that right.

Williams waited behind the barrier. Her suit remained crisp despite the late hour, her hair perfectly arranged. She embodied competence in a place where competence felt foreign, impossible. Everything about her screamed control, order, solutions.

Chris slumped into the metal chair. It scraped against linoleum with a sound like nails on a chalkboard. He couldn't meet her eyes. Couldn't bear to see his reflection in those professional lenses.

"We need to discuss bail," Williams said, her voice filtering through speakers that made everything sound hollow, distorted. "Your father-in-law has been coordinating with me since last night. We've arranged everything for the arraignment tomorrow morning."

Her words should have brought relief, but Chris felt only the hollow weight of undeserved mercy. John Miller—a man he barely knew, whose daughter he'd married, whose resources he'd never wanted to need—was orchestrating his release while he sat here drowning in self-loathing.

"I don't deserve bail."

The words emerged from some place deeper than rational thought. They carried the weight of self-condemnation that had been building since the handcuffs closed. Since Louise's face crumpled in understanding.

"I attacked him. In front of children. At my daughter's art celebration."

Each word felt like swallowing glass. Cutting him from the inside out. But they needed to be said. Needed to be acknowledged. He had crossed a line that couldn't be uncrossed.

"She was so proud," Chris continued, his voice breaking. "The district showcase. Only five students selected. And I turned her moment into—"

"A response to systematic provocation," Williams interrupted, though her tone carried understanding rather than dismissal. "The circumstances were—"

"There are no circumstances that justify what I did."

His voice cracked like breaking ice. The force of his certainty surprised him. How could he feel so empty and so full of conviction simultaneously?

"I became what they said. Violent. Dangerous to Louise."

Everything reduced to rubble in thirty seconds.

"Ryan Matthews engineered this outcome. Every word was calculated to provoke exactly this response. You walked into a trap."

Williams spoke with her characteristic firmness. Each syllable measured, weighed, delivered with the authority of someone who understood legal strategy. But strategy felt irrelevant now. Tactics couldn't undo what had been done.

"I chose to swing my fists."

Chris's hands clenched in his lap. Muscle memory of violence still fresh beneath his skin. The weight of Ryan's head snapping back. The sound of his own breathing, harsh and animal.

"No one forced me to become a monster."

Monster. The word hung between them like a physical presence. It felt accurate in a way that terrified him. He'd glimpsed something in himself that he'd never suspected existed. Something primitive and savage and utterly destructive.

The silence stretched. Mechanical ventilation hummed through ductwork overhead. Somewhere in the distance, other inmates processed their own failures. Their own moments of discovering who they really were beneath the surface.

Williams studied his face. Her assessment carried the weight of someone who had seen countless clients destroy themselves with guilt that served no productive purpose. Who understood the difference between productive remorse and destructive self-flagellation.

"Louise needs her father. Leah needs her husband. Self-flagellation won't undo what happened, but it might prevent you from fixing it."

Fixing it. As if violence could be repaired like a broken toy. As if trauma could be undone with the right words, the right actions, the right penance.

"How do I fix terrorizing my daughter?"

The question scraped his throat raw. How did someone come back from that?

"How do I explain to a five-year-old that her daddy lost control and hurt someone? That the man she trusted to protect her became something she should be protected from?"

The image of Louise's face haunted him. Those wide eyes, brown like her mother's, filled with an understanding no child should possess. The moment innocence died. The moment safety became conditional.

"You explain that even good people make terrible mistakes when they're pushed beyond their breaking point," Williams said, her voice dropping to the register reserved for clients teetering on emotional precipices. Soft but firm. Professional but human. "That you're sorry. That you're getting help. That you love her more than your shame."

Love her more than your shame.

The words cut through his self-pity like a blade through tissue. Clean and sharp and necessary. They forced him to confront an uncomfortable truth: his wallowing served his needs, not hers.

"She saw me hit him."

Chris buried his face in his hands. The gesture provided no real protection from the memory. Louise's shocked expression burned behind his closed eyelids. The way her small body had jerked backward, as if his violence was a physical force pushing her away.

"She watched me draw blood. Violence was never supposed to touch her world."

He'd built their life with such care. Chosen their neighborhood for its quiet streets and good schools. Screened movies for age-appropriate content. Protected her from the sharp edges of adult reality. And then he'd become the thing she needed protection from.

"But it did. And now the question is whether you let that moment define everything that follows, or whether you fight to preserve the family Ryan Matthews is trying to destroy."

Williams tapped the glass with one manicured finger. The sound echoed in the small space like a gavel falling. Like judgment being rendered.

"Wallowing in guilt might feel like appropriate penance, but it's actually selfish. Louise doesn't need your guilt. She needs her father."

The accusation struck like a physical blow. *Selfish.* His guilt felt pure, righteous, necessary. But she was right. Self-condemnation was easier than action. Shame was simpler than strategy. Wallowing was a luxury he couldn't afford.

Not when Louise was processing trauma he'd caused. Not when Leah was handling fallout he'd created. Not when their family hung in the balance of decisions he'd make in the days ahead.

"What if the judge sees the video?"

The question emerged from his deepest fear. Phone cameras had captured everything. His loss of control. His violence. The moment he'd forfeited any claim to moral high ground.

"What if those phone recordings end up in court?"

The technology of modern humiliation. His worst moment preserved in digital amber, ready to be replayed endlessly. Evidence of his unfitness as a father, as a husband, as a human being.

"Then we explain the context. Ryan's provocation. His calculated cruelty. The systematic campaign to destabilize your family."

Williams's voice carried the authority of someone who had navigated similar crises. Who understood that context mattered, even when the facts were damning. Especially then.

"Violence is hard to defend, but it's not impossible when the circumstances are properly presented."

Properly presented. Legal alchemy. The transformation of inexcusable into understandable. But some things couldn't be spun, couldn't be reframed. Some moments demanded accountability without qualification.

"Ryan called her a mistake, and instead of walking away, I tried to beat the words out of his mouth."

The memory played in slow motion: Ryan's calculated cruelty, delivered with surgical precision. The words designed to find the deepest wound and tear it open. And his response—primitive, violent, utterly predictable.

"Because you're her father. Because you couldn't tolerate someone reducing your daughter to an accident or burden."

Williams's tone gentled without losing its authority. She understood the landscape of protective instincts, the way love could become violence when pushed past breaking points.

"That protective instinct isn't evidence of unfitness. It's evidence of love."

Love. The word felt foreign now, tainted by what it had driven him to do. Could love and violence coexist? Could protection and destruction spring from the same source?

Chris raised his head. Met her gaze through the scratched bulletproof barrier that separated them. The glass was scarred by years of desperate conversations, last chances, failed redemptions.

"What if I lose her? What if this gives them everything they need to take Louise away?"

The possibility hollowed him out. Louise, raised by strangers. Growing up believing her father was a violent man who'd abandoned her. The life they'd built together reduced to memory, to photographs, to scheduled visitation in sterile rooms.

"Then we fight harder. We document Ryan's provocation. We show the court that one moment of poor judgment doesn't erase years of devoted parenting."

Williams gathered her papers with decisive movements. Each gesture conveyed purpose, direction, the possibility of moving forward despite everything that had happened.

"But first, we get you out of here. John Miller has coordinated everything with the court. The bail hearing is set for tomorrow morning. Leah needs you home. Louise needs you home."

Home. The word carried weight that felt crushing and essential simultaneously. Their house with its carefully chosen furnishings, its photographs chronicling Louise's growth, its quiet routines that created safety through repetition.

"Is Leah okay? Is Louise?"

The question tore from his chest. He'd been so focused on his own guilt that he'd barely processed their trauma. They'd watched him become something unrecognizable. They were processing their own version of this catastrophe.

"Leah is... focused. She's called her father."

Something in Williams's expression suggested this development carried significance beyond family support. A subtle shift in her posture, a careful choice of words that implied deeper meaning.

"I think you'll find she's approaching the situation differently now."

"Differently how?"

Williams stood, preparing to leave. Her movements carried the efficiency of someone with urgent business elsewhere. Plans being made, strategies being implemented while he sat in this concrete box.

"She's stopped playing defense. Which means you need to stop playing victim."

Her eyes held his through the glass. The message was clear, uncompromising. Self-pity was a luxury they couldn't afford. Not when the stakes were this high.

"Ryan Matthews wanted to provoke you into violence. Mission accomplished. But he may have underestimated the resources at your disposal now."

The words carried implications that sent electricity through Chris's nervous system. He'd married into the Miller family knowing their reputation for strategic thinking, for protecting their own with ruthless efficiency. But he'd never needed their particular skills before.

The conversation ended, leaving Chris alone with the weight of decisions made and opportunities lost. His reflection stared back from the darkened window—hollow-eyed, stubbled, wearing the particular expression of someone who had discovered their capacity for destruction.

But beneath the guilt and shame, something else stirred. Williams was right about one thing—wallowing served no purpose except self-indulgence. Louise needed her father to be more than his worst moment. Leah needed her husband to fight rather than surrender.

The guard appeared to escort him back. Keys jangled with mechanical rhythm, the sound of institutional control. But it was temporary. John Miller had coordinated his release. The family he'd built through daily acts of love was permanent, even if thirty seconds of violence had threatened to eclipse years of devotion.

Ryan had engineered this outcome, pushed every button, exploited every vulnerability, created the perfect storm of provocation and response. But he'd miscalculated one crucial element—the Miller family's capacity for strategic warfare.

The cell door closed behind him with metallic finality. Tomorrow would bring arraignment, bail hearings, the beginning of legal consequences for his actions. But it would also bring reunion with the family worth fighting for, regardless of the cost to his pride or reputation.

As the fluorescent lights hummed their mechanical lullaby, Chris settled onto the metal bench that would serve as his bed. Outside these walls, his wife was planning war. His daughter was processing trauma. His family was learning to survive without him.

But not for long. Tomorrow, the real fight would begin.

The fight to prove that love could survive violence. That families could heal from trauma. That thirty seconds of failure didn't have to define a lifetime of devotion.

The fight to come home.

The Wallace & Associates conference room existed in that peculiar liminal space between midnight and dawn, where fluorescent light transformed polished surfaces into mirrors of ambition. Ryan Matthews settled into the leather chair at the table's head, his reflection fracturing across the mahogany surface like a kaleidoscope of vindication.

His suit jacket hung abandoned on the chair back, the crisp navy wool a stark contrast to the clothes he'd worn during the confrontation. The bandage above his left eyebrow pulled at his skin with each micro-expression. His swollen lip throbbed in rhythm with his pulse.

These wounds were not injuries but investments, capital gains in a war economy where pain converted directly into custody rights.

James Wallace entered last, his movements carrying something Ryan hadn't seen before—a flicker of surprise wrapped in professional assessment, the expression of someone who had underestimated his client's capacity for independent strategy. He settled into his chair with the deliberate care of someone recalibrating expectations, his eyes moving from Ryan's visible injuries to the tablet displaying video evidence that had begun circulating within hours.

"I have to admit," Wallace began, his voice carrying grudging admiration threaded with concern, "when we discussed potential scenarios for documenting instability, I never anticipated you'd take matters into your own hands quite so... directly."

Ryan met his gaze without flinching, the satisfaction of his engineer's mind having identified a problem and solved it burning beneath his careful composure. "You said we needed recent evidence. Something that couldn't be dismissed as family gossip or coordinated testimony."

"I did." Wallace's fingers drummed once against the mahogany, a rare gesture of uncertainty from a man who had built his reputation on unshakeable confidence. "But provoking someone into assault at a child's celebration carries risks I wouldn't typically advise a client to undertake." He paused, studying Ryan with new respect that bordered on wariness. "It was very good thinking. Strategically brilliant, actually. But also extraordinarily risky."

The acknowledgment landed like validation Ryan hadn't realized he'd been seeking. For months, he'd followed Wallace's carefully orchestrated campaign, playing the role of concerned biological father according to scripts refined through hundreds of custody cases. But standing in that backyard, watching Chris's protective instincts war with mounting rage, Ryan had recognized an opportunity that no lawyer could have engineered for him.

"Risk implies uncertainty of outcome," Ryan replied, his voice carrying the particular confidence of someone who had calculated variables and achieved predicted results. "I knew exactly which words would break his

control. I've watched him long enough to understand his triggers—the protective instincts that override rational thought, the fear of being seen as inadequate, the guilt about raising another man's child."

Wallace leaned back, reassessing the man across from him with the intensity of someone realizing their client possessed capabilities beyond what initial consultations had revealed. "Most people can't execute that kind of psychological manipulation under pressure. The fact that you maintained composure while saying things designed to provoke violence..." He shook his head slowly. "That requires a particular kind of discipline."

Ryan's hand moved unconsciously to his swollen lip, pride warming his chest despite the throbbing pain. He had proven himself capable of more than signing checks and following legal advice. He had identified the weakness in their opponents' armor and struck with the precision his engineering training had taught him to value above all else.

"But help me understand," Ryan said, leaning forward with the intensity of someone who had taken enormous personal risk and needed confirmation it had been worth the cost. "How does this actually help our case? Yes, we have documentation of violence. But their lawyer will argue provocation, will present my words as calculated cruelty designed to force exactly this response. How do we counter that narrative?"

Wallace's expression shifted, the brief moment of uncertainty dissolving as he moved back into familiar territory—the strategic interpretation of evidence, the transformation of messy human conflict into clean legal advantage. His smile returned, sharper now, carrying the satisfaction of someone who recognized a gift even when it came wrapped in unexpected packaging.

The junior associates entered, settling into their positions with the quiet efficiency of people who understood their roles in the machinery of legal warfare. One began taking notes, capturing every word for the record that would justify their strategy. The other activated the digital recorder, preserving this strategic session for whatever appeals or challenges might emerge.

"The beauty," Wallace said, pulling up the tablet and swiping through video files with practiced efficiency, "is that provocation is extraordinarily difficult to prove in ways that matter legally. Multiple angles showing a grown man vaulting a fence to physically attack you at a child's celebration. Witnesses who will testify to the terror those children experienced. Parents who documented their own children's trauma from witnessing domestic violence."

Ryan watched the footage play across the screen—seven confirmed videos from different perspectives, each one showing the same devastating sequence. Him presenting a gift. Chris's explosion into violence. Children scattering in fear.

"The legal standard," Wallace continued, his voice taking on the pedagogical tone of someone educating a client about complex principles, "isn't whether you said things that upset him. It's whether a reasonable person in his position would have responded with violence. And the answer, in the eyes of the court, will be no."

Ryan felt something loosening in his chest—the residual anxiety that perhaps he'd overplayed his hand, that his independent action might have created complications his expensive legal team couldn't navigate. But Wallace's confidence, the methodical way he was already constructing their narrative, suggested otherwise.

"Even if they prove you deliberately provoked him," Wallace said, warming to his theme as the strategy crystallized, "that actually strengthens our case rather than weakens it. Because it demonstrates that Chris Johnson cannot maintain composure under stress. That he prioritizes his own emotional satisfaction over Louise's wellbeing. That when challenged or upset, his default response is violence rather than walking away."

The female associate looked up from her tablet, her earlier uncertainty replaced by recognition of the strategic gift Ryan had delivered. "The provocation itself becomes evidence of poor judgment on his part. Any reasonable adult, especially one caring for a child, should be able to disengage from verbal conflict without resorting to physical assault."

"Exactly." Wallace's satisfaction deepened, his initial surprise at Ryan's independent action transforming into appreciation for the results it had achieved. "You've given us something we could never have manufactured through legal strategy alone—genuine, documented evidence of violent instability that no amount of character witnesses or family testimony can refute."

Ryan's engineering mind processed this with the same analytical rigor he brought to complex technical problems. The variables had aligned perfectly: his calculated provocation, Chris's predictable response, the presence of witnesses with recording devices, the particular setting of a children's celebration that amplified the horror of violence. Each element had been necessary, and he had orchestrated them all through intuitive understanding of human psychology that his legal team couldn't have guided him toward.

Documents spread across the table like tarot cards predicting an inevitable future. Wallace consulted his calendar with the satisfaction of someone scheduling inevitable triumph. "Emergency custody modification filed within forty-eight hours. We argue Chris Johnson represents immediate threat to Louise's wellbeing."

Ryan leaned back, feeling leather conform to his spine. Chris was probably sitting in a holding cell right now, concrete walls closing around him like the logical consequences of poor impulse control. While his opponent wallowed in guilt and self-recrimination, Ryan was already three moves ahead.

"Pattern of escalating violence. Inability to control aggressive impulses. Exposure of the child to traumatic domestic violence," Wallace articulated, each phrase building their narrative with architectural precision.

The male associate glanced up from timeline charts. "Emergency hearing within thirty days. The assault evidence is so compelling that opposing counsel will likely recommend settlement."

Ryan's pulse quickened. Settlement meant acknowledgment of defeat. It meant Chris and Leah recognizing that their manufactured family couldn't withstand contact with biological reality.

"What terms?" Ryan asked.

"Supervised visitation. Every other weekend, assuming anger management completion and psychological evaluation." Wallace's smile carried the particular satisfaction of someone describing unconditional surrender. "You'd have primary custody with full decision-making authority."

The female associate added, "No adoption proceedings for Chris Johnson. Violence eliminates any possibility of judicial approval."

Ryan nodded, though privately he intended to pursue complete termination of Chris's access once Louise was established in his care. Why settle for primary custody when total victory remained achievable?

His phone buzzed against the table. A text from Judge Matthews: *Heard about the incident. This isn't what we discussed. Call me immediately.*

His father's sharp tone cut through Ryan's satisfaction like cold water. The judge had been reluctant about the custody battle from the beginning, warning that any harm to Louise would end his support entirely. Ryan deleted the message without responding—some conversations required careful timing.

"Character witnesses?" the female associate asked. "Previous family members might be reluctant after today."

Ryan's expression darkened momentarily. Terry's spectacular courtroom implosion had eliminated his most useful family witness. But today's events more than compensated for that loss—video evidence spoke more eloquently than any relative's testimony.

"We won't need family witnesses," Ryan said, the phrase tasting like vindication. "Facts speak for themselves."

The female associate's fingers danced across her tablet, harvesting social media documentation. "The video is already circulating. Local parenting groups are sharing it. Parents who witnessed the violence posting their concerns about child safety."

The organic spread through social networks felt powerful. The narrative wrote itself—concerned biological father versus violent stepfather creating dangerous environment.

The conference room fell silent as each participant contemplated the transformed landscape. What had begun as an uphill battle against established family bonds had become straightforward argument about child safety.

Ryan studied his reflection in the darkened windows. The bandage and swollen lip would heal within days, but video evidence would last forever. Perfect documentation of Chris Johnson's unfitness as a parent.

The associates gathered their materials, preparing for the coordinated campaign that would begin at dawn. Emergency petitions. Media statements. Home preparation for custody transition. Each element choreographed to create overwhelming momentum toward inevitable conclusion.

The strategy session wound down as midnight gave way to the small hours before dawn. By the time the associates departed, their plan had crystallized into devastating simplicity.

Ryan remained alone in the conference room, studying his reflection in the darkened windows. The building's height offered perspective on the city below—sleeping neighborhoods where families existed in blissful ignorance of the legal machinery that could reshape their lives overnight.

His mind drifted to the guest room he had prepared weeks ago. Child-appropriate furniture arranged like a showroom. Educational toys selected for their developmental value and visual appeal during home evaluation visits. Every detail orchestrated to demonstrate superior parenting environment.

Somewhere in that urban landscape, Louise was probably sleeping in a bed that didn't belong to her, in a house that couldn't provide the advantages his success offered. Soon, she would wake up in her proper home, learning to appreciate the stability that biological connection and financial resources could provide.

His phone buzzed again. A message from his assistant: "Story spreading on neighborhood social media. Three parents already shared video." The incident was gaining organic momentum through digital whispers and shared outrage.

Ryan touched his swollen lip again, savoring the connection between temporary pain and permanent gain. Chess masters understood that sacrificing pieces could win games. The bruises were tactical losses that had achieved strategic victory.

The elevator descended through fourteen floors of sleeping ambition. Tomorrow, this building would pulse with renewed energy as lawyers and paralegals executed the plan refined in tonight's session. Emergency filings would initiate the legal machinery that would deliver Louise to her rightful home.

His car waited in the parking garage, expensive German engineering that would soon transport Louise to weekend visits, then custody exchanges, then permanent residence. He started the engine, feeling the machinery respond to his commands.

The highway stretched ahead like an illuminated pathway toward the future he had engineered. Louise would learn to appreciate the advantages his patience and strategy had secured for her. The confusion and instability of her life with Chris and Leah would fade like dreams upon waking.

He didn't look back at the corporate tower diminishing in his rearview mirror, didn't second-guess the strategy that had transformed his custody petition from desperate claim into inevitable victory. Tomorrow would bring the beginning of Louise's true family life, regardless of whatever resistance remained from those who couldn't accept biological reality.

CHAPTER 21

Evidence and Anguish

The glass tower of Wallace & Associates rose against the late afternoon sky like a monument to legal warfare. Chris sat in the passenger seat of their car, watching the building's reflective surface fracture the dying sunlight into sharp, angular pieces. His right hand bore faint bruising across the knuckles—evidence of the night that had transformed their family crisis into something far more dangerous.

Leah's fingers drummed against the steering wheel. "We don't have to go in," she said for the third time since parking.

Chris studied the building's entrance. "He'll press charges if we don't show. Two nights in county was enough preview."

The conference room stretched before them like a battlefield prepared for surrender negotiations. James Wallace rose as they entered, his silver hair catching the light. Ryan sat to his right, avoiding eye contact with practiced care.

Elizabeth Williams sat across from them, her presence a reassuring counterweight to Wallace's theatrical authority.

"Thank you for coming," Wallace began, opening his portfolio with practiced movements. "My client has drafted a resolution that benefits everyone involved."

He slid documents across the mahogany table. "Mr. Matthews will drop the assault charges. In exchange, Mr. Johnson drops the adoption petition. Joint custody."

"Joint custody means what?"

"Alternating weekends. Shared holidays. Standard divorce arrangement."

"We're not divorced parents," Leah said, her voice sharp. "We're married parents, and he's a stranger."

Ryan spoke for the first time, his voice carefully controlled. "I won't be a stranger much longer. Louise will learn who I am."

"She already knows who you are," Chris said quietly. "You're the man who scared her at her art celebration."

Wallace intervened quickly. "Mr. Johnson, we understand this is difficult. But consider the alternative—criminal conviction, job loss, Louise watching her stepfather go to prison."

"Stepfather?" Chris's voice carried dangerous quiet. "Interesting choice of words."

Elizabeth leaned forward. "What's the timeline on this alleged generous offer?"

"Seventy-two hours," Wallace replied. "After that, we proceed with assault charges and emergency custody modification based on Mr. Johnson's violent behavior."

Ryan pulled out his phone, scrolling to a video. "Would you like to see what the jury will see? You, punching me while children screamed in the background?"

Leah's hand shot out, stopping Chris from lunging across the table. "Put that away."

"Why? Because it shows who he really is when his temper snaps?" Ryan's confidence was building. "How many times has this happened at home, I wonder?"

"You son of a—" Chris started.

"Chris." Leah's voice cut through his rage like ice water. "Don't give him what he wants."

Wallace sensed the shift. "Mrs. Johnson, surely you can see the wisdom in avoiding a lengthy court battle. Think of Louise's welfare."

"I am thinking of Louise's welfare," Leah said, her voice steady as steel. "Which is why I need to ask Mr. Matthews something directly."

She turned to face Ryan. "What's your endgame?"

Ryan blinked. "I want to be part of my daughter's life."

"After you get custody. After you disrupt everything. Then what?"

"She'll adjust. Children are resilient."

"That's not an answer." Leah's medical training kicked in, her voice taking on clinical clarity. "You're asking us to traumatize a young child for your benefit. What's the long-term plan that makes that worthwhile?"

Ryan's composure flickered. "She deserves to know—"

"She deserves stability," Chris interrupted. "Which you're threatening to destroy because you can't live with your own choices."

Leah leaned forward, her eyes searching Ryan's face with the particular intensity of someone trying to understand how a human being could arrive at such cruelty. "What happened to you, Ryan?"

The question landed differently than the others—not accusatory, but genuinely bewildered. Ryan's defensive posture faltered slightly.

"What do you mean?"

"I mean, what happened to the person I knew?" Leah's voice carried something between grief and disbelief. "The man I met in high school wasn't cruel. He was scared, yes. Selfish, absolutely. But this?" She gestured at the documents spread across the table. "Engineering a child's trauma at her own art celebration? Calling her a mistake to provoke violence? Using a young child as a weapon in your personal war for redemption?"

Ryan shifted uncomfortably, his jaw tightening.

"When did you become someone who could look at a little girl—your own daughter—and decide her suffering was acceptable collateral damage for your guilt?" Leah's words carried the surgical precision of a diagnosis delivered without anesthesia. "Because that's what this is, Ryan. You're not fighting for Louise. You're fighting to feel less terrible about abandoning her. And you're willing to traumatize her to achieve that."

Something flickered across Ryan's face—recognition, perhaps, or the ghost of conscience not yet completely calcified. His hands unclenched slightly on the table's edge, his breathing shifting into a pattern that suggested her words had found their target.

"My choices?" Ryan continued, his defensiveness rebuilding itself brick by brick. "My choice was supporting myself instead of becoming a teenage father with no prospects!"

"Your choice," Elizabeth said calmly, "was signing legal documents terminating all parental rights. Documents you're now asking the court to ignore."

Wallace shuffled papers nervously. "The law allows for reconsideration under changed circumstances—"

"What circumstances?" Leah demanded, her voice carrying the accumulated fury of watching that momentary remorse evaporate. "That he finally has money? That he's lonely? That he regrets his decision?"

"All valid considerations," Wallace said, but his voice lacked conviction.

Chris studied Ryan's face, seeing something he'd missed before. "You don't actually want joint custody, do you?"

"Of course I do."

"No." Chris's voice carried sudden understanding. "You want me to say no. You want to be the victim here, the wronged father denied access to his child."

Ryan's silence stretched too long.

"That's it, isn't it?" Leah said, pieces clicking into place. "If we agree to joint custody, you actually have to be a father. But if we refuse, you get to play the martyr forever."

"You're being ridiculous," Ryan said, but sweat had appeared on his forehead.

"Am I?" Leah leaned forward. "Because joint custody means real responsibility. School conferences, medical decisions, discipline, daily care. Are you actually prepared for that?"

"I've prepared extensively—"

"Buying furniture isn't parenting," Chris said. "When's the last time you changed a diaper? Handled a sick child? Stayed up all night with fever watch?"

"I can learn—"

"From a young child who doesn't know you?" Leah's voice carried devastating logic. "You want to practice parenting on a traumatized child who's being forced to spend weekends with a stranger?"

Wallace tried to regain control. "These concerns can be addressed through supervised transition—"

"Supervised by whom?" Elizabeth asked. "And for how long? Months? Years? Until Louise accepts that her family has been legally dismantled for Mr. Matthews' emotional needs?"

Ryan stood abruptly. "I have rights!"

"You had rights," Chris said, rising to meet him. "You signed them away. This is about wants, not rights."

"Fine." Ryan's voice turned cold, any trace of his earlier vulnerability completely erased. "Then you go to prison. Louise watches her precious 'daddy' get handcuffed again. See how that trauma serves her best interests."

Leah stood slowly, her movement carrying finality. "There it is. When reason fails, threats. When logic fails, emotional manipulation. This is who you want Louise to spend weekends with."

She gathered her purse with deliberate calm. "We're done here."

Wallace half-rose from his chair. "Mrs. Johnson, if you walk away from this offer—"

"When," she corrected. "When we walk away from this offer, you'll discover that the Miller family doesn't negotiate with people who threaten children."

Chris felt something shift in the room's atmosphere. Leah's voice carried new authority he'd never heard before.

"Seventy-two hours," Ryan called as they reached the door. "Then your husband becomes a convicted felon."

Leah paused at the threshold, her hand on Chris's arm. "Mr. Matthews? When you're sitting alone in that house you've prepared for a daughter who will never come, remember that you chose this outcome. Not us."

The elevator doors closed on Ryan's stunned silence and Wallace's frantic attempts at damage control.

"That felt different," Chris said quietly.

"It was different," Leah replied, her voice carrying steel he'd never heard before. "They just threatened the wrong family."

Outside the corporate tower, the late afternoon air felt clean after the suffocating atmosphere of legal manipulation. Chris and Leah walked toward their car in contemplative silence, processing the magnitude of what they'd just refused—security offered in exchange for their daughter's happiness.

"Daddy! Mommy!" Louise's voice carried across the plaza as she ran from the babysitter, her joy untouched by adult complications.

Chris scooped her up, feeling her small arms circle his neck with absolute trust. In that moment, every threat Ryan had made felt insignificant compared to this—the weight of a child who called him Daddy because he'd earned it.

"How was your meeting?" Louise asked with her natural curiosity about grown-up business.

"Productive," Leah said, her hand finding Chris's free one. "We made some very important decisions about our family."

They reached their car as sunset painted the sky in brilliant oranges and purples. Louise chattered about her afternoon adventures while Chris secured her in her car seat, her innocent happiness serving as reminder of what they were protecting.

"We did the right thing in there," Leah said quietly as they pulled away from the corporate district.

"Even knowing what comes next?" Chris asked, though his voice carried conviction rather than doubt.

"Especially knowing what comes next." Leah's fingers intertwined with his across the console. "We're stronger than whatever they throw at us."

At a red light, Chris brought her hand to his lips, pressing a soft kiss to her knuckles. The gesture was simple, automatic, but it carried the weight of partnership tested by fire and emerging unbroken.

"I love you," he said, the words encompassing gratitude, commitment, and absolute certainty about the path they'd chosen.

"I love you too," she replied, her eyes bright with unshed tears that spoke of relief rather than fear. "All of us. This family we've built together."

Louise's sleepy voice drifted from the backseat: "Are we going home now?"

"Yes, sweetheart," Chris said, his reflection in the rearview mirror showing a man who understood exactly what home meant. "We're going home."

Behind them, the corporate tower grew smaller in the distance, its glass surface no longer intimidating but merely irrelevant. Ahead lay whatever consequences their refusal would bring, but they would face them as they always had—together, united by love that no legal threat could diminish.

The evening stretched before them, golden with possibility and weighted with the particular peace that came from choosing principle over convenience, family over fear. They had rejected Ryan's offer not because it was easy, but because it was right.

And that made all the difference.

Monday evening arrived with exhausted relief—Chris home from jail but carrying the weight of what he'd done, Louise finally asleep after clinging to him since his return. The doorbell's soft chime made them both freeze, hypervigilance still raw from seventy-two hours of separation and uncertainty.

"I'll get it," Leah whispered, recognizing Mary's silhouette through the frosted glass. Her mother-in-law stood on the porch clutching her phone, her usually composed face bearing traces of tears and something else—a fragile hope wrapped in determination.

"I need to show you something." Mary's voice shook. "About Louise's art celebration. I didn't even realize until this morning."

Chris looked up from the couch, confusion replacing dread. "What do you mean, Mom?"

Mary stepped inside, her fingers trembling around her phone. "When Ryan arrived, something felt wrong. The way he stood at the gate, the look in his eyes—I don't know. I just felt this dread in my stomach." She took a shaky breath. "So I pulled out my phone and started recording. I wasn't thinking clearly. I just... I needed to document whatever was about to happen."

Leah guided Mary to the armchair, recognizing the exhaustion of someone who had been carrying a burden alone. "You recorded the confrontation?"

"I didn't mean to." Mary's voice cracked slightly. "After everything happened—the police, Louise crying—I completely forgot. The whole thing was so traumatic that I couldn't bear to think about it, let alone watch it again." She looked at Chris with regret. "For days, I've been carrying this phone around not even remembering what was on it."

Chris moved to sit on the coffee table facing his mother, his hands clasped between his knees. "What changed?"

"Last night, I couldn't sleep. I kept thinking about Ryan's lawyers claiming you attacked him unprovoked, about those distant videos everyone else took." Mary's fingers worked nervously across her phone screen. "I finally forced myself to look through my photos from that day, thinking maybe there was something—anything—that could help. And then I saw it. A video file I didn't remember taking."

She paused, gathering courage. "I almost didn't watch it. I was terrified of reliving that moment. But I made myself put in headphones and press play."

The weight of her confession settled around them. Leah reached out, touching Mary's knee with gentle encouragement.

"The video was running when Ryan started talking to you," Mary continued, her voice gaining strength. "I must have been standing closer than I thought—maybe by the porch pillar, I can't quite remember. The audio is muffled, not perfect, but with headphones..." She looked between them. "You can hear everything he said. Everything he did to provoke you."

Leah felt her heart rate quicken. She had been there, had heard every calculated word Ryan had spoken, every deliberate strike designed to destroy Chris's control. But hearing it was different from having it documented, preserved as evidence that could counter the narrative Ryan's lawyers were building.

"Can we hear it?" Leah asked gently, though she already knew what the recording would contain—those same words that had been replaying in her mind for days.

Mary nodded, her hands steadying as she pulled out earbuds from her purse. "It's not crystal clear—there's background noise, children playing, wind—but his words are there. Audible. Deliberate." She offered the earbuds to Chris first. "I thought... I thought maybe this could help. Show that he wasn't there to celebrate. That he came with a purpose."

Chris took the earbuds with hands that had forgotten how to be steady. The small speakers settled into his ears, creating an intimate connection to that terrible afternoon. Mary pressed play.

Party sounds emerged first—familiar and painful. Louise's laughter somewhere in the distance. Then Ryan's voice, slightly muffled but unmistakable in its cold precision: *How long do you think this little arrangement will last when Louise realizes her mother trapped you into raising another man's child?*

Leah watched Chris's face as he listened, saw the moment the word "mistake" landed like Ryan had intended—a blade finding the most vulnerable spot. She remembered standing just feet away, frozen as she'd watched Ryan systematically dismantle Chris's control with surgical precision. The memory of her own helplessness in that moment still burned.

Chris pulled out the earbuds, passing them to Leah without speaking. His mother's face swam in his vision, tears he didn't remember shedding blurring the edges of her concerned expression.

Leah took the earbuds, though she didn't need to hear the words again—they were seared into her memory. But she listened anyway, letting the clinical detachment of her medical training analyze the recording's quality, the clarity of Ryan's voice, the unmistakable calculation in every syllable. When she finally removed the earbuds, relief washed through her.

"It's clear enough," she said, something hardening in her voice. "Every word designed to break Chris. To force exactly the reaction Ryan needed for his custody case. And it's captured. Evidence."

She felt tears threatening—not of sadness but of fierce gratitude. She had heard it all happen, had been powerless to stop it in that moment. But now they had proof, documentation that could counter the carefully edited videos Ryan's team would present.

Mary reached forward, taking both their hands. "I didn't know what I'd captured until this morning. And even then, I wasn't sure if it would be clear enough, if anyone would be able to hear what he said through all the background noise." Her grip tightened. "But this morning, I listened again. And again. Making sure I wasn't imagining it, that the words were really there."

"They're there," Leah confirmed, her voice carrying both relief and renewed determination. "Every calculated word. I heard them when it happened, but I couldn't prove what he'd said. This changes everything."

"What should we do with this?" Mary asked, her earlier fragility replaced by steady purpose. "I know it's not perfect quality, but it's the truth. It shows what really happened."

"We call Williams first thing in the morning," Leah said, already organizing the next steps. "She'll know how to present it, how to use it to counter Ryan's narrative."

"And Judge Erikson needs to hear it," Chris added, something loosening in his chest as shame began to unravel. "Compare what you captured to those distant videos showing just my reaction."

Mary nodded, relief washing over her features. "I'm sorry I didn't remember sooner. If I'd known days ago—"

"You were traumatized too," Leah interrupted gently. "We all were. Louise's celebration became a crime scene. Your mind protected you by letting you forget until you were strong enough to face it."

Mary had witnessed her son's violence, her granddaughter's terror, the systematic destruction of a child's celebration. Of course she'd needed time before confronting the evidence of what had unfolded.

"Thank you," Chris said, the words inadequate for the magnitude of what his mother had given them. "For being brave enough to watch it. For trusting that we needed to see it."

Louise stirred upstairs, her small voice calling for water. Leah rose automatically, but paused at the base of the stairs.

"This changes everything," she said to Mary. "Not just the legal case, but what Chris has been carrying. The belief that he became a monster at our daughter's celebration."

"You didn't become anything," Mary said firmly, looking at her son. "You were provoked. Deliberately. Systematically. By someone who knew exactly which words would destroy your control."

After Mary left, Chris and Leah sat together in the darkened living room, processing the evening's revelation. The recording existed. The truth had been captured, even accidentally, even imperfectly.

"She didn't even mean to document it," Chris said wonderingly. "Just felt something was wrong and started recording."

"Maternal instinct," Leah replied. "The same thing that made her forget for a few days—trauma protection. Our minds are remarkable at knowing what we can handle and when."

Chris reached for her hand across the couch cushions. "Ryan studied us. Identified our vulnerabilities. I heard every word he said, even in the middle of it all. But I couldn't stop myself."

"Because he knew exactly what to say," Leah said quietly, her own memory of standing helpless surfacing. "I was right there. I heard it happening. I saw your face change when he called Louise a mistake. I wanted to intervene, to stop it somehow, but it all happened so fast."

She squeezed his hand. "That's why this recording matters so much. I can testify that I heard what he said, but my word as your wife might

380

be dismissed as bias. Mary's recording is objective proof of what we both witnessed."

The distinction mattered—the difference between testimony that could be questioned and evidence that spoke for itself.

"We have the truth now," Chris said, his voice carrying cautious hope. "Documented. Preserved."

Outside, the night settled over their neighborhood with deceptive tranquility. Inside, understanding had shifted, not just legally, but emotionally. Chris wasn't the monster he'd feared becoming. Ryan wasn't the wronged father seeking connection. Mary wasn't the passive grandmother but a protector who had accidentally captured truth when it mattered most.

Tomorrow they would call Williams. Submit the evidence. Begin the process of countering Ryan's narrative with the truth that had been there all along, waiting for someone brave enough to listen—and fortunate enough to have captured it on video, however accidentally.

CHAPTER 22

The Weight of Recorded Truth

M orning arrived with the particular clarity that follows sleepless nights spent processing impossible revelations. Less than twelve hours had passed since Mary's revelation, since they'd discovered that evidence of Ryan's calculated provocation had existed all along, waiting for courage to uncover it.

Elizabeth Williams's office building rose against the late morning sky like a monument to second chances. They arrived together—Chris, Leah, and Mary—carrying the small device that held evidence of psychological warfare.

The reception area's neutral beige and chrome spoke of professional detachment, but Williams emerged from her office carrying the particular energy of someone who sensed their case was about to transform. Her handshake was firm, her gaze moving between them with swift assessment.

"You sounded urgent on the phone," Williams said, gesturing them into her office. "What's happened?"

The conference room's familiar mahogany table stretched before them. Mary's hands trembled slightly as she placed her phone on the polished surface, its black screen reflecting fragments of their anxious faces.

"I recorded the art celebration confrontation," Mary said, her voice carrying exhaustion. "I didn't remember until the other night—the trauma made me forget—but the audio captures everything Ryan said to provoke Chris."

Williams's expression shifted into something sharper, more focused. She leaned forward with the attention of someone recognizing strategic advantage. "Everything?"

"Every word," Chris said quietly, his voice steadier than it had been in weeks. "Every pressure point he tested."

Mary's finger hovered over the play button. Leah reached across the space between them, her palm settling against Mary's forearm with gentle encouragement.

"It's okay," Leah whispered. "This is what we came here to do."

The video began with celebration sounds—Louise's distant laughter, the bounce house's mechanical hum, the ordinary percussion of an art showcase gathering. Williams frowned, leaning closer to the phone.

"The audio's quite faint with all the background noise," she said. "Do you have earbuds?"

Mary pulled them from her purse with shaking hands. "I had to use headphones to hear it clearly. There's wind, children playing, but his words come through."

Williams inserted the earbuds, her face immediately transforming as Ryan's voice emerged with clarity that the phone's speaker couldn't provide. Her pen stilled against her legal pad, her entire posture shifting as she absorbed what she was hearing.

"How long do you think this little arrangement will last when Louise realizes her mother trapped you into raising another man's child?"

Leah watched her lawyer's face cycle through recognition and assessment. The recording continued, Ryan's voice carrying deliberate precision as he dismantled Chris's deepest insecurities with surgical accuracy.

"Tell me, Chris, what do you think will happen when Louise starts asking the hard questions? When she realizes you're just the man her mother settled for because she needed someone—anyone—to help raise her mistake?"

Williams's knuckles whitened around her pen. On the small screen, Chris's face transformed as control finally shattered, the moment when provocation achieved its intended result captured in devastating clarity.

The recording ended. Williams removed the earbuds slowly, her expression carrying grim satisfaction.

"This changes everything," she said. "Ryan wasn't there to celebrate Louise's achievement. He came to conduct psychological warfare designed to provoke exactly this response."

Chris exhaled slowly, accumulated tension finally finding release. "So I'm not the monster I thought I'd become."

"You're a father who was pushed beyond his breaking point," Williams replied, her tone carrying both professional assessment and human compassion. "The video shows premeditation on Ryan's part, not on yours."

Williams was already reaching for her phone. "I need to get this file immediately. Mary, can you email it to me?"

"I'm not very good with technology," Mary said, her fingers moving uncertainly across her screen. "How do I do that?"

Williams reached across her desk and pressed a number on her desk phone.

"David? Elizabeth Williams. I need you in my office immediately with your equipment." She paused. "Audio file extraction from a cellphone, plus cleanup work afterward. High priority—it's custody case evidence."

She hung up and turned back to them. "Our IT specialist will extract the audio and clean it up—remove background noise, isolate the voices,

385

enhance clarity. That way we can present it to Judge Erikson without requiring headphones to hear the provocation."

"How long will that take?" Chris asked.

"An hour, maybe two for something this important." Williams made notes with rapid movements. "But the raw file is already powerful. Combined with the betting jar evidence and the café recording, it reveals a campaign rather than spontaneous paternal concern."

"Will it be admissible?" Leah asked.

"Absolutely. Mary was recording events at a family gathering where she had every right to be present. The audio quality actually strengthens our case—it shows this wasn't professional surveillance but a grandmother's instinct to document something that felt wrong."

A knock at the door interrupted them. A young man in glasses entered carrying a laptop bag.

"David, I need you to extract a video file from this phone," Williams said as she handed Mary's phone to him. "I'll also need audio cleanup—noise reduction, voice isolation. Can you work on it here?"

"Give me an hour," David said, already setting up his equipment on the conference table's far end.

Williams turned her attention back to them. "This video doesn't just change our legal strategy, it changes the narrative entirely. Chris, you've been carrying the belief that you became violent without cause. But this proves you were responding to systematic psychological torture."

Leah felt recognition flickering through her chest. The precision in Ryan's attack carried familiar architecture—her father's voice from memory, explaining competitor analysis over dinner as if destroying livelihoods was mere business strategy. She glanced at Chris, seeing him process similar recognition from his own childhood, the bewilderment in his father's voice when trust had been weaponized against him.

Williams gathered her notes with decisive movements. "We submit this as evidence in both the assault case and the custody proceeding. We show that Ryan's campaign has been calculated destruction rather than genuine paternal awakening."

"What happens next?" Chris asked.

"We wait for the cleaned audio, then I file motions to introduce new evidence. The assault charges should be dropped or reduced significantly given the provocation. And Ryan's custody petition..." She smiled grimly. "Judge Erikson will see this for what it is—an attempt to reward the very behavior family courts exist to prevent."

As they prepared to leave while David worked, Mary paused at the door. "I'm sorry I forgot for so long."

Chris embraced his mother with careful gentleness. "You remembered when you were ready. That's exactly when we needed it."

They walked to their car in contemplative silence, each processing what Mary's forgotten video had revealed.

"The way Ryan tested each pressure point," Leah said quietly as they reached their car. "It's the same methodology my father uses in business. Clinical."

Chris's hand found hers across the space between them. "Your father," he said carefully, understanding dawning. "You said you called him for help?"

Leah nodded, her throat tight with the complexity of what she'd set in motion the night Chris was arrested. "I did. After watching you get handcuffed at Louise's art celebration, I realized we couldn't win this battle by playing defense. We needed someone who understood Ryan's tactics because he'd perfected them himself."

"Do you regret it?" Chris asked, though his voice carried no judgment.

"No." The certainty in her response surprised them both. "But I'm learning the difference between using strategic thinking and becoming someone who views people as chess pieces. Dad knows how to dismantle campaigns like Ryan's because he's run them himself. But I get to choose how we use that knowledge—whether we destroy Ryan or simply protect Louise."

Chris studied her face, seeing the woman she'd become through necessity and choice. "You're meeting with him today, aren't you?"

"This afternoon. He's been investigating Ryan's funding sources, his legal team's vulnerabilities, the network supporting his custody campaign." Leah's fingers tightened around his. "Mary's video gives us the truth about what happened. Dad's investigation will show us how to make sure that truth is heard."

"And you're okay with that?" Chris asked. "With using his methods?"

"I'm okay with protecting our daughter using every ethical tool available," Leah replied, her voice carrying conviction that transcended doubt. "The difference is, I'm not trying to destroy Ryan for my own gain. I'm trying to end his campaign so Louise can grow up feeling safe."

Chris pulled her closer, his arms circling her waist as they stood beside their car in the parking lot. "We're not rejecting who our fathers are," he said, understanding crystallizing. "We're choosing to be different versions of strength."

"Exactly." Leah leaned into his embrace, drawing comfort from his steady presence. "I can be strategic like Dad without being cruel. You can be strong without being violent. We get to write our own definitions."

As they drove home, Leah's phone buzzed with a text from John Miller: *Investigation complete. Free this afternoon to discuss findings?*

She typed her response: *2pm. Your office.*

The path forward had split into two streams that would converge toward the same destination—Williams wielding Mary's video in court while John Miller's investigation dismantled the infrastructure supporting Ryan's campaign. Legal truth and strategic intelligence working in concert to protect what mattered most.

"Thank you," Chris said quietly, his eyes on the road ahead. "For being willing to ask for help, even when it meant facing complicated feelings about your father."

"Thank you," Leah replied, "for trusting me to know the difference between fighting like him and fighting with his help."

The distinction mattered more than the words could express—the choice to use inherited wisdom without inheriting its cruelty, to be strategic without being destructive, to protect their family with every tool available while maintaining the moral boundaries that made their family worth protecting.

By afternoon, Leah would sit across from her father and learn what his investigation had uncovered. But for now, she carried the knowledge that love sometimes required wielding uncomfortable weapons, that protecting innocence occasionally demanded engaging with those who understood how innocence got destroyed, and that breaking generational patterns didn't mean rejecting every lesson those patterns had taught.

The afternoon light filtered through her father's office windows, casting amber shadows across the mahogany desk where a single manila folder waited like a door to uncomfortable truths. Leah settled into the familiar leather chair, her fingers unconsciously tracing the worn armrest where her teenage self had once sat through serious conversations about college choices and future directions.

A few days had passed since she'd called her father from their darkened kitchen, Chris arrested and Louise's art celebration destroyed by Ryan's calculated cruelty. The transformation within her felt both gradual and sudden, like discovering muscles she'd never known she possessed, now flexing with the particular authority that came from choosing to fight rather than merely endure.

John Miller moved with deliberate care, each gesture economical and purposeful. His hair had gained more silver at the temples since their last real conversation, but his eyes retained the analytical sharpness. He poured coffee from the service tray with movements that spoke of patience earned through decades of strategic thinking.

"How's Louise processing everything?" he asked, settling across from her with careful attention.

"She keeps asking when the 'mean man' is coming back." Leah's voice carried the hollow exhaustion of a mother who had spent nights explaining adult cruelties to a young child's mind. "Chris tries to reassure her, but she can sense our fear. Children always do."

John nodded, his expression reflecting recognition of patterns that transcended generations. He opened the manila folder with movements that suggested both reluctance and necessity, revealing documents that spoke of investigation conducted with corporate thoroughness—financial records, professional assessments, the kind of intelligence gathering that followed money trails and observed behavior rather than intercepting private conversations.

"I've had my people look into Ryan Matthews," he began, his tone carrying measured delivery of verifiable facts rather than speculation. "What we found explains the escalation in his custody campaign, though the psychological motivations require some educated assessment."

Leah leaned forward, studying the documents that painted a portrait through observable evidence—bank statements, professional evaluations, timeline analyses that revealed patterns without claiming impossible knowledge of private conversations.

"Ryan's consulting firm is successful enough, but his personal life tells a different story," John continued, his finger tracing documented evidence. "Social media activity showing increasing isolation, professional contacts noting erratic behavior during business meetings. But there's something particularly telling about his career trajectory."

He turned to another set of documents, timeline charts that revealed patterns of decision-making. "Ryan left Tesla months ago—not because he was fired or because his consulting firm was thriving, but because he relocated specifically back to this area. His business address puts him within a short drive of Louise's school."

The revelation settled around Leah like pieces of a puzzle that revealed calculated proximity disguised as career advancement. Ryan's geographic choices hadn't been driven by business opportunities but by the gravitational pull of regret and the particular emptiness that came from watching happiness from a distance.

"The consulting firm's client base supports this assessment," John observed, consulting records that painted a portrait of professional decisions driven by personal rather than strategic considerations. "He could have maintained his California connections, expanded his Tesla network, built something substantial on the West Coast. Instead, he established himself here with smaller clients, less prestigious work, but closer access to the family he'd abandoned."

Leah felt something cold spreading through her chest as the psychological architecture of Ryan's campaign became visible through documented choices. Not sudden paternal awakening but systematic positioning, the methodical approach of someone who had spent months observing their life while building the infrastructure necessary to disrupt it.

"But there's a financial component that explains the legal resources," John said, consulting records that revealed the practical architecture supporting Ryan's campaign. "Judge Matthews has been paying Wallace & Associates' fees. The financial trail is clear—direct transfers from his personal account to cover Ryan's legal expenses."

Leah felt something cold settle in her chest as she processed the implications. Not ideological warfare but financial enablement, a grandfather's money funding a campaign whose methods he might not fully understand.

"How do you know Judge Matthews' involvement?" she asked, her medical training automatically seeking logical connections between observable facts and psychological conclusions.

John turned to documents that revealed investigative methods behind his assessment. "Financial records, primarily. But also professional observations from colleagues in the legal community. Judge Matthews has been making inquiries about family law precedents, consulting with family court attorneys about custody cases involving biological versus adoptive parents. The professional chatter suggests someone deeply conflicted about a personal situation."

The systematic nature of Ryan's approach suddenly made sense through this evidence-based analysis—not coordinated family conspiracy but individual desperation guided by Wallace & Associates' expertise in family court warfare. The legal firm's reputation for aggressive tactics explained Ryan's sophisticated strategy far better than any family coaching could.

"Ryan is essentially acting against his father's explicit warnings," John observed, his voice carrying measured weight. "Judge Matthews wanted careful, respectful contact that prioritized Louise's wellbeing. He agreed to fund the petition through his old friend, James Wallace, not knowing that his firm uses an aggressive playbook in family warfare. The art celebration assault, the systematic provocation, the psychological manipulation—that's all Wallace & Associates' strategy, not something Judge Matthews would ever endorse."

Leah felt pieces falling into place with uncomfortable clarity. Ryan's sophisticated approach hadn't come from judicial coaching but from a legal firm that specialized in exactly this kind of calculated family destruction. Judge Matthews had provided funding believing he was supporting reconnection, not enabling systematic manipulation designed by professionals who treated children as strategic assets.

"What else did you find?" Leah asked, steeling herself for whatever additional revelations waited in that manila folder.

John hesitated, his expression carrying particular reluctance. "Terry O'Donnell approached Wallace & Associates on her own. She volunteered to provide information about your family, claiming she wanted to protect Chris from what she saw as a harmful situation."

Terry's willingness to share family concerns suddenly made sense through this lens—not Ryan's manipulation but her own misguided protective instincts, seized upon by lawyers who understood how to weaponize family dysfunction for their client's benefit.

"Ryan didn't seek her out?" Leah asked, processing this shift in narrative.

"According to our sources within the legal community, Ryan was initially reluctant to use Terry's information. He apparently felt it was 'borderline unethical' to exploit family tensions." John's voice carried weight. "But

Wallace & Associates convinced him that winning custody required using every available advantage, regardless of personal reservations."

The complexity of manipulation operating through genuine emotion became visible through this realistic investigation framework. Terry's betrayal hadn't been pure malice but misguided loyalty exploited by someone who understood how to weaponize good intentions against the very people they claimed to protect.

"They're not going to stop," Leah said quietly, understanding settling around her like inevitability. "Even if we win the current legal battle, Ryan has resources and determination to continue this campaign."

John's expression shifted to something she recognized from childhood, the particular focus he brought to problems requiring systematic solution rather than temporary fix. "Which brings us to strategy. We have several leverage points, but we need to think three moves ahead."

He pulled out a legal pad, his movements deliberate as he began mapping their options. "First, Judge Matthews is increasingly horrified by what his funding has enabled. The art celebration incident, in particular, crossed ethical lines that make his continued support untenable. Our sources indicate he's been expressing serious concerns to colleagues."

Leah watched her father work, seeing the strategic mind that had built his business empire now turned toward protecting his granddaughter. "You're talking about turning Judge Matthews into an ally."

"I'm talking about helping him understand that Ryan's campaign has become exactly what he feared—harmful to Louise rather than beneficial." John's voice carried strategic thought wrapped in genuine concern. "Judge Matthews never wanted this level of conflict. He wanted to meet his granddaughter, not watch her become collateral damage in legal warfare."

He tapped the legal pad with his pen. "But here's what we need to understand about the broader picture. Wallace & Associates operates on a specific model—they take cases with wealthy backers, knowing that most custody battles end in settlement once legal fees become prohibitive. Their entire strategy depends on the opposing party running out of resources or will before they do."

"So they're betting Judge Matthews will keep funding Ryan indefinitely," Leah said, following the logic.

"Exactly. But what if we remove that assumption?" John leaned forward, his analytical mind now fully engaged in problem-solving. "Judge Matthews is a respected jurist. His reputation matters to him. If we can show him that continuing to fund this campaign associates his name with tactics he's publicly condemned from the bench—child manipulation, provoked assault at family events, psychological warfare against a young child—his moral compass will override his familial loyalty."

Leah felt something quickening in her chest—not excitement but recognition of an elegant solution. "You're suggesting we appeal to his judicial ethics rather than his family ties."

"I'm suggesting we provide him with a mirror," John corrected. "Show him what his money is actually funding. Not in accusatory terms, but as a fellow jurist and grandfather who surely didn't intend for his support to enable trauma to a child."

He pulled out another document, this one showing patterns of Wallace & Associates' past cases. "Here's what my people found. Wallace has a history of taking aggressive family law cases, but he's careful about his public reputation. Most cases settle before reaching trial because he makes the process so expensive and psychologically devastating that families capitulate. But when cases do go to trial, his record isn't as strong as his reputation suggests."

"Why?" Leah asked, leaning forward to study the data.

"Because judges don't like manufactured crises," John explained, pointing to specific case outcomes. "Once Wallace's tactics become visible in open court—the provocation, the manipulation, the weaponization of family relationships—judges tend to rule against his clients. He wins through intimidation and attrition, not through judicial approval of his methods."

Understanding crystallized for Leah. "So Ryan's strongest weapon is actually his greatest vulnerability."

"Precisely. Wallace's entire strategy depends on keeping the ugliest parts of his playbook invisible. But Mary's video recording, the betting jars, Ashley's café recording—these are exposing the machinery in ways that make judicial approval increasingly unlikely." John's voice carried conviction. "If we can get Judge Matthews to see what we see, he'll withdraw support not because we forced him, but because continuing to fund this campaign would violate everything he's stood for professionally."

Leah absorbed this, recognizing her father's particular genius—not forcing confrontation but creating conditions where the right choice became obvious. "What about Ryan himself? Even without his father's funding, he could liquidate assets, continue fighting on his own."

"He could," John agreed. "But here's what the financial analysis shows. Ryan's consulting firm generates decent revenue, but it's largely tied up in operational costs and growth investments. His liquid assets would cover maybe two months of Wallace's fees. After that, he'd be choosing between his business and this custody battle."

He pulled out another document, this one showing Ryan's financial structure. "More importantly, Ryan is an engineer. He thinks in systems and solutions. Once he understands that the system supporting his campaign is collapsing—his father's funding withdrawn, Wallace's tactics exposed, the financial reality of continuing alone—his analytical mind will likely calculate that continued pursuit is irrational."

"You're betting on his practicality overriding his emotional need," Leah said.

"I'm betting on giving him the information he needs to make a rational choice," John corrected. "Right now, he's operating on false assumptions—that his father will fund him indefinitely, that Wallace's tactics will work, that biological claims trump demonstrated parenting. We're not attacking him; we're removing the false foundations his campaign is built on."

Leah felt her mind working through this strategy, recognizing both its elegance and its risks. "What if he doubles down instead? What if exposing the truth makes him more desperate rather than more rational?"

John's expression grew more serious. "That's always a risk when you corner someone. Which is why timing matters. We need to approach Judge Matthews while Ryan still has options—while withdrawing feels like wisdom rather than surrender forced by circumstances."

He stood, moving to the window that overlooked the city. "I've already made preliminary contact with someone in Judge Matthews' chambers. Not direct approach—that would put him on defensive—but through a mutual colleague who can frame this as concern rather than accusation."

"What did you say?" Leah asked.

"That I've been made aware of a custody case that appears to violate principles Judge Matthews has championed throughout his career. That I'm reaching out not as an adversary but as someone who believes he'd want to know what his support is enabling." John turned back to face her. "The conversation is scheduled for tomorrow afternoon. Not in his chambers—too formal—but at his club where he can speak freely without judicial constraints."

Leah felt something settling in her chest. Her father wasn't proposing warfare but wisdom, not destruction but illumination. "And if he refuses to see the problem?"

"Then we proceed with legal remedies—presenting all our evidence in open court, letting Judge Erikson see the full scope of manufactured crisis and psychological manipulation." John's voice carried resolve. "But I don't think it will come to that. Everything I know about Judge Matthews suggests he has a conscience that can be reached."

He returned to his seat, pulling out one final document. "There's one more element we need to discuss. Wallace & Associates has a pattern of using family dysfunction as ammunition, but they're careful about crossing certain legal lines. What they did at the art celebration—Ryan's calculated provocation captured on video—may actually constitute witness tampering or obstruction if we can prove premeditation."

"Can you prove that?" Leah asked.

"My people are working on it. If Wallace coached Ryan on specific provocations to use, if there's any documentation of that strategy session, it would be grounds for ethics complaints that could affect Wallace's entire practice." John's tone carried careful hope. "Not vengeance—professional accountability through proper channels."

Leah absorbed all of this, feeling the weight of multiple strategies converging toward the same goal: ending Ryan's campaign not through mutual destruction but through revealing truth that made continued aggression untenable.

"What do you need from me?" she asked, the question carrying commitment that surprised them both.

John's expression softened with something approaching pride. "Permission to proceed. This approach offers Judge Matthews the chance to be the grandfather he originally wanted to be—but only if he chooses Louise's wellbeing over family loyalty to Ryan's destructive campaign."

"He made his choice when he ignored his own instincts about Ryan's methods," she said quietly. "When he continued funding tactics he'd warned against."

Her voice gained strength with each word, conviction crystallizing into action. "But he still has a chance to choose Louise's wellbeing over family loyalty. That's more than Ryan has done."

John nodded, understanding passing between them that balanced justice with compassion. They were no longer just father and daughter but strategic partners protecting the same essential truth—that Louise deserved to grow up in peace, with family members who earned their place through love rather than demanded it through manipulation.

"I'll reach out to Judge Matthews carefully," he promised. "Frame it as an opportunity for him to fulfill his original intention—protecting Louise—rather than as confrontation. Give him the information he needs to make the right choice, then trust his judgment."

"And Wallace & Associates?" Leah asked.

"The ethics investigation proceeds through proper channels. If there's evidence of coaching Ryan to provoke assault, the bar association will handle it. If not, at least we tried to address systemic abuse through legal means rather than personal vendetta." John's tone carried resolve tempered by ethics. "Either way, we're using the system correctly—not for revenge, but for accountability."

As Leah prepared to leave, she felt the particular lightness that followed difficult decisions made with clear conscience. She had chosen to fight with weapons her younger self would have rejected, but she had done so in service of protecting innocence rather than accumulating power.

"One more thing," John said as she reached the door. "Whatever happens with Judge Matthews, whatever Ryan ultimately decides, you've already won the only battle that matters."

"What's that?" Leah asked.

"You've proven that love isn't about biology or legal claims or who can afford better lawyers." His voice carried pride wrapped in hard-won understanding. "You've proven that family is what you build through daily choice, through showing up when it's hard, through choosing your child's wellbeing over your own need to win."

Leah felt tears threatening but refused to let them fall, not here, not now. "Thank you," she whispered. "For understanding what we needed and helping us get it without becoming people we'd be ashamed to be."

"That's what real strength looks like," John replied. "Knowing when to fight and when to show mercy. When to destroy and when to simply illuminate truth and let others choose."

As Leah walked through the late afternoon shadows toward her car, she carried with her not just information but transformation. The woman who drove home to her family was someone who understood that love sometimes required strategic thinking, that protection occasionally demanded calculated response, that fighting for family meant choosing effectiveness over purity—but never choosing cruelty over compassion, never choosing victory over her daughter's wellbeing, never choosing revenge over the possibility of redemption.

Chris and Louise waited at home with their evening routines and bedtime stories and all the ordinary miracles that comprised the life Judge Matthews and Ryan were trying to dismantle. But they were no longer defenseless against systematic manipulation disguised as parental concern.

The Miller family had entered the battle with wisdom rather than weapons, and the rules of engagement had just shifted decisively in favor of love that knew how to protect itself without becoming what it fought against.

That made all the difference.

CHAPTER 23

The Arithmetic of Love

R yan's sedan idled beneath the oak tree across from Maple Elementary, engine marking time he couldn't reclaim. Days of surveillance, and the 72-hour ultimatum he'd delivered through Wallace & Associates now weighed like a stone. The deadline approached when Chris and Leah would accept his terms or face assault charges and emergency custody modification based on documented violence.

Wallace had been confident—the art celebration video was damning, witnessed by dozens of parents. Victory was within reach. His father's continued funding, despite Judge Matthews's growing discomfort, meant the legal machinery could grind forward with relentless efficiency.

Yet something had drawn him here this morning. Perhaps to see Louise before the deadline forced capitulation. Perhaps to reassure himself that systematic destruction of a young child's security was worth it.

Or perhaps you need to see what you're actually destroying.

He silenced that thought. Louise was his daughter. Biology wasn't just relevant—it was foundational. The law recognized this. His father had recognized it enough to fund Wallace & Associates' aggressive strategy.

Even Chris and Leah's desperate adoption filing acknowledged the threat his biological claim represented.

Chris emerged from the school entrance, Louise skipping beside him like sunlight given motion. Her purple backpack drooped from one shoulder, books creating abstract sculptures of a day fully lived. Ryan's hands tightened on the steering wheel.

Louise gestured with uninhibited enthusiasm, small hands painting invisible pictures. Chris bent to her level, attention complete, undivided. The posture spoke of thousands of similar moments, muscle memory carved by daily devotion.

Ryan's chest tightened. When had anyone last looked at him with such unguarded trust? His engineering team respected his expertise, clients valued his problem-solving, but no one needed him the way Louise needed Chris—not for what he could provide, but simply for who he was.

That's exactly why you're fighting. She should need you that way.

He rolled down his window, catching fragments of their conversation.

"—and then Marcus said his hamster could swim, but I told him hamsters don't like water because you said—"

"That's right, Sunshine. Some animals are better suited for different environments."

Sunshine. The endearment hit like physical impact. Not "Louise" or "sweetheart" but something intimate, earned, specific. He'd never had a pet name for her. Had never stayed long enough to develop one.

Because you made a choice years ago.

But people changed. He'd been twenty-one, terrified, unprepared. Now he was established, stable, capable of providing everything a child could need. The Tesla years had taught him that complex systems yielded to systematic analysis and persistent effort. Why should fatherhood be different? Mistakes could be corrected. Biology created connections the law should honor, regardless of intervening years.

Wallace had assured him: joint custody wasn't about erasing Chris—it was creating space for Louise to know her real father, to benefit from resources and stability Ryan's success could provide.

Real father. The phrase circled his mind like a mantra, pushing back against uncomfortable observations accumulating during these surveillance sessions.

Louise stumbled over the uneven sidewalk, enthusiasm overriding coordination. The purple backpack flew from her shoulder as she pitched forward.

Chris moved before Ryan could process the sequence. No thought, no hesitation—pure parental reflex honed by years of vigilant protection. His frame folded instantly, arms extending to catch her before concrete could, body forming a shield between her vulnerability and the world's sharp edges.

But Louise's knee scraped against the rough sidewalk, drawing a thin line of blood.

"Daddy!" The word tore from her throat with absolute trust that comfort would come. Her arms circled Chris's neck with desperate gratitude, world tilted but finding its balance again.

Ryan felt something cracking inside his chest—not clean break but the slow fracturing of assumptions supporting his understanding of what he was fighting for. Chris's face transformed with concern that erased every other expression, hands moving with unconscious competence to check injuries, calculate comfort.

That's what I should be doing. I should be the one she calls for. I should have the muscle memory that makes protection automatic rather than theoretical.

But his absence hadn't been malicious—it had been survival. He'd chosen Tesla believing career success would validate his existence in ways teenage fatherhood never could. The consulting firm, financial security, professional respect—these were real accomplishments providing advantages Chris's music teacher salary never could.

Except she doesn't need your money. She needs years of accumulated trust, daily presence, learning her fears through lived experience rather than legal discovery.

No. Defeatist thinking. Children were resilient. Wallace had shown him studies about successful joint custody, biological fathers reclaiming relationships after years of absence. Louise would adjust. Within months of regular visitation, she'd learn her real father could provide stability transcending emotional bonds formed with Chris out of necessity.

"It hurts," Louise whispered against Chris's shoulder, voice carrying vulnerability that only surfaced in genuine need.

"I know, sweetheart. But look—it's just a little red line. Your body is already starting to fix itself." Chris's voice carried absolute certainty, calm transforming panic into manageable disappointment. "And you know what the best medicine is for scrapes like this?"

Louise lifted her head, tears clinging to dark lashes. "Ice cream?"

"Ice cream," Chris confirmed, smile carrying relief the injury wasn't serious, joy he could provide easy comfort. "But only after we get home and clean this properly."

Ryan felt something twisting as Louise's face brightened with anticipatory pleasure. The ease of it—how Chris knew exactly what would comfort her, how she trusted his promises without question—spoke of relationship built through countless similar moments.

I could learn that. Given time, I could learn her patterns, needs, what makes her feel safe.

The thought felt hollow even as he formed it. Louise wasn't a system to be optimized. She was a person with years of accumulated experiences shaping her understanding of love, safety, family. Experiences he'd had no part creating.

But that was precisely the injustice he was fighting to correct. He'd been denied those years. Leah had pushed for termination papers, made him believe walking away was responsible. Wallace had suggested she'd manipulated him, gotten him to sign away rights so she could find someone else to play father to his daughter.

Chris helped Louise to her feet, movements gentle but efficient. He shouldered her backpack without being asked. When she reached for his hand, their fingers intertwined with unconscious harmony of people who'd walked together through countless school pickups, playground accidents, ordinary moments accumulating into unshakeable bonds.

This isn't performance. This isn't convenience. This is what love looks like when tested daily and never found wanting.

But acknowledging that truth felt like surrendering everything he'd fought for. Years of guilt waking him at three in the morning. Years imagining what Louise might look like, sound like, need from a father she'd never known. Years building justifications—career advancement was providing for her future, success would circle back to benefit the daughter he'd temporarily set aside.

Temporarily. The word mocked him. Years wasn't temporary. Years was Louise's entire conscious memory, foundation of her understanding about who belonged in her life and why.

"Daddy, will you carry me?" Louise's request carried exhaustion following adrenaline crashes.

Chris lifted her without hesitation. Louise's legs wrapped around his waist, head settling against his shoulder with boneless trust of someone who'd never doubted she'd be caught, held, protected. Her arms circled his neck like anchors, securing her to absolute safety.

Ryan's vision blurred. He blinked rapidly, refusing to acknowledge moisture gathering at the corners of his eyes.

Grief. This is grief for something you never actually had.

But grief could transform into rage. Why should Chris reap rewards of fatherhood Ryan had earned through biology? Why should years of presence outweigh fundamental truth of genetic connection? Wallace would argue exactly that in court—biological bonds, Ryan's transformation, Louise's right to know her heritage. The art celebration assault had given them the perfect weapon.

You're not fighting for her. You're fighting against the reality that someone else became her father while you were busy becoming successful.

Ryan started his car, hands moving through familiar sequences while his mind continued civil war. The 72-hour ultimatum stood. Wallace & Associates waited for final confirmation. His father's money continued funding the campaign.

He could still win this. The law was on his side. Biology mattered. His father's judicial experience confirmed judges recognized children deserved relationships with both parents. Chris's assault provided perfect leverage.

Except he's not unfit. He's human. He lost control after systematic provocation designed to make him snap. And now you're using his one moment of weakness against years of demonstrated strength.

The thought hardened his resolve instead of shaming him. This was war. Wars required ruthless tactics. Louise would understand someday—her real father had fought through every obstacle to claim his rightful place in her life.

Will she? Or will she remember her daddy was taken by a stranger claiming biology mattered more than love?

They moved toward the crosswalk, Louise chattering against Chris's ear. "—and tomorrow I'm going to tell Marcus that hamsters can't swim but daddies can catch little girls who fall down."

Ryan's breath caught. The casual possessiveness—*my daddy*—spoke of ownership transcending biology. Not legal claim but emotional reality, built through years of daily choice.

He knows her weight. How she feels when tired. The exact pressure that comforts her.

This wasn't substitute parenting. Chris knew Louise's body language, comfort needs, emotional rhythms with intuitive understanding that could only come from thousands of shared moments. Moments Ryan had sacrificed for quarterly reviews and client presentations.

He pulled away from Maple Elementary, GPS offering efficient route toward the office where Wallace waited. Saturday would bring their decision—accept joint custody disrupting Louise's world, or watch Chris face criminal charges destroying their family differently.

You're lying to yourself. You watched her call for her daddy, and you know it wasn't you. It will never be you, no matter how many court orders you accumulate.

But Ryan couldn't afford to listen to that voice. Not when he'd come this far. Not when victory remained achievable through legal channels vindicating his years of absence by proving biology ultimately trumped choice.

The office building rose ahead. Wallace waited inside with documents requiring signature, final confirmation Ryan was ready to deploy legal assault forcing surrender.

The seed of doubt planted during surveillance had begun germinating, sending uncomfortable roots through careful justifications. But doubt wasn't certainty. Questions weren't answers. And watching Chris catch Louise wasn't the same as understanding some bonds, once formed through years of devotion, couldn't be severed without destroying the very person he claimed to love.

Ryan parked and walked toward the building carrying uncertainty like a briefcase full of documents he didn't want to examine. Saturday's deadline approached. Wallace's confidence remained unshaken. His father's funding continued despite growing discomfort.

You can still win this.

But even rehearsing familiar arguments, Ryan couldn't silence the voice that had watched Louise call for her daddy and recognized he was fighting to destroy something he'd never understood. Something that looked remarkably like love when stripped of legal definitions and strategic maneuvering.

The elevator ascended, carrying him toward decisions determining Louise's future and his own. The doubt traveled with him, a quiet passenger asking questions he wasn't ready to answer about the difference between claiming and earning, between legal rights and emotional reality.

But he would continue fighting. The deadline stood. The machinery was in motion. Whatever discomfort he felt would fade once joint custody allowed building his own relationship. Time would prove him right. Biology would assert itself.

Even if it destroys the connections she's already chosen?

Ryan stepped into Wallace's office without answering, because answering might require acknowledging truths he'd spent years avoiding. The hours would pass. The ultimatum would expire. Decisions would be made. Lives reshaped.

The doubt would have to wait. Victory came first.

The familiar mahogany desk stretched between them like a chasm carved by accumulated disappointment. Judge Matthews sat in the same leather chair where Ryan had confessed Louise's existence months ago, but the man behind the bench bore little resemblance to the grandfather who had once promised support.

Evening light filtered through the windows, casting amber shadows across photographs of Ryan's achievements. Engineering degree graduation. Tesla corporate headshots. Professional milestones that had once seemed to define success but now felt hollow as museum pieces—beautiful, distant, irrelevant to the wreckage spreading across the desk between them.

A manila folder lay open like an autopsy report. Timeline analyses. Witness statements. Evidence that documented the psychological toll on a young child.

Ryan leaned forward, his hands pressed flat against the desk's cool surface. "Dad, you have to understand—we have him on video. Multiple angles. Witnesses. Parents with their phones out recording everything." His voice carried desperate urgency. "Chris Johnson assaulted me at a children's art showcase. That's not manipulation or legal maneuvering—that's documented fact."

Judge Matthews remained motionless, his judicial mask revealing nothing as his son built his case like a prosecutor convinced of victory through overwhelming evidence.

"Wallace says the footage is devastating," Ryan continued, momentum building. "You can see him vault the fence, see his fist connect, see me trying to defend myself while children scattered. Every parent there witnessed it." His finger jabbed the desk for emphasis. "This isn't about my past mistakes anymore—it's about proving he's unfit to raise Louise. Violent. Dangerous. Unable to control his temper around children."

The words hung between them like smoke from a controlled burn—deliberate, designed to obscure rather than illuminate. Judge Matthews studied his son with the particular attention he'd brought to thousands of custody cases.

"You're quite confident about this video evidence," Judge Matthews said quietly.

"Confident?" Ryan's laugh emerged sharp with vindication. "Dad, it's ironclad. Wallace has already started drafting emergency custody modification papers. The judge will see a man who can't control his rage, who traumatized children at an art celebration, who—"

"Who was systematically provoked by someone who knew exactly which psychological buttons to push."

The interruption landed like cold water on Ryan's building momentum. His expression flickered—confusion, then defensive calculation.

"What are you talking about? I brought a gift to my daughter's art showcase. I was attempting reconciliation, and he attacked me without—"

"Without provocation?" Judge Matthews opened the manila folder, sliding documents across polished wood. "Is that the story you're planning to tell in court?"

Ryan's eyes tracked to the papers. Audio transcripts. Timeline analyses. A single line highlighted in yellow: *"When she realizes you're just the man her mother settled for because she needed someone—anyone—to help raise her mistake."*

"That's out of context," Ryan said quickly, though sweat had appeared on his forehead. "I was having a conversation—"

"You were conducting psychological warfare. Deliberately. Systematically. Using words specifically chosen to provoke exactly the response you needed for your legal strategy."

Ryan's hands clenched into fists against the desktop. "Even if I said things in the heat of the moment, that doesn't justify violence. He's an adult. He should have walked away."

"You called Louise a mistake." The words fell between them like stones into still water. "You reduced your daughter to a burden, calculated the exact phrasing that would destroy Chris's control, and now you want to use his thirty seconds of humanity against years of devoted fatherhood."

"It was a figure of speech—"

"It was provocation. Mary Johnson recorded the entire encounter. Not professionally, not with legal intent, but because her grandmother's instincts told her something dangerous was about to happen."

Ryan stared at the documents spread before him, his mind racing. "How do you know all this?" The question emerged sharp with suspicion. "These transcripts, the timeline analyses—where did you get these?"

Judge Matthews leaned back in his chair, his expression carrying something that might have been reluctant admiration. "John Miller reached out through a mutual colleague."

The name landed like a physical blow. Ryan felt the air leave his lungs. "Miller? Leah's father contacted you?"

"Through proper channels. Professional courtesy between men who've both practiced law long enough to recognize when a situation requires intervention." Judge Matthews tapped the folder. "He didn't threaten or demand. He simply provided the results of his investigation and asked if I was aware what my financial support was enabling."

Ryan's throat constricted as understanding crystallized. Miller hadn't launched an attack—he'd conducted reconnaissance, gathered evidence, and delivered it with surgical precision to the one person whose withdrawal of support would dismantle the entire campaign.

"He framed it as an opportunity for me to fulfill my original intention," Judge Matthews continued, his voice carrying something that might have been shame. "Which was protecting Louise, not funding psychological manipulation. He provided documentation of everything—the café recording between you and Terry, the betting jars, the provocation at the showcase. He suggested I might want to know what Wallace & Associates' tactics actually look like when deployed against a child."

"He's trying to turn you against me," Ryan said, but the words lacked conviction.

"He's trying to help me see what I should have recognized months ago." Judge Matthews opened the folder wider, revealing page after page of meticulously documented evidence. "That I've been funding exactly the kind of family destruction I've spent my career condemning from the bench."

Ryan's eyes moved across the documents—financial analyses showing the trail of his father's payments to Wallace & Associates, witness statements from the art showcase, timeline analyses revealing the systematic nature of his campaign. Miller's investigation had been thorough, clinical, devastating.

"This is everything?" Ryan's voice emerged hollow.

"Everything relevant." Judge Matthews closed the folder with quiet finality. "Miller's investigation revealed patterns I was too close to see. Or perhaps," he added with brutal honesty, "patterns I didn't want to see because you're my son and I wanted to believe your campaign served Louise's interests rather than your guilt."

The silence stretched between them, broken only by the grandfather clock marking time that felt suddenly precious, suddenly finite.

"He didn't have to share this with me," Judge Matthews said. "He could have used it all in court, exposed my funding publicly, made this a scandal that would taint my reputation. Instead, he gave me the chance to withdraw support with dignity intact. That's not warfare, Ryan. That's grace."

Ryan sank deeper into his chair as the magnitude of Miller's strategic approach became clear. Not destruction but illumination. Not attack but intervention. The most effective move was one that didn't feel like aggression at all—just truth delivered with enough care that the recipient had to acknowledge it.

"My funding ends now," Judge Matthews said, the words carrying absolute finality. "Which means you have hours, not days, to decide whether you're willing to bankrupt yourself pursuing a custody case that will expose your manipulation to public scrutiny."

"Hours?" Ryan's voice cracked.

"The ultimatum you gave them expires soon." Judge Matthews's tone carried no sympathy. "You created this timeline. You weaponized urgency against them. Now you'll discover what it feels like when time becomes your enemy."

Ryan's hands trembled as reality crystallized. Without his father's funding, Wallace & Associates would require immediate payment—retainers that would drain his business accounts. Everything he'd built sacrificed on the altar of claiming a daughter who had never been his to possess.

"What if I choose to fight?" The question emerged as both challenge and plea. "What if I liquidate everything, pay Wallace myself, proceed with the charges?"

Judge Matthews studied his son with eyes that had witnessed countless defendants make life-defining choices. "Then you'll learn whether winning custody is worth losing yourself in the process." He paused, letting the words settle. "But remember—being Louise's father would have required presence years ago. What you're fighting for now isn't fatherhood. It's absolution for abandonment. And absolution doesn't come through custody petitions."

Ryan felt tears threatening—not calculated emotion but genuine grief for something he was only beginning to understand he'd never actually possessed. But admitting defeat felt impossible, unbearable.

"I can't just walk away," he whispered. "If I give up now, what does that make me? The man who abandoned her twice?"

Judge Matthews moved around the desk, his hand settling on Ryan's shoulder. "It makes you the man who finally chose her wellbeing over his own needs. That's not abandonment—that's the most parental act you've ever contemplated."

The door closed with quiet finality, leaving Ryan alone in the hallway with fluorescent truth and diminishing time to choose between bankruptcy and surrender, between possessing his daughter and releasing her to the family she'd already chosen.

He descended the stairs slowly, each step marking minutes toward a deadline when his ultimatum would expire and demand an answer to the question he'd been avoiding: what was he actually fighting for, and was winning worth the cost of everything it would require him to destroy—including himself?

The evening stretched ahead, vast with possibility and suffocating with proximity to decisions that could no longer be delayed. Behind him, his father's office held its silence like a confessional after difficult truths had been spoken. Ahead waited hours of reckoning.

What he would decide remained unknowable—even to himself.

The house held its breath in the particular stillness that followed Louise's bedtime—the careful quiet of parents navigating around sleeping children, their voices automatically dropping to whispers that carried more intimacy than shouts ever could. Lamplight pooled across the living room in warm circles, transforming familiar furniture into soft sanctuaries against the darkness pressing at the windows.

Leah sat curled in the corner of their sofa, her father's call still echoing in her mind. The information John Miller had shared moved through her consciousness—symptoms presenting, patterns emerging, diagnosis crystallizing with devastating clarity.

Chris moved through their evening routine with unconscious grace, checking locks and switching off lights, his musician's hands creating small symphonies of domestic security. But Leah watched the tension in his shoulders, the way his gaze lingered on Louise's artwork covering the refrigerator, as if memorizing proof of their family's happiness before it could be threatened again.

"Dad called," she said quietly, her voice cutting through the whispered domesticity. "Judge Matthews withdrew funding from Ryan's legal team."

Chris paused in his nightly ritual, coffee mug halfway to the sink. The ceramic caught lamplight like a prayer, suspended between ordinary gesture and extraordinary news. His reflection in the kitchen window showed a man processing victory that didn't feel quite real.

"It's over?" The question emerged carefully, as if speaking too loudly might shatter whatever fragile peace had descended upon them.

"The money is gone. But Ryan..." Leah set down the medical journal she'd been reading, its pages forgotten as her mind worked through implications that transcended legal strategy. "He's not going to stop. Not because of money."

She rose from the sofa, her movements carrying the particular restlessness of someone whose understanding had just shifted fundamentally. The living room felt different now—not a sanctuary but a launching point, a place where difficult truths would be acknowledged and acted upon.

"He can't afford Wallace & Associates without his father's backing," Chris said, but doubt colored his voice. "The emergency custody modification hearing—"

"Will be postponed, probably dismissed. But Chris, this was never really about custody law or legal rights or even Louise." Leah moved to the window, her palm pressing against glass that separated their warm sanctuary from the uncertain world beyond. "It's about Ryan trying to fix something inside himself that broke years ago."

The revelation hung between them, gradually taking shape as Chris processed the psychological landscape Leah was mapping. His wife's abandoned medical training had given her tools for understanding human motivation that transcended legal strategy, the ability to see wounds beneath aggressive behavior, to recognize desperation masquerading as determination.

"When I was eight," Leah continued, "I watched my father destroy a competitor's family business. Not through illegal means—through perfectly legal psychological warfare that identified every emotional vulnerability and exploited them."

Chris joined her at the window, his reflection merging with hers in the glass. Outside, their neighborhood slept in suburban tranquility, houses glowing with gentle domestic light, families existing in the comfortable illusion that love alone could protect them from such destruction.

"The man tried to fight back through lawyers, through publicity, through every conventional method available. But Dad had studied him—understood that his pride in craftsmanship was his weakness, that his loyalty to employees could be turned against him." Leah's voice carried inherited shame wrapped in hard-won wisdom. "The battle ended only when Dad got what he really wanted—not the contract they were competing for, but validation that he was stronger, smarter, more worthy of success."

The parallel crystallized between them. Ryan's custody campaign had followed identical patterns—identifying vulnerabilities, exploiting emotional pressure points, using Louise herself as both weapon and prize. But the true target hadn't been Chris and Leah's marriage; it had been

415

Ryan's own sense of unworthiness, his need to prove he deserved the love he'd abandoned.

"You think this is about redemption," Chris said quietly. "Not possession."

"I think it's about a man who made the worst decision of his life and has been running from that choice ever since." Leah turned from the window, her medical mind continuing its diagnostic process. "The consulting firm here instead of California. The surveillance. The campaign—none of it serves Louise's interests. It serves his need to feel like her father without actually earning that relationship."

The understanding settled around them like a weighted blanket, offering both comfort and responsibility. If Ryan's campaign was driven by psychological need rather than legal strategy, then conventional legal defense would never truly end it. Victory in court might silence him temporarily, but the underlying wound would continue festering until it found new ways to express itself.

"So what are you thinking?" Chris asked, though something in his voice suggested he already sensed the direction of her thoughts.

Leah moved to Louise's artwork on the refrigerator, her fingers tracing bright crayon lines that spoke of a child's unguarded joy. The family portraits showed stick figures holding hands beneath enormous suns—a young child's vision of love that transcended biological complexity or legal definitions.

"I'm thinking we've been fighting the wrong battle," she said finally. "Trying to defend against someone who's really attacking himself."

The words carried implication that made Chris's protective instincts flare. His wife was building toward something that would require her to leave their sanctuary, to engage directly with the man who had spent months trying to destroy their family.

"Leah, no." The refusal emerged before conscious thought could shape it. "Whatever you're considering—no. He's manipulated you before. He'll do it again."

She turned to face him, her expression carrying the particular calm that had first drawn him to her—the steady competence of someone who could make difficult decisions under pressure, who could see solutions others missed because she wasn't afraid of emotional complexity.

"He manipulated the girl I was years ago," she said quietly. "Someone who believed love meant accommodating others' needs above her own, who thought devotion required accepting betrayal with understanding. That woman doesn't exist anymore."

The transformation was visible in her posture, in the set of her shoulders, in eyes that had learned to recognize manipulation without being wounded by it. The frightened medical student who had been abandoned while pregnant had evolved into someone who understood that compassion could be strategic, that healing sometimes required confronting rather than avoiding difficult truths.

"I'm not suggesting we trust him," Leah continued, moving to sit beside Chris on the sofa. "I'm suggesting we give him a chance to choose differently than he has before. Not through legal pressure or family intervention, but through honest conversation about what Louise actually needs."

Chris felt resistance rising like physical nausea, his every instinct screaming against exposing his wife to someone who had already proven his capacity for psychological cruelty. The art celebration assault had revealed Ryan's willingness to traumatize Louise for strategic advantage—what might he do to Leah if given the opportunity?

"He engineered violence at our daughter's celebration," Chris said, his voice carrying all the accumulated protective fury of months spent watching his family under siege. "He deliberately traumatized Louise to gain legal advantage. And you want to give him another chance to hurt you?"

"I want to give him a chance to recognize what he's actually fighting for," Leah replied, her hand finding his across the cushions between them. "Because right now, he's fighting to possess our daughter. But what he really needs is permission to let her go."

The distinction rippled through Chris's consciousness. Possession versus love. Claiming versus releasing. The recognition that sometimes the most parental act was stepping away rather than stepping forward.

"This conversation we should have had years ago," Leah continued, her voice carrying conviction that transcended fear. "Not about custody or rights or legal obligations, but about responsibility and hurt and what it means to love someone enough to choose their wellbeing over your own needs."

Chris studied his wife's face in the lamplight, seeing determination wrapped in compassion, strategy infused with genuine care. The woman who had once accepted betrayal with resigned understanding had developed the capacity to offer redemption without requiring it, to extend grace while maintaining boundaries.

"You think you can reach him," he said finally. "Get him to see Louise as more than a prize to be won."

"I think I can help him see himself clearly enough to make a real choice about her future. Not driven by guilt or legal strategy or family pressure, but by genuine understanding of what serves her best interests." Leah's fingers tightened around his, grounding them both in the physical reality of their connection. "But only if you trust me to do this."

The request hung between them like suspended breath. Chris felt every protective instinct screaming against sending his wife into emotional combat with someone who had already proven his capacity for cruelty. But beneath the fear ran something stronger—their years together that had taught him to recognize Leah's strength, to trust her judgment even when it led into territory that terrified him.

"What if he tries to manipulate you again?" The question emerged from his deepest fear. "What if this is just another strategy to get close enough to inflict more damage?"

"Then I'll handle it." Leah's response carried quiet certainty that spoke of transformation earned through trial. "Because I'm not fighting to win anymore, Chris. I'm fighting to end this—truly end it—in a way that serves Louise's long-term wellbeing rather than just our short-term legal victory."

The wisdom in her approach settled around them like morning light, gradually illuminating corners that legal strategy had left in shadow. Court victories could silence Ryan temporarily, but only psychological resolution would address the underlying wound that had driven his campaign from the beginning.

Chris felt his resistance crumbling not through argument but through recognition—the same intuitive understanding that had drawn him to Leah originally, the sense that she possessed emotional intelligence capable of seeing solutions others missed.

"When?" he asked quietly, surrender carrying its own relief.

"Soon. Before he finds new lawyers, new funding, new ways to continue this campaign." Leah leaned against his shoulder, her weight grounding them both in physical reality while their minds processed emotional complexity. "While he's still shaken by his father's withdrawal of support, still questioning whether this battle is worth fighting."

Chris felt fear and trust warring in his chest like competing musical themes, each carrying its own validity, its own emotional truth. But ultimately, the deeper melody was love—for Leah, for Louise, for the family they had built through daily choice rather than biological accident.

"I love you," he said quietly, the words carrying both benediction and promise. "I trust you to handle this. But if he hurts you again—"

"He won't," Leah replied with conviction that transcended hope. "Because I'm not the same person he hurt before. And because this time, I'm not fighting for his love—I'm fighting for his humanity."

Outside their window, the night painted their neighborhood in shades of sleeping tranquility. Inside their living room, surrounded by Louise's artwork and the accumulated detritus of family life, they held each other against whatever tomorrow would bring—understanding that sometimes the most courageous act was extending grace to those who least deserved it, trusting that redemption remained possible even for those who had chosen destruction.

The path forward required faith rather than certainty, compassion rather than strategy. But as Chris felt Leah's breathing slow toward sleep against his shoulder, he knew they had found their way to something beyond legal victory—the possibility of healing that served everyone involved, especially the little girl whose laughter would fill their house again tomorrow morning, blissfully unaware of the adult conversations that would determine her future.

CHAPTER 24

Conversations Beneath the Oak

Dawn painted their bedroom in watercolor fragments, pale light bleeding through curtains that had witnessed almost a year of married mornings. Leah's eyes opened without alarm, her body attuned to the particular silence that preceded difficult choices.

Chris slept beside her, one hand resting across the space she'd occupied moments before. His breathing carried the deep rhythm of someone whose conscience remained untroubled by what morning would bring. She envied that peace, even as she drew strength from his unconscious trust.

The phone call to Ryan waited on her nightstand. Three attempts at dialing, each time her finger hovering over the final digit before courage abandoned her. Today would be different. Today required the conversation that should have happened five years ago.

Louise's room exhaled the particular sweetness of childhood sleep—lavender fabric softener and the lingering scent of bedtime stories. Her daughter's face held the boneless peace of someone whose world remained unshattered by adult complexities. Dark curls spilled across mermaid pillowcases, creating abstract art against purple cotton.

This is what I'm protecting.

The thought crystallized with absolute clarity as Leah studied her daughter's sleeping form. Not just Louise's physical safety, but this innocence, this unguarded trust in the stability of love. Ryan's legal campaign had threatened to weaponize that trust, transform it into uncertainty and fear.

Her reflection in Louise's bedroom mirror showed a woman she barely recognized from five years ago. Gone was the frightened medical student who had accepted abandonment as somehow deserved. In her place stood someone who understood that compassion could be strategic, that healing sometimes required confronting rather than avoiding difficult truths.

The kitchen welcomed her with familiar shadows, coffee maker gurgling to life with mechanical devotion. Steam rose from her mug, offering small comfort against the weight of what lay ahead. Her hands steadied around ceramic warmth, muscle memory of countless mornings when this simple ritual had anchored her to ordinary life.

She dialed Ryan's number before rational thought could intervene.

His voice answered after three rings, cautious and sleep-roughened. "Leah?"

"We need to talk." The words emerged steadier than expected, carrying authority she'd forgotten she possessed. "Not through lawyers. Not through family members. Just us."

Silence stretched across the digital connection. She imagined him processing the unexpected directness, calculating potential traps or strategic advantages in her request.

"When?" His voice carried surprise wrapped in wariness.

"Today. This morning. Riverside Park, by the old oak near the walking trail. Ten o'clock."

The park where they'd walked together through high school and early college, where everything had begun before it all collapsed. The symmetry felt appropriate—returning to the beginning to finally find an ending.

"Leah, I don't think—"

"I'm not asking for your permission, Ryan." Her voice cut through his hesitation with quiet finality. "I'm telling you I'll be there. Whether you come or not is your choice."

She ended the call before he could respond, before doubt could creep in and poison her resolve.

Upstairs, Chris stirred as she slipped back into bed. His arm circled her waist automatically, drawing her against the warmth of his sleeping body. She pressed her face into the familiar curve of his shoulder, breathing in the scent of home and safety and love freely given.

"Where did you go?" His voice carried the particular roughness of someone surfacing from deep sleep.

"To make the call."

Chris's body tensed against hers as understanding penetrated the fog of awakening. His arms tightened reflexively, holding her as if physical proximity could protect her from what she'd chosen to face.

"I don't like this." The admission emerged muffled against her hair. "I don't like you going anywhere near him."

"I know." Her fingers found his, intertwining with the intimacy of their marriage and the deeper bond forged through years of building their family together. "But this is the only way to truly end it. Not just the legal battle, but the psychological wound that's driving it."

Louise's laughter drifted from the hallway, bright and unguarded as she padded toward the bathroom. Their daughter's joy served as reminder of what they'd built together, what they'd fought to protect, what today's conversation would either preserve or threaten.

Leah rose to meet her daughter's morning needs, her movements carrying new purpose. The coffee grew cold on the nightstand, abandoned in favor of more important rituals—breakfast prepared with extra care, clothes selected for the comfort they offered, kisses dispensed with the precious understanding that some mornings felt more fragile than others.

By nine-thirty, she stood at their front door, keys trembling in her hand. The woman reflected in the hallway mirror bore little resemblance to the girl who had told Ryan about her pregnancy with quiet dignity, expecting nothing and receiving exactly that. This woman had learned that love sometimes required letting go, that healing sometimes demanded facing the person who had caused the wound.

Chris appeared behind her reflection, his presence both anchor and blessing. His hands settled on her shoulders with gentle weight, transmitting strength without demanding she abandon her course.

"Come home to us," he said quietly, the words carrying both permission and plea.

She turned in his arms, memorizing his face with the particular intensity of someone preparing for battle. When their lips met, the kiss tasted of morning coffee and absolute certainty—not about what waited ahead, but about what waited for her return.

The air carried crisp promise as she walked to her car. Behind her, their house held the accumulated weight of years spent building their family—love and laughter and small daily miracles that had transformed three separate lives into something unshakeable. Ahead waited the conversation that would determine whether that sanctuary could finally exist without the shadow of threats and legal manipulations.

Her hands no longer trembled as she started the engine. The frightened medical student was gone, replaced by someone who understood that courage meant facing difficult truths rather than avoiding them. Someone who had learned to fight for love without becoming destructive in the process.

The drive to Riverside Park passed in a blur of familiar neighborhoods and morning traffic, each mile carrying her closer to the reckoning six years in the making. In her rearview mirror, their life grew smaller but remained unshakeable—the foundation she would return to regardless of how this conversation unfolded.

Ten o'clock approached with inevitability as she parked along the tree-lined street beside Riverside Park. Today, she would discover if redemption remained possible even for those who had chosen destruction, if healing could emerge from honest confrontation with shared wounds.

The woman who stepped onto the sidewalk carried herself with quiet dignity earned through years of choosing love over fear, of building a family despite the wounds of the past. Whatever waited in that park, she would face it with the strength of someone who had learned that real courage meant protecting what mattered most, even when protection required walking directly into the storm.

The old oak stood sentinel beside the walking trail, its branches reaching toward morning sky like arms stretched in supplication. Saturday morning had arrived with the weight of Ryan's ultimatum—the 72-hour deadline expiring this afternoon, forcing a decision that would reshape all their futures. Leah arrived first, her hands steady against the rough bark as she traced patterns carved by decades of lovers and dreamers who had believed their marks would last forever.

Footsteps crunched through fallen leaves, measured and hesitant. Ryan emerged from the tree line wearing his engineering confidence like ill-fitting armor, his suit jacket crisp despite the morning chill. But his eyes held something new—uncertainty that no amount of strategic planning could disguise.

"You came," Leah said, turning to face him across five years of accumulated silence.

"I wasn't sure you would." His voice carried the careful neutrality of someone expecting ambush. "Your lawyer finally ready to negotiate?"

Leah studied his face, noting the lines that stress had carved around his eyes, the way his shoulders held themselves ready for battle. He had dressed for war but found himself facing something he didn't recognize—a woman who no longer needed his approval to exist.

"I'm not here as a client, Ryan. I'm here as Louise's mother."

The distinction rippled through him visibly. His posture shifted, engineer's mindset giving way to something more human and far more vulnerable. The oak's shadow fell between them like a line he couldn't cross.

"What do you want?" The question emerged softer than intended, stripped of its edge.

Leah settled onto the weathered bench beneath the oak's protective canopy. The wood held morning coolness that seeped through her jeans, grounding her in physical sensation when emotional vertigo threatened. She gestured to the space beside her.

"I want to have the conversation we should have had five years ago."

Ryan remained standing, his body language screaming flight instincts barely held in check. But something in her voice—the absence of anger, the presence of something deeper—kept him rooted to the spot.

"We talked five years ago. You told me about the pregnancy. I made my choice."

"No." Leah's voice carried quiet authority. "You ran. There's a difference."

The words hit him with unexpected force. His careful composure cracked, revealing glimpses of the panic that had driven him to sign termination papers without reading them, to choose career advancement over confronting the magnitude of what he was abandoning.

"I was twenty-one years old," he said, the defense sounding hollow even to his own ears. "I had Tesla waiting, my whole future mapped out—"

"I was twenty-one and pregnant." Leah's interruption carried no heat, only the weight of lived experience. "My future disappeared the moment I saw those test results. But I didn't run."

Ryan finally sat, the bench suddenly feeling too small to contain the space between them. His hands clasped and unclasped in his lap, seeking occupation for energy that had nowhere productive to go.

"You don't understand the pressure I was under—"

"Tell me." The invitation emerged gently, without the accusation he'd been bracing for. "Help me understand what was so important that you had to erase us completely."

The request disarmed him utterly. For months, he'd prepared for legal arguments, character assassinations, strategic maneuvering. He had no defense against genuine curiosity about his motivations.

"Tesla was everything I'd worked toward. Four years of engineering school, internships, networking. The offer came with relocation requirements, sixty-hour weeks, total commitment to company culture." His voice gained momentum as familiar justifications aligned themselves. "I couldn't split my focus between career advancement and—"

"And your child."

The words fell between them like stones into still water, ripples spreading outward until they touched every corner of Ryan's carefully constructed narrative. His mouth opened and closed, seeking explanations that suddenly felt inadequate.

"I thought you'd be better off without me," he confessed. "Young, single mother with medical school dreams versus absent father working hundred-hour weeks in California. The math seemed obvious."

Leah absorbed this with clinical detachment. She recognized the logic, even appreciated its surface reasonableness. But logic hadn't kept her warm during those first terrifying months of pregnancy.

"Did you ever wonder what happened to me after you left?"

Ryan's throat worked silently. He had wondered, especially in those first months when guilt made sleep elusive. But wondering required confronting what he'd abandoned, and confrontation threatened the psychological architecture he'd built around his choice.

"You had your family. Your father's resources. I figured—"

"You figured." Leah's voice remained steady, but something dangerous flickered beneath its surface. "You figured I'd be fine, so you didn't have to think about it anymore."

She turned to face him fully, her brown eyes holding depths he'd never bothered to explore when they were younger. "Do you want to know what actually happened, Ryan? Not what you figured, but what I lived through?"

He nodded, though every instinct screamed against hearing what came next.

"I dropped out of pre-med school at sixteen weeks pregnant. The morning sickness was so severe I couldn't keep water down, much less attend anatomy lectures." Her voice carried the weight of dreams abandoned by necessity rather than choice. "I decided to keep her—termination was not an option, not for me."

Ryan felt something cold spreading through his chest as the reality of her experience began to penetrate his careful rationalizations. He had imagined her supported, cushioned by family wealth. The truth carved different pictures entirely.

"I worked as an art therapy instructor until I was nine months pregnant, helping children process trauma through creativity while dealing with my own." Leah's hands rested calmly in her lap, but Ryan could see the cost of these memories in the set of her shoulders. "Kate was my pillar through all of it—the one person who never questioned my choice to keep Louise."

The images assembled themselves in Ryan's mind with devastating clarity. Leah, young and pregnant and alone, working while he attended company parties and celebrated his advancing career. The comparison made his stomach twist with something approaching nausea.

"Leah—" Ryan's voice cracked around her name.

"I'm not telling you this for sympathy," she continued, her tone cutting through his attempted interruption. "I'm telling you because you need to understand what abandonment actually looks like. What it costs the people left behind."

Ryan's hands trembled in his lap as the magnitude of his choice began to penetrate the psychological barriers he'd constructed. He had told himself she would be better off, that his absence was somehow protective. The reality felt like drowning.

"I learned how to survive that abandonment," Leah continued, her voice gaining strength. "I learned how to be both mother and father, how to make medical decisions at three in the morning when fever spiked, how to build a life for her from nothing but love and determination. And then Chris came along and showed me what it looked like when someone stayed instead of running."

She straightened, her posture carrying a transformation Ryan was only now beginning to recognize.

"So when you ask me what I want from this conversation, here's the truth: I want you to understand that I'm not the frightened girl you abandoned anymore. I'm a mother who would burn down the world before letting anyone hurt my daughter the way you hurt me."

The declaration hung between them like a drawn blade—not a threat, but a promise. Leah's eyes held something fierce and uncompromising that made Ryan suddenly aware of how profoundly he had miscalculated.

"Do you understand what you're really trying to do?" Leah's voice carried steel. "You're not claiming what was stolen. You're stealing what Chris built. Because you can't live with your choices."

"Why?" The question emerged raw and desperate.

"Because you'd made your choice so completely that it would have been cruel to both of us." Leah turned back to him, her expression carrying hard-won wisdom. "You didn't want to be her father, Ryan. You wanted the problem to disappear."

The truth of it settled into his bones. He had approached her pregnancy as an engineering problem requiring elegant solution. Termination papers had offered clean resolution, legal protection, freedom to pursue the future he'd planned. Louise herself had been incidental to the equation.

"Your legal campaign, your surveillance, your systematic attempt to dismantle our family..." She paused, making sure each word landed. "I let it continue because I wanted to believe you might choose differently this time. That somewhere inside you was a person capable of putting Louise's wellbeing above your own need for redemption."

"I never wanted to hurt her," Ryan began, but Leah's raised hand stopped him.

"Intention doesn't matter when the outcome is trauma." Her voice carried authority earned through lived experience. "You engineered assault at her art celebration. You called her a mistake to provoke Chris into giving you exactly the ammunition you needed. Those aren't the actions of someone prioritizing her wellbeing."

Ryan opened his mouth, then closed it, recognizing that any defense would only prove her point.

Leah nodded, her expression carrying compassion rather than condemnation. "You thought claiming her would somehow undo the choice you made five years ago. But you can't rewrite history, Ryan. You can only decide what to do with the present."

The distinction rippled through him, reshaping the landscape of his understanding. For months, he had told himself that asserting biological rights would somehow validate his worthiness as a father. The truth felt simpler and more devastating—Louise already had a father.

"What am I supposed to do with this?" The question emerged broken, desperate. "How do I live with knowing I threw away something irreplaceable?"

Leah studied his face, seeing not the engineer who had manipulated their family for months, but the young man who had panicked when faced with responsibility he wasn't ready to accept. The difference felt crucial.

"You forgive yourself," she said quietly. "Not because what you did was acceptable, but because carrying that guilt for the rest of your life won't serve anyone, especially Louise."

"How?" The single word contained multitudes of pain.

"By choosing what's best for her, even when it costs you everything you thought you wanted." Leah's voice carried authority earned through similar impossible choices. "By letting her keep the family that's loved her unconditionally instead of forcing her into one that's conditional on your need for redemption."

The path Leah was suggesting crystallized before him—walking away from his legal campaign, letting Louise keep the family that had raised her, accepting that he'd forfeited his right to fatherhood through his own choices. But everything in him rebelled against that surrender.

"I can't just disappear from her life again," he said, desperation creeping into his voice. "I can't pretend she doesn't exist."

Leah studied him carefully, seeing the war between growing understanding and desperate need. "I'm not asking you to pretend anything. I'm asking you to consider what's truly best for her versus what you need to feel better about your choices."

"And if those aren't the same thing?"

Leah considered this carefully, recognizing the genuine concern beneath his question. "She'll know her story. When she's old enough to understand, Chris and I will tell her about biology and choice, about the difference between creating life and raising it. But that conversation will happen in love, not courtroom conflict."

"And if she wants to meet me someday?"

"Then she'll make that choice as an adult who's secure in her identity rather than a child caught between competing claims of ownership." Leah's answer carried wisdom earned through thinking through every possibility. "But that's her decision to make, not ours to force."

Ryan felt tears threatening for the first time in months. Not the frustrated rage that had fueled his legal campaign, but genuine grief for everything he'd lost through his own choices. Louise would grow up knowing she was loved completely by the family who'd chosen her, free from the shadow of his regret.

"I don't know how to let go," he admitted, the confession emerging from depths he'd never acknowledged.

"You start by stopping the legal campaign." Leah's response carried gentle firmness. "You call Wallace & Associates and withdraw the custody petition. You choose Louise's peace over your pain."

The practical steps seemed impossibly simple and utterly devastating simultaneously. Ryan could end the legal warfare with a phone call, but he couldn't undo the psychological architecture he'd built around claiming his daughter. Learning to live without that hope would require reconstructing his entire understanding of who he was and what his life meant.

"What if I can't?" The question emerged barely audible.

"Then you have to decide which one matters more," Leah said quietly. "Your healing or her happiness."

Ryan felt something cracking inside him, but he wasn't ready to surrender everything he'd fought for. The conversation had shown him truths he'd spent months avoiding, but accepting them meant admitting he'd been wrong about everything.

"I need time to think," he said finally, his voice hoarse with exhaustion. "This isn't... I can't just..."

"I know." Leah's voice carried unexpected gentleness. "But while you're thinking, remember that every day you continue this legal battle is another day Louise lives with uncertainty and fear."

They sat in silence as wind moved through the oak's branches, scattering leaves like benedictions around their feet. Other park visitors passed on the walking trail—joggers and dog walkers and families creating the kind of ordinary memories Ryan had forfeited when he chose advancement over presence.

"I need to ask you something," Ryan said finally, his voice steady for the first time since arriving. "And I need you to be honest, even if it hurts."

Leah nodded, prepared for whatever final reckoning he required.

"Do you think I could have been a good father to her? If I'd made different choices five years ago?"

The question hung between them like a prayer waiting for answer. Leah studied his face, seeing not the man who had engineered psychological warfare against a child's art celebration, but the frightened boy who had chosen career over connection because he genuinely didn't understand what fatherhood required.

"I think you could have learned," she said finally, her honesty wrapped in compassion. "But that's not the choice you made. And the man you became while trying to claim her isn't someone any child should have to love."

The assessment hit him with the force of absolute truth. His custody campaign had revealed character he didn't recognize—manipulative, willing to traumatize a child to achieve strategic advantage. That man had no business raising Louise, regardless of biological connection.

Ryan's composure finally shattered completely. His shoulders shook as tears he'd been holding back for months—years—finally broke through. When he spoke again, his voice was raw, stripped of all pretense.

"I thought about you," he whispered, the confession tearing from somewhere deep. "During your pregnancy. After I signed those papers. All those months in California." His hands covered his face, muffling words that had been buried for five years. "I'd be in meetings and suddenly wonder if you were showing yet. If you were sick. If you were scared."

Leah remained silent, allowing him space for this final unburdening.

"There were nights I'd pull up my phone, start typing a message." Ryan's voice cracked. "Ask how you were. Tell you I'd made a mistake. That maybe I could—" He stopped, breath hitching. "But I'd already done the damage. Signed the papers. Made my choice so publicly, so completely. I convinced myself it was too late. That reaching out would only make things worse for you."

He looked up at her, his face wet with tears. "So I stayed silent. Told myself I was being noble by not interfering. That you'd moved on, that my guilt didn't give me the right to disrupt whatever peace you'd found." His laugh was bitter, broken. "I was a coward, Leah. I thought about my daughter every single day and did nothing because I was too afraid to face what I'd thrown away."

The confession hung between them, years of suppressed regret finally given voice. Leah felt her own eyes burning, not for the man he'd become, but for the young father he might have been if courage had matched his conscience.

"Thank you," she whispered finally, the words carrying surprising weight. "For telling me the truth instead of what I wanted to hear."

Ryan nodded, exhausted by honesty that had cost him everything he'd been holding onto. But something in his expression suggested that this unburdening, however painful, was also the first step toward whatever healing might eventually be possible.

Leah rose from the bench, her movements carrying new lightness. The conversation she'd dreaded for five years had somehow become the key to a freedom she hadn't known she was missing. Forgiving Ryan didn't absolve his choices, but it freed her from carrying the weight of his abandonment.

Ryan remained seated, staring at his hands as if they belonged to someone else. The conversation had shattered assumptions he'd built his entire campaign around, but he couldn't process it all at once. Everything Leah had said contradicted the story he'd told himself for months.

"What will you do now?" Leah asked, though she sensed his internal struggle was far from resolved.

"I don't know," he admitted, the honesty feeling foreign on his tongue. "I thought I knew what I was fighting for, but now..."

His voice trailed off, unable to complete thoughts that might lead to admissions he wasn't ready to make.

Leah felt compassion stirring despite everything he'd put them through. She recognized the agony of having your entire worldview challenged in a single conversation. She stood, her movement carrying finality that suggested this conversation had reached its natural conclusion.

"You asked me once what I wanted," she said, her final words carrying truth distilled to its essence. "I want you to understand that love isn't about possession or redemption or proving you've changed. It's about knowing when to hold on and when to let go. It's about choosing what serves the beloved, even when—especially when—that choice costs you everything you thought you needed to make yourself whole."

She turned to leave, then paused, offering one last observation.

"Maybe the most profound act of fatherhood you'll ever perform is choosing not to be one, not because you don't love her, but because you love her enough to leave her unbroken."

Ryan nodded without looking up, his mind already churning through everything she'd told him. The weight of truth felt heavier than the burden of self-deception had been.

"Goodbye, Ryan," Leah said, the words carrying both finality and possibility, the chance for him to choose differently than he had before.

"Goodbye," he replied, his voice barely audible.

Leah walked away without looking back, her steps carrying her toward the parking lot and the life waiting beyond this confrontation. Behind her, Ryan remained on the bench beneath the old oak, alone with truths he'd spent months running from.

The morning sky stretched overhead, vast and clear, offering no answers but infinite space for whatever decision would be made by the time afternoon shadows lengthened toward the ultimatum's expiration. And as morning progressed toward that inevitable hour, Ryan remained on that bench, alone with the echo of words that had stripped away every justification he'd constructed, leaving only the raw question of who he would choose to become when all comfortable illusions had been burned away.

What he would ultimately decide remained unwritten, suspended in the terrible freedom of choosing between the man he'd been and whoever he might yet become—if courage existed somewhere beneath the accumulated weight of five years spent running from the consequences of abandonment disguised as pragmatic necessity.

The old oak held its silence like a witness to transformation. Ryan remained on the bench long after Leah's footsteps had faded into memory, the afternoon stretching around him with the particular weight of moments that divided life into before and after.

His hands lay open in his lap, palms up as if waiting to receive something he'd been refusing for years. The cellular memory of Louise's weight against Chris's chest haunted him—the way her small body had fit so perfectly into the curve of his shoulder, the absolute trust in her cry of "Daddy!" The word hadn't been about him. Had never been about him. The recognition arrived not as fresh wound but as old injury finally acknowledged, the pain of setting a broken bone that had healed wrong and must be broken again to mend properly.

I've been grieving the wrong thing.

The thought emerged with devastating clarity. He'd spent years mourning his absence from Louise's life while never confronting the harder truth: he had chosen that absence. Chosen Tesla over three AM feedings. Chosen quarterly reviews over first words. Chosen professional advancement over the messy, terrifying, beautiful work of becoming someone's father.

A jogger passed on the trail, her breathing steady and purposeful. Ryan watched her disappear around the bend, envying the clarity of her trajectory. When had his own path become a labyrinth of justifications, each turn promising redemption while leading deeper into self-deception?

His phone buzzed. Wallace & Associates: *Emergency hearing scheduled for Monday. Victory within reach.*

Victory. The word crumbled like ash in his mind. What would he be winning? The legal right to shatter Louise's sense of safety? The privilege of forcing her to learn that love could be weaponized, that family could be torn apart by adults who claimed to be protecting her?

He deleted the message.

The memory rose unbidden—not the elementary school scene he'd replayed obsessively, but something older. His own father, the Judge, sitting in this exact park decades ago. Ryan couldn't have been more than seven, crying about a science fair project he'd destroyed in frustration. His father had said something that echoed now with uncomfortable resonance: *"Son, sometimes the bravest thing you can do is admit you're wrong before you've caused damage you can't repair."*

Ryan reached into his jacket pocket, his fingers finding the slim leather portfolio he carried everywhere. Beneath business cards and emergency contacts lay a single sheet of personal stationery—cream-colored, expensive, entirely inadequate for what he needed to say. Yet somehow appropriate for the gravity of what he was about to surrender.

He smoothed the paper across his knee, and the words that emerged weren't the careful explanations he'd rehearsed in his head. They were something rawer, more honest.

Dear Louise,

I won't begin with apologies, because apologies are for mistakes you can fix. What I did—what I failed to do—can't be undone with words.

By the time you read this, you'll be old enough to understand that DNA is just chemistry. It creates possibilities, not promises. It gave you your mother's eyes and maybe my stubbornness, but it didn't make me your father.

The wind lifted the corner of the paper, and Ryan pressed it flat, protective of words that felt like the first honest thing he'd written in years.

Your real father is the man who learned your weight, your rhythms, your particular brand of joy. The one who knows which nightmares require holding and which require space. Who can tell from your footsteps in the hallway whether you need comfort or celebration.

I watched him catch you outside your school—did you know that? Probably not. You fell and he was there before you could be afraid, before gravity could translate into pain. His body knew yours in ways that don't come from genes. They come from years of showing up, of choosing you every morning, of building trust one patient moment at a time.

A couple passed with a young daughter balanced on her father's shoulders. The man's hands held her ankles with unconscious certainty, his body automatically adjusting to her shifting weight. Ryan's pen paused as understanding crystallized: that security couldn't be faked or claimed or demanded. It could only be earned through the accumulated weight of presence.

I tried to steal something that wasn't mine. Not your love—I don't deserve that. Your safety. Your trust in the family that's held you from the start. I wanted to believe showing up now could erase years. That biology could trump daily choice.

The words flowed now without the careful architecture of justification. Just truth, stark and unadorned.

Your mother told me today that love isn't about possession. She's right, though I'm only beginning to understand what that means. Real love makes space for another person to exist fully, safely, joyfully. It doesn't try to force itself into places where it will cause harm just to satisfy its own need for validation.

I created you, Louise. But Chris became your father. Those are two completely different things, and I spent years pretending otherwise because accepting that truth meant accepting responsibility for choosing wrong.

Ryan paused, his throat tight with grief that felt clean for the first time in years—not the corrosive guilt that had driven his custody campaign, but honest sorrow for what he'd lost through his own choices.

This letter is my gift to you, though you won't understand that for years. I'm stopping the legal battle. Not because I don't care about you, but because I finally understand that my love—whatever that means from someone who was never there—doesn't give me the right to dismantle the family that's loved you perfectly all along.

I hope you grow up knowing that some people fight for what they want, and some people fight for what's right. Your mother and Chris fought for what was right. I'm finally learning to do the same.

A leaf detached from the oak above, spiraling down to rest beside his hand. Ryan watched it settle, its golden surface catching afternoon light like a small benediction.

The man you call Daddy earned every single day of that title. He earned your trust when I was busy earning money. He earned your love when I was busy earning success. And he earned the right to be your father in ways that no court could ever grant me, even if I won every legal battle.

Someday, if you want to know about the man whose biology you share, I'll answer any questions you have. But that conversation will happen—if it happens—on your terms, in your time, when you're old enough to understand that families are built through love, not genetics.

Until then, I'll be the person I should have been years ago: someone who puts your wellbeing above his own need for redemption.

With more love than I earned the right to claim, Ryan

He folded the letter with careful precision, each crease a small act of letting go. Tomorrow he would give it to his lawyer with instructions for delivery when Louise turned eighteen. Tonight he would call Wallace & Associates and dismantle the legal machinery he'd set in motion, ending the campaign that had cost everyone involved more than any victory could justify.

The sun had begun its descent, painting the park in shades of gold that transformed ordinary trees into something transcendent. Ryan stood slowly, his body carrying the particular ache of someone who had held tension for so long that its release felt almost like injury.

He didn't look back at the bench where his understanding of fatherhood had been rebuilt from its foundations. The old oak would stand long after this afternoon became memory, its roots deep enough to weather whatever storms came next.

His car waited in the lengthening shadows. The GPS would guide him home to an empty house where he would begin the long work of building a life that didn't depend on taking what belonged to someone else. But for the first time in years, the destination felt honest rather than strategic. The path forward wasn't about proving he deserved to be Louise's father. It was about finally becoming the kind of man who understood that love sometimes meant stepping back, that the most profound act of caring was knowing when you'd cause more harm than good.

Ryan started the engine and pulled slowly away from Riverside Park. In his rearview mirror, the old oak grew smaller but remained visible, its branches still reaching toward sky with the patient endurance of things that understood their purpose.

He drove toward home through the golden hour, no longer fighting against the current but finally allowing himself to be carried toward whatever healing waited on the other side of letting go. The letter rested in his jacket pocket—not an explanation or an excuse, but a bridge between the father he had failed to become and the man he was finally ready to be.

The evening stretched ahead, vast with possibility and weighted with grief that felt paradoxically like freedom. He had lost Louise, but perhaps in losing her, he had found something more essential: the understanding that real love didn't take, didn't demand, didn't try to force itself into spaces where it would cause harm.

Real love knew when to hold on and when to let go. And sometimes, the most fatherly thing you could do was choose not to be a father, not because you didn't care, but because you cared enough to leave something beautiful unbroken.

The highway offered no answers, only the steady progression of mile markers leading away from the life he'd tried to claim. His GPS showed two addresses: California, where his Tesla career had taken him, and this city, where Louise would grow up without him. He didn't know which one to choose as his destination.

Staying meant watching from a distance, a silent presence in the same city but never part of her daily life. Leaving meant putting geography between them, making it easier for both of them to build separate futures. Neither choice felt clean or certain.

Leah had given him a gift in that park—not absolution, but possibility. *If* Louise wanted to know him someday. *If* the time was right. *If* she chose to seek him out when she was old enough to understand the difference between creating life and raising it.

Ryan didn't know if he would stay or go. He didn't know if Louise would ever want to meet the man whose DNA she carried. He only knew that for the first time in years, he was making decisions based on her needs rather than his guilt.

The rest would unfold in its own time, following its own logic. Some endings weren't meant to be resolved, only accepted.

CHAPTER 25

The Art of Letting Go

T he conference room at Wallace & Associates held different energy this morning—not the predatory anticipation of victory, but the hollow echo of surrender. Ryan sat across from James Wallace, the custody petition spread between them like funeral arrangements. His hands rested flat against the mahogany table, steady for the first time in months.

"You understand what you're doing?" Wallace's voice carried professional disappointment wrapped in concern. "This withdraws all claims. Permanently. No future recourse."

Ryan's throat worked silently. Through the floor-to-ceiling windows, morning painted the city in shades of ending. Somewhere below, Louise was probably eating breakfast, Chris helping her tie her shoes, the ordinary magic of family continuing without him.

"I understand completely."

The words emerged cleaner than he'd expected. No tremor. No hesitation. The certainty felt foreign after months of desperate grasping, but it fit like clothing he'd forgotten he owned.

Wallace gathered the documents. "Your father's funding withdrawal makes this financially prudent, but—"

"This isn't about money." Ryan's interruption surprised them both. "It's about letting Louise keep the family that chose her."

The pen felt weightless in his hand as he signed each page. His signature transformed legal warfare into legal peace, possession into protection, his need into Louise's security. The ink dried like medicine absorbed into wounded skin.

Ryan stood, his reflection fragmenting across the polished table's surface. The man looking back carried different eyes—not the calculating engineer who had entered this building months ago, but someone who understood that love sometimes meant stepping away.

"Send this to Williams immediately," he said, gathering his jacket. The fabric felt lighter, unburdened by strategies that had never served anything except his guilt.

Wallace nodded, already calculating billable hours lost. "And if you change your mind—"

"I won't."

The elevator descended fourteen floors, each number marking distance from the person he'd been. The lobby's marble echoed with footsteps heading toward battles he was choosing to abandon. Through revolving doors, morning air felt clean after the suffocating atmosphere of legal manipulation.

His car waited in the parking garage, expensive engineering that would take him home to begin building a life that didn't depend on claiming someone else's family. The GPS offered multiple routes, but for the first time in months, the destination mattered less than the direction.

Away from Wallace & Associates. Away from custody petitions. Away from the systematic destruction of a young child's security. The rearview mirror held the building until he turned the corner, carrying with him only the weight of truth and the unexpected lightness of surrender.

RHYTHMS OF RESILIENCE

The kitchen held its familiar morning rhythm: coffee brewing, sunlight streaming through windows that had witnessed months of whispered fears and guarded hopes. Leah stood at the sink, watching steam rise from her mug like prayers finally answered. Louise's chatter filled the space between heartbeats, her observations about squirrels and swing sets creating the soundtrack of ordinary life.

Chris sat with the newspaper spread before him, but his eyes tracked Louise's movements rather than headlines. The hypervigilance had become second nature, muscles trained to expect attack from angles they couldn't predict. Even victory in court felt temporary.

The phone's ring sliced through domestic tranquility.

"Williams," Chris answered, his voice carrying automatic tension.

Leah turned from the sink, coffee forgotten as she read disaster in his posture. Months of living under siege had taught them to interpret each other's reactions with care. His eyebrows lifted, confusion replacing dread.

"Say that again?" Chris pressed the phone closer, as if proximity could make impossible news more believable. "He what?"

Louise paused mid-bite, cereal dripping from her spoon as adult tension commanded her attention. The kitchen crystallized around them, sunlight and shadows holding their breath while everything changed.

"Complete withdrawal. No conditions. Effective immediately." Chris's voice carried wonder that bordered on disbelief. He looked at Leah across the kitchen island, their eyes meeting with the particular electricity of shared impossibility becoming real.

"The adoption petition?" Chris asked, though his expression already carried the answer.

Williams' response transformed his face. Months of accumulated tension dissolved like snow in spring rain. His free hand found Leah's across the granite surface, their fingers intertwining with desperate gratitude.

"Thank you," he whispered into the phone. "Thank you for everything."

445

The call ended, leaving silence that felt different from before—not the hollow quiet of waiting for attack, but the profound stillness of peace finally arrived. Louise resumed eating, unaware that her world had just become infinitely more secure.

"It's over," Chris said, the words experimental on his tongue. "Ryan withdrew everything. The custody petition, the appeals, all of it."

Leah's knees buckled slightly. Chris rose to catch her, their bodies coming together with the desperate relief of survivors who had weathered the storm and found themselves still standing. Still whole. Still family.

"Really over?" she asked against his shoulder, her voice muffled by emotion and fabric softened through countless similar embraces.

"Really over." His arms tightened around her waist, holding her as if she might evaporate if he relaxed his grip. "Williams said he walked into Wallace & Associates this morning and signed withdrawal papers. No negotiation. No conditions."

Louise looked up from her cereal, brown eyes bright with curiosity about adult tears that carried joy instead of sadness. "Why are you crying happy?"

Chris knelt to her level, his hands framing her face with the tenderness of someone who had fought to keep this exact moment possible. "Because no one is going to try to take you away from us anymore, Sunshine. Ever."

"Good," Louise said with the practical certainty of childhood. "I don't want to go anywhere. Can I have more cereal?"

Laughter erupted from both parents, the helpless, cleansing sound of people whose worst fears had been lifted like stones from their chests. Normal life resumed around them, but nothing would ever be the same.

Chris settled onto the stool beside Leah, his coffee forgotten as he processed the magnitude of Ryan's complete surrender. The kitchen held their victory like a blessing, but curiosity flickered beneath his relief.

"What did you say to him?" Chris asked quietly, his voice carrying the particular intimacy reserved for conversations that happened in spaces their daughter couldn't overhear. "Yesterday at the park. What made him change his mind so completely?"

Leah's hands stilled around her coffee mug, steam rising between them like the ghosts of difficult truths finally spoken. She met his eyes across the granite surface that had witnessed months of whispered fears and careful hopes.

"I told him what he was really fighting for," she said finally, her voice carrying the weight of recognition that had shifted everything. "Not Louise. His own guilt."

Chris moved closer, drawn by the quiet devastation in her tone—not cruelty, but the surgical honesty of someone cutting through years of self-deception.

"I asked him directly: 'Do you understand what you're actually trying to do?'" Leah's fingers found his across the counter, needing the anchor of his touch to steady herself through the memory. "I told him he wasn't trying to claim a relationship that was stolen from him. He was trying to steal one from the man who earned it."

"How did he react?" Chris asked, though he could imagine the devastation of having comfortable lies stripped away in a single sentence.

"Like someone whose entire foundation just crumbled." Leah's voice softened with something that might have been compassion, though it carried no absolution. "I told him I'd let his campaign continue because I wanted to believe he might choose differently this time. That somewhere inside him was a person capable of putting Louise's wellbeing above his own need for redemption."

She paused, her medical training bringing clarity to psychological diagnosis. "But everything he'd done—the surveillance, the provocation at her art celebration, calling her a *mistake* to destroy your control—none of it was about protecting her. It was all about him trying to feel less guilty about abandoning her years ago."

"What did you tell him to do?" Chris asked, sensing there was more—a path forward that Leah had offered even to someone who had tried to destroy their family.

Leah's eyes held his with the particular intensity of someone sharing words that had cost her to speak but needed saying anyway. "I told him he couldn't rewrite history. That he couldn't undo the choice he made years ago by forcing his way into Louise's life now." Her voice carried both steel and unexpected gentleness. "I told him he could only decide what to do with the present."

"And the guilt?" Chris asked quietly. "How does someone live with that?"

"I told him he forgives himself." Leah's answer emerged with the particular wisdom of someone who had done similar work with her own wounds. "Not because what he did was acceptable, but because carrying that guilt for the rest of his life won't serve anyone—especially Louise."

She turned to face him fully, her hands framing his face with the tenderness of someone delivering difficult truth wrapped in love. "I told him that real forgiveness comes through choosing what's best for her, even when it costs him everything he thought he wanted. That the most profound act of fatherhood he could perform was stepping back—not because he doesn't love her, but because he loves her enough to leave her unbroken."

The weight of those words settled between them like benediction. Chris felt tears threatening—not for Ryan, but for the particular grace Leah had shown in offering a path toward healing even to someone who had wounded her so deeply.

"You gave him permission to let go," Chris said wonderingly, understanding crystallizing. "You showed him that walking away could be love instead of abandonment."

"I showed him the difference," Leah corrected gently. "Years ago, he walked away to serve himself—to preserve his career, his freedom, his comfortable future. Yesterday, I asked him to walk away to serve Louise—to preserve her security, her family, her peace."

Her thumb traced circles on his palm, grounding them both in the physical reality of their connection. "The first abandonment was about him. This choice—if he made it—would finally be about her."

Chris felt something profound shifting in his understanding of what had happened beneath that old oak tree. Leah hadn't defeated Ryan through legal strategy or emotional manipulation. She'd offered him something far more valuable and far more costly: the truth about what he was really fighting for, and the chance to make a different choice.

"He must have known," Chris said quietly, "that this was his last chance to be anything resembling a father to her. Even if it meant never being one at all."

"I think that's exactly what he finally understood." Leah's voice carried the weight of witnessing transformation that came through pain rather than comfort. "That sometimes love means recognizing you'll cause more harm than good. That biology gives you DNA but doesn't obligate a child to your presence. That real fatherhood—" her eyes held his with fierce certainty, "—is what you've been doing every day since you chose her. Not claiming. Not demanding. Just showing up and choosing her over and over again."

Louise's laughter drifted from the living room, untouched by adult conversations about the forces that had threatened her security. The sound reminded them both what they'd protected and why yesterday's difficult conversation had been necessary.

"Thank you," Chris whispered, the words encompassing gratitude for her courage, her wisdom, her willingness to walk into that park and offer Ryan redemption at the cost of everything he thought he wanted. "For knowing what to say. For seeing what he needed to hear even when he'd spent months trying to destroy us."

"He destroyed himself," Leah said softly, her medical training offering final diagnosis for psychological wounds that had driven destructive behavior. "I just helped him see it clearly enough to stop."

Chris brought her hand to his lips, pressing a kiss to her knuckles that spoke of reverence rather than simple affection. "You gave him what he actually needed instead of what he thought he wanted."

"I gave him the truth," Leah replied, her eyes bright with tears that spoke of relief rather than fear. "That he's been fighting against his own guilt all along, not for his daughter. And that the only way to finally forgive himself was to make the right choice now—even if it meant losing everything he'd been fighting for."

The morning stretched ahead, golden with possibility and weighted with the particular peace that came from choosing principle over convenience, honesty over comfortable lies, healing over holding grudges. Ryan's withdrawal wasn't defeat, it was the first genuinely paternal decision he'd made in years, choosing Louise's wellbeing over his own need for absolution.

That made all the difference.

The church parking lot held Sunday's particular quiet, cars arranged in neat rows like congregants in pews, waiting for service to release them back into ordinary time. Terry O'Donnell stood beside her car, hands clasped around her purse with the white-knuckled grip of someone preparing for confession.

Chris approached across the asphalt, still warm from the morning sun. His steps carried new authority, the particular confidence of someone whose deepest fears had been lifted. Behind them, church bells chimed the hour with bronze tongues that had marked time through generations of Henderson family worship.

"Chris." Terry's voice carried something that might have been humility, though her posture remained straight. "Thank you for agreeing to talk."

He stopped three feet away, the distance deliberate. Close enough for conversation, far enough to maintain the protective space Louise's wellbeing required.

"I owe you an explanation," Terry continued, her fingers working the handle of her purse. "About the betting jars. About working with that lawyer. About everything." She paused, drawing breath like someone preparing to dive into cold water. "I've been thinking a lot these past weeks. About what happened. About my role in it."

Chris said nothing, his silence creating space she felt compelled to fill.

"I see now that Leah really does love you," Terry said, the admission emerging with visible effort, each word costing her something she'd spent decades hoarding: the certainty of her own judgment. "That I was wrong about her intentions. I made a mistake interfering in your marriage."

The acknowledgment hung between them for a moment before Terry's familiar patterns reasserted themselves. "But you have to understand—I was watching you repeat your father's mistakes. Falling for someone whose family had destroyed ours. After Tom's business collapsed, I was the one who held this family together. I made sure you had stability when your parents couldn't function. I couldn't just stand by and watch history repeat itself when I had the power to prevent it."

"Stop," Chris said quietly.

Terry blinked, the interruption clearly unexpected. "I'm trying to explain—"

"You're trying to justify." His voice carried no anger, only exhausted clarity. "You acknowledged you were wrong about Leah, then immediately spent the next thirty seconds explaining why you were actually right to be wrong."

"That's not fair," Terry protested, but Chris raised his hand gently.

"You believe a big part of you is still right," he said, not as question but as diagnosis. "You think your only mistake was being 'too obvious' or 'not subtle enough.' You've convinced yourself that if you'd just executed your plan better, I'd have eventually agreed with your assessment."

"Chris, I'm trying to take ownership—"

"No, you're trying to distribute blame while maintaining the appearance of humility." His voice carried the particular sadness of someone recognizing patterns that couldn't be broken. "You'll always find faults in everyone around you except yourself. Dad was too trusting. I'm too naive. Leah is too manipulative. Everyone has fatal flaws except Terry, who only makes 'mistakes in execution.'"

A couple passed between parked cars, their conversation about potluck assignments creating bizarre counterpoint to the reckoning unfolding beside Terry's sedan. Terry's shoulders pulled back defensively, chin lifting with familiar certainty.

"I came here in good faith—"

"You came here hoping I'd validate your version of events," Chris interrupted, his tone remaining steady. "Hoping I'd say 'You were wrong but your heart was in the right place' so you could walk away feeling absolved without actually changing anything fundamental."

"I love you," Terry said, tears gathering in her eyes—not remorse for harm caused, but grief for authority lost. "I love you enough to have made myself the villain in your story if it meant keeping you safe. Everything I did came from love. Doesn't that count for something?"

Chris let the silence stretch, watching her cycle through hope and defensiveness as she waited for validation.

"Are you finished?" he asked finally.

Terry hesitated, then nodded uncertainly.

"Save your breath," Chris said gently, the phrase carrying surgical honesty. "You're still the same manipulative person you've always been."

The words landed without heat, delivered as observation rather than accusation. Terry's face cycled through shock and defensive anger, her mouth opening to protest.

"I love you," Chris continued before she could speak. "I always will. You helped raise me when I needed raising. But Louise is my daughter, and I won't let anyone hurt her. Not even you. Especially not you, because you'll hurt her while convinced you're protecting her, and you'll never understand why that makes it worse."

"What are you saying?" Terry whispered.

"I'm setting boundaries," Chris replied, each word deliberate. "You can be Louise's great-aunt at family gatherings. You can send birthday cards and gifts. But you don't get unsupervised time with her. You don't get to question our parenting decisions. You don't get to have opinions about our marriage."

"That's not fair," Terry protested, the words automatic.

"Fair would be cutting you off entirely after you collaborated with lawyers trying to steal my daughter," Chris replied, his voice still carrying that devastating calm. "This isn't fair—this is mercy."

The distinction carved the air between them. Forgiveness without reconciliation. Love without trust.

"I love Louise too," Terry said quietly, one final appeal. "Despite what you think, everything I did came from love."

"I know," Chris replied, the acknowledgment carrying more weight than any accusation could. "That's what makes it so dangerous. You love your certainty about what's best for people more than you love their actual happiness."

Terry opened her mouth to protest, then closed it, some part of her recognizing that denial would only prove his point.

"Can you forgive me?" The question emerged broken.

Chris studied her face, seeing both the woman who had helped raise him and the person who had wagered money on his marriage failing. "I can forgive the woman who loved me enough to help raise me. I can't trust the woman who loved me enough to betray my family while convinced she was protecting it."

He turned toward the church entrance, where Leah and Louise waited with Mary and Tom. "If you want to rebuild trust, start by taking ownership without justifying. Start by loving people enough to let them make their own mistakes."

"And if I can't?" Terry asked.

"Then we have what we have," Chris said simply. "It may have to be enough forever."

He walked away without looking back, leaving Terry alone beside her car with truths she couldn't quite accept but could no longer avoid.

The music studio held afternoon light like amber preserving prehistoric moments. Chris sat at his piano, fingers moving across keys with the muscle memory of a man who had learned to express through melody what words couldn't carry. Tyler stood in the doorway, his large frame carrying none of the aggressive confidence that had characterized his recent presence in Chris's life.

"Congratulations," Tyler said finally. "On winning the custody battle."

Chris's hands stilled on the keys. "Winning." The word emerged like something foreign in his mouth. "Is that what you think happened?"

Tyler shifted uncomfortably. "Ryan withdrew. The adoption will be finalized very soon. Legally—"

"Legally, we're exactly where we started," Chris interrupted, exhaustion threading through his voice. "Except now Louise knows that families can be torn apart by strangers in suits. That her art celebration can turn into a crime scene."

You think this is about winning. But we all lost something in this.

The words landed with more force than Chris intended, but Tyler needed to hear what his "protection" had cost.

"You're right," Tyler said, the admission costing him something he hadn't expected to surrender. "Winning isn't the right word."

Chris turned on the piano bench, his eyes holding depths Tyler had never bothered to explore. "Are you here as my brother or as Morrison's client?"

"I let Morrison go. I no longer needed his services." Tyler stepped deeper into the studio, his movements careful. "I was wrong about Leah. About her family. About everything."

At least you can admit that much.

Chris felt the sting of betrayal but also recognized genuine remorse in his brother's voice. Tyler was trying, even if he didn't fully understand what he was apologizing for.

"You were protecting yourself," Chris said quietly. "From watching me get hurt the way Dad did."

Tyler settled heavily into the student chair, furniture creaking in the studio's acoustics. "I spent months believing she was a threat. Then her father ended the nightmare within days." He looked at his brother with something approaching wonder. "Because they're not the enemy. They never were. I created the threat I was protecting you from."

You did. But at least you can see it now.

Chris felt the weight of his brother's realization—that good intentions didn't erase damage done, that fear had driven Tyler to hurt the very person he claimed to protect.

"How do I fix this?" Tyler asked, the question stripped of pride.

I wish I knew.

"You start by acknowledging that Leah is my wife, not a threat to be neutralized," Chris said, his fingers finding their mother's favorite melody on the keys. "Then you learn to know them. Not as Miller family representatives, but as the people I chose to love."

It's going to take time. But maybe we can get there.

The music provided a bridge between them, something familiar when everything else felt uncertain. His mother's hymn had always been about forgiveness, about grace extended even when it wasn't deserved.

Tyler nodded, understanding that reconciliation required more than apology—it demanded fundamental reconstruction of everything he thought he knew about protection and love.

"Louise asked about you yesterday," Chris said. "She wanted to know why Uncle Tyler was mad at Mommy. I told her that sometimes grown-ups make mistakes about who's safe to love." He paused. "She said maybe Uncle Tyler just needed to meet Mommy for real instead of being scared of her."

The wisdom of a child's observation cut through Tyler's defenses like light through darkness. "She's right," he admitted, tears threatening for the first time in years. "I've been scared of losing you to people I never bothered to actually know."

At least you can admit you were scared. That's something.

Chris felt his resistance softening slightly. Tyler's tears were real, his remorse genuine. That had to count for something.

"You can't lose me," Chris said gently. "But you can lose the right to make decisions about my life."

The distinction clarified their path forward—relationship without control, brotherhood without tyranny.

"Can I take you to dinner sometime?" Tyler asked, vulnerability threading through the invitation. "All of you. As a family."

He's really trying. Maybe that's enough for now.

Chris studied his brother's face, seeing genuine hope there, genuine desire to make amends. The betrayal still hurt, but he could also see the path toward healing if they were both willing to walk it.

"We'd like that," Chris said, his voice carrying warmth that felt more natural now. "Fair warning—Louise talks through the entire meal, and Leah's become quite the cook."

"I'd like that," Tyler said, the words carrying hope rather than strategy. "To really know them."

To really know them. That's all I've ever wanted—for you to give them a chance.

"Then we'll make it happen," Chris promised, finding the final notes of their mother's hymn. "We'll all learn to be family together. The right way this time."

The afternoon light painted the studio in shades of reconciliation—not complete but possible, not easy but worth pursuing. Tyler rose to leave, understanding that healing would be measured in shared meals and patient conversations, in learning to know rather than protect.

At the door, he paused. "I'm sorry. For all of it."

I know you are. And I'm choosing to believe that.

Chris nodded, accepting without pretending it erased months of betrayal. "Show me through actions instead of words."

Tyler left carrying both hope and humility. Behind him, Chris returned to his piano, fingers finding melodies that spoke of damage survived and healing beginning—family bonds tested by fire but not destroyed.

His fingers moved across the keys with practiced ease, the music expressing what words couldn't quite capture. The betrayal had hurt deeply, but Chris understood why Tyler had done it. Fear of losing another family member to the Millers. The scars from their father's business collapse. The protective instinct that had twisted into something destructive.

Understanding doesn't erase the hurt. But maybe it makes forgiveness possible.

The melody shifted into something lighter, more hopeful. Chris let his fingers express the complex truth—that love and hurt could coexist, that healing was possible even when trust needed rebuilding, that family bonds could survive being tested if both sides chose to fight for them.

He's my brother. We'll figure this out. It'll just take time.

Tyler needed to heal from his past wounds against the Millers—the history that had shaped his distrust, the damage he'd inherited from their father's business collapse. Chris needed to heal from his brother's betrayal—the knowledge that protection had become control, that love had been expressed through harmful means.

But unlike the darkness he'd feared, Chris found something approaching peace in this understanding. Tyler had been wrong, but he was trying to make it right. That was more than Chris had dared to hope for weeks ago.

We're not there yet. But we're starting. That's enough for now.

The studio held his truth, his acceptance that forgiveness was a process rather than a moment. Tomorrow, he would respond to Tyler's texts and plan family dinners and work toward the healing they both needed. Tonight, he let himself acknowledge both the wound and the possibility of recovery.

As the last light faded from the studio windows, Chris finally rose from the bench, carrying hope alongside the hurt—a wound that would scar but was already beginning to heal.

That was more than enough.

Maple Hill Cemetery held afternoon light like a cupped palm, golden rays filtering through oak branches onto weathered headstones that marked the passage from presence to memory. Leah walked the familiar path between graves, her steps automatic after over a year of monthly visits that had become sacred ritual rather than obligation.

Kate's headstone sat beneath the oak they'd chosen together—or rather, that Kate had chosen during one of those terrible final conversations when pain medication couldn't quite mask the approaching reality. "Something with roots," she'd insisted, her voice papery but determined. "So you'll know I'm growing into something else."

The granite surface reflected afternoon light, its polished black surface engraved with words that could never contain the magnitude of what had been lost. *Katrina May Anderson. Beloved daughter, friend, and light.* Below that, the quote Kate had insisted upon: *"Love never ends."*

Leah settled onto the granite bench facing the grave, her body finding the position that had become habit through seasons of one-sided conversations. The air carried the scent of earth and leaves, nature's constant cycle that had claimed her best friend too early.

"I know you already know everything," Leah began, her voice carrying the conversational tone she'd developed for these visits. "But I need to tell you anyway, because I can't process it without saying it out loud to someone who understands the whole story."

A squirrel chattered from the oak's branches, creating a soundtrack for confession that felt both absurd and essential. Talking to granite and air about custody battles and family warfare, seeking counsel from someone whose wisdom lived now only in memory and the particular way love echoed forward through time.

"Ryan withdrew his petition yesterday. Completely. No conditions, no appeals, no future threats." The words felt strange on her tongue, victory that had come through grace rather than battle. "The lawyer said he walked into their office and signed papers like someone finally understanding what love actually means."

The breeze shifted, stirring leaves that scattered across the grave like nature's applause. Leah felt Kate's presence in the movement, not supernatural visitation, but the way love persisted in small moments that carried meaning beyond explanation.

"You would have been proud of Chris," she continued, her voice strengthening with emotion that needed expression. "He learned to fight for our family without becoming someone Louise couldn't recognize. Remember how you always said he had that rare combination of strength and gentleness? It took a custody battle to prove you right."

Memories surfaced unbidden: Kate holding newborn Louise while Leah slept, exhausted from labor and abandonment. Kate teaching Louise to blow bubbles in the backyard, her laughter mixing with the baby's delighted squeals. Kate promising to be the aunt who spoiled Louise with art supplies and encouraged messiness that drove structured parents insane.

"She's almost in kindergarten now," Leah said, tears beginning to blur the afternoon light. "Reading chapter books and writing stories about princesses who rescue themselves. She asked me last week why people put flowers on stones, and I told her it's how we keep talking to people whose bodies stopped working but whose love keeps going."

The conversation continued through golden minutes that felt both endless and too brief. Leah shared details Kate would never witness firsthand—Louise's first loose tooth, her growing confidence in swimming lessons with Ashley, the way she'd handled the custody crisis with resilience that amazed everyone who watched her navigate adult complexity with wisdom beyond her years.

"You were right about everything," Leah continued, her voice breaking slightly. "About Chris being worth the risk. About love being the only thing that really mattered when everything else fell apart."

A couple passed on the path beyond the trees, their quiet conversation about grandchildren creating a backdrop for grief that had evolved into something approaching peace. Death remained incomprehensible, but love's persistence had become fact rather than hope.

"I miss you every day," Leah said, the admission emerging with the simplicity of absolute truth. "Not just the big moments like Louise's art celebration or my wedding, but the small things. Coffee conversations about nothing important. Your terrible taste in romantic comedies. The way you could make me laugh when everything felt impossible."

She reached into her jacket pocket, withdrawing the small bundle she'd brought for this visit. Kate's favorite pen, the purple one with silver stars that she'd used for everything from grocery lists to the journal she'd kept during treatment. Leah had found it weeks after the funeral, tucked between couch cushions where Kate had dropped it during one of their last visits.

"I brought this back," Leah said, placing the pen against the headstone's base where flowers usually rested. "I kept it for over a year, thinking I might need it for something important. But I realized today that talking to you is the most important thing I use words for now."

The pen looked small against granite, insignificant except for the weight of memory it carried. Kate's fingers had held it while writing birthday cards and thank-you notes and the letters she'd left for Louise to read, love letters to a goddaughter who would grow up hearing about her Aunt Kate through stories rather than shared experiences.

"Louise wants to plant flowers here in the spring," Leah said, settling back against the bench with the particular exhaustion that followed emotional honesty. "She picked out seeds from a catalog, wildflowers that will grow back every year without needing much care. She said they should be the kind that make bees happy because you always liked gardens that helped other living things."

The wisdom of a child's logic struck Leah with its perfect appropriateness. Kate had always been drawn to beauty that served multiple purposes, kindness that helped others while creating joy for herself, relationships that grew stronger through mutual support rather than one-sided dependence.

"I think you'd approve of our custody victory," Leah continued, her voice growing lighter as afternoon shadows lengthened across the cemetery's careful landscape. "We won through honesty instead of manipulation. Through presenting truth instead of destroying opposition. Very Kate-like approach to conflict resolution."

The conversation wound down as the day progressed, painting the sky in colors Kate had always claimed were too beautiful for photography to capture. Leah rose from the bench reluctantly, knowing that leaving never felt complete but that staying too long transformed comfort into something approaching avoidance of life that continued beyond this sacred space.

"Watch over us," she said, the words carrying quiet certainty. "I know you can hear me, Kate. I know you're there in Heaven, probably already assigned to guardian angel duty because you couldn't resist looking after people even in the afterlife."

A soft breeze moved through the oak's branches, and Leah smiled through her tears. She touched the small crucifix at her neck—the one she'd worn through pregnancy and abandonment and finding Chris.

"Keep whispering good advice when I don't know what I'm doing," she continued. "Keep watching over Louise as she grows. And whatever the future holds for our family, be there for that too. I know you will be. Angels don't miss the important moments."

She made the sign of the cross, the gesture automatic from childhood. "Thank you for loving us so well when you were here. Thank you for continuing to love us from where you are now. I'll see you again someday, but not for a long while—I have too much living left to do."

The oak's branches moved again, sunlight breaking through the leaves in a way that felt like benediction, like Kate's laughter transformed into light. Leah touched the pen she'd left at the base of the headstone one more time.

"Pray for us, Kate. The way I know you do. The way I know you always will."

Leah walked back toward the parking lot with the certainty that death was not ending but transformation. Kate wasn't gone. She was simply somewhere Leah couldn't follow yet, watching with the eyes of angels, loving with a heart made perfect by Heaven's touch.

Behind her, Kate's pen rested against the granite like a promise that their conversations would continue—through prayer and memory and the particular grace that connected the living and the dead across the veil that separated earth from Paradise.

CHAPTER 26

Foundations and Futures

T he family courthouse wore a different atmosphere than their last visit. Chris adjusted his tie—the same charcoal gray from their wedding—while Louise skipped between him and Leah with the particular energy of someone attending an important event she sensed meant celebration without fully understanding why.

"Is the judge scary?" Louise asked, her hand finding Chris's.

"Judge Erikson is very nice," Leah assured her, smoothing the purple dress Louise had insisted on wearing.

"Does he have a big hammer?"

"It's called a gavel. But he only uses it for important announcements."

"Like ice cream?"

"Exactly like that," Chris agreed, earning a delighted giggle.

Elizabeth Williams waited outside the ceremonial courtroom, her arms full of documents that would transform emotion into law. Her smile carried triumph rather than strategy, celebration rather than defense.

"Ready to make it official?"

The courtroom held perhaps twenty people scattered across pews like witnesses to a wedding. Mary and Tom Johnson occupied the front row, Mary's hands clasped around a tissue she wouldn't need for sorrow. Susan Anderson sat beside them, Kate's continued presence felt through love that persisted beyond absence. Behind them, John and Claire Miller occupied adjacent seats with the careful arrangement of divorced parents who had learned to navigate shared family moments with grace.

Judge Erikson entered with measured steps, his black robe carrying authority that felt protective rather than threatening. The man who had presided over their custody hearing bore different expression today—judicial gravity softened by recognition that some proceedings celebrated love rather than arbitrated its destruction.

"This court convenes to hear the petition for stepparent adoption filed by Chris Johnson regarding Louise Danielle Miller."

Louise straightened, her four-year-old sense of importance activated by official attention. She tugged Chris's sleeve and whispered loudly, "Do I gotta raise my hand?"

Chris bent down. "No hand-raising today, Sunshine."

"Even for potty?"

"Especially for potty."

Judge Erikson's lips twitched before he schooled his features back to judicial dignity. Williams presented their case—Chris's years of presence, his financial and emotional support, his consistent parental role unmarked by biological obligation.

"Mr. Johnson," Judge Erikson addressed Chris directly, "do you understand that this adoption creates permanent legal relationship with all attendant responsibilities and privileges?"

"Yes, Your Honor." Chris's voice carried steady conviction. "Those responsibilities and privileges already exist. This proceeding simply recognizes what's always been true."

Judge Erikson nodded, then turned to Louise, his demeanor softening. "Louise, do you understand that Mr. Johnson wants to adopt you?"

Louise tilted her head, considering seriously. "Like my library card?"

Judge Erikson blinked. "I'm sorry?"

"The library lady already knows it's me." Louise's voice carried patient logic. "But I still gotta show the card. So the papers match."

Laughter rippled through the courtroom. Judge Erikson's professional composure cracked into genuine smile. "That is... remarkably accurate, young lady."

Louise looked up at Chris, her brown eyes holding no doubt. "He's already my daddy. The papers are just catching up."

The courtroom dissolved into soft laughter. Judge Erikson wiped at his eyes, his judicial dignity thoroughly demolished. "Mrs. Johnson, do you consent to this adoption?"

"Completely and enthusiastically, your honor" Leah replied.

Judge Erikson straightened, his demeanor shifting back to ceremonial formality. The courtroom fell into expectant silence.

"By the power vested in me by the State, I hereby grant the petition for adoption. Chris Johnson is now the legal father of Louise Danielle Johnson." He paused, allowing the new name to settle like a blessing finally spoken aloud. "Effective immediately, Louise Danielle Miller shall be known as Louise Danielle Johnson, with all rights and responsibilities pertaining to this legal relationship."

Louise's head tilted. "Did my name change?"

"You're a Johnson now, Sunshine," Chris whispered, his voice thick with emotion. "Just like me and Mommy."

Louise's face lit up with understanding. "Oh! We all match now."

Judge Erikson lifted his gavel. "Welcome to your new name, Miss Johnson."

The gavel's sound marked transformation from intention to reality. Louise clapped, then whispered loudly, "That was really loud!"

Williams approached with final documents. Louise watched Chris sign beside her new legal name. "That looks like scribbles."

"Very fancy scribbles," Chris agreed.

Judge Erikson descended from the bench with unusual informality, crouching to Louise's level. "I've been doing this for twenty-three years, and that is the first time anyone has compared adoption to getting a library card. You've made my day, Miss Johnson." He rose, addressing the small gathering. "You've formalized what any observer could see was already true. Louise is fortunate to have parents who fought for her rather than over her."

The courthouse steps held different meaning than their previous exit— no drama, no sense of battle concluded. Just family walking into sunlight that felt warmer for carrying the security of official recognition.

Tom lifted Louise onto his shoulders. "How does it feel to be officially adopted, sweetheart?"

"Good," Louise said, then added after consideration: "Can we get ice cream now?"

Light painted their kitchen in warm tones, transforming familiar surfaces into something approaching sanctuary. The dinner hour unfolded with orchestrated ease—Leah stirring pasta sauce while Chris helped Louise with homework, their domestic symphony unmarked by the hypervigilance that had characterized recent months.

Louise sat at the kitchen island, tongue protruding with concentration as she traced letters across lined paper. Her assignment required writing three sentences about family, and she approached the task seriously.

"How do you spell 'happy'?" Louise asked, her pencil hovering above paper.

Chris spelled the letters slowly, watching her careful formation of each character. The word emerged in crooked but legible script, followed by the sentence: "My daddy adopted me." Simple. Complete. Everything that mattered.

"What's next?" Chris asked, settling onto the stool beside her while Leah's cooking provided gentle background percussion.

"About ice cream!" Louise announced, already writing before he could help. "We got ice cream after."

Chris smiled at the priorities of childhood—official proceedings and frozen desserts weighted with equal significance. "One more sentence," he prompted gently.

Louise chewed her pencil eraser, thinking hard. "I'm happy we match now." She wrote carefully, her letters large and uneven but determined.

Leah moved to Chris's shoulder, reading over his arm while her hand settled against his neck. "Perfect," she said, though whether she meant the homework or this moment remained beautifully ambiguous.

"Dinner's ready."

They moved to the dining room table with easy coordination. The routine felt both familiar and transformed—ordinary actions suddenly precious for their very ordinariness.

"Tell me about your day," Chris said as they settled into their seats.

Louise launched into elaborate exposition about playground politics and art class achievements, her narrative including voices for different characters and hand gestures that made tomato sauce slide dangerously close to plate edges.

"And then Marcus said his hamster can swim, but I said no 'cause hamsters don't like water. Like how you said some animals are different." Louise took a large bite of pasta, satisfied with her zoological wisdom.

"Very true," Chris agreed, his eyes meeting Leah's across the table with shared appreciation for their daughter's confidence.

Leah watched this exchange with quiet contentment. The phone remained silent on the counter—its lack of interruption notable after months when every ring carried potential crisis. No lawyers. No family members reporting concerns. Just ordinary quiet.

"After dinner, can we make pictures?" Louise asked between bites. "For Grandma Mary about today?"

"That's a wonderful idea," Leah agreed. "I'm sure she'd love pictures from our special day."

"Can I use the good crayons?"

"Absolutely," Chris said. "Special day pictures deserve the good crayons."

They finished dinner with unhurried pleasure, conversation flowing between practical matters and whimsical observations. Louise excused herself to gather art supplies, leaving Chris and Leah alone with dishes and the particular intimacy that emerged when their daughter's attention focused elsewhere.

"How does it feel?" Leah asked, beginning to clear plates.

Chris rose to help, their movements synchronized through years of practice. He was quiet for a moment, considering. "Like standing on solid ground for the first time in months. I keep waiting for the floor to drop out, but it doesn't."

"It won't," Leah said, and the certainty in her voice carried more weight than reassurance—it was promise.

They moved around the kitchen together. Chris scraped plates while Leah loaded the dishwasher, their bodies navigating the space with unconscious choreography.

"I've been thinking," Leah said, pausing mid-motion with a serving bowl in her hands. "About what comes next."

Chris looked up, catching something in her tone—not worry, but anticipation wrapped in careful consideration. "Next?"

"We've spent so long defending what we have." She set down the bowl, turning to face him fully. "I forgot what it feels like to simply... build. To imagine forward instead of protecting backward."

The distinction rippled through Chris with unexpected force. She was right—their entire marriage had been lived in defensive crouch, every decision filtered through the lens of potential threat. The idea of moving through life without that constant vigilance felt almost foreign.

"What does forward look like?" he asked, genuinely curious about her answer.

Leah leaned against the counter, her expression shifting into something more vulnerable. "That's what scares me." She paused, her fingers tracing patterns on the granite. "I've spent years telling myself that wanting anything beyond this—beyond us—was selfish. Dangerous, even. That if I let myself want more, I'd somehow ruin what we'd built."

Chris moved closer, sensing they were approaching territory she'd been circling but never quite entering. "But?"

"I keep catching myself." Leah's voice dropped. "Looking at medical journals. Extension catalogs. Art therapy workshops." She met his eyes. "I start planning every detail. Then I stop. Because I'm doing it again."

"Doing what?"

"Trying to make it perfect before I even start." The confession emerged with the weight of old patterns finally named. "It's the same thing I did before Louise—I had every semester mapped out through residency, every rotation planned, every contingency accounted for. I wouldn't let myself actually apply to medical school until I had a flawless plan. And then Ryan happened, and pregnancy happened, and none of my perfect planning mattered."

She turned back to the dishes, needing the distraction of movement. "I'm almost twenty-seven years old, and I still can't just... try something without knowing exactly how it will turn out. If I can't do it perfectly, I won't let myself do it at all."

Chris's hands stilled her restless movements, turning her to face him. "What if you did it anyway?"

"Did what?"

"Started something without knowing the ending. Tried something that might not be perfect."

Leah's laugh emerged hollow. "You know me better than that."

"I know you're terrified of failing," Chris said gently. "I also know you're brilliant at everything you actually let yourself attempt. The problem isn't capability—it's permission."

"Permission to be mediocre?" Leah's voice carried the particular edge of someone whose perfectionism had been both shield and prison.

"Permission to be human," Chris corrected. "To want things. To try things. To be something more than Louise's mother and my wife, even though you're extraordinary at both."

Leah felt tears threatening. "What if I start something and can't finish it? What if I finally let myself want something and discover I'm not good enough?"

"Then you'll know," Chris said simply. "Which is better than spending the rest of your life wondering."

Louise's voice drifted from the living room, talking to herself with the concentration she brought to important artistic projects: "Purple for the judge's coat... yellow for ice cream... big heart for everyone..."

Leah listened to her daughter's unconscious narration, hearing the fearlessness of someone who hadn't yet learned to be afraid of imperfection. Louise drew without erasing. Sang without caring if the notes were right. Lived without the paralysis of perfectionism that had defined Leah's entire existence.

"I don't want to be afraid anymore," Leah whispered, the admission costing her something she hadn't known she was holding. "I don't want to reach forty and realize I never tried because I was too scared of not being perfect."

"So don't be," Chris said, making the impossible sound simple.

"It's not that easy."

"It's exactly that easy. And exactly that hard." He pulled her closer. "You spend so much energy trying to figure out the perfect path that you never actually walk any path at all."

The observation landed with uncomfortable accuracy. How many nights had she spent researching programs she'd never apply to? How many conversations had she rehearsed with advisors she'd never actually contact? How many dreams had she polished to perfection while keeping them safely theoretical?

"What if I choose wrong?" The question contained multitudes—wrong career, wrong timing, wrong priorities.

"What if there is no wrong?" Chris suggested. "What if you're allowed to try something, discover it doesn't fit, and try something else?"

The concept felt foreign, almost transgressive. In Leah's world, choices were permanent, mistakes were failures, and perfection was the only acceptable outcome. The idea that she could experiment, explore, even abandon one path for another—it contradicted everything she'd believed about how life was supposed to work.

"What are you two doing?" Louise appeared in the doorway, purple crayon in hand and curiosity written across her face.

"Planning," Leah said, though the answer encompassed more than Louise could understand. "Planning all the wonderful ordinary things we get to do now."

"Like what?" Louise asked, practical as always.

"Like tomorrow," Chris said, scooping her up until she giggled. "And the day after that. And every day that comes."

"That's a lot of days," Louise observed with four-year-old wisdom about infinity.

"It is," Leah agreed, her hand finding Chris's free one. "And we get to fill them however we want."

But as the words left her mouth, Leah felt something shift inside her chest—not resolution, but the first trembling steps toward it. The evening stretched ahead with promise rather than anxiety, and for the first time in years, she allowed herself to imagine a future that included more than survival. Perhaps even included dreams she'd been too afraid to pursue, paths she'd been too paralyzed to walk, versions of herself she'd kept safely theoretical rather than risk discovering they were beyond her reach.

The question wasn't what she would do. The question was whether she'd finally be brave enough to try.

Morning light filtered through kitchen windows, painting familiar surfaces with silver. Two months had passed since the adoption papers had transformed love into law, and their household had settled into rhythms unmarked by the hypervigilance that had once characterized every ordinary moment.

Leah stood at the bathroom mirror, her reflection catching morning light as she brushed her teeth with the automatic routine of established habit. But something had shifted in recent weeks, a subtle awareness that her body felt different in ways she was only beginning to acknowledge.

Her hand paused, toothbrush suspended, as realization crystallized with startling clarity. The missed cycles. The exhaustion. The way her clothes had been fitting differently, changes so gradual she'd dismissed them at first.

How long has it been?

Her medical training kicked in, mental calendar calculations reaching back. Her periods had always been irregular, but this felt different. More deliberate. Like her body was trying to tell her something she'd been too distracted to hear until now.

She set down the toothbrush, her hand moving unconsciously to her stomach. The possibility bloomed in her chest—not with fear or anxiety, but with something that felt surprisingly like hope.

"Chris?" she called softly through the bathroom door.

He appeared within seconds, coffee mug in hand and wearing the particular expression of someone whose life had found its proper balance. His eyes immediately found hers with the intuitive awareness of a partner who had learned to read her subtle signals.

"I think..." she began, then stopped, a smile threatening at the corners of her mouth. "Chris, I think I might be pregnant."

His coffee mug froze halfway to his lips. "Really?"

"I don't know for certain yet," she said, her voice carrying wonder rather than worry. "But I've been feeling different. And I just realized I can't remember my last period. It's been weeks, maybe months."

Chris set down his coffee with careful deliberation, his eyes never leaving her face. "How do you feel about that?"

Leah considered the question, searching her emotions for the fear that had characterized her first pregnancy discovery. But it wasn't there. Instead, she felt something closer to excitement, possibility, readiness.

"I feel..." she paused, finding the right words. "I feel like maybe this is exactly what we were talking about. About not needing to plan everything perfectly. About being brave enough to just... live."

Chris's face transformed into something radiant. "We talked about this possibility," he said, moving closer. "About expanding our family when the time felt right."

"And it does feel right," Leah whispered, surprised by her own certainty. "Doesn't it?"

"It feels perfect," Chris agreed, his hands finding her waist. "But we should probably confirm it before we get too excited."

Leah laughed, the sound carrying pure joy rather than nervousness. "Too late for that. I'm already excited."

Louise's voice drifted from the kitchen, singing to herself while she arranged cereal. Her contentment provided a soundtrack to the moment that was reshaping Leah's understanding of their family's immediate future.

"Should we tell Louise we're going to the store?" Chris asked.

"Let's bring her," Leah said, her hand finding his. "This is a family moment, whether the test is positive or not."

They moved to the kitchen where Louise sat surrounded by artwork that had evolved into elaborate family portraits—stick figures holding hands beneath houses that looked more like castles, their windows blazing with crayon sunshine.

"Mommy, Daddy, look!" Louise announced, holding up her latest creation. "I drew our forever family with extra hearts."

The timing of her artistic choice felt like the universe offering commentary on what they were about to discover. Leah knelt beside her daughter, her heart full with possibility.

"Louise," Leah said gently, "we need to go to the store for a few minutes. Want to come with us?"

"Can we get cookies?" Louise asked.

"We can get anything you want," Chris said, his voice thick with emotion he wasn't trying to contain.

The drive to the pharmacy passed in contemplative excitement, Louise chattering while Chris and Leah exchanged glances that spoke of shared

474

hope. At the store, Leah selected two different tests—one with traditional pink lines, another with a digital display that would remove all ambiguity.

"Just to be sure," she said, placing both boxes in the basket.

Chris squeezed her hand. "However it turns out, we're okay."

"I know," Leah replied. "But I really hope it's positive."

Back home, the bathroom felt smaller with all three of them crowded inside, anticipation making the air feel electric rather than anxious. Leah opened the first box with steady hands, her medical training now partnered with genuine excitement rather than warring against it.

"What's that for?" Louise asked as they settled together.

"It helps us find out if there's gonna be a baby in Mommy's tummy," Leah explained.

Louise's eyes widened with delight. "Like when I was growing?"

"Exactly like that," Chris said, his arms circling Leah from behind while they waited.

Three minutes stretched with anticipation rather than dread. When the timer on her phone buzzed, Leah lifted the test stick to examine it.

One clear pink line. And beside it... something. Maybe. A shadow that might have been the faintest whisper of a second line.

"I can't tell," she said, though her voice carried hope rather than frustration. "There's something there, but it's so faint..."

Chris leaned closer. "Is that...?"

"I think so." Leah moved toward the window, pulling back the curtain to let natural light flood across the plastic stick. In the morning sun, the second line became slightly more visible—definitely present, but so pale it felt like a whisper.

"It's there," Chris said, his voice carrying wonder. "I see it."

Louise peered at the stick with four-year-old curiosity. "What's it supposed to look like?"

"Two pink lines means yes," Leah explained, her heart beating faster. "But let's try the other one to be completely sure."

She reached for the digital test, her hands steady but her pulse racing with hope rather than fear. This time, the waiting felt different—not weighted with anxiety but filled with possibility.

The test sat on the counter between them, its small digital window blinking with a processing cursor. Louise watched with fascination while Chris's hand found Leah's, fingers intertwining.

"Why's it doing that?" Louise asked.

"It's thinking," Chris said softly.

"Like when my tablet loads?"

"Something like that."

The cursor continued its hypnotic blinking. Leah found herself counting Chris's breaths, drawing strength from his steady presence. They had talked about this possibility. Imagined it. And now, maybe, it was becoming real.

Louise shifted restlessly. "Is it done thinking yet?"

"Almost, Sunshine," Leah whispered.

And then, between one blink and the next, the cursor disappeared. In its place, a single word materialized:

PREGNANT

Leah's breath caught in her throat, tears springing to her eyes—but these were tears of joy, pure and uncomplicated. Chris's arms tightened around her from behind, his own breathing gone ragged with emotion.

"We're having a baby," Leah whispered, the words feeling like celebration rather than confession.

Chris pulled her into his arms with sudden force, lifting her off her feet as he held her against him. His face buried in her neck, his shoulders shaking with emotion he didn't try to contain. When he set her down, his hands moved to cup her face with infinite tenderness, his thumbs brushing away the tears that streamed down her cheeks.

"I love you," he said, his voice thick with wonder. "I love you so much."

And then he kissed her—deeply, passionately, a kiss that spoke of years of partnership and love tested by fire and dreams finally coming true. His hands tangled in her hair while hers gripped his shoulders, both of them pouring every ounce of joy and gratitude and hope into that single moment.

When they finally broke apart, both breathless, Chris pressed his forehead against hers. "We're having a baby," he whispered again, as if saying it out loud would make it more real.

"We are," Leah said, her smile so wide it hurt. "Our family is growing."

Louise tugged at Chris's pant leg, her voice carrying impatient curiosity. "So there IS a baby?"

Chris scooped her up, including her in their embrace. "There is, Sunshine. You're going to be a big sister."

Louise's face lit up with pure delight. "When will the baby come?"

"In several months," Leah said, joy making her feel weightless. "You'll be finishing kindergarten, and the baby will be learning to smile and laugh."

"I can teach the baby stuff!" Louise announced. "Like how to draw and how to make Daddy laugh."

Chris's laughter emerged thick with emotion he didn't try to disguise. "You're going to be the most wonderful big sister in the world, Sunshine."

They moved back to the kitchen as a transformed unit, their movements carrying different energy than they had an hour before. The morning light seemed more precious, familiar surfaces weighted with new significance.

477

Leah settled onto her stool with both hands pressed against her stomach where life was reshaping her understanding of what their future would hold. Both pregnancy tests sat on the counter beside Louise's family portraits—the barely-there pink line and the definitive digital word, twin evidence that their circle was growing.

"Should we call Grandma Mary?" Louise asked.

"We will," Chris agreed, his hand finding Leah's across the granite surface. "But first, let's just be here together and let this feeling settle in."

The kitchen held their wonder like a blessing, morning light transforming ordinary surfaces into sacred space. Coffee grew cold beside Chris's elbow while Leah traced patterns on countertops, her other hand never leaving her stomach.

"Are you scared?" Chris asked softly.

Leah considered the question, searching for the fear she'd expected to feel. "No," she said, surprised by her own answer. "I'm not scared at all. I'm excited."

"Me too," Chris said, his voice carrying wonder. "This feels right. Like we're ready."

"We are ready," Leah agreed. "We're not the same people we were with Louise. We're stronger now. Together."

She looked at their daughter, at the purple crayon in her small hand, at the artwork spread across the table that showed a family of four with such uncomplicated joy. And for the first time, Leah felt no fear about the future—only anticipation for all the beautiful, messy, imperfect moments that lay ahead.

Chris squeezed Leah's hand across the counter, reading in her expression the peace that had finally settled over her. The pregnancy tests sat beside Louise's artwork, tangible evidence that their family was expanding at exactly the right time, in exactly the right way.

Outside their windows, morning continued its progression, indifferent to human plans. Inside their kitchen, three peopl· soon to be four, stood at the threshold of possibilities they were finally bra· enough to embrace.

Louise returned to her drawing, humming contentea·. ·s she added details to her family portrait. Leah watched her daughter's t· ·less strokes, the way she added color without hesitation, created withou· ·e paralysis of perfectionism.

Her gaze drifted to the stack of mail on the counter: university ·ension catalogs, community center brochures, medical journals Sus· had dropped off. Each one a path she'd researched obsessively withou· ·er taking a single step forward. Her hand moved unconsciously to ı· stomach, where new life was already growing—unplanned in its timing, uncontrolled in its arrival, yet somehow exactly right.

"What are you thinking?" Chris asked quietly, following her gaze between the catalogs and her protective hand on her stomach.

Leah's fingers traced the edge of the nearest catalog, her mind connecting the dots between the life growing inside her and the life she'd been too afraid to pursue. "I'm thinking about this baby," she said slowly. "How we didn't plan the exact timing. How we talked about being brave enough to just live, and then... this happened. This beautiful, unplanned blessing."

She looked up at Chris, something crystallizing in her expression. "I've spent years researching these programs, planning the perfect moment to start. But this pregnancy just taught me something." Her voice gained strength. "Life doesn't wait for perfect plans. This baby didn't wait for me to have everything figured out. It just... became. And I'm so happy about it."

Chris moved beside her, understanding dawning in his eyes as he watched her revelation unfold.

"Maybe that's what I've been doing wrong with everything else," Leah continued, her hand still resting on her stomach as if drawing courage from the life within. "Waiting for the perfect plan before I'm allowed to begin. But if we'd waited for the perfect time to have another baby, we might have waited forever. And we would have missed this."

She picked up one of the catalogs, really looking at it for the first time. "What if I applied the same courage to this? To pursuing something for myself? Not waiting until I have every detail planned, not requiring perfection before I start. Just... beginning. The way this baby is beginning right now, without permission or guarantees."

Chris's hand covered hers on her stomach. "You're ready to start."

"I think I am," Leah said, wonder threading through her voice. "This pregnancy is showing me that beautiful things can happen without perfect planning. That I can handle the unknown. That maybe the goal isn't to have everything figured out—it's just to be brave enough to take the first step."

She looked at the pregnancy test, then at Louise's artwork showing a building with many windows blazing with light, then back at the catalogs. "I don't know if it will be medical school or art therapy or something I haven't even discovered yet. But whatever it is, I'm going to start exploring. Because if I can grow a whole human being without having every detail controlled, I can certainly explore a career path without having the next ten years mapped out."

Chris pulled her close, his arms circling both her and the new life growing between them. "This baby is already teaching you things."

"Teaching both of us," Leah corrected softly. "That families expand in unexpected ways. That love makes room for new dreams. That we're stronger than we knew."

Louise looked up from her drawing, holding up her latest creation. The stick figure family now included four people, the newest member cradled in loving arms while the others stood in a protective circle. But in the corner of the page, she'd drawn something else—a building with many windows, each one blazing with light. Not a house. Something larger. Something undefined.

"What's this building, baby girl?" Leah asked, pointing to the structure.

Louise studied her own artwork. "I don't know yet," she said, her words echoing Leah's earlier thoughts with uncanny timing. "But it's important. See all the lights? That means lots of people need it."

Leah felt tears threatening as she studied the drawing—a child's intuitive understanding that the future held spaces yet to be discovered, purposes yet to be defined, possibilities that didn't require perfect planning to be worth pursuing.

"It's beautiful," Leah whispered. "Just like our growing family. Just like all the possibilities ahead."

Chris's arm circled her waist, pulling her close while Louise returned to her drawing with the fearlessness of someone who hadn't yet learned to be afraid of blank pages.

Inside their kitchen, a woman who had spent almost twenty-seven years believing she needed perfect answers before taking any steps finally understood that perhaps the bravest thing she could do was begin walking without knowing exactly where the path would lead. The baby growing inside her was proof that life's most beautiful blessings often arrived unplanned, uncontrolled, yet exactly when they were meant to.

The pregnancy tests remained on the counter beside Louise's artwork and the stack of catalogs—tangible evidence that life didn't wait for perfect planning. That families expanded in unexpected ways. That new beginnings, whether in the womb or in career aspirations, carried invitations to become someone you'd been too afraid to attempt.

And as morning stretched toward afternoon, Leah felt something shifting in her chest—not the weight of decisions made, but the lightness of finally giving herself permission to begin. The catalog sat within reach. The journals waited. The blank applications beckoned. The future spread before her like Louise's drawing, undefined but full of light, unknown but no longer terrifying.

Whatever came next—whether growing this baby or growing into a new version of herself—she would finally let herself try. Not perfectly. Not with every contingency mapped and every risk calculated. But courageously, messily, humanly.

The way her daughter lived, adding color without hesitation, creating without fear.

The way this new life was already growing inside her, following no blueprint, requiring no permission, simply becoming what it was meant to become.

Perhaps it was time to learn from that wisdom. To grow without knowing the final shape. To become without requiring perfection. To start without guarantees of how the story would end.

The catalog gleamed in the morning light, one possibility among many. Not an answer, but an invitation—one that a woman carrying new life inside her was finally brave enough to accept.

For the first time in her life, Leah was ready to begin.

**** END OF BOOK TWO ***

More from this series

Healing Hearts

Book 1

Harmonies
of
Hope

Book 2

Rhythms
of
Resilience

Book 3

Coming Soon!
Fall 2026

Follow the series
on Amazon

www.ingramcontent.com/pod-product-compliance
Lightning Source LLC
Chambersburg PA
CBHW052330110726
47901CB00005B/1183